I HOPE you ~~...~~ ithout saying good-bye. ~~Clay Madison~~ had rolled down his driver's-side window as well.

"Sorry. I have an afternoon flight out of Baltimore and am running a little late." Lucy cleared her throat. "Besides, I thought we said good-bye after the wedding on Saturday."

"I thought we'd only said good night." He paused, then added, "I was hoping for a chance to sit and talk, you know. Catch up."

"We did that on Saturday," she replied, suddenly aware that she'd sounded somewhat prim, and wished she hadn't.

"We only touched the surface, LuLu." He took off his sunglasses and held them in the hand that hung out the window. His eyes were an odd mix of blue and gray, and they studied her face with what she'd first thought might be amusement, but now wasn't quite sure. Looking into them, Lucy felt a spark of guilt. Over the weekend, she'd had an opportunity to say things to him that needed to be said, and she had let it slip away.

"Maybe next time," she told him, hoping she'd have found the nerve by then, but suspecting that she might not.

Home for the Summer

The Chesapeake Diaries Book 5

Mariah Stewart

BALLANTINE BOOKS • NEW YORK

A Ballantine Books Mass Market Original

Copyright © 2012 by Marti Robb
Excerpt from Book 6 in the Chesapeake Diaries series copyright © 2012 by Marti Robb

Published in the United States by Ballantine Books, an imprint of The Random House Publishing Group, a division of Random House, Inc., New York.

BALLANTINE and colophon are trademarks of Random House, Inc.

This book contains an excerpt from the forthcoming Book 6 in the Chesapeake Diaries series by Mariah Stewart. This excerpt has been set for this edition only and may not reflect the final content of the forthcoming edition.

ISBN 978-0-345-53122-3
eBook ISBN 978-0-345-53465-1

Cover art: Chris Cocozza

Printed in the United States of America

www.ballantinebooks.com

9 8 7 6 5 4 3 2 1

Ballantine Books mass market edition: June 2012

To Cole—you are our sunshine

ACKNOWLEDGMENTS

Because writing the book is only the beginning, I must send many thanks to the amazing team at Ballantine Books—Kate Collins, Gina Wachtel, Scott Shannon, Libby McGuire, Linda Marrow, Junessa Viloria, Ania Markiewicz, Alison Masciovecchio, Kristin Fassler, Scott Biel—I sure hope I didn't forget someone! These are the folks who do the heavy lifting, and they do a phenomenal job of making what I send them into a book, and then getting it out there and making sure people *know* that it's out there. I owe them all big time.

Thanks also to my agent, Loretta Barrett, and her crew—Jennifer Didik and Nick Mullendore—for all the years of working so hard on my behalf.

The book you're holding in your hands is number thirty-five for me! I know! I can hardly believe it myself! But without the support of my friends and family, I'd never have finished that first one. So huge thanks to Helen Egner and the late Carole Spayd for cheering me on back in those early days—and to Bill, Becca, Katie, Mike, and the newest member of the family, our darling Cole, for giving meaning to the journey.

Many thanks to Marianne McBay, Wed Accompli—Weddings and Events, Savannah, Georgia, not only for years of friendship and laughter (we don't need to say how many years), but for sharing her knowledge of the world of wedding planning that made this book possible.

Karyn Park won the right to have a character named after her in the annual ADWOFF raffle benefitting the Nora Roberts Foundation (thanks and love, as always, to Phyllis Lannik). Hopefully, Karyn is enjoying her new career as a celebrity photographer.

Lastly, since we have three cousins named Bonnie, it was only a matter of time until I named a character after them. So here you go, Bonnie Slavin-Walls, Bonnie Bricker Almquist, and Bonnie Shafer Sayette (whose maiden name was so good I poached it all!).

Home for
the Summer

Diary ~

What a whirlwind these past few days have been, what with the big weddings here at the inn over the weekend, and all the comings and goings! Why, you'd think I'd be dead to the world with exhaustion—and frankly, I am. So why, one might ask, am I sitting at my desk at twenty minutes to three in the morning?

For one thing, Lucy leaves tomorrow morning to head back to L.A. after a full ten days here at home, working downstairs when she should have been sleeping. And there's been something in her behavior this past week that has been unsettling to me . . . nothing I've yet been able to put my finger on, but I'm worried about that daughter of mine, and I don't know why.

Oh, I am grateful for the time we've spent together these past days, but it saddens me every time she leaves because I never know when I'll see her again.

I admit there's some small amount of irony in the fact that both Dan and I tried so hard to raise our children to be independent, to have open minds, and to follow their own stars—and now here I am, lamenting the fact that my girl has done exactly that.

To add to my misery, my dearest friend, Trula, who's been here for the weekend, leaves tomorrow as well. I'm not by nature a lonely person, but right now I'm feeling lost without their company—and here neither has left yet!

Perhaps I'm simply feeling the crush of the years, the warm breath of my mortality breathing down my neck. I will be seventy . . . well, seventysomething on my next birthday. So many friends of my youth never made it this far, and I should be grateful, not anxious, about my advancing age. I've never been particularly afraid of dying—I've held the hand of several loved ones as they passed from this world into the next, including my darling Dan, whom I still miss every day. And yet, right now I feel a loneliness I haven't felt since the days immediately after he left me.

Of course, if Dan were here, he'd say something like, "Oh, Gracie, you know you never sleep well after eating egg-plant" . . . and that would be that. Perhaps I should take this up with Alice and see if she has any thoughts on the matter . . . and I will, as soon as Lucy leaves, so I can get the Ouija board out of the closet in her room.

~ Grace ~

Chapter 1

WHEN Lucy Sinclair was twelve years old, she packed a suitcase to go away by herself for the first time. There had been something exciting and so grown-up about folding her clothes and tucking them inside the plaid fabric travel bag next to her sneakers and sandals and the plastic cosmetic case she borrowed from her mother for her toothpaste, toothbrush, dental floss, and shampoo. She'd also packed a diary—in which she planned to write every day—and a pen with which she could record the anticipated noteworthy moments as well as write postcards home.

She'd returned from those two August weeks at her aunt and uncle's Pennsylvania farm without having opened the diary and all but three of her postcards were still secured in the rubber band. As instructed, she'd sent one to her parents at the end of the first week ("Aunt Clarissa and Lydia were both stung by yellow jackets yesterday and we spent the whole afternoon in the emergency room. Jake got poison ivy from playing in the weeds. I don't think I have it yet. Love, Lucy"). The other two went to her younger brother, Ford, who at eight was deemed too young to go away by himself ("Uncle Pat says you can come when you're ten, which is totally unfair because I had to wait until I was twelve"), and to her best friend, Clay Madison ("I went fishing in the lake and caught three bass in one day! We found a cool old cemetery that has graves from the Revolutionary War! I took lots of pictures—can't wait to show you!").

Now, at thirty-five, packing had become so routine she could do it with her eyes closed, and these days, her trips rarely promised such adventure. The old plaid suitcase had been banished years ago to the attic, and, knowing her mother, was probably still tucked up under the eaves, and she couldn't remember the last time she'd gone fishing. The one thing that hadn't changed was the look on her mother's face when Lucy entered the lobby of the Inn at Sinclair Point, suitcase in tow and her computer bag over her shoulder, and announced that she was ready to leave for the airport.

"Do you have everything?" Grace Sinclair asked her daughter.

Lucy opened her handbag and checked for her plane ticket, her sunglasses, and the keys to her rental car. "Got it all. And if by chance I did forget something, you can always send it out or hold on to it until I come back next month to meet with Robert Magellan.

"I'm still having a hard time convincing myself that's really going to happen." Lucy shook her head as if still in disbelief that one of the wealthiest men in the country wanted to talk to her about planning his wedding. "Thanks for arranging it, Mom."

"Thank Trula. She's the one who's insisting that Robert not even consider another event planner," Grace reminded her. "Or another venue."

"I did thank her." Lucy slid her sunglasses to the top of her head. "I thought I'd get to thank her again this morning, but she doesn't seem to be up yet."

"I'm glad she's sleeping in." Grace lifted Lucy's computer bag. "She never gets a chance to—"

"Baloney. I've been up for hours." Trula Comfort, Grace's best friend for just about as long as either could remember, marched down the steps and joined them near the information desk. "I thought I'd be gracious and allow you two to have a nice breakfast together without me hanging around."

"Trula, you can hang around as much as you want." Lucy hugged the older woman. "I'm so happy you were here this weekend."

"I was glad to be here. Thought it would be good to see your work product before I browbeat Robert and Susanna into having their wedding here, with you at the helm."

"Ha." Grace grinned. "You just admitted to browbeating."

"One does what one must when one must." Trula gave Lucy one last hug, then looked around for something to carry.

"I'll take that." Daniel, Lucy's brother and the inn's proprietor, grabbed the handle of Lucy's suitcase just as Trula was about to. "You weren't planning on sneaking out on me without saying good-bye, were you?" He put a hand on his sister's shoulder.

"Have I ever?" Lucy asked as she fished in her bag for the keys she'd had just a moment ago but dropped when she hugged Trula. "I'm just trying to get organized. It appears I need a committee to get on my way."

Daniel wheeled the suitcase toward the inn's double doors and held one side open for the trio who trailed behind him.

"Thanks, Danny." Lucy smiled as she stepped outside into a crisp early winter morning. "Brrr. I keep forgetting how chilly it gets here in December. Remind me to bring a coat back with me next time."

"Any chance next time might be Christmas?" her mother asked. Lucy could tell that Grace was trying her best not to appear too hopeful.

"It doesn't look like it, Mom." Lucy paused at the car and opened the doors and trunk with the remote. "We have so many parties lined up, and several weddings, including two on Christmas Eve and another on Christmas night. Bonnie had two big events this past weekend that she had to handle on her own, and I think her last nerve is just about gone. I can't take off again in two weeks."

"Well, I doubt either of those shindigs was as 'big' as the wedding of Dallas MacGregor." Grace handed over the computer.

"That wedding was big even for us, and we've handled some big affairs over the years." Lucy put her bag on the front seat and turned to hug her mother. "I don't even know how to thank you for helping me to land that."

"All I did was set the wheels in motion, dear." Grace held on to her daughter for a long moment before patting her on the back and releasing her. "The 'landing' was all your doing."

"Mom's right, Luce." Daniel placed her suitcase in the trunk. "The inn never would have gotten the MacGregor wedding without you." He paused. "Sorry.

The MacGregor weddings. We can't forget that Dallas's brother got married on Saturday, too. I've been running the inn for a long time and I've seen a lot of really spectacular weddings here, but nothing like Saturday's affair." He slammed the trunk. "It's going to be a long time before people stop talking about it. And since all those stories and photographs started flooding the Internet on Sunday, our phone has been ringing off the hook and we can't keep up with the emails."

"Great. It's about time the inn was recognized as *the* destination venue on the Eastern Shore." Lucy reached out for her brother. "You run one hell of a business, bro."

"We do our best." Daniel planted a kiss on the top of his sister's head. "But we never could have pulled off what you did this weekend. Madeline is a good event planner, but she doesn't have your skill and creativity or your experience. We wouldn't have gotten this job if you hadn't agreed to come back and handle the planning."

"Well, remember that I've been doing this for thirteen years now. I've made a lot of contacts." She jangled her keys softly in her hands, a nervous habit. "It's all in the contacts, Danny-boy."

"I appreciate that you dug in and pulled it off with so little time. I know it was stressful," he told her.

"It was so worth it, are you kidding me? Bonnie says our phones have been ringing nonstop since yesterday, too. What a plum for the résumé."

"And perhaps an even larger plum awaits," Trula said.

"From your lips, Trula." Lucy kissed the older woman, then kissed her mother, and pretended not to see the touch of sadness in Grace's eyes. "I'll be talking to you, Mom. And I'll be back soon enough. Maybe we could have our Christmas in January this year."

"That's a fine idea. We'll leave the tree up." Grace nodded and stepped back from the car. "Safe trip, love."

"With any luck, I'll be sleeping the whole time." Lucy angled behind the wheel and her brother closed the door for her. "Take care, everyone."

"Bye, Lucy."

"Thanks again . . ."

Lucy turned the key in the ignition and headed around the circular drive to the long lane that led from the inn to the main road, trying to swallow the lump in her throat. For her, coming home was both agony and ecstasy. She loved her family more than anything, cherished the time she spent with her mother and brothers—but staying at the inn brought back her most painful memory. The irony was not lost on her that her childhood home, the place where she'd been raised with so much love and laughter, also housed her worst nightmares. The place where she should have felt most secure was where she had been most vulnerable.

She blinked back tears, knowing that her long absences hurt her mother, and yet she could never explain why she stayed away, why even this time around she'd slept more nights at the home of one of the brides, Steffie Wyler, than she had at the inn. Grace would all but die if she knew the truth, if Lucy were to tell her why she was more comfortable sleeping under another roof—any roof—than the inn's. Keeping her secret was Lucy's way of shielding her mother from an even greater pain, and so she'd moved to the opposite side of the country and came home only for those family events she could not avoid.

Turning her back on the inn with a conflicting sense of both relief and regret, Lucy negotiated the first broad curve in the road just as a dark Jeep rounded the bend at the same time. Pulling as far to the right as she could, Lucy slowed to pass the oncoming car on the narrow drive.

Daniel should have this widened, she was thinking, when she realized the driver of the Jeep had stopped next to her. She stared at the driver through her dark glasses against the glare of the morning sun, then reluctantly hit the brake and rolled down her window.

"I hope you weren't going to leave town without saying good-bye." Clay Madison had rolled down his driver's-side window as well.

"Sorry. I have an afternoon flight out of Baltimore and am running a little late." Lucy cleared her throat. "Besides, I thought we said good-bye after the wedding on Saturday."

"I thought we'd only said good night." He paused, then added, "I was hoping for a chance to sit and talk, you know. Catch up."

"We did that on Saturday," she replied, suddenly aware that she'd sounded somewhat prim, and wished she hadn't.

"We only touched the surface, LuLu." He took off his sunglasses and held them in the hand that hung out the window. His eyes were an odd mix of blue and gray, and they studied her face with what she'd first thought might be amusement, but now wasn't quite sure. Looking into them, Lucy felt a spark of guilt. Over the weekend, she'd had an opportunity to say things to him that needed to be said, and she had let it slip away.

"Maybe next time," she told him, hoping she'd have found the nerve by then, but suspecting that she might not.

"When's that going to be?"

"I might be back in January to talk to . . . to a potential client."

"Yeah, I heard Robert Magellan was interested in booking the inn for his wedding this summer but only if you'd do your wedding planning thing."

Lucy frowned. "Where'd you hear that?"

"Trula mentioned it last week when she stopped in with your mom for coffee at Cuppachino."

"There's no such thing as discretion in this town," she grumbled, and he laughed, the sound touching something inside her, the way his laughter always had. "I need to go if I'm going to make my plane."

"This is where you're supposed to say, 'It was great seeing you, Clay.'" He slid his glasses back onto his face.

"It *was* great seeing you again." Lucy nodded. It *had* been great.

"Thanks, LuLu. You, too. See you next time around." He rolled up his window and continued on the drive toward the inn.

"You need to stop calling me 'LuLu,'" she muttered, though he was gone.

It took a moment for her to realize that her foot was still on the brake. She hit the accelerator and followed the lane to Charles Street, where she made a left, trying not to think about Clay and the fact that when he wanted to get her attention, he still called her by the name he'd given her when they were in kindergarten, for crying out loud. No one, but NO ONE, had ever been permitted to call her that, except Clay, her onetime best friend.

All weekend long, the guilt from knowing that she still owed him, if not an apology, certainly an explanation for something she'd done long ago, hung between them. He'd not asked, and she'd not offered, but it was there nonetheless. It rankled that even now, so many years later, she was unable to bring it up and out into the open. Perhaps if she could, she'd be done with it, once and for all, and the nightmares would stop. Maybe then she could come home and sleep in her old room and not wake up in the middle of the night, cold with sweat and shaking with fear. Maybe just telling someone after all these years would make a difference . . .

She was mulling that thought over as she drove through the center of town and past the shops that had helped to rejuvenate this small bayside community when renewal had been needed most. For several hundred years, the town had quietly grown on the shores of the Chesapeake Bay, the crab and oyster industries supporting the residents for generations. But time, overfishing, and polluted waters had taken their toll on the famed Chesapeake Blue crabs and the Bay's oysters alike, and the local watermen had to turn to other means to make their living. As their businesses began to die, so did the town. Soon an exodus began, as more and more families moved away in search of a life that could sustain them. For years, it was said that Charles Street only led *out* of town.

And now new businesses were thriving: Bling, for upscale women's clothing and accessories; Cuppachino, for the best coffee on the Eastern Shore and darned good light lunches; the Checkered Cloth for tasty takeout; Let's Do Brunch, for quick breakfasts through elegant brunches; One Scoop or Two, for incredible homemade ice cream; and Bow Wows and Meows, the pricey shop for pampered pets (after all the years she'd spent in L.A., dogs wearing sundresses and pearls no longer gave Lucy pause) which, rumor had it, was being turned over to the present owner's daughter—Clay's sister, Brooke—who was converting the shop into a bakery to be called Cupcake, which would sell only, well, cupcakes.

Charles Street represented an all-new St. Dennis to Lucy, and she was just fine with that. When she was growing up, many of those same shops were single-family homes, and others were boarded-up storefronts. There'd been fewer businesses and hardly any tourists, though the inn had always been packed in the summer, and of course, the crabbing and oyster fishing had had some good years along with some not so good. The *St. Dennis Gazette*—owned and operated for over a century by her mother's family—was still the only local newspaper, but the inn was no longer the only place in town to book a room. Now, Lucy mused, it seemed like every other house that had been built before 1900 had been turned into a bed-and-breakfast.

But it was all good, she reminded herself, because it meant that her hometown was alive and growing.

St. Dennis had always had charm, even when it had been little more than a tiny watermen's village on the Bay. Houses that back then had been plagued by peeling paint and sagging porches were now the stars on the annual Christmas Tour. While in some parts of town the rejuvenation was still a work in progress, efforts had been made to offer something that would bring the tourists—and their dollars—coming back twelve months of the year. Certainly her family had benefited—the inn was slowly becoming *the* place for destination weddings on the Eastern Shore, and the *St. Dennis Gazette* was kept in print by virtue of the advertisements the local businesses were only too happy to place.

The big news, of course, was Dallas MacGregor's decision to form her own production company and establish a film studio right there in St. Dennis. She'd purchased several old warehouses on some good acreage down near the river on the way out of town, and was already renovating them to suit her needs. In a million years, no one would have predicted that one day major feature films would be produced and made right there in St. Dennis.

Well, that was progress, Lucy thought, and thank heaven for it. Just as she was proud of herself for her own accomplishments, she was proud of her family and friends—including all the newcomers she'd gotten to know—for their ability to adapt and meet the needs of a changing world. It was the rare St. Dennis family that could survive solely as watermen anymore.

The divide between the commercial and residential districts was gradual, but soon Lucy passed the last of the businesses. Charles Street narrowed where it crossed Old St. Mary's Church Road, and from that point, the homes were larger and more ornate, and set upon bigger lots that were increasingly farther apart. A mile farther, however, well-maintained homes gave way to woods that led down to the New River on the right side of the road, and fields of now-harvested corn on the right.

Lucy slowed as she rounded the curve that she knew from memory marked the beginning of the Madisons' farm. From the road, she could see that the orchard where the apple trees grew was almost completely bare, only a few leaves and some over-looked fruit hanging on. Behind the orchard was the pond where all the kids skated when it froze over. Mrs. Madison and some of the other mothers would bring folding chairs so they could sit and watch their kids and socialize at the same time. There would be thermoses of hot chocolate and always a snack—rich brownies or gingerbread—and some nights, bonfires in a nearby field where they'd toast marshmallows.

Lucy remembered her first time at the farm, sitting on her mother's lap, sniffing back a runny nose while she watched her marshmallow turn black and crispy.

"Hey, you're not supposed to let it burn." Clay had grabbed the stick on which her marshmallow had been speared and pulled it from the fire. He'd tossed the charcoaled nugget into the dark field and stabbed another on the stick for her. "Here, try again," he'd said. "Don't hold it so much in the flame. Just get it close . . ."

She'd leaned forward, her face flushed with embar-rassment. For some reason, it was suddenly very im-portant to her that she get it right this time.

"There you go." Clay had smiled at her accomplishment. "It's just right."

Lucy had nodded and pulled the stick from the fire. With cold fingers she'd popped the marshmallow into her mouth and grinned when the white goo spilled out onto her lips and chin. She'd laughed and licked the sticky mess from her fingers, and Clay had laughed with her. The scene had remained in her memory all these years for two reasons: that night had been the first time Lucy had really laughed since the death six weeks earlier of her best friend, Natalie Wyler, and it had marked the beginning of her friendship with Clay.

The blast of the horn from the car behind her made Lucy jump, and she realized she'd all but come to a stop in the middle of the road. She waved a hand out the window, a gesture she hoped would be understood as an apology, and she stepped on the gas.

Get a grip, Lucy. She shook herself from her reverie.

LuLu. She could almost hear Clay's voice, and in spite of herself, Lucy smiled. Hearing the name from his lips had brought back memories of the best time in her life, a time when everything had been so simple, so uncomplicated. Growing up in this place, at that time, could have spoiled her for living anywhere else. Would have spoiled her, but for that one thing . . .

The light up ahead turned green as she approached, and she breezed through it, made a left onto the highway, and headed toward Baltimore, her flight back to the West Coast, and the life she'd made for herself far from the shores of the Chesapeake Bay.

Chapter 2

CLAY eased the Jeep into the circle that led to the inn, looped around, and flowed into the lane that headed back toward Charles Street. He slowed as he rounded the first curve and paused, waiting for Daniel to finish taking a photograph of Grace and her friend Trula Comfort on the front porch. After a moment, Daniel turned and waved Clay on. Clay parked near the porch, right next to the NO PARKING AT ANY TIME sign, and turned off the engine while Daniel, Grace, and Trula descended upon the Jeep.

" 'Morning," Clay greeted them as he opened the car door and swung his legs out.

"Good morning," Daniel and Trula echoed.

"You're out and about early," Grace noted.

"Got to get a head start on the day, Miz Grace," Clay replied. He opened the back of the Jeep and pulled out a bushel basket of apples, which he set on the ground before closing the hatch. "I thought I'd drop these off for Franca while I was out this way."

Grace smiled. "I see apple pies in our future." She turned to Trula. "Our new pastry chef makes a mean apple pie."

"Sorry I won't be around to taste it." Trula glanced at her watch. "I fear I've already overstayed my welcome."

"Never," Grace assured her friend. "You know you're welcome to stay as long as you like."

"That's nice of you, Gracie, but I need to be getting back home. Everyone's going to think I ran away. Not that I haven't been tempted at times." Trula turned to Daniel. "Perhaps you could get one of those bellhops of yours to bring my bags down for me. I'm all packed."

"I'll take care of it myself," Daniel told her. He turned to Clay. "Great-looking apples, by the way. Are they the last of the season?"

Clay nodded. "Pretty much. We'll have some into January, but after that, we'll be done until next year. I've had everything in cold storage, but we're down to just a few more weeks."

"We'll take whatever you have left," Daniel told him. "Any cider?"

Clay nodded. "I have raw and pasteurized. Not a whole lot of each, but there's some."

"I'll take both." Daniel smiled. "Nothing like fresh, mulled cider on Christmas Eve, right, Mom?"

"Nothing like it," Grace agreed.

"You get many folks staying here over Christmas week?" Trula asked.

"You'd be surprised," Daniel told her. "Ten years ago, I couldn't have guessed we'd be such a year-round hot spot. Who knew that the business would grow the way it has."

"Since St. Dennis was 'discovered' a few years ago, every business is doing well, in spite of the economy.

This past year was a little tight, but for the most part, the tourists have really kept the town running in the black." Clay took off his glasses and held them up to the sunlight, then wiped at a spot with his T-shirt. "There's always some grumbling about how the town isn't the same anymore, things aren't the way they used to be, that the tourists take over the town in the summer, but for a lot of the shops in town, the tourists have meant the difference between an end-of-the-season sale and a going-out-of-business sale."

Grace nodded. "We've seen more shops open in the past three years than we have in the last twenty. Your mother's is the exception, of course."

Clay laughed. "My mother opened that pet supply place on a whim when she first moved back to give her something to do. As soon as my sister expressed an interest in opening her bakery, my mother couldn't arrange to have her signs taken down fast enough. Brooke's going to have the interior fitted with what she calls a baker's kitchen so she can get her business up and running by February."

Grace turned to Trula. "You met Clay's sister, Brooke, at the wedding on Saturday. Her cupcake shop is due to open just in time for Valentine's Day."

"If everything she bakes is as delicious as the cupcakes she baked for the wedding, she can't miss," Trula said. "I wish I could have smuggled some out of the reception to take back home to Robert."

"Brooke bakes for One Scoop or Two, the ice-cream shop down near the marina," Clay told her. "I'm sure you could pick up a few cupcakes there if you get there before noon. Steffie mentioned that she sells out early most days."

"I will stop on my way out of town. Which needs to be soon." Trula tapped Dan on the arm. "I'll take you up on that offer of assistance now."

"Clay, leave your invoice for the apples with Franca and we'll take care of it." Dan took Trula's arm.

"Good seeing you, Trula," Clay said.

"Always nice to see you, Clay." Trula looked back over her shoulder.

Clay bent to pick up the basket of apples.

"Now, how come you call Trula by her first name, but you always call me 'Miz Grace'?" Grace asked after her son and her friend disappeared into the lobby to gather her bags.

"I guess because I've called you 'Miz Grace' all my life." He grinned as he lifted the basket. "Old habits die hard. You're the mother of one of my friends from school. I couldn't call you just 'Grace.'"

"Speaking of your friend from school, you just missed Lucy," she told him. "She had to leave to catch a plane."

"I didn't miss her. I ran into her coming up the lane."

"So you had a chance to say good-bye," Grace said. "That's good. It was nice seeing you dancing together at the wedding the other night."

When Clay didn't respond, she continued: "Nice that the two of you had some time to catch up."

"We didn't really catch up all that much." Clay set the basket back on the ground. "She was working. You know, trying to keep everything running smoothly."

"I wish she'd . . ." Grace began, then stopped.

"Move back and take over the event planning here, I know." Clay finished the sentence for her.

"I just don't understand." Grace shook her head. "Especially since we need her . . ."

"I guess she's made a life for herself in California and she's happy out there."

"Did she tell you that?" Grace asked.

"More or less." Clay bent again to pick up the basket. "You know Lucy, Miz Grace. She's going to do what she wants to do."

"True enough." Grace sighed and walked with Clay to the door of the inn.

"Clay." She reached out a hand to touch his arm. "You and Lucy used to be so close. You were inseparable all those years—then it seemed like one of you pulled the plug on your friendship. If you don't mind my asking . . . what happened?"

Clay shifted the basket in his arms. "You're going to have to ask Lucy, Miz Grace. I wasn't the one who pulled the plug."

"I'm sorry. I probably shouldn't have even asked."

"It's okay. I've asked myself the same question for years." He turned toward the service area. "See you later."

He was almost to the kitchen door when she called to him.

"Have you ever thought of asking her?"

Clay went on into the kitchen, pretending not to have heard.

He wasn't trying to be rude. The truth was, he had tried to work his way into asking Lucy on Saturday night, but every time he thought he knew exactly what to say, something intervened. When they'd been dancing and he thought he finally had her attention—and captive, it had occurred to him—the slow song had stopped abruptly and the band started to play some line-dance thing he'd never heard before and Lucy excused herself "to see about the cake cutting." And later, when he found her alone out on the portico looking chilly, he'd slipped out of his jacket and draped it over her shoulders.

"Did you see where they remade *The Karate Kid*?" he'd asked casually.

"I did see that."

"You saw the announcement or you saw the movie?"

"Just the trailers for it."

"Reminded me of how much we both loved that movie when we were kids. Remember how we went to see it over and over?"

Lucy had nodded.

"And we made your dad buy the video when it came out and we sat in the lobby and played it over and over again on the TV in there because it was the biggest one in the inn." He'd glanced at her from the corner of his eye. "We were both going to take karate lessons and become black belts, remember?"

"I remember."

"Did you ever . . . ?"

"Earn a black belt? No."

"Me neither."

Clay had leaned both elbows on the railing and followed her gaze out toward the Bay.

"Beautiful night," he'd said.

She'd merely nodded.

"Everything seemed to go very smoothly today." He'd thought to try a different tack. "With the weddings, I mean. Must have been some job, getting two weddings off without a hitch."

"The day wasn't without its challenges," she'd admitted, "but that's my job."

He'd started to say something but she cut him off.

"I need to get back inside and keep this show moving," she'd said.

"Any chance we could get together for one more dance before the night's over?" he'd asked.

"We'll see how it goes," she'd told him.

"You're the wedding planner. Don't you decide how it goes?"

"There's a schedule." She'd smiled and slid his jacket off and handed it to him. "Thanks," she'd said, and then she was gone.

They never did have that one last dance after all.

When he came out of the kitchen, Clay was surprised to see Grace still in the lobby. She stood on the Bay side of the room, staring out a window, watching Trula's car disappear down the drive.

"Did Lucy mention to you if something was bothering her?" Grace asked.

He hesitated, because he, too, had sensed something in Lucy that hadn't felt quite right.

"Would you tell me if she had?"

"Depends on what it was, I guess." Clay tried to sound casual.

"Did she?" Grace turned to him.

"No, she didn't. But . . ." Again, he paused.

"But . . . ?"

"But . . . there were times when . . . I don't know, she seemed to be somewhere else." He thought about what he'd said, and added, "Maybe I misread her. I haven't seen her in a long time. Maybe I just don't know her anymore. Besides, I didn't see that much of her. I'm sure you spent a lot more time with her over the past week than I did."

Grace shook her head. "No. That's part of what's bothering me. I was hoping to spend some time alone with her, but she was so busy all week. Most nights, she slept at Steffie's, said she had to help get things ready for the weddings." Grace sighed. "I miss her. I don't know what's going on in her life anymore, and I guess I was looking forward to catching up. She just didn't seem to have much time."

Grace's disappointment was almost palpable.

"Well, she was here to do a job." Clay tried to rationalize on Lucy's behalf. "And you know it must have taken a lot of work to pull off what she did this past weekend. I'm sure she would have rather spent the time with you, but she was pretty busy."

"Do you really think that's all it was?" Grace looked up at him, her eyes searching his face.

"Yeah, I'm sure." He put his arm around her reassuringly even as he questioned his own words. "That's why she's so successful, Miz Grace. She takes her business very seriously." That much, he felt was true.

"I suppose you're right." Grace still looked concerned.

"She's the party planner to the stars," Clay reminded her. "You have to work hard if you want to be the best, and Lucy always did want to be the best at whatever she did."

"Well, that much is certainly true." Grace smiled. "Thank you, dear."

She patted his arm and walked toward her office.

Clay wanted to say something else reassuring but couldn't get his thoughts together before she'd closed the door behind her. He left the inn and got back into his Jeep.

He played the radio as loud as he could on the way back to the farm to keep himself from thinking too much about Lucy, about the things they'd said and the things they hadn't said. He switched off the eighties station when they started playing a New Kids on the Block song. It reminded him of the decision he'd made back then to form his own boy band because he knew Lucy was enamored of them. He was going to be the lead singer. (So what if he couldn't carry a tune? A lot of the singers didn't sound much better.) He would make albums and go on tour with his group and then Lucy would wish she'd never stopped being friends with him. But school—and soccer— started before he could get that idea off the ground, and his dreams of rock stardom were replaced by ones in which he scored the winning goal in the state championship and became a whiz at algebra so he could spend more time on the soccer field and less on his homework.

He drove around his sister's old Toyota and parked close to the barn. Brooke was coming down the steps from the back porch as he was walking toward it.

"Hey," he called to her. "Where are you off to?"

She pointed beyond the field next to the barn.

"I'm meeting Cameron at the tenant house to go over his schedule of the renovations." She paused. "I suppose I shouldn't call it the tenant house anymore, since it's going to be *my* house."

"True enough." Clay met her halfway along the

worn path between the barn and the farmhouse where they'd both grown up, left, and come back to. "Did Cam give you his final estimate?"

Brooke nodded and pulled her blond hair into a ponytail, which she held in place with an elastic she'd had on her wrist.

"It's pretty much what we talked about. Right now I'm dying to see the work schedule. I won't be moving in until well after Christmas, which is fine with me. I have almost a thousand cupcakes to bake between now and New Year's Eve and the new kitchen at the shop to put together, so I don't really have time to pack."

"Just as well," Clay told her. "Let Logan have a Christmas here in the farmhouse with Mom and me."

Logan was Brooke's almost eight-year-old son and the apple of Clay's eye. Since the death of Brooke's husband, Eric, in Afghanistan almost three years ago, Brooke and Logan had been living on the family farm, which Clay had taken over when their father retired.

"Mom was hoping to be into her new house by then," Brooke told him, "or hadn't you heard? She's looking forward to hosting a New Year's Eve party for some of her friends."

"She shouldn't move before Christmas." Clay frowned. Their mother, also a widow, had just bought herself a spiffy town house in which everything was brand spanking new.

"That's her decision, not ours." Brooke shrugged.

"Do you think she'll miss us after she moves out?" Clay asked.

"You're kidding, right?" Brooke laughed. "She's

not moving to Canada, Clay. She's only going across town."

"By herself," he reminded her. "She's never lived alone before."

"Maybe it's time she did. She married young, had her kids young. Devoted most of her life to Dad and to us. She went from her parents' house to her husband's, and after Dad died, Logan and I moved in with her. She's looking forward to having her own place, to having some time to herself." Brooke fell in step with her brother. "She's really excited about her new house and I'm not surprised she wants to share it with her friends, but I do agree, it would be nice if we were all together on Christmas morning. Who knows where any of us will be this time next year."

"You've got plans that I don't know about? You and your boyfriend planning on running away together?" he teased. Before she could answer, he added, "Okay, then, leave if you must, but the kid stays here."

Brooke laughed. "I doubt I'd ever be able to get Logan to leave the farm now. I've never seen him so happy. But no, Jesse and I aren't planning on leaving town, and I'm not going any farther than right here." She pointed up ahead to where the path ended at the front porch of the cottage that had been their destination.

Long known as the tenant's house, the two-story clapboard had been scraped clean of its old paint and awaited a new coat. The shutters had been removed, scraped, and sanded, and leaned up against the front of the building. The small front porch had also been prepped for painting.

"Looks like Cam's guys have been busy," Clay noted approvingly.

"The entire exterior has been prepped," Brooke pointed out. "Cam said the painters will start tomorrow out here while the carpenters continue inside. Come on in, and I'll show you what they've done so far."

Brooke unlocked the door and pushed it open.

"Wow, it sure looks different from when I lived here." Clay walked around the large front room, nodding at the work that had already been done. "New windows, I see. That's a real improvement. That first winter I stayed here, I thought I'd freeze to death. The wind whipped right around those sashes, so the house was always cold. I took to watching TV upstairs after that."

"New windows, new insulation." Brooke walked around the big room, her footsteps echoing.

"And we're starting on that new kitchen tomorrow." Cameron O'Connor, their contractor, pushed open the front door and joined them. "Brooke, did you tell Clay about what we're doing in the kitchen?"

"Only about seventeen times," Clay told him.

Brooke nodded, her eyes shining. "Lots of counters, two ovens, a big freezer—"

"I'm outta here." Clay laughed. "She's all yours, Cam. I've got work to do."

"How are those plans for the brewery going?" Cam asked.

"Great. As soon as Wade gets back from his honeymoon, we're going to start mapping out what equipment we'll need and how to turn that first barn into a brewery."

"Still planning on growing all your own hops and

barley?" Cam followed Clay to the door, Brooke's project momentarily forgotten.

Clay nodded. "We found a great source of seed for both. It'll be a few more years before the hops are ready, so we'll buy some this year and experiment. Wade has some formulas he's used before that we can work with. I love farming, but I have to admit, I'm excited about this new venture."

"Hey, we're all excited to have some local brew to look forward to," Cam told him.

"Stay tuned," Clay said. He waved to his sister. "See you back at the house."

Clay smiled all the way back to the house. Mad-Mac Brews was still a working plan in progress, but he had no doubt that he and Wade MacGregor, who'd owned a brewery in Texas not too long ago, would make some of the finest beer on the Eastern Shore. Once they got up and running, that is.

And as he'd told Cam, they'd be growing a lot of the ingredients that would go into their beer. Clay's success with his organic produce over the past few years encouraged him to try growing what they needed to brew organic beer as well. Wade had some pretty interesting ideas for beer flavors.

Flavored beer. Clay had laughed when Wade first mentioned it, but once he saw the numbers Wade had from his previous venture, Clay was sold. Why not beers flavored with herbs or fruits? The possibilities, it would seem, were endless.

And if it kept Clay's farm profitable, well, that was the bottom line, wasn't it? He paused midway to the barn and looked out over the fields that his family had farmed for over two hundred years. His ancestors had settled here and built the earliest section of the farmhouse he grew up in, the same one he now shared—however temporarily—with his mother and sister.

Clay had never wanted to do anything but farm, never wanted to be anything but a farmer. It was in his blood and in his heart, and over the past few years, he'd found ways to make Madison Farms relevant to the community in ways his forefathers could never have imagined. He grew for the farmers' markets and he grew for restaurants from D.C. to Manhattan. Certain famous chefs requested that he grow herbs and vegetables for them, and he grew rows of flowers that he sold to a number of restaurants for their tables. There was the orchard that still produced some of the finest apples and pears in the region, and the fields of wheat and rye that provided nearby Autumn Mills with the raw product they ground and made into breads and other products that they sold to some of the best restaurants on the East Coast. Thanks to Clay's foresight in recognizing the direction the food market was headed, Madison Farms was thriving. Growing organic hops and grains to make beer in his own microbrewery—well, his and Wade's—was just one more way to keep the farm intact. It was a promise he'd made to his father when the farm passed to him, and it was a promise Clay intended to keep.

Chapter 3

Lucy opened her eyes and glanced at her watch as she stretched as much as one could within the confines of an airplane seat. Disappointed to find she was still three hours from L.A., she sat up, opened her bag, and pulled out the paperback novel she'd picked up at BWI, a thriller by one of her favorite authors. She'd had trouble concentrating on the first few pages and gave up and tossed it back into her handbag and traded it for the folder containing notes she'd made regarding upcoming events.

The sheer number of holiday parties was enough to give her a headache, but toss in the six weddings they'd booked between now and New Year's Day and she could feel a migraine closing in. What in the name of all that's holy were they thinking when they booked not one, but two weddings for Christmas Eve, one on Christmas night, two on New Year's Eve, and one on New Year's Day, which pretty much guaranteed that neither Lucy nor her partner, Bonnie Shaefer, would have much of a holiday this year. Since Bonnie had been left to deal with the business over the past ten days on her own, Lucy figured it was only fair that she take the New Year's Day wedding and give Bonnie at least one day off.

She sighed and checked her calendar for potential dates to meet Robert Magellan and his fiancée, Susanna Jones. The second week in January looked good, weather permitting a trip back east. The last really big deal they had booked was a Twelfth Night party on January 6. After that, they were clear for almost two full weeks. What to do with all that free time? she wondered wryly. Of course, there'd *be* no free time. There were two weddings at the end of January, a wedding and a sweet sixteen on Valentine's Day, and full bookings almost every weekend beginning in March.

Might be time to bring in another pair of hands, Lucy thought as she closed her date book. Her assistant, Ava, would be the logical person to promote, if they could only get her to organize her time better . . .

Lucy closed her eyes for what she thought would be a moment while she visualized each of the upcoming events, starting with the Christmas party the following Saturday. In her mind's eye, she saw the venue ready to receive guests, everything from place cards to flowers to the table linens, the food, the band, the photographer. By the time she was midway through the January events, the plane was landing.

It was almost seven P.M. when Lucy turned into the parking lot at the small pink stucco building that served as the office of Shaefer & Sinclair. Noting that Bonnie's car was still in its assigned spot, she grabbed her bag and got out of the car, locked it, and went in through the back door.

"Honey, I'm home," she called out.

"Luce?" Ava called from the small conference room.

"Yup." Lucy opened her office door, dropped her bag on the floor near her desk, and walked the short hall to the conference room.

"Hey, you sure caused a stir." Ava met her in the doorway. "Did you see all the press coverage for your big gig?"

"I saw the Internet coverage, which was awesome." Lucy followed Ava into the conference room, where Ava tossed a handful of tabloid newspapers across the table, all of which had coverage of Dallas MacGregor's wedding on their front pages.

"Well, I'm not surprised. The security at the inn on Saturday was ridiculous. As in practically nonexistent. Dallas said she didn't want her guests to feel as if they were in an armed camp, so she just told the few guards she did hire to look for people who looked like they didn't belong there." Lucy skimmed the photos, noting that the photographers had managed to get shots of not only the famous bride and her groom, but plenty of the decor as well. "This is like good news and bad news. The bad news, of course, is that there are too many photos floating around out there. The good news, however, is that the shots that were taken certainly do justice to the old inn."

"It all looks glorious." Bonnie breezed into the room. "Either the inn is one of the most beautiful places on the planet, or you're a genius."

Lucy grinned. "Perhaps a bit of both."

Ava sorted through the stack of papers until she found what she was looking for. She folded the tabloid in half and held up a photo. "This one of the ballroom before anyone arrived? We've had seven calls today from brides who want this look for their wedding. *Seven,*" she repeated for emphasis.

"Including Marlena Missoni." Bonnie made a face.

"Marlena Misso—oh." Lucy frowned. "You mean my Christmas Eve bride?"

Bonnie nodded and pulled a chair out from the table. "Yes, that Marlena Missoni. She left voice mail for me three times yesterday—that would be Sunday—wanting to know why you didn't suggest those pretty trees with the twinkling white lights for her reception. Now, of course, she wants them. Must have them. Daddy says money is no object."

Daddy, as Lucy knew, was Enrico Missoni, the Italian director.

"So she wants, what, the decor changed at the last minute? Is she crazy?" Lucy sat on the edge of the table.

"No. She's spoiled and she's jealous that someone else had something beautiful that she doesn't have, so she wants it." Ava sighed. "Any chance you could line up some of those trees . . . ?"

"I'll call around in the morning and see what I can find." Lucy thought for a moment. Leafless trees weren't all that easy to come by in Southern California in December. Especially on short notice. "I'll call Olivia—she's the florist back in St. Dennis—and ask her who her supplier was for the trees we got for the inn."

"I hope the supplier has lots of them," Bonnie told her, "because Marlena wasn't the only bride who called about them. I think we're going to have to buy the trees and rent them out."

"That many?"

"Every one who saw those photos loved those tiny white sparkly lights," Bonnie said.

"And all the white flowers," Ava added. "One of the New Year's Eve brides wanted to know if she could change her flower order to all white."

"You told her no, I hope."

Ava nodded. "I told her the order was already in with the florist and she'd have to pay for the ones she ordered as well as the new order. She said she'd get back to us."

Lucy rolled her eyes. "I knew that doing Dallas MacGregor's wedding was going to be good for business, but I didn't think it would be this good."

"As bad as the phones were this morning, this afternoon was worse." Bonnie slipped off her shoes and rested her feet on the chair next to the one she was sitting in. "Angela stopped answering the phone by three o'clock and just let all the calls go to voice mail. She said she'd come in early tomorrow and listen to them."

"It's not like we've never done a celebrity wedding before," Lucy said.

"Ah, but this is Dallas MacGregor, and she's always news. Especially after all the scandal her ex-husband caused last year with that stupid sex tape of his," Bonnie reminded her.

"At which time she went back to her old summer haunt and reunited with her childhood love." Ava smiled. "Who doesn't love a story like that?"

"Dallas is really a very nice woman," Lucy told them, "and she deserves her happy ending. And as you can see from the photos, she was a beautiful bride."

"Well, she's helped to move Shaefer and Sinclair up a few notches in the event planning hierarchy." Bonnie straightened up, slipped her shoes back on, and stood. "We do need to thank her for that."

"Thank my mother," Lucy told her. "It was her idea."

"The same mother who also arranged for you to meet with Robert Magellan. We should all be so lucky." Bonnie waved from the doorway. "I'll see you in the morning."

"How does your mom know all these famous people?" Ava asked. "Is she, like, famous or something, too?"

"No, she just knows a lot of people who know people. Mom's lived in St. Dennis forever and knows everyone, including Dallas and her great-aunt, Berry Eberle."

"And Robert Magellan? Does he live in St. Dennis, too?"

"No. His . . . I guess you'd call her his surrogate grandmother, for lack of something better . . . is one of my mom's oldest friends. Trula has a lot of influence where Robert is concerned. She wants him to have his wedding at my family's inn, so unless I propose something totally unsuitable, or if he or his fiancée hates me on sight, we could very well land that wedding."

"And we move up another notch. Not bad for a few months' work."

"Well, first we have to get through the holidays," Lucy reminded her. "With all the parties and the weddings we booked, we're going to be near crazy come January. I'll need a trip back home just to unwind."

"Don't count on relaxing for too long. Beverly Tolliver called about her daughter's sweet sixteen party."

"The one we booked for Valentine's Day?"

Ava nodded. "She's had what she called a 'flash of brilliance.'"

Lucy covered her face with her hands. "I don't think I want to hear this."

Ava laughed. "Since it's in February, she thinks it would be fun to have an old-fashioned skating party."

"Roller skating?"

"Ah, that it would be too simple." Ava paused. "Ice skating."

"Okay, well, I'm sure there are rinks—"

"No, no, not inside. She wants it outside. Like on a pond."

"There are no frozen ponds in Los Angeles in February." Lucy stated the obvious.

"I pointed that out. But she has faith in you. She wants the pond built on their estate grounds. She's sure you can arrange for that."

"Possibly. But not tonight." Lucy gathered the newspapers into a neat stack and left them in the middle of the conference table. "I'll think about the Tollivers tomorrow."

"A little jet-lagged, are we?"

"A little." Lucy walked to the door. "You coming?"

"In a few. I just want to finish up the checklist for the Saturday morning wedding. I'll email it to you when it's finished."

"No hurry. Tomorrow is soon enough." Lucy stifled a yawn. "I'll see you in the morning."

"I'll be here."

Lucy stopped in her office long enough to pick up the printout of phone messages that Angela had left for her, took one long look at it, then put it back on her desk. There was no way she was going to return calls tonight. She grabbed her handbag and turned off the light. She would check the emails she'd received while she was on the plane once she got home, assuming she could stay awake long enough to read them. If not, well, there was always tomorrow.

Lucy's condo was dark when she arrived home, the air still and slightly stale from the place having been closed up for over a week. She turned on the unit's air conditioner and a few lights as she passed through the living room, where one end served as a dining area; the kitchen, where she checked the wall phone for the blinking light that announced she had messages, and left the bag containing her takeout dinner on the counter; the small spare bedroom that served as a home office, where she left her briefcase; and her bedroom, where she kicked off her shoes and changed from her skirt and shirt to shorts and an oversize tee.

Back in the kitchen, she opened the bag from Giatta's and took a whiff of the lasagna, which caused her mouth to water. Using the plastic fork that the server had tossed into the bag, Lucy ate from the container, leaning against the counter. It had been hours since she'd eaten, and until she'd walked into Giatta's, she hadn't realized how hungry she was. She ate half the lasagna before opening the refrigerator and grabbing a bottle of water, which she carried, along with the rest of her dinner, out onto the balcony that looked out over the valley.

Watching the sun set over the hills was the best part of her apartment, as far as Lucy was concerned, though being back in St. Dennis for more than a long weekend had reminded her of just how much she loved the views of the water and the change of seasons. When she first met with the brides, Dallas and Steffie, it had been autumn, and the Maryland countryside had been in full glorious color. The trees lining the drive that led to the inn were decked out in golds and reds and oranges, the colors reflected in the Bay. There was nothing in Southern California, she'd had to admit, that could compare with that show of color and light. This past weekend, those same trees, now stripped of their leaves, stood silhouetted against the late afternoon sky like perfectly sketched charcoal drawings. Even in winter, with the Bay a gunmetal gray, there was a beauty to the landscape of the Eastern Shore that had never been equaled anywhere in Lucy's eyes.

Not that she didn't love her adopted state, and in all fairness, she reminded herself, California could boast considerable geographic diversity. She just didn't have time for the traveling it would take to experience it all.

She finished her dinner and set the empty container on the small table to her left, then rested her bare feet atop the balcony railing, closed her eyes, and breathed in the gentle evening air. For a few moments, she permitted herself to relax, but it wasn't long before lists of things to do began to march through her brain. There were a dozen phone calls to answer, emails to read and respond to, and last-minute details to go over before her Saturday-afternoon affair, a small wedding at the home of the bride's mother. Meetings to set up. And, oh yes, she needed to figure out how quickly she could have a pond installed, and how to keep it frozen for a four- or five-hour party in Glendale, where the temperatures in February ranged from the high sixties to the low fifties—definitely not skating weather where Lucy came from. Perhaps, Lucy thought, they would settle for an outside skating rink instead of a pond. Maybe there was some way to have it made with cooling pipes under the surface that could keep the ice frozen. Surely there was someone who knew how to make that happen.

For the second time that day, her mind drifted back to the Madisons' pond and the many afternoons and evenings she'd spent there. In winter, most of the cattails had turned brown and lost their fuzzy tips, and Canada geese had taken up residency along the shore. She smiled in spite of her fatigue, wondering how the Tollivers would react if thirty noisy, aggressive geese accompanied her when she arrived to set up for the skating party. Surely they wanted authenticity . . .

She jerked awake in her chair. After allowing herself a moment to wake up, she gathered her dinner container and her water bottle and went back into her apartment. Feeling only slightly refreshed following her impromptu nap, she opened her laptop on the table in the dining area and turned it on. While she waited for it to boot up, she made herself a cup of tea. Her email was waiting for her when she returned, and she sat and scanned the list.

Clients with last-minute questions. Vendors with

order confirmations. A floral designer in West Hollywood who wanted to know how to get onto her
"preferred" list. A Realtor who was selling an old
Hollywood mansion with an eye toward having it
turned into a party venue asking for her suggestions.
A heartfelt thank-you from Dallas and Grant for the
bang-up job she'd done on their wedding. And an incoming email from CMadfarms. She hesitated before
opening it.

Hey, LuLu, let me know when you're coming back to St. Dennis and I'll
take you to Captain Walt's for some oysters and rockfish. See you then—

Clay hadn't signed his name but the salutation gave
him away. Not that he'd been trying to be anony-
mous. He would have known she'd know it was from
him. She read the email again, then saved it as new
without replying, and shut down the computer. If she
couldn't think of a snappy response, she was obviously more tired than she'd thought. She turned off
the lights in the quiet apartment and went to bed.
Tomorrow she'd deal with everything she missed
while she was in Maryland, and maybe even deal
with Clay's email, if she could come up with something that was suitably witty.

The next morning found her no more capable than
she'd been the night before. She'd dreamed she was
at the inn and of snow that fell so fast and thick that
she couldn't see the Bay. Someone was on the lawn
building a snowman, rolling each section to gigantic
heights until the head reached the inn's roof. She
stood on the porch in her bare feet and gazed up at
the snowman, wondering how its creator had man-

aged to get the head section atop the torso, and where a black hat that size could have been found. The snow continued to fall until it had piled up around her like a fortress, but still she stood and stared at the snowman. From somewhere inside the inn, she heard Christmas carols being sung and she turned to join the carolers, but the snow was too deep around her and she was trapped. In her dream, she called first for her mother, then both of her brothers, then for Clay, but no one came to help. Finally, the snowman leaned over and scowled at her.

"Stop yelling! I can't hear the music." He drew closer, his face morphing into the one that had haunted her for decades.

She awoke with a start, sweating and disoriented and annoyed to find she'd forgotten to set her alarm. She stumbled into the bathroom for a quick shower, dressed, and set out for the office with the sure knowledge that she'd just had what was likely to be the most sleep she'd have for at least a month. She consoled herself with the fact that the less she slept, the fewer nightmares she'd have.

Chapter 4

WHERE are you off to?" Clay stood in the doorway watching his sister buzz around the kitchen looking for her keys.

"Jesse and I are helping his grandfather decorate his house for the Christmas Tour, which as you know, is tomorrow." Brooke paused to pat the pockets of her jacket, then smiled. "Success."

"I'm still trying to absorb the fact that Curtis Enright has agreed to have his mansion on the tour this year." Clay raised an eyebrow. "What do you suppose has gotten into him? You could probably count the number of living people who have been inside that place on the fingers of both hands."

"I don't think he was ever asked to be on the tour before." Brooke shrugged. "He certainly doesn't have a clue about what he's supposed to be doing, and Jesse, being relatively new to St. Dennis, doesn't either."

"Which effectively puts you in charge."

"Right." Brooke grinned. "How often in the life-time of the average person does one get to dress up a real mansion in Christmas finery? Not an opportunity I'm going to pass up, that's for sure. I've only been in a few of the downstairs rooms, and I can tell you, what I've seen is gorgeous. And perfectly preserved, with everything just as it was when his wife died, or so I hear." She paused. "Which may be very romantic or very creepy, depending on how you look at things."

"Maybe the guy just doesn't like change. Maybe he just likes things the way they are." Clay glanced around the kitchen, which looked pretty much the way it did when he and Brooke were growing up. "Let's face it, some people are comfortable with the status quo."

"True. But Jesse seems to think it's a little more than that."

"What does he think it is?"

"He thinks his grandmother is still in the house."

"Now might be a good time to remind Jesse that Rose has been dead for, oh, I dunno, I'm guessing maybe twenty years."

"Jesse knows that. But he's said a couple of times when he was over there, he heard his grandfather talking to her when Jesse wasn't in the room."

"Hey, old habits die hard. A lot of people who live alone talk to someone who's not there."

"Do you suppose you'll do that? When Mom leaves and I move into my little house?"

"I wouldn't rule it out." Clay took an apple from the bowl on the table and polished it on his shirtsleeve before taking a bite. "My point was that Curtis and Rose were married for a long time and he probably misses talking to her. So maybe he still does. Doesn't mean that she's really still there."

"He still keeps all her orchids and ferns and plants growing in her greenhouse. Mr. Enright calls it the 'conservatory.' Jesse said it's like a jungle." She opened the refrigerator door and took out a box of cupcakes.

"Everyone needs a hobby." Clay shrugged.

"Jesse said sometimes you can smell gardenia in the room and sometimes not."

"Air freshener?"

"Mr. Enright told Jesse that gardenia was Rose's favorite fragrance." Brooke grabbed her handbag, started for the door, changing the subject in midstride. "Is it okay if I cut some branches off the blue spruce and the holly bushes? We might need some greens to decorate with, and I don't know what trees Mr. Enright has on his property."

"Take whatever you need," Clay replied. "You don't have to ask."

"Thanks." Brooke opened a drawer under the counter and removed a pair of garden snips.

"There is, of course, a tariff on the snips."

"And that would be?"

"A cupcake or two should do it."

"If you want cupcakes, you're going to have to work for them. You can follow me over to the Enright place and help out." She opened the back door. "Better yet, head over to the inn and give Grace a hand with the downstairs. Mom volunteered to help this morning, but she has her card group's holiday luncheon today and that's been planned for months."

"Will there be cupcakes at the inn?" he asked.

"If any are left. Mom took some with her this morning. I don't know if anyone else showed up to help." Brooke went through the door and out onto the back porch, her "see you" trailing behind.

"See you," Clay called back.

With Brooke gone, her son, Logan, at his friend Cody's house, and his mother off for the day, the farmhouse was eerily silent. Clay remained in the doorway for a few moments before following his sister out back. The Inn at Sinclair's Point was an awfully big place for Grace to tackle, and while he was sure some friends other than his mother showed up to help, it wouldn't hurt to ask. Maybe he'd just take a drive over there and see if there was anything he could do.

"Need a hand with those greens?" Clay paused in the drive and called to his sister, who already had a modest pile of blue spruce branches on the ground near her feet.

"No, I'm good, thanks," she replied.

Clay got into the Jeep and turned on the windshield wipers. The day had started off with a cold misty drizzle that left pin-drops of rain on the windows. He paused at the foot of the drive and glanced across the road at the trees that formed the woods. The last of the leaves dropped two days ago when a rough rain fell, and now the river beyond was exposed, and would remain so until spring came back around. Having farmed all his life, Clay was more attuned than many to the rhythm of the seasons, and while he much preferred summer to the other three, he trusted in that rhythm, and knew it was only a matter of time before the trees would be in bud once again.

The road was slightly slick and the air still cool, but the center of town bustled with shoppers. Every storefront on Charles Street was decorated with garlands

and wreaths and colored lights. The sidewalk plant-
ers that overflowed with bright annuals in summer
now were filled with greens and boughs of red berries, and huge red-and-white fake candy canes were
placed at jaunty angles on each utility pole. Even
the dampness didn't seem to depress the spirits of the
visitors who traipsed from shop to shop, their arms
overloaded with their purchases. Many were tourists,
not a few of whom were there for the weekend and
the house tour the following day. Judging from the
number of people standing at the light at Charles and
Kelly's Point Road, St. Dennis's merchants were having a very good day.

Things looked pretty lively at the inn, too. Clay
parked in his usual "No Parking" spot and went into
the lobby, where Santa's elves had already decorated.
The tree in the far corner was easily twelve feet tall
and completely decked out in garlands and lights and
what must have been hundreds of decorations. The
mantel was festooned with greens and a swag, and
even the sconces wore bunches of holly and red plaid
bows.

"Smart move to lie low for the morning shift," Dan
Sinclair told him, a gaily decorated wreath in one
hand and a silver bowl of pinecones in the other.
"That's when all the craziness took place. Musta been
about fifty women in here, each one trying to outdo
the others when it came to decorating." Dan faked a
shiver. "I'll be having nightmares for weeks."

"That's what happens when you're a successful
widower with no steady girl. Every woman in town
wants to be on your short list."

"What short list? Who has time for a list?" Dan

snorted and handed Clay the silver bowl and the wreath. "Assuming you're here to help, you can take these into the library. You know the way?"

Clay nodded. "I used to do my homework in there just about every afternoon."

"Oh, right. I remember. You and Lucy used to walk home from school together, but you never seemed to make it past the inn."

"What can I say? There were always freshly baked cookies here."

"The cook we had back then really doted on us kids. She baked just about every day."

"Lucy and I would stop in the kitchen and grab a snack, then we'd go into the library and spread our books out on that old table." Clay paused. "You still have that old table in there?"

"Go on back and see for yourself. I think my mom might still be working in there. Tell her to let me know what else she needs."

"Will do." Clay headed for the library. He went through the big double doors that separated the lobby in the back of the building from the big reception hall in the front. Once in the hall, he went through the first door on his right.

He found Grace fussing over something on the mantel. She looked up when Clay came in.

"What do you think?" she asked. "The red plaid bows or the gold?"

Clay scratched his head. He really didn't think too much about bows, but pretended to give it considerable thought to please Grace.

"I think maybe the plaid ones," he told her.

"I think you may be right." She tossed the gold

bows onto the table and tied the plaid ribbons around the brass candlesticks.

"Dan said you wanted this wreath hung over the mantel." He sat the bowl of pinecones on the table. "Shall I take down that painting and hang this in its place?"

"That would be most helpful, Clay. Thank you." Grace stepped back to give him room.

"Where would you like the painting?" he asked after he made the exchange.

Grace paused, then pointed to a closet. "We'll put it in there for now."

Clay opened the door and stood the painting up against the side wall of the closet.

"What else can I do for you?" he asked as he closed the closet door.

"You could help me find a few more hours in this day." Grace sighed and leaned against the side of the table, her arms folded across her chest, her face weary. "I've been working since early this morning and we still have miles to go before we're finished."

"Why don't you tell me what else you want done in here, then go grab yourself a cup of tea and a chair and sit and put your feet up for a few minutes," Clay suggested.

"That's a lovely idea. Are you sure you wouldn't mind . . . ?"

"Just tell me what you need, then go relax for a while."

"Well, there's a tree out there on the porch that needs to be brought in and put in that stand." Grace pointed to the red-and-green tree stand in one corner.

"Where would you like the tree?"

"I think in the alcove there near the window." She studied the space, then nodded. "I usually put it over there in the corner, but I think this year we'll try something new."

"Your wish, my command," he said. "And after I have the tree in place?"

"Well, if it wouldn't be too much trouble, there are some strings of lights in one of those boxes near the window. You could put those on the tree. There's more of that plaid ribbon on the table that you could use as garland." She held up a spool of the plaid. "Oh, and there are also some ornaments in the boxes near the door, but I'll be back before you get to them. I'll only be a moment."

"Take as much time as you want, Miz Grace. I can handle the tree, the lights, and the ornaments."

"You're a dear. Could we get you some coffee or a glass of wine?"

"Coffee would be fine, but no hurry."

"I'll send someone in with it," Grace promised as she left the room.

Alone in this room where he'd spent so much time as a child, Clay walked around the table to the first chair from the wall, the one that faced the windows. The one he always used to sit in when they did homework. He pulled the chair away from the table and sat for a moment just looking around the room, trying to see it as he'd seen it then. Back then, the room with its two walls of bookcases that reached to the ceiling had been cavernous, and the table had seemed enormous.

Funny how the room—and the table—had become so much smaller over the years.

He pushed away from the table and leaned over until his face was almost parallel to it, and smiled when he found that the initials he'd scratched into the wood when he was nine—CTM, for "Clayton Thomas Madison"—were still there. He found it strangely satisfying to know that for all the years that had come and gone, this little bit of him had remained.

The last time he'd sat in that chair, at that table, he and Lucy were studying together for exams, and he'd had a really hard time keeping his mind on his notes. Every time he looked up, there she sat, dressed in a tee and cutoff, ripped jeans that were so popular that year, her curly, pale auburn hair piled on top of her head. When she looked up and smiled, his heart beat nearly out of his chest and scared the bejesus out of him because the feelings he was starting to have for her seemed, well, *wrong*. Lucy was his *best friend*. He wasn't supposed to be thinking about what it would be like to kiss her now, but the fact that when they were thirteen, they'd practiced kissing—on each other—in this very room wasn't lost on him. It still annoyed him to think that Lucy had wanted to practice on *him* so she'd know what to do if the object of her affection at the time wanted to kiss her at Sherry Marshall's birthday party.

Clay got up from the table, walked to the window, and looked out. The shrubs that had barely touched the window ledges back then were almost to the top of the window frame, and he was sure they'd been pruned many times over the years to keep them from taking over the entire front of the inn. When he and Lucy were kids, there'd been bird feeders outside the windows. When they were in fourth grade, the two of them moved the feeders closer to the other side of the front door and replaced them with a hummingbird feeder. They'd made hummingbird food from water and sugar and filled the little plastic disk and watched, but that first day, no tiny birds had arrived. By the next afternoon, however, their feeder had been discovered, and over the summer and into early fall Clay and Lucy spent so much time watching the hummingbirds that they could recognize one from another, and had gone so far as to name them.

They'd started out by giving them names that began with *H*.

"Harry," Clay said aloud, remembering. "Hortense. Horatio. Helene. Higgins. Hester. Hilary. Hank . . ."

Before the summer was over, there'd been more birds than *H* names, and they'd started over with the *A*s.

"Agatha. Amadeus. Archimedes . . ."

Damn, but they'd had fun when they were kids, hadn't they?

"What happened, LuLu?" Clay heard himself say, then looked over his shoulder to see if anyone else had walked in and maybe heard him, too.

Didn't his father always say that you couldn't change the past, so it was a waste of time to dwell on it?

He didn't have to dwell on it, but there was no harm in acknowledging it, he reasoned. His friendship with Lucy had been a big part of his childhood, and there was no getting around that. They'd done just about everything together growing up, and much of it right here in this room. They made science projects and wrote book reports, excitedly sharing their newest favorite books with each other. They quizzed each other before tests and shared notes they took in class. They played music here, purloined albums Lucy had lifted from Daniel's room. As nine-year-olds, they'd learned all the words to every song on Springsteen's *Born in the U.S.A.* album. Later that year, they took turns singing all the parts of "We Are the World."

They learned how to dance by practicing with each other.

Lucy had really aced dancing, he recalled. She was petite and light on her feet, whereas he was always too tall for his age to be anything but awkward. She never seemed to mind, though, and by the time their first junior high dance rolled around, they were ready.

His eyes narrowed as he remembered how he'd felt when Kevin McMillan had asked Lucy to dance, how something hot and fierce had risen in his chest and his hands had fisted all on their own. He hadn't had enough experience back then to recognize that first brush with jealousy, and had convinced himself that he was only annoyed because Kevin was such a jerk and, as such, had no business asking Lucy to dance.

Not for the first time, Clay wished he understood what had caused the rift between them. He'd spent hours thinking about it, back then, but had never come close to knowing.

One of these days, he promised himself, he was going to find out. In the meantime, there was a Christmas tree that needed to be set up.

Clay set the stand in the alcove where Grace had indicated and went through the big front door to the porch, where he found a Scotch pine leaning against the wall. He brought it inside and wrestled it into the tree stand in the alcove, then stepped back to see if it was straight.

"A little to the left maybe," Dan noted as he joined Clay and handed over a cup of black coffee. "You still take it black?"

Clay nodded. "Sometimes. Thanks." He took a sip, then set the cup and saucer on the table. "You're right. It's leaning toward the left."

"Let's see if we can fix that."

After several tries, they were both satisfied that the tree was as straight as it was going to be.

"Nice of you to help out Mom," Dan told him. "She's running herself ragged, trying to achieve perfection for the tour."

"Judging by the way the lobby looks, I'd say she's well on her way to succeeding." Clay opened a box and started to unwind the lights. "How many more rooms is she going to do?"

Dan shrugged. "I'm trying to talk her into limiting the tour area to the two lobbies, this room, and the sitting room across the way. I don't see any reason to do anything else."

"I saw some trees going into the dining room," Clay noted.

"I'll do those later. Otherwise the dining room is almost done, thanks to your mother and a few of her friends who pitched in yesterday and again this morning to do centerpieces and the mantel. Tomorrow it's only going to be open to guests who have bought tickets to the tea that follows the tour." Dan watched Clay struggle to untangle the lights for a moment, and was looking about to give him a hand when his cell phone rang. He answered it, listened, then said, "All right. I'll be there in a minute."

Dan dropped his phone into his pocket. "Diana needs to be picked up from her sleepover at a girlfriend's. How 'bout I give you a hand with those lights?"

"I've got it." Clay held up the bundle of wires and searched for an end. "I'm good at this. Really. Go get your daughter."

"If you insist."

"I do," Clay said without looking up. Normally he *was* good at untangling things. He stared at the jumble, then placed it all on the table, where he proceeded to unknot the tiny white lights, one at a time. When he was finished, he draped the strands on the tree, then stood back to admire his work.

"Nice," he said aloud.

Grace had said something about using the plaid ribbon as garland, but he didn't have a clue about that, so he passed directly on to the ornaments. He was just sorting through the boxes when Grace returned.

"I feel much refreshed," she told him. "Thanks so much for giving me a little time off."

"Don't mention it." Clay glanced up from the box he'd just opened.

"My, but you certainly accomplished a lot in a short period of time." Grace went right to the tree. "The lights are lovely. You did a great job." She walked around the three exposed sides. "I like the way you draped them. Very nice."

"I didn't understand the ribbon-thingy, so I put that aside."

"We can save that until the decorations are on the tree." Grace came closer to see what he'd uncovered. "Oh, I love these ornaments."

She reached around him to pick up a blue-green glass ball. "Dan and I bought this in Maine one year. It was the first time the two of us went on a vacation together—just the two of us—since Ford was born. We'd left Daniel in charge of Lucy and Ford—he was home from college—and I was a nervous wreck the whole time that something was going to happen." She held the ball up to the light. "But apparently nothing did. That was one of those times when my instincts proved unreliable."

"How long ago was that?" Clay unpacked a few more glass balls and handed them to Grace, who hung them on the tree.

"Oh, dear, let's see . . . well, it was the year that Ford started junior high. The year between Lucy's freshman and sophomore years at the high school." She searched in a box for some ornament hooks, and paused for a moment, a gold glass ball in her hand, her gaze fixed outside the window. She sighed loudly. "Of course, I was so happy that everything had gone well in our absence, and yet . . ."

"And yet?" Something in her voice drew his attention. Clay stopped unwrapping and turned to her. She was still staring out the window.

She shook her head as if to shake off whatever it had been that had bothered her. "Oh, it was nothing, I suppose. In retrospect, I have to think I'd misunderstood what I'd been feeling."

"What had you been feeling?" Clay had heard the stories about Grace having some kind of sixth sense, some kind of "sight," though no one seemed quite sure exactly what it was that she could sense or see. He'd never had the opportunity to ask her directly, though, and his curiosity got the best of him.

"Just that something was happening here that had been very bad." Her voice dropped to a near whisper, and her hand clenched around the glass ball she was holding. "But obviously I was wrong, and everything was fine when we got back. Still, I never can seem to think back on that summer without having that same feeling of dread that I'd felt as we'd driven away, that same sense of panic and fear and pain . . ." She shook her head as if shaking off a bad dream, and her hand tightened around the glass ball she'd been holding until it cracked.

Grace looked down at her right hand and opened it. Shiny gold shards were embedded in her palm.

"Oh, for heaven's sake," she muttered. "Would you look at that? I wonder how I managed to do that . . ."

"Miz Grace, your hand is bleeding," Clay told her. "I'll get some towels from the kitchen."

"There are paper towels in the restroom right through that door." Grace pointed to a door directly across the hall. "If you wouldn't mind . . ."

"Not a bit." Clay went into the bathroom, grabbed some paper towels, and held a few under cold running water in the sink. He returned to the library and asked, "Do you think you got all of the glass out?"

Grace nodded. "I'm pretty sure. Here, give me those." She reached for the wet paper towels and cleaned her palm of the blood that had puddled there. "I don't know what I was thinking to have broken that ball like that."

Grace wrapped one of the paper towels around her hand and cleared her throat. "Well, then, I suppose I should probably get a bandage of some sort, shouldn't I?"

"Would you like me to—"

"No, no. I'm fine, dear. I'm sure there's a first-aid kit in Daniel's office . . ." Her voice trailed away as she passed through the door and into the hall beyond.

Clay gathered up the discarded shards of broken glass that had fallen onto the floor, wondering what had spooked Grace back then that had been so powerful that it still frightened her just to think of it, all these years later.

Chapter 5

L UCY held the phone between her shoulder and her ear. It kept slipping, and every time it did, she dropped the place cards she was trying to artfully drape over the miniature orchids in their little pots. Tomorrow's bride had been very specific: her calligraphied seating cards had to be hung by thin silver cords from the stems of tiny white orchids in little terra-cotta pots spray-painted silver. The paint job had gone to Ava, but since Bonnie had taken their assistant with her for tonight's event, the job of making the cards work perfectly fell to Lucy.

"So it sounds like the inn is decked out to the teeth," Lucy replied to her mother's lengthy description of what had gone where in preparation for the Christmas Tour.

"And then some. Oh, I do wish you could see it, Lucy. The old place has never looked so elegant." Grace paused before adding, "Well, excluding the MacGregor-Wyler weddings."

"It all sounds grand, Mom. Make sure Danny takes lots of pictures. I'm glad you had so many volunteers to work with you."

"Yes, but we could have used your touch. You always know how to make things look special."

"Hey, I learned everything I know from you."

"That's very sweet of you, dear, and I appreciate the thought, but I've never had your artistic touch."

"Nonsense. I remember how you always came up with something new, every year, for the mantels and the tables. How you used whatever was still green in the garden and how, when there wasn't anything left that was green, you sprayed whatever you could find—twigs and pinecones and ivy and acorns— silver or gold and put them in glass bowls with those vintage Christmas decorations."

Hmm, Lucy thought. *Vintage Christmas decorations . . .*

"Well, I'll send you some pictures so you can see how pretty everything is," Grace told her.

"I can't wait. Tell Danny to email them to me." Lucy opened a storage closet and began to look for the box of old decorations she'd bought at an estate sale a few years ago. If there were enough of them, they'd add just the right touch to the two-foot Christmas trees her Christmas Eve bride had wanted for centerpieces. Lucy had plenty of silver ornaments on hand, but a few of the very delicate glass balls could lend a special touch. She found the box on one of the top shelves and had a dickens of a time getting it down without dropping the phone or her train of thought.

"I'll have him send the pictures from the Enright mansion, too. I hear it's magnificent. Barbara from the bookstore stopped in there for a peek before she came here. She said Brooke and Jesse are doing an amazing job. I just may have to sneak over there tomorrow and take some pictures for the *Gazette*." Grace yawned, then excused herself for having done so.

"You sound tired, Mom."

"It was a long day," Grace admitted. "But it wasn't too bad. I had a lot of help from the Historical Society and, of course, some friends stopped by to lend a hand. Oh, and Clay came by and he—"

"Clay?" Lucy made it to the conference room table with the box, which she tried not to drop. "Clay helped you with the Christmas decorations?"

"Yes, he stopped by to see if I needed a hand, and it was perfect timing on his part. I have to admit, I was starting to fade, but he took over in the library so that I could grab a quick cup of tea and put my feet up for a few minutes."

"Huh." Lucy opened the box and started to unwrap a few of the ornaments.

"He brought in the tree for the library and put it up," Grace continued, "hung the lights and the ornaments on it. Hung the wreath over the fireplace, cut some greens for the centerpiece on that old library table. Wasn't that nice of him?"

"Huh," Lucy said, then realized it was her second "huh" in less than thirty seconds. She knew she could do better. "Well, yes, that was very nice."

"Very nice indeed. He's such a nice boy."

"Clay's not a boy anymore, Mom."

"He'll always be a boy to me, dear. Just like you'll always be a girl in my eyes."

"Mom . . ." Lucy sighed and hoped her mother wasn't working herself up into trying to sell her on Clay again. Lucy got it. Her mother wanted her to give up her business, move back to St. Dennis, marry someone local—Clay would do nicely—and have babies.

"Oh, I'm going to have to run," Grace said. "We have guests who want to check in and Andrea is not at the desk. Good luck with tomorrow's wedding, dear. I'm sure it will be a smash."

"Thanks, Mom. You, too. I know the inn will be . . ." Lucy heard her phone disconnect but finished her thought aloud anyway. ". . . the star of the show tomorrow."

She slid her phone back into her pocket, trying to process the fact that Clay had spent the afternoon helping her mother decorate the inn. The concept raised a number of reactions. On the one hand, it really *was* nice of him to pitch in and help her mother. Grace might not want to admit it, but she wasn't as young as she used to be, and between the newspaper that she ran almost single-handedly, and whatever she got involved in at the inn—not to mention all of her community projects—she could very easily run herself into the ground. So for Clay to just stop in and offer to help, well, Lucy had to admire him for that. On the other hand, the fact that anyone else in town had to give of their time to help get the inn ready for the holidays only reinforced the feeling Lucy got every once in a while—like now—that she—not Clay, not family friends or members of the Historical Society—should be the one taking on those tasks for her aging mother.

And how, Lucy wondered, would Grace react if she knew her daughter thought of her as "aging"?

Putting aside her guilt and all thoughts of being an

unworthy daughter, Lucy focused on counting the old ornaments in the box only to find there weren't enough. As nice a touch as the antiques would have been, she'd have to be content with the ones she'd purchased for the occasion. Unless, of course, she could find others. Making a mental note to check a few online sites, she started to rewrap them, then paused.

She really should thank Clay for helping her mother. Call, or email? She pondered the choices. A phone call is more personal, would require a different level of engagement than email. If she called him, she'd have to say something other than thank you. What else did she really want to say to him? Knowing Clay, he'd want to talk. He'd ask her how things were going, and then she'd have to be polite and ask him how things were going for him, and before she knew it, they'd be engaged in conversation.

Better to just reply to his email. No chitchat necessary. No polite inquiries. Just a short and sweet "thank you."

She went into her office, opened her laptop, and began to type. But once she'd typed "thank you," she realized it wasn't enough. It was too cool, too impersonal. The words looked too lonely on the screen. She deleted what she'd written and tried again.

> Clay—I don't know how to thank you for helping Mom get the inn ready for the house tour. So nice of you.
> Lucy

There, she thought. That should be just fine. She reread it, reconsidered, and added, Hope you have a wonderful holiday.

She reread it again, then grumbled, "For crying out loud, you're thirty-five years old. Just send the damn thing and be done with it."

She hit send, vowed to not second-guess herself again, and was on her way back to the conference room when she heard the *ping* that announced incoming email. She stopped, then went back into her office and turned the laptop around to face her.

My, that was fast.

> You can thank me by having dinner with me the next time you're home.
> Clay

Lucy sat on the end of the desk and reread his note. In her mind's eye, she saw Clay in the library, the room where they had spent so many hours together, the room that had, years later, become her safe place. She thought of the bookshelves that all but reached the ceiling, that held the books in which, as a troubled teenager, she had sought refuge, some books brought there by her great-great-great-grandmother Cordelia when she married the first Daniel Sinclair, the one who'd built the original section of the inn. There were the books Cordelia had brought with her from her native England, volumes of Shakespeare and Jane Austen and Charles Dickens, their leather bindings dry and fragile but always handled with great care. Mark Twain and Jonathan Swift sat beside Longfellow and Hawthorne, and on lower shelves, Hemingway and Faulkner. The Sinclairs had always been lovers of literature, and as a young girl, Lucy had been the beneficiary. She'd loved that room for as long as she could remember, and she recalled that

Clay had loved it, too. Enough, apparently, to have spent a Saturday afternoon helping her mother dress it up for Christmas. Hanging wreaths. Cutting greens. Stringing lights on the tree. She could almost see his tall lanky self dragging in the tree, could almost hear his deep voice humming the Christmas carols she knew would have been playing. Something about the scene brought a lump to her throat.

It's just nostalgia, she told herself. *That's all.*

She sat at her desk, and pulled the laptop closer. Clay's email was still open on the screen. Lucy hit reply, typed, "It's a date," then hit send before she could change her mind.

She closed her laptop and returned to the conference room and the preparations for the wedding that would keep her up for most of the night.

On the second of January, Lucy smacked her alarm clock when it had the audacity to ring at six A.M. She'd worked nonstop for the past month, and this morning, damn it, she was sleeping in until at least eight. She rolled over and kept her eyes closed, but the damage had been done. Once awake, she stayed awake, so after twenty minutes of trying unsuccessfully to fall back to sleep, she got up and headed for the shower. Another twenty minutes and she was in the kitchen, towel wrapped around her wet hair, hunting for the coffee beans she knew she'd bought the last time she'd gone food shopping. When that had been, she wasn't certain, but she did know she'd bought the coffee. When her search proved fruitless, she gave up and put a kettle of water on the stove to boil for tea. While the water heated, she checked email on her phone.

Most fabulous wedding EVER, wrote the mother of the New Year's Eve bride. Total perfection! Your reputation is well earned!

"Not to mention *hard* earned, after having to deal with you and your nut-bar daughter—not to mention your two sisters and their idiot daughters—for the past eight months," Lucy muttered.

Gorgeous right down to the last tiny detail, enthused her Christmas Eve bride. I'll cherish the memory of every moment forever!

"Except, perhaps, for the moment your maid of honor found her fiancé on the coat-closet floor with one of the waitstaff."

The teakettle began to whistle. She poured water into a mug and dropped in a tea bag. When her phone rang, she glanced at the number, then answered the call.

"What are you doing up so early?" she asked.

"Probably the same thing you're doing," Bonnie replied. "Old habits die hard."

"I was thinking of coming in late today," Lucy told her.

"I was thinking of closing the office completely. What do you think?"

"I think it's the best idea you've had in a very long time. I'm exhausted," Lucy admitted.

"Me, too, and I didn't even have to work yesterday. How'd the Palmer wedding go, by the way?"

"Without a hitch, for the most part. But the band the groom insisted on using, the one we weren't familiar with?" Craving caffeine, Lucy blew on the tea, hoping to cool it. "They lived up to my worst fears."

"That bad, eh?"

"Just dreadful. I hope we don't get blamed for them."

"Of course we will. Live and learn."

"I learned that lesson a long time ago, but neither the bride nor the groom wanted to hear it. Anyway, it's done, and we don't have another gig until Saturday."

"Hallelujah." Bonnie sighed. "By the way, have you heard from Mr. Gazillionaire?"

"Robert Magellan?" Lucy took her mug into the living room and eased herself into a chair. "He wants to meet with me next week."

"What did you tell him?"

"I told him whatever was most convenient for him was convenient for me," Lucy replied. "Which turned out to be Thursday."

"Fabulous. Coming on the heels of Dallas MacGregor's wedding, this is huge. We've enjoyed a great reputation for years, Luce, but these two weddings are the icing. One of the first things I want to do is revise our fees for 2012."

"One of the first things I want to do is hire a few more people. We just can't keep trying to do everything ourselves, Bon. Neither of us will make it to forty if we don't slow down."

"I've been thinking the same thing. We need at least three more assistants just to handle the events we have on the calendar going right on through until the fall."

"I think Ava is ready to start taking on events by herself, and I heard that Corrine over at Walton's firm is looking to move on," Lucy told her.

"Can't say that I blame her. Yvonne Walton is a

witch. I worked for her when I first came out here. I shudder every time I think back on those days. Who told you about Corrine, anyway?"

"We have the same hairdresser."

"Always a reliable source."

"Okay, so let's talk to Corrine, and let's talk to Ava and see if we can staff up. And we need a few more day-of hands, while we're at it. I think it's likely that Robert Magellan's wedding will be sometime in June, and I imagine that will keep me busy for a while."

"That's prime time," Bonnie acknowledged. "June is still the most popular month for weddings. So yeah, we'll see if Corrine really is interested in making a move, and we'll offer Ava a promotion. How 'bout we meet with her in the morning at nine?"

"Perfect. She's earned it. We just need to remind her that she needs to enhance her time management skills." Lucy covered a yawn. "Gosh, maybe next year one of us will get to have a real Christmas. Could that really happen?"

"If we play our cards right, maybe both of us will have Christmas," Bonnie mused. "How long has it been since you were home during the holidays?"

"Too long."

"Let's make an executive decision right now not to take on any event for Christmas Eve or Christmas Day, 2012, unless Ava or Corrine—or whoever we end up hiring—is the consultant."

"Wow. That's a revolutionary concept."

"I know. Let's do it. Agreed?"

"Agreed." Lucy paused, then said, "I'd like to take a few extra days off next week while I'm home. I feel guilty about not being there with my mom, especially with my brother Ford being away for so long."

"Go 'head and take the time."

"There's a twenty-fifth anniversary party that weekend, Bon."

"I booked it, I'll handle it. Besides, it's a small affair," Bonnie assured her. "We owe your mother bigtime for the weddings she's steered our way. When you come back, maybe I'll take a few days off myself, fly up the coast to see my ex."

"Seriously? Are you talking about Bob?"

"He's the only ex I have. But yeah, we've been talking on the phone for a month or so now, and we're both wondering . . . well, we're just wondering if we did the right thing when we split up."

"Take a week," Lucy told her. "Take two."

"A few days, maybe. Anyway, I'll see you in the morning. Get some sleep. That's what I'm going to do."

The first thing Lucy did after she hung up the phone was to call her mother and tell her she'd be staying on for a few days after her meeting with Robert Magellan. The second thing was to send an email to Clay.

Meeting potential client at the inn on Thursday morning, staying through the weekend. Thank-you dinner at your convenience.

Lucy.

Within minutes came his reply.

Thursday night. Will pick you up at seven. Your mother wants you to bring home a coat this time. Baby, it's cold outside.

Clay

Lucy hit reply.

You told my mother we were going to have dinner?

A quick tap to send, and she stared at the screen awaiting his response.

Don't shoot the messenger. Saw her at Cuppachino yesterday & she mentioned you were coming home soon & she hoped you'd remember to bring a coat with you.

Lucy breathed a sigh of relief. The last thing she wanted was for her mother to get ideas about her and Clay. More than she already had, that is. She figured she wouldn't mention it at all until she got home, lest her mother read more into this dinner than was there.

After all, she reasoned, it was only a friendly dinner with an old classmate, right?

Chapter 6

HIS coffee mug refilled and half a fat croissant on its plate nearby, Clay took a folder from his briefcase and spread it open on the table. At ten o'clock on a January morning, Cuppachino was much more subdued than it had been at eight. His table was one of only three that were inhabited.

"This," he said as he removed a piece of graph paper, "is what we need to be thinking about."

Wade MacGregor, Clay's partner in MadMac Brews, stared at the hand-drawn structure. "It looks like one of those old-fashioned hop barns."

"That's exactly what it is. And it's what we're going to be working on once we get the hops in the ground."

Wade picked up the sketch and studied it. "What do you mean 'we'?"

"I mean you and me." Clay leaned back in his seat and took a sip of coffee. "We can't afford to hire someone to build it, so we're going to have to do it ourselves."

"I have no carpentry skills," Wade said bluntly.

"Fortunately, I do," Clay assured him. "And since

you seem like a reasonably intelligent guy, I'm betting you can learn."

"Maybe we can get Cameron O'Connor to give us a hand."

"And we'll pay him . . . how?"

"We'll pay him in beer." Wade grinned. "We both know that Cam really likes a good beer."

"Which we won't have in any real quantity for about, oh, three years if we're lucky. If the Eastern comma larvae don't eat our hops and we don't get hit with powdery mildew."

"Someone's been studying up," Wade said.

"Someone has to."

"Hey, give me a break. I just got married, been back from my honeymoon for all of"—Wade looked at his watch—"sixteen hours."

"Time enough to get to work."

"Okay, supposing I agree that the two of us should build a hop barn. I'm assuming we'd build it there on your farm?"

Clay nodded. "Plenty of room."

"So what are we going to use as material? As you pointed out, we don't have a whole lot of discretionary funds to work with."

"Barn boards." Clay took a bite out of his croissant.

"Barn boards?" Wade frowned.

"Sure. Those, I have plenty of." He leaned forward. "There are three barns on the farm. One I use primarily to store equipment. The other—the biggest one—we're going to turn into our brewery."

"For which we're borrowing the money from my sister."

"Right. And the third barn, the one that's seen better days, we're going to tear down and reuse the boards to build the hop barn."

Wade nodded. "I guess I know better than to ask who's going to take the barn down."

Clay laughed. "The dismantling process will take some planning so that we don't pull it down on top of ourselves. I think we'll need Cam's help there, too."

"Maybe if we asked him to be our official taster, he won't charge us too much."

"The idea has possibilities. But it just occurred to me to offer him some of the old barn boards that we don't use."

"What would he want with those?"

"We're talking about heart-pine boards that are over one hundred years old here, champ."

"Okay, so you'll have a lot of old wood left over. Still don't get why Cam would want that instead of cash."

"In his spare time, Cam makes furniture. Tables, mostly. He prefers to work with old woods. Old heart pine if he can get it, which is rare."

"So what you're saying is that the barter system is alive and well in St. Dennis."

Clay nodded. "I bet Cam would jump at the chance to get his hands on all that old pine. The tables he makes are works of art, by the way. My mom just bought one for the dining room in her new house. It really is one of a kind. My sister liked it so much, she asked him to make one for her." He paused as a thought occurred to him. "It would be really cool if Cam made one for her from the boards from our old barn."

"Nice housewarming gift," Wade noted.

"Yeah, I'll have to talk to him about that, sooner rather than later. Brooke's planning on moving into the old tenant house as soon as it's finished. She's hoping maybe as soon as next month."

Wade pulled Clay's sketch closer and took another look. "What about this rounded top piece? How would we make that?"

"Traditionally, a cupola sits over the drying area, and I thought it looked pretty cool. I think we can make it with shingles, maybe a metal roof. That's something we'd need Cam for."

"So okay, we meet with him as soon as we can set it up. Meanwhile, while I was away, I ordered some barley seed."

"You were ordering barley seed while you were on your honeymoon?" Clay stared at Wade. "What did Steffie have to say about that?"

"Nothing, since she went off in search of a wholesaler for macadamia nuts. She had some while we were in Hawaii that she thought were superior to the ones she was using, so of course, she had to track down the source."

"You two deserve each other." Clay laughed. "You're two of a kind."

"Hey, the woman makes the best ice cream on the eastern seaboard. I make . . ." Wade paused, and a cloud momentarily crossed his face. "I made one of the best beers in the country."

"And as soon as we get MadMac off and running, you'll be making the best once again," Clay assured him.

"That's the plan, Stan." Wade glanced at his watch.

"I gotta run. Time to pick up Austin from preschool." He stood and finished his coffee in one long gulp. "How long do you suppose I have to live in St. Dennis before Carlo's wife makes me a mug with my name on it?"

He pointed to the shelf behind the counter where a line of handmade mugs stood.

Clay shrugged. "She only makes them for regular customers."

"I could be a regular customer."

"Put up or shut up." Clay turned his mug around so that his name was front and center.

"Or we could buy mugs with our names on them and hold our morning meetings out at the farm, or over at my place. Steffie makes her ice creams early, so she's usually at Scoop before seven."

"True enough, but we both make lousy coffee."

"Good point. Okay, tomorrow. Same time. Same place. See you then." Wade nodded in the direction of the kitchen, where Carlo, the owner, was bellowing at one of the busboys. "A real friend would put in a good word for me where it counts."

"I'll think about it."

Clay waved off the waitress who roamed the room offering refills.

"Your friend's leaving already?" the waitress asked.

"He has to pick up his son from school."

Before Wade's late business partner died, he'd married her to give her young child a home and a parent who could be counted on. Austin had just turned two, and had been welcomed into the MacGregor family—and all of St. Dennis—with open arms.

Clay returned the sketch of the hop barn to the

folder and was just about to drop it into his briefcase when the door opened and Grace and Lucy came in. They were both a bit windblown by the wind coming off the Bay, and they both paused to chat with Wade. Lucy having served as planner on Wade's recent wedding, Clay figured there would be a round of thank-yous all over again.

Well, that was all right. He liked looking at Lucy.

Right now she stood with her hands in the pockets of her coat—apparently, she'd heeded her mother's directive—her head tilted at an angle as she looked up at Wade and smiled. Clay guessed Wade was telling her once again how much he and Steffie had loved everything Lucy had done to pull off their wedding in a very brief period of time. Grace was beaming like the proud mama Clay knew her to be, so he figured it was safe to say the praise was still being heaped on.

Again, okay by Clay. He could look at Lucy all day. She had always had the best smile, still did. It lit her face and deepened her dimples and, well, it was just a pretty sight to see.

Lucy had always been petite—some of the kids in their class had nicknamed her "Runt"—but after Clay grew to his full height at sixteen, she seemed even tinier. Her hair was darker now, he noticed. When they were kids, it had been equal parts of gold and red. Now it was more a light auburn. The red and gold still there, but the mix was different. Today, it looked more . . .

She stood across the table, one hand waving in front of his face. "Clay, you in there?"

"Yeah. Hey, Lucy." He tried to cover up the fact

that he'd not only been tuned out, but tuned out thinking about her. "How was your flight?"

"Okay. I got here." She smiled, and for a moment, he could have sworn he'd heard his heart thump onto the floor. If she'd heard it, too, she gave no sign.

"Glad you did. So when's your meeting?"

"Tomorrow at ten at the inn. Wish me luck."

"Of course, but I'm sure you'll knock 'em dead."

"I hope so." She leaned on the back of the closest chair. "I don't know either of these people, so it's going to be very tentative. All I do know is that Trula wants them to have the wedding here. I don't really know what *they* want. For all I know, they're only humoring Trula by meeting with me."

"Nonsense." Grace came up behind her daughter and handed Lucy a takeout cup of coffee. "Robert would tell her if he wasn't interested."

"I don't know." Lucy turned to her. "Trula's awfully tough sometimes."

"Robert and Susanna have been to the inn and they loved it," Grace reminded her. "I'm sure when they see what sort of ideas you have for their wedding, they'll be very pleased."

"That's just it, Mom, I have no ideas. I don't know them, don't know what they like and what they don't like." She turned back to Clay. "Anyway, keep your fingers crossed for me."

"Will do."

"Well, I guess I'll see you tomorrow night. Seven, right?"

"Right. Lola's or Captain Walt's?"

"Captain Walt's. You promised me rockfish and oysters, and I intend to make you deliver."

"Walt's it is. See you then."

"So nice that you two are going on a date after all these years." Grace smiled.

Lucy frowned. "It's not a date."

"Sure it is." Clay grinned.

She turned back to him, the frown still in place. "No, it isn't. It's just dinner."

"If you say so." He was still grinning, and had the overwhelming feeling that she wished he'd stop.

She took her mother's arm and steered her toward the door. He watched from his seat until her red coat disappeared from sight, then got up, took his mug over to the counter, and handed it to the waitress to be washed and replaced on the shelf, then waved good-bye to Carlo, who was on the phone. When he stepped out onto the sidewalk, Lucy and Grace were nowhere to be seen.

Funny her insisting they weren't going on a date, he mused as he walked back to his car, his keys jingling in his pocket, wondering if he should read something into it. He'd just unlocked the door with the remote when the thought occurred to him: Maybe to her, this wasn't a date. Maybe it really was just a thank-you-for-helping-my-mother.

And maybe—he had to face this possibility even though he didn't like it one bit—maybe she's involved with someone in California. Maybe that's why she spends so little time here, why whenever she's here, she acts like she can't wait to leave.

Bummer, he thought as he started the car. That would be a real bummer. He'd always had a thing for Lucy. It had taken him a long time to accept it. A lot of women had come and gone through his life in the years since they'd been friends, but he'd never felt the same sense of, well, *fate* that he had when he looked at her. When he thought of her. And, he had to admit, over the years, he'd thought of her often.

This dinner—date or nondate—had been a long time coming. He damn well better make the best of it.

Chapter 7

L UCY cleared her throat for about the fifth time and paced along the window wall in the library. She checked her phone for a possible text, voice mail, or missed call, but nothing.

Robert Magellan and his fiancée, Susanna Jones, were ten minutes late. Had they decided to skip this morning's meeting and just hadn't gotten around to letting her know?

Nah, Trula would never permit such a thing, and Lucy knew that Trula had tremendous influence over Robert. It never failed to amuse her that her mother's old friend held such sway over one of the country's wealthiest self-made men. Trula was a seventy-something-year-old woman who wore her white hair tucked into a bun at the back of her head and favored polyester pant suits and coffee mugs with pithy quotes. Robert was a dot-com millionaire who'd started up several enormously successful companies over a fifteen-year period of time and had profited from each of them, but it had been his search engine, aptly named the Magellan Express, that literally made his fortune. Following the sale of Express and his subsequent retirement, he'd organized the Mercy Street Foundation, a nonprofit investigative firm that searched for missing people at no expense to the loved ones of the victims. Susanna Jones had been his right hand in each of his ventures, and to hear Trula tell it, had been in love with Robert for years. Susanna had stood by him even when he'd married another woman and started a family, and after his wife, Beth, had gone missing with their infant son, Ian, Susanna continued her personal search for them. Months later, Susanna was the one who located the place where Beth's car had gone off the road and into a deep ravine in the mountains of western Pennsylvania, Beth's remains still strapped behind the wheel. Ian, however, had been nowhere to be found, and it was partly through Susanna's diligence that Robert's child eventually was located and returned to him. According to Trula, it had taken a while, but Robert had finally come to the realization that Susanna was his happily-ever-after.

"Once he came to his senses," Trula had told Lucy, "he was hell-bent for the altar, would have had his cousin, Father Kevin, perform the ceremony right then and there. But I told him there was going to be a proper wedding, that Susanna deserved the whole shebang, and that was what she was going to have, and that if he had any sense, he'd be having the wedding right here in St. Dennis."

Trula does have a way of getting people to see things her way, Lucy mused.

She walked to the front window, stepping around the Christmas tree—the one Clay had decorated— and tried to ignore his unseen presence in the room.

Well, it was hard to pretend there was no trace of him here. She walked around the table and knelt down, her fingers feeling along the side of the table until they connected with the carved letters. She smiled to herself. Yes, even without the Christmas tree, a little of Clay remained. She remembered the day he'd put them there, and how she'd admonished him for marking up the table. She wondered if he knew that his initials were still there.

There were footsteps in the hall, and Lucy straightened up, pushed thoughts of Clay aside, and went into the lobby, where the prospective bride and groom were accompanied by Trula and Grace.

Lucy had done her homework, spent much of the previous day and night reading about Robert online; she'd have recognized him anywhere. Susanna Jones, on the other hand, had made herself somewhat scarce as far as the press was concerned. There'd been few photos of her online; Lucy never did find one that showed the woman's full face.

They make such a striking couple, Lucy thought as she walked from the library to the lobby to greet them, Robert classically tall, dark, and handsome, and Susanna willowy, her dark hair framing an oval face into which were set dark blue eyes that took in Lucy and their surroundings with quick scrutiny. Once the introductions were made, Trula and Grace went off to have tea and Lucy invited her potential clients to have a seat at the table.

After the obligatory congratulations to the engaged couple, Lucy got down to business, opened her notebook, and took a pen from her bag. Three things became obvious very quickly: Susanna knew exactly what she wanted, Robert completely deferred to her, and money was not going to be an issue.

"We want our wedding to walk that line between formal and informal." Susanna took a leather folder from her bag. She removed several sheets of paper and placed them in front of her on the table.

"As long as it's not stuffy," Robert added. "I hate stuffy."

"Right." Lucy made a note: *Formal/Informal.* "Got it."

"Here's a copy of my list." Susanna passed one of the sheets to Lucy. "I will email a copy to you for your electronic file."

"Thank you." Lucy shouldn't have been surprised. Given that Susanna was the person who, according to Trula, had been handling Robert Magellan's affairs for years, nothing less than efficiency would be expected.

"We'd like the wedding and the reception both outside," Susanna continued. "We're thinking white tents partly open to the sky and to the Bay. Long tables—not round ones—and lots and lots and lots of flowers. Everywhere."

"So you don't want anything at all in the inn itself?" Lucy glanced at Susanna's list. The open tent was right there near the top at number two.

"Maybe if it rains we'll have to move the ceremony inside, but we really want as much outside as possible, since we'll be here all week."

"All week?" Lucy looked up from her own notes. "You mean after the wedding?"

"No, no. Before. We want to have a great week

with our friends. Like a big happy vacation that we can share with everyone."

"You're planning on having some of your guests arrive a few days before the wedding?" Lucy made a note to check with Daniel about holding rooms and offering a special rate for guests who'd be attending the wedding. "I'll talk to Daniel about blocking off some rooms."

"We want all of them," Robert said.

Lucy's head snapped up. "All of them?"

Robert nodded. "We want the entire inn. The grounds, the tennis courts, the children's playgrounds."

"Do you have a date in mind for the wedding?" Lucy hoped there wouldn't be a conflict with those regular guests who returned for the same week or two weeks and had been doing so for years. How would her brother handle that?

"June something. Maybe the last Saturday, if it's available," Susanna told her. "Grace said she thought it might be."

"I'll have to check with Daniel," Lucy said, "but I'm sure the inn will do everything possible to accommodate you."

"Great." Susanna smiled, then asked, "Could we take a walk outside? I'd like to go over what I had in mind for the ceremony and the reception with you. I have a list."

"Of course." Lucy stood and gathered her notes, then grabbed her coat from the back of the chair where she'd previously tossed it. When they'd all bundled up, Lucy led the way out through the lobby and the door that faced the Chesapeake.

"Such a majestic building," Susanna noted.

"She is a beauty," Lucy agreed. "The earliest section—the large main section—was built in the 1800s and added onto over the generations. It's been in my dad's family all that time."

"Trula told me." Susanna fell into step between Robert and Lucy. "One of the things that drew me to the inn was the strong sense of history here. I love that one family has lived here all that time. Most people don't stay in one place for all that long."

"It's pretty unique, that's for sure." Lucy glanced over her shoulder and admired the three-story white building that rose behind them.

"Are there ghosts?" Susanna asked.

"Ghosts?" Lucy laughed. "I hope not."

"Damn. I was hoping for ghosts. I was sure that in a building this old . . ." Susanna paused. "You wouldn't tell me even if there were, would you?"

"Probably not. But rest assured. No ghosts." *None but my own . . .*

They reached the area where the lawn was flattest and led to the Bay.

"This is where I'd like the ceremony to be." Susanna stopped twenty-five feet from the water's edge and looked around. "I thought I remembered that there was a gazebo here."

"There's one around the corner of the building," Lucy pointed out. "That's the only gazebo."

"Any chance we could have it moved over here for the ceremony?" Susanna asked. "I sort of pictured it here, with the Bay behind us. I wanted our guests to have a view of the water."

"I can discuss that with Daniel," Lucy told her. "I don't know exactly what that would entail."

"And I was hoping for roses all around the gazebo," Susanna continued, staring at the designated space as if she could see it already in place. "Tons of climbing roses growing all around and over, sort of like they do on Nantucket. Do you think we could have roses?"

"Any particular color?" Lucy wished she'd opted to record the meeting lest she forget something.

"Pink roses," Susanna went on. "Lots of pink roses. And if I'm getting to choose—not light pink, not hot pink. That medium shade, you know the ones I mean? Pretty and sophisticated but not overly girlie."

Lucy checked Susanna's list. Yes, right there under the heading CEREMONY and the subheading GAZEBO, Susanna had typed *Roses—preferably pink (medium shade).*

Lucy nodded and made a note to herself, *Can plant pink (medium) climbing roses around the gazebo to bloom in time for wedding?*

"Susanna, is there a theme?"

Robert frowned. "It's a wedding. Isn't that the theme?"

Susanna ignored him. "Just something fun. Lots of great music, fabulous food . . . you do have a great chef here, don't you?"

"Of course." *And if we don't have one now, we will have one by June.* "I'm sure Daniel's chef will be happy to work with you on your menu, then you'll come back for a tasting."

"Actually, we'll want to work on menus for the entire week," Susanna pointed out. "We'll want meals and snacks for the kids, too. I'd like a tea one afternoon and Robert would like to do some fishing with his friends one day." She paused. "Can you arrange to rent a boat with a crew and some gear?"

"I'm sure that Daniel would know—"

"Oh, and we keep hearing about the tasty Maryland blue crabs. Do you think a few of us could go crabbing sometime that week?" Susanna paused, as if a thought had just occurred to her. "Maybe we should have crab served at least once a day. Rob, how do you feel about having—"

"Great." Robert strolled off toward the water. "Wow, take a look at that sailboat out there. Carry on, you two. You don't need me for any of this stuff." To Lucy, he said, "Whatever Suse wants . . ."

"Rob isn't much of a planner when it comes to things like this. He just wants to show up and have everything perfect."

"I'm sure everything will be," Lucy assured her. It would be a challenge to coordinate everything from the opposite side of the country, but she could probably talk Dan into letting her use the services of Madeline, the inn's own event planner, to tackle some of the details when Lucy was in L.A. Even so, the Magellan-Jones wedding had all the signs of a massive undertaking.

"We'll need lots of things to keep the little ones happy." Susanna consulted her list. "Oh, and swimming and tennis for the older kids. And maybe sailing lessons. Can we arrange for that? Golf? Is there a course nearby?"

Before Lucy could respond, Susanna added, "And speaking of the little ones—can we have a story hour in the afternoons? Maybe a puppet show one day. And pony rides." Lucy opened her mouth to speak but Susanna wasn't finished. "Would it be possible to hire some babysitters for the afternoons and the evenings?"

"I'm sure we can arrange that." *Note to self: ask Mom to find out who the most reliable babysitters are these days.* "As for golf, there's a brand-new course that just opened last summer on Cannonball Island, which is at the end of Charles Street. I'm sure they'd be more than happy to accommodate your group."

A quick wind blew off the Bay. Susanna pulled up the collar of her jacket and asked, "Lucy, you can see what I'd like out here, right? I mean, as far as the gazebo and the roses and the aisles are concerned?"

"I get the picture."

"Great. Then let's go back inside. I'm freezing." Susanna turned toward the water and cupped her hands to call to Robert, who was walking toward the marshy side of the property. "Rob, are you coming in?"

He waved to her, shook his head, and kept walking.

"Guess not," Susanna noted. "Just as well. He starts to twitch when we start getting into the little details, and for me, the details are everything."

"I couldn't agree more." Lucy started toward the building, wondering how many more little details Susanna had yet to share with her.

"Look, I know I must sound like one of those awful brides you see on TV. 'I want this' and 'I want that.'"

Lucy began to protest, but Susanna held up her hand.

"No, I know it sounds like a lot. But we just want to make sure our guests have the time of their lives. We want to make sure that everyone is as happy as we are, that everyone has a great time, one they'll never forget. We're trying to think of every detail."

"I don't think you've missed too many."

Susanna laughed. "There's more to come."

"Go for it."

"We're going to want welcome gift bags for our guests' rooms when they arrive. Can you put those together for us?"

"Of course. Just tell me what you'd like to go in them, and I'll—"

"I already know. It's on the list, second page. Did I not give you page two?" Susanna frowned. "I'll get you a copy. At the top of the list are some really good chocolates. Is there a good chocolatier in the area? I like to keep things as local as possible. And maybe some vouchers—like tickets—for boat rides. And a bottle of wine. Is there a local vineyard? Oh, I just had another thought: maybe a wineglass for each guest with his or her initials on it. A map of the Eastern Shore. Gift certificates for some of the local shops, like maybe a discount or something. I bought some darling shorts at Bling when we were here before and I know some of my friends would love that place."

"I'm sure our merchants will thank you."

Lucy was happy to see the inn's front door. She'd been trying to run a rough tally of what all this was going to cost, and had just given up.

"I'm definitely going to have to write all this down," Lucy said as they went back into the library. "I'll never remember it all."

"Let me know when you think you have it," Susanna said as she took off her coat, "because there's still more."

"Let me get all the items down for the gift bags before we move on." Lucy jotted down as much as she could remember.

"I wasn't done with the gift bags," Susanna told her. "I keep thinking of other things."

"You have to be kidding." The words were out of Lucy's mouth before she realized it. "Sorry, I mean—"

"Look, I know it's a lot. It's going to be excessive. But you know, I've known Robert since I was nineteen. I worked for him for years. I've waited for him almost my entire adult life, and now I can hardly believe we're really going to be married. I'm so happy, I just want to share it all with everyone who means something to me and to Rob. I want everyone to be happy that they came and to fall in love with St. Dennis the way I have. I want this wedding to be flawless, something people talk about forever."

"I understand." Lucy nodded. "I just want you to know up front that this will be . . . well, put bluntly, one pricey affair."

"I know." Susanna grinned. "Isn't it grand?"

Lucy laughed. "We'll do our best to make it absolutely grand."

"I know you will." Susanna reached out and patted Lucy on the arm before launching back into her list of wants. "Did I mention that I wanted tokens of some sort made up? You know, things our guests can use for an ice-cream cone, or a cup of coffee and a muffin. The sort of things that would draw people into the town to discover St. Dennis the way we have."

"That's the town motto. 'Discover St. Dennis,'" Lucy told her.

"Trula has some mugs that have that written on

them," Susanna said thoughtfully. "Your mom sent them to her."

"Some of the merchants in town sell them, along with T-shirts with the slogan."

"Do you think we could get some of those—the mugs and the T-shirts—for the gift bags?"

"I don't see why not." Lucy made a note.

"Oh! And maps of St. Dennis! Wouldn't it be fun if the gift bags had maps of St. Dennis?"

"Maps to go into the bags," Lucy spoke aloud as she wrote.

"No, no. Not in the bags. *On* the bags. On the front. Canvas bags with the map of the town on the front that shows where all the shops are located. And a picture of the inn on the back." Susanna showed no sign of slowing down. "And postcards of some sort." She paused, then snapped her fingers. "I know! We'll have postcards made up with some of those beautiful historic buildings on them! We can give each guest a set tied up with a pretty ribbon."

Lucy cleared her throat. "Susanna, I think we need to talk about some of the basics."

"Like what?"

"Like, nailing down a date and how many people are on the guest list. What flowers you want. If you want a DJ or a live band."

"Maybe both. The band for the adult tent and we're thinking about a DJ for the kids."

Lucy scribbled down that information.

"Now, about the guest list—"

"And I know what flowers. Lots of peonies and roses and hydrangea everywhere. I want garlands of ivy and magnolia and those pink roses we talked about wound all around the gazebo. I want the chairs set up outside with a center aisle and flowers on the end of each, set up like a church. Flower petals sprinkled up the aisle. Oh, and for the rehearsal dinner, a great seafood feast with—"

Lucy laughed and held up one hand. "Let's make the rehearsal dinner a separate conversation. Right now let's focus on the wedding."

"Sorry." Susanna looked anything but. "I do have a tendency to get carried away sometimes. I'm so excited about this."

"I totally understand. And that's why I want to go step-by-step so that we don't miss anything."

"All right." Susanna motioned to Lucy to do her thing. "We'll start from your beginning . . ."

They were halfway through the wedding ceremony when the door opened and Daniel wheeled in a cart of coffee, tea cakes, tea, scones, and fruit. Lucy couldn't remember if she'd ever been happier to see her brother.

"I thought you might be ready for a bit of a break." Daniel looked around the room. "Where's Robert?"

"He's out walking the grounds," Susanna told him. "I think all the details just bore the hell out of him."

"Daniel, we need you to check some availability dates for the wedding," Lucy said.

"I'm sure we'll be able to work it out, regardless of the date you've chosen," Daniel assured Susanna.

"Well, that's just it." Lucy diverted his attention back to her. "The date may have to depend on the availability of—"

"We'll work it out, Luce," he repeated.

"They want to book the entire inn for a week, Daniel," Lucy said pointedly.

He paused and tilted his head to one side, as if not certain he'd heard her correctly.

"You mean . . ."

"Yes," Lucy told him. "The entire inn, one entire week."

"Oh." His sister could tell he was having a good news/bad news moment. "That could be awkward, depending on the week."

"Hence we're working the date around the availability." Lucy pulled a calendar out of her bag. "Let's look at the last weekend in June. Why don't you check to see if you have any bookings for the week before?" Lucy glanced up at Susanna. "Sunday through Sunday?"

Susanna nodded.

Lucy tried to make eye contact with her brother, but he still looked a bit uncertain he'd heard correctly. "Will you check into that and get back to me as soon as you can?"

Daniel nodded. "I'll do that. Good to see you, Susanna."

"We'll be talking again soon, I'm sure." Susanna smiled as Daniel left them.

"Susanna, would you like coffee?" Lucy asked.

"Love some. Thank you."

"How do you take it?"

"I'll fix it, thanks." Susanna joined Lucy at the end of the table where Daniel had left the cart. Lucy poured and handed off the first cup to her guest, then poured one for herself.

"These little tea cakes are amazing," Lucy noted. "The pastry chef here is exceptional."

"They look delicious." Susanna smiled and placed one on a plate along with one of each of the cookies. "I should sample, of course."

"Of course." Lucy waited until Susanna had made her selection, then picked up two of the petits fours before returning to her seat.

"As our wedding planner, can you order the invitations for us?"

"Yes, and you should send out save-the-date notices as soon as we can settle on the wedding date, and let people know of your plans so they don't book their vacations for that same week. Do you have a guest list yet?" Lucy sipped her coffee.

"Sort of. I suppose I should finalize that."

"That should be your priority right now. Get your guest list drawn up and settle on a date. The rest should be relatively easy." Lucy tried to smile but had the feeling she'd be eating her words before too long. Something told her that nothing about this long-distance extravaganza was going to be easy. "Once we have those two things done, you can pick out your invitations."

"I've been looking but I haven't seen anything I really liked. I wanted something different, but something that still has a traditional feel to it." Susanna bit into one of the cakes. "These are delicious. Can we have these for the ladies' tea I mentioned earlier?"

"I don't see why not." Lucy made another note.

"Do you have any suggestions for the invitations? I'd really like something unique."

"I've used someone in the past who does exquisite work, all hand done."

"One of a kind?"

"If you like."

"Invitations designed just for us," Susanna mused. "I love it."

"Think about possibly playing up the Bay theme," Lucy suggested, realizing that she would need to take charge if she was going to handle this wedding. Susanna had so many ideas she was all over the place. "Maybe something with a cream-and-navy combo, with maybe a tiny sailboat in gold at the top, and—"

"As long as it isn't too girlie," Robert said as he joined them.

"I'll speak with the designer and see if we can get some samples for you." Lucy was scribbling like a madwoman. "Robert, help yourself to coffee."

"I just had some. Ran into Trula and your mom in the back lobby, but thanks." He rested his forearms on the back of the chair that stood next to Susanna's. "How's everything going?"

"I think we're finished for one day," she replied happily. "We'll have to meet again very soon, but Lucy is going to take care of absolutely everything for us. I'm so happy, Rob. Our wedding day—"

"Our wedding week," he corrected, and twirled a strand of her dark hair between his fingers.

"Our wedding week is going to be everything we talked about. Everyone is going to have such a great time. Lucy is going to make it all happen."

"Well, then, Lucy, we're leaving it all in your hands." Robert looked somewhat amused, as if he understood that what his fiancée wanted was going to be a monumental undertaking.

"So, you've decided to have your wedding here?" Lucy asked.

"Wedding week," Susanna reminded her. "But yes, I very much want to have the wedding here. Rob?"

"Whatever you want," he agreed.

Susanna turned to Lucy. "So that's that. All we need is a date."

"I can get back to you on that as soon as Daniel gives me the green light." Lucy suspected that the fact that her brother hadn't already done so meant that they had more than a few "regulars" already committed for that week. "Just in case there's a conflict, I have to ask: is June the only acceptable month?"

"I always wanted to be a June bride . . ."

"June it is, then," Robert said to Lucy.

"But I can be flexible if I have to." Susanna turned to Robert. "Let's see what dates Daniel has available."

"I'm sure we can come to an agreement on the date." Robert stepped aside while Susanna stood, then helped her into her coat.

"Lucy, when can we get together again?"

Before Lucy could respond, Susanna added, "Soon, I hope. I'm going to finalize the guest list this week, so we should be able to get things moving along as soon as we have a firm date."

"We can do a lot by phone, and email—" Lucy began.

"Oh, but that's so impersonal," Susanna interrupted. "I really like having the time to sit and go over things with you in person. It's so much better.

You don't get the same exchange of ideas on the phone or with email."

Lucy hesitated. She hadn't planned on another trip back to St. Dennis for a while. "How about I get some sample invitations and I'll overnight them to you?"

"Great."

Lucy sighed with relief.

"And then we can look them all over when we get together." Susanna swung her bag over her shoulder.

Lucy wanted to protest but knew it was useless. Susanna wanted hands-on. Face time. Well, she was going to be paying a premium for it.

"This is going to be quite the production." Lucy stood as well.

"But it can't look like it's a production." Robert frowned. "I don't want it to look like it's been orchestrated."

"I understand," Lucy assured him. "I think I know what you want."

"Good. Then let's get a contract drawn up so we can sign it."

"Not until we have a firm date," Lucy told him. "We'll need to settle that first, then we'll go over everything else."

"Great." He extended his hand to Lucy to shake. "Everything's under control . . ."

"Of course." Lucy forced a smile of confidence she wasn't sure she felt. It was clear that neither of her new clients had any clue as to how monumental an undertaking this wedding would be. "Totally under control . . ."

Chapter 8

I COULD easily see this whole thing spinning totally out of control unless someone keeps a foot on the brake." Lucy called Bonnie the minute the car Robert was driving disappeared down the driveway. "It obviously won't be the bride. She wants . . . well, pretty much everything."

"Like what?" Bonnie asked.

"Name something. Anything. Chances are it's on her list." Lucy sighed. "From one-of-a-kind invitations to moving the gazebo so her guests can look out over the Bay. And dear Lord, the list of things she wants in the gift bags is going to make your head spin. Organizing those is going to be a project in itself. But Susanna's such a sweet person, it's going to be a pleasure to work with her."

"Nice that she's so generous and can afford to be."

"You have no idea just how generous she is."

"Hey, we've handled huge complicated affairs before," Bonnie reminded her. "Huge, complicated, expensive affairs. They're our specialty. Our bread and butter."

"True, but those events only lasted one day. Two at

the most. I've never done a weeklong event like this before. Still, it's all good news for us."

The phone went silent.

"Bon? Are you still there?" Lucy asked.

"Go back to the 'weeklong' part," Bonnie said. "I don't remember you mentioning that."

"I hadn't gotten to it yet." Lucy sat at the library table and flipped through her notes. "They have their hearts set on a week's stay for everyone involved—everyone on the guest list. Every blessed man, woman, and child. Activities for each of the seven days. Special activities for the kids. Golf lessons. Sailing. A chartered fishing boat—"

"You're making this up."

"I swear, I am not. Susanna has a whole list of things she wants for her guests, starting with treating them all to a full week at the inn. Sunday to Sunday, a weeklong party complete with all manner of wonderful things to do and eat and see."

"So she's a real bridezilla?"

"No, no, not at all. She's very down-to-earth, actually. A total sweetheart. But she knows what she wants, and one of the things she wants is to share her happiness with all of their friends and family. Except for relocating the gazebo, almost everything she wants us to do is for the comfort and entertainment of their guests. It's just that she wants a lot."

"For an entire week."

"Right."

"I'm guessing there's no budget . . ."

"None whatsoever. Robert says whatever Susanna wants is fine with him. It's going to be a real challenge to put all the pieces together." Lucy rubbed her eyes, then realized she'd probably just rubbed mascara onto her cheeks.

"Well, between the Internet and the phone, you should be able to handle it."

"Uh-uh. One of the things Susanna wants is lots of face time. She wants meetings. She wants sit-downs. She wants me to be there with her when she goes through sample invitations. However, Robert does have a plane, so hopefully she'll be willing to fly out to L.A. if necessary."

"You've held the hand of many a bride before. You'll do what you have to do. This will be one big payday for Shaefer and Sinclair." Bonnie hesitated. "You do have a contract signed, right?"

"Not until we pin down a date. Daniel's still trying to work something out for June, but he told me he has two blocks of rooms for the last weekend who really don't want to switch. Both are families that have been coming to the inn for their vacations for well over twenty years."

"And if they won't change the dates?"

"Then we'll have to look at July. Every other weekend in June is already one-half to three-quarters booked. They get a lot of regulars here, people who have standing reservations or who book for the following year while they're signing out at the end of their stay."

"Nice that the inn has such a following, but I'd hate to see this job slip away from us because we can't agree on a date."

"It would be a lot easier to accommodate the happy couple if they weren't insistent upon booking the entire inn."

"I don't believe you mentioned that detail."

"Oh, well, that's part of it. The whole inn for the whole week."

"That's . . . huge."

"It is to my brother."

"I'm leaving it in your hands," Bonnie told her. "I know you'll wow them with your organizational skills and your creativity. And I trust you're still planning on coming back on Sunday?"

"I am. I'll be in the office bright and early on Monday morning. In the meantime, if anything comes up—"

"I'll call. Oh, and I'll email the report we received today regarding the ice-skating sweet sixteen party. You can have a rink built instead of a pond, which the contractor you called is recommending. He's gone over the Tollivers' property and says there's no good place to build a pond, what with runoff and all that. I told him you'd be in touch."

"I'll read over the report and give him a call before I call the Tollivers."

Lucy opened her laptop and scrolled through her mail. She found and read the note from the contractor, then reworded it in less technical terms to send to her client. Surely Beverly Tolliver would understand the difference between over $100,000 to have a pond constructed—not counting maintenance—and the number the contractor brought in for the rental and setup of the temporary ice rink. She hit send, scanned the rest of her emails, then opened a new general file for the Magellan-Jones wedding.

Using her scribbled notes as a guide, she typed all of the bride and groom's wishes for their big week. Then she organized her notes under different headings and set up a separate page for each day, listed the day's events, then started a new page for each separate event. By the time she was finished, she had more questions than answers—especially after reading Daniel's most recent text message that said simply, *No luck*.

June wasn't looking good.

July and August were notoriously hot and often steamy on the Eastern Shore. Would Robert and Susanna agree to postpone their wedding until later in the summer if Daniel continued to be unsuccessful in convincing his regular guests to reschedule their vacation weeks? Some of the flowers that Susanna wanted might not be available late in the season— peonies, for one, were all but impossible to find in August and didn't stand up to heat very well. Hydrangeas and roses, she could get. She'd have to speak with Olivia and find out what would be in abundant supply. Susanna did mention she loved flowers and wanted them everywhere. It was going to be tough enough to tell the happy couple that their choice of month wasn't going to work, but telling Susanna that her flowers wouldn't be available was only going to make things more difficult. If Lucy had fabulous floral alternatives to offer, it might dull the pain a little.

Of course, that could be the deal breaker. Lucy was well aware that they could easily go elsewhere, someplace where Susanna could have her first-choice date *and* her flowers.

This could be tricky.

Lucy made notes reminding her to talk to her mother about finding babysitters for that week— hopefully Grace or some of her friends would know of high school girls in town who'd be available—and lining up tennis, swimming, and golf teachers. A charter boat and a captain . . . next to that, she added a reminder to herself to talk to Hal Garrity about chartering his cruiser, the *Shady Lady*.

Of course, she paused to reflect, she'd need a definite date before she could line up any of the events and vendors that Susanna wanted. And she'd have to get Daniel on board to allow her to delegate some tasks to Madeline, and she'd need someone in her L.A. office to do as much research as could be done by phone or email as possible. Lucy knew that with their event schedule she couldn't possibly do it all herself. Not if she wanted to maintain any semblance of sanity.

She made a few more notes. Invitations (*Contact Molly Nixon about sending some samples*). Tokens for the local shops (what amount was Susanna planning on designating for each token?). Lucy needed to talk to the shop owners directly about this and get them on board.

She had just finished listing the shops that Susanna had mentioned—Scoop, Bling, Cuppachino, Book 'Em—when Grace poked her head into her room.

"I just wanted to see how you were doing," her mother said. "It's getting late and I didn't know if you were going to want to change before your date with Clay."

"Mom—"

"It's a prearranged meeting to get together for dinner. Therefore, it's a dinner date." Grace shooed away Lucy's protest before she could voice it. "I don't know what the big deal is. He's a wonderful guy and darned good-looking, too. There's not a single girl in St. Dennis who wouldn't be more than happy to take your place tonight."

"I've no doubt." Lucy smiled. No point in reminding her mother that most of the "girls" she referred to were, at the very least, over thirty, the ones from her own class having hit thirty-five this past year. Grace was old school: women Lucy's age would forever be girls.

"You just keep that in mind when you're busy brushing him off," Grace said.

"I didn't brush him off. It's just that . . ." Lucy paused. What, exactly, was it? "Well, it's just that I live out there, and Clay lives here."

"So?" Grace came into the library.

"So, it's really impossible to have any kind of relationship with someone who lives so far away. Too difficult to get together, and all that." She hastened to add, "Not that I want a relationship with Clay. I'm just saying."

"But you'll be in St. Dennis a lot this year," Grace reminded her. "So you won't always be on the other side of the country."

"But when I'm here, I'll be working on the wedding."

"You'll have time for the occasional dinner, though," Grace noted. "Like tonight."

"Mom."

"I know. I'm giving you a headache." Grace smiled. "I just thought you might need reminding of the time."

"I do." Lucy glanced at her watch. "I had no idea it was so late. I need to run up and change."

"Wear that lovely green sweater Trula sent you for Christmas, why don't you?"

"I just might do that." Lucy started toward the door, then turned and kissed her mother on the forehead. "Thanks, Mom."

"For . . . ?"

"For reminding me about the time. And . . . for caring that I have a life."

"Of course I care. I care about everything that touches you. You're my girl." Grace reached out and straightened a strand of Lucy's hair that had worked its way from her ponytail.

"I know, Mom. And I am grateful to have you as my mom. It might not always come across that way, but I am." Lucy paused once more before leaving the room. "By the way, I think you and Clay did a great job decorating in here."

"Clay did most of the work," Grace pointed out. "By that hour of the day, I was winding down."

"It's all lovely. I love the way you moved that big leather chair to stand between the tree and the fireplace. It looks homey and warm. Christmas-y."

"Clay's idea."

"It was a good one."

"Maybe you might want to tell him that."

"Maybe I will . . ."

Clay parked the Jeep outside the inn and turned off the wipers. Of course it would rain on the night he was taking Lucy out. He just hoped the cold front the local weather forecaster mentioned on the six o'clock news would hold off until they'd had dinner and he'd gotten her back home. He'd hoped to take a walk along the pier with Lucy after dinner and didn't know how she'd feel about a stroll in the snow. It was the sort of thing she'd liked when they were younger, but he didn't know if she still did. There was a lot about her now that he didn't know.

He went into the lobby and was surprised to find her there waiting.

"Right on time," Lucy noted.

"Wow. You look great. Wow." The words tumbled from his mouth before he could stop them. *Way to sound like a fifteen-year-old,* he silently chided himself.

"Thanks." She smiled and picked up her jacket from a nearby chair. "Shall we?"

"Let me give you a hand with that." Clay reached out to help her on with the jacket, but she had already slipped her arms into the sleeves.

"Got it, but thanks." Lucy buttoned up and tied the jacket's belt around her waist. "Is it still raining? Do I need to find an umbrella?" She frowned and stepped behind the registration desk. "Mom used to keep a few back here but I don't see any . . ."

"It's raining but not too hard, and I'm parked right outside the door," he told her. "If it's still raining when we get to the restaurant, I can drop you off in front while I park the car."

"That'll be fine." She walked to the door and he trailed just slightly behind her, thinking that she really did look pretty, well, *wow,* in that green sweater that set off her coloring and her eyes, jeans that were just skinny enough, and black boots. She wore sparkly earrings that swung just a little when she moved her head, and her hair curled around her face and made her look almost cherubic. He caught up with her to open the door but she was already through it.

She was, he was beginning to realize, a woman who was used to doing things for herself.

"So how did your meeting with Magellan go?" Clay asked after they'd arrived at the restaurant and were seated, at his request, at a table overlooking the Bay. They'd given their waitress, Candace, their drink orders, and Clay was hoping to avoid any awkward silences. Talk about her work, he thought. That might break the ice. "What's he like?"

"The meeting went really well," Lucy replied. She closed the menu she'd been scanning and placed it to the side. "And he's . . ." She paused as if to think. "He's very different from what one might expect from one of the dozen wealthiest men in the country."

"In what way?"

"He's very much allowing his fiancée to take over the wedding planning. As long as it isn't too formal or too girlie—his words—he's fine with whatever she wants."

"Aren't most men like that? They don't care about the details as long as she's happy? I mean, aren't most weddings all about the bride?"

Lucy smiled. "I've done weddings where the groom called all the shots, and I've had weddings where both parties had to be in perfect agreement about every little detail. And of course, I've had weddings where the bride is the one who decides what's what. Sometimes the bride's mother gets involved, and sometimes her sisters, her best friends . . ." She made a face. "Those are the toughest."

"Too many cooks?"

"Way too many. Frankly, any more than two is too many. Everyone's vision is different, and the only vision that really matters to me is that of the bride and the groom. I always want what my clients want, but life is so much easier when I can sit down with just the couple being married. So I have to admit I was relieved when Robert totally deferred to Susanna. When you're talking about an affair as elaborate as this one is going to be, the fewer opinions you have to navigate, the better."

"But that's your specialty, right? Big, elaborate, fancy affairs?" He'd learned this much from the tabloid reports following Dallas MacGregor's wedding in December. Secretly, he'd read every one of them that mentioned Lucy or her company.

"I've done fancy in more ways than you can imagine, but this one isn't fancy in the way you're thinking. At least, it isn't starting out that way, but then again, who knows? I've seen wedding plans take crazy turns between the first meeting with the clients and the actual day. Right now Robert and Susanna just want fun, sort of casual but elegant."

"How can you be casual and elegant at the same time?" Clay asked.

Lucy looked around the room for a moment, then nodded toward the window. "See that sailboat in the first slip?"

"Doc Benson's *Tonight Tonight*. She's a beauty."

"She is," Lucy agreed. "All that lovely wood, and that graceful mainsail. Would you consider her elegant?"

He thought about it for a moment, then nodded. "Yeah, very elegant. She has beautiful lines, and if you saw her skimming the water, you wouldn't even have to ask."

"So she's elegant, but you wouldn't take her out for a spin around the Bay wearing a tux, would you?"

"Well, there have been some fancy parties on some of the boats out there in the marina, but no, I would not want to crew her in a tux." He nodded. "I get it. Elegant and casual."

"The inn is that way. She dresses up very nicely, but she does casual just beautifully, just like that boat out there," she noted. "This wedding is going to be outside, overlooking the Bay. There will be flowers everywhere and a string quartet and champagne and waitstaff in black tails—just as elegant as you please—but the vibe will be low-key."

"The MacGregor wedding was sort of like that." He took a sip of wine. "Well, Wade and Steffie's was. Dallas and Grant's was more formal."

"The best weddings reflect the personalities of the bride and the groom. In Dallas's case, we had an A-list Hollywood star, a very sophisticated guest list, and then there was the fact that she and Grant were older and were both married before. You expect some glamour there. For Wade and Steffie, you had a younger bride and groom, first-time wedding for each—well, if you don't count Wade's marriage in Texas to his business partner—and a younger guest list. Different personalities. Different vibes."

"Are you allowed to talk about what your new clients are going to have or is that a breach of wedding planner etiquette?"

"So far, there's not much to talk about. We only talked in generalites for the most part. We'll talk

more about the specifics the next time we get together."

"When will that be?" he asked casually, as if it
didn't really matter when she'd be back in St. Dennis
again.

"I'm hoping to put it off until the week after next.
Susanna would be happy if I met with her every week,
but I do have other clients who are getting married or
having some special life event that they've paid me to
organize, so I can't put everyone aside for Magellan.
But Susanna wants to meet often, so somehow I will
have to accommodate her, whether or not it's a hardship for me to keep coming back here."

"Is it a hardship? Coming back here?" He leaned
back in his chair to watch her face. If it attracted him
in sunlight, by candlelight it mesmerized. He couldn't
look away if he tried.

"Not in the sense that I don't like St. Dennis. It's my
hometown. My family is here, my roots. But I lose a
day of work traveling each way, there's no way of getting around that. Plus, there's a lot on the to-do list
for this wedding, and it would be easier for me if the
wedding was in L.A. instead of St. Dennis. But I'm
lucky to have landed this one. It's huge." She paused.
"At least, I'm hoping I have it. We can't sign a contract until we have a date and Danny's still working
that out. There's a lot I could be doing right now, and
I feel pretty secure that it's going to work out, but
until we've all signed, I hate to invest the time."

"Makes sense." He took another sip of beer just as
the waitress appeared at the table.

"Are you ready to order now, Clay?" she asked,
pad in hand.

"Rockfish and oysters for both of us," Clay told her. Turning to Lucy, he said, "Unless you changed your mind."

"No, no. That's what I'm here for." Lucy handed her menu to the waitress.

"Fried or raw?" the waitress asked. Smiling at Clay, she added, "I know you like yours fried."

Clay nodded. "Nothing like a fat, lightly fried Chesapeake oyster the way they do them here."

"How can I resist? I'll have the same," Lucy said.

"Two fried oyster and rockfish dinners." Clay gave his unopened menu to the waitress.

After the waitress disappeared with their orders, Lucy said, "And speaking of beer, why don't you tell me more about this new venture of yours?"

"Not much to tell at this point. We'll be putting in our first crop of barley and hops as soon as the ground is right. We're going to turn one of our old barns into a brewery so we'll have the entire operation right here in St. Dennis."

"It sounds very ambitious. Converting the barn, growing everything yourself. You're going to be a very busy man," she observed.

"Well, the barn conversion isn't going to happen overnight, and the crops have to be planted and harvested, and that takes time, too. These first couple of years, we'll be buying from other growers. The hops are going in this year, but they take a few years to mature."

"So you buy seeds or plants from someone else . . ."

"From several someone elses, actually. There are hundreds of different varieties of hops, and we're going to want to experiment with several."

"What makes them different, and how will you decide which ones to grow?"

"The best varieties are disease-resistant, they have the right aroma, they have a high yield, they store well." He studied her face as he spoke, watched for the telltale sign of her eyes glazing over. When they did not, he continued: "I've learned more about beer in the past six months than I have in my lifetime before Wade and I started talking about the possibility of going into business together. He knows so damned much about every stage of the process. I'll be the one doing the planting, but he'll be the one who decides which varieties of hops we grow."

"You had the land, he has the knowledge," she observed. "Sounds like a good partnership."

"I think it's going to be. I've had some dozens of acres lie fallow for a couple of years now, so I'm not losing anything in that regard. Wade's got several years' experience brewing, says he has a really good nose for it. Judging by the success of his last company, I'd have to say he knows his business."

"I heard about how that business went down, about his partner falling for some con man who ripped off her and the business, left her pregnant, and disappeared."

"Left her pregnant and pretty much penniless at that point. Wade said even with the money gone, they were willing to borrow and start over again—he really believed in his products—but then they discovered that Robin had terminal cancer. That took all the wind out of his sails. He spent the next couple of months taking care of her—she'd declined treatment that could have prolonged her life for a short time because it would have caused the death of the baby."

"Steffie told me Wade married her before she died so that he could raise her baby." Lucy met his eyes. "That takes a big man with a big heart."

Clay nodded. "If you didn't know the story, you'd never suspect that Austin wasn't Wade's biological son. And to see Steffie with the kid, you wouldn't know that she wasn't his birth mother."

"I like a story that has a happy ending, don't you?"

"I do." He raised his glass and tilted it toward hers. "Let's drink to happy endings, LuLu."

"Don't call me . . ." She paused, then laughed and lifted her wineglass. "I give up. All right, to happy endings." She took a sip of wine. "Though why I didn't come up with a silly nickname for you when we were little—"

"You did," he reminded her. "You called me Clay Pot Head."

Lucy laughed. "Only until someone told me what that meant. Back in first grade, it just meant, you know, a clay pot. In fifth grade, it meant something entirely different, as Kevin McMillan explained to me one day on the playground. And that," she said, her eyes twinkling, "was the end of Clay Pot Head."

"Kevin McMillan." Clay grumbled. "Sneaky little weasel was always trying to get your attention."

"He succeeded. I went on my first date with him. Seventh-grade dance. He brought me flowers. Yellow and white daisies."

"Don't remind me."

She laughed again. "Kevin was nice."

"No, he wasn't. He was nice to you because you

were the prettiest girl in the class and all the guys had a crush on you."

"Jessie Linton was the prettiest girl in the class," she corrected him. After a few seconds, she added, "And if memory serves, it was every guy but you."

"Not true." Clay shook his head. "At least, it wasn't true after eighth grade."

"Then what happened?" She rested her forearms on the table and leaned forward, her lips curved in a soft smile.

"Then hormones kicked in and you turned into a girl."

"I was always a girl." Her smile widened. "I never tried to pretend otherwise."

"Yeah, but once we hit puberty, it got harder and harder to remember that we were buddies." He put his glass down and caught her gaze. "Especially when the other guys would be fighting over who was going to ask you to go to so-and-so's party, or to the movies."

"Why didn't you ever ask me?"

"Because we were supposed to be friends. Best friends."

"We *were* best friends, Clay. You were the best friend I ever had."

"So what happened, LuLu?" he asked softly. "Why did we stop being friends?"

For a moment, she looked stricken. Then she broke eye contact and stared at her wineglass for a long moment. When it looked as if she was about to speak, Candace appeared to serve their dinners.

"Okay, we have two rockfish and fried oyster combos," the waitress said as she placed a platter in front of both Lucy and Clay.

She put her hands on her hips. "What else can I get you? Another beer, Clay? Another glass of wine for you?" she asked Lucy.

"Oh, yes. That would be fine. Thank you." Lucy nodded.

"I'll take another beer, thanks, Candace," Clay said.

"I'll be right back with those." Their waitress refreshed their water glasses before disappearing into the crowded dining room.

Clay and Lucy ate in silence for several moments.

"The fish is delicious," she said at last. "Just the way I remember it. And the oysters are perfect. They just don't taste the same from anywhere else."

"True enough." He'd thought about pressing her on his unanswered question—he'd thought for a moment she was going to finally shed some light on that subject—but decided to let it go. For now.

"Mom told me that you've been growing produce for some restaurants these past few years," Lucy said, apparently happy enough to have been let off the hook. "Are you abandoning farming in favor of brewing beer?"

"No, growing barley and hops will be in addition to my produce business." He put down his fork. "I was thinking the other day about how the farm has evolved since my ancestors arrived and claimed that land. You know, for almost three hundred years, the farm sustained my family. Today, it's a hybrid operation of mostly organic produce that I sell to farmers' markets and restaurants—including the inn. Tomorrow, with luck, it will be as successful providing the raw product for MadMac Brews."

"You don't sell anything directly?" she asked.

"I sell directly to the restaurants. Almost all of the ones here in town buy from me, some in D.C., others in New York."

"I meant, don't you have a little veggie market on the farm?"

"No one to operate it," he replied. "I work the fields, my mother's moved out, and my sister is going to be moving in another few weeks."

"Where's Brooke going?"

"She's moving into the old tenant house. Cam O'Connor's doing the renovations, and he's just about finished."

"I remember that old place. There used to be an old guy who lived out there . . ."

"Mr. Littleton." Clay nodded. "He worked for my dad back when we were kids. Sort of helped run the place."

"I guess he's moved on by now."

"He died when we were in high school, don't you remember? He was killed in a hit-and-run accident out on Charles Street. They never did find the car who hit him. My dad always suspected one of the politicians from D.C. who has a vacation home across the Bay. He figured any one of them would know how to hide the evidence."

"I'd forgotten that." Lucy frowned. "It's not the type of thing I usually forget."

"Well, you've been gone for a long time, Luce. It's not surprising that some things have slipped your mind."

"I guess."

There was another silence that was only minutes away from becoming awkward when Lucy said, "Oh, by the way. I loved the tree you decorated in the inn's library. It was perfect."

"Is it still up?" He speared an oyster and raised the fork halfway to his mouth. "I'd have thought all the decorations would have been taken down and stored away by now."

"Everything's coming down tomorrow, but Mom left it all up for me to see. We had our Christmas last night. Ford called and we all got to talk to him for a few minutes, so I got to thank him for these." She flicked a finger at one of her earrings and made the dangling part dance. "He sent these to Mom to hold for me."

"I noticed them," Clay told her. He *had* noticed. They caught the light of the candle much the way her eyes did, and brought his gaze back to her face again and again. "They're very pretty."

"I love them." She touched them once more before picking up her fork. She seemed to aim at a piece of broccoli, but put the fork back down again. "Mom worries about me being in California alone—even after all this time—but it's hell on her worrying about Ford. She can go weeks without hearing from him. It just breaks my heart sometimes when I think about how all she really wants is to have both Ford and me back here in St. Dennis, and neither of us seems to be able to make the move."

"You both have your reasons," Clay said. "You've invested a lot of time and hard work in your business. I'm sure that Ford believes in what he's doing, and you have to admire him for giving up what could be a much easier life to do something he thinks is right and important. Being a UN Peacekeeper isn't the path most of us would choose to follow, but he has. He had all that special training while he was in the service, so he has skills that most of us don't have."

"All true." Lucy nodded. "He's well equipped for the places they send him, but still, you never know . . ." She picked up her wineglass and swirled the last bit of liquid around. "My mom worries that he'll be in a bad situation someday and that he'll be the one who saves everyone else but doesn't get out alive himself. Even a cat only has nine lives."

"Has he told you that he's used up a few?"

"He tells Danny things, but he won't tell me much. He'll just say he's in Africa, for example, but he won't say that the country he's in is in the midst of political turmoil and that villages are being annihilated and women and children murdered and raped and that he's having a hard time keeping the lid from blowing off." She stared at her glass. "I get all that from the news. I always hope to God my mom isn't watching the same broadcast."

"Where is he now?"

"He didn't really say. Just sort of hemmed and hawed and talked past it. Which worries me as much as it worries Mom," she admitted.

"Maybe he didn't want to say too much in front of your mother," Clay suggested. "Maybe you could give him a call when you get back to California."

"I thought about that." She nodded. "That's probably what I'll do."

Clay looked down at his plate and was surprised to find he'd eaten pretty much everything on it.

"Wow," he said. "I didn't realize how hungry I was."

"Me either. I haven't eaten this much in . . . I don't remember the last time I ate so much." She laughed. "Oh, yes, I do. Last night. Huge dinner last night."

"Christmas dinner, right."

"I'll need two seats on my flight back home." She touched her napkin to her lips then folded it and placed it on the table.

"Which is when?"

"Sunday."

"That's great." He grinned. "That means we get to do this again."

"I think your email called for 'dinner,' not 'dinners,'" she reminded him.

"A technicality." Clay saw their waitress approaching. "Luce, do you want dessert? They still make the best cheesecake in town. It's amazing stuff."

"The best, is it? Sounds like we'll have to get the inn's new pastry chef to up her game," Lucy replied good-naturedly. "But thank you, no. If I ate one more thing . . ."

"Just the check, please, Candace," Clay told her.

She brought the bill and he paid it. At the coatroom, he picked up Lucy's jacket and held it as she slipped her arms in. It was the closest he'd been to her all night, and for just a moment, he caught the scent of her hair when she flipped it out from under her collar. She smelled faintly of flowers and sunlight, even on this wintry night.

"Looks like the rain has stopped," he said when

they stepped outside. "Want to take a stroll along the pier?"

"Wouldn't hurt to try to walk off a bit of dinner. It really was a treat, Clay. Thanks so much."

"My pleasure." He took her hand and tucked it under his arm. "I waited twenty years for this date—and don't break my heart by insisting this wasn't a date, all right? Play along with me if you must. But don't say—"

"I wasn't going to. And for the record, it's the best date I've had in a long time."

"Now you're just being nice. But I'll take it."

"No," she insisted. "Really. It's a pleasure to be with someone you've known all your life. Not at all like a first date with someone you've just met."

"Ha! You said first date. The implication being that there will be another."

"Yeah, well, don't let it go to your head." In the dark, he could see that she was smiling.

"This is what I think of when I think of the Bay at night," she went on. "The moon reflected on the water, that gentle, rhythmic sound of the waves lapping against the side of the boats. I love that sound. I'm glad they weren't all put in dry dock."

"Most of the boats you see still in the water will be heading south through the Intercoastal Waterway within the next week or so."

She stopped and took a deep breath. "It smells like winter in Maryland. It smells like snow."

"It's in the forecast." He stopped when she did, and followed her gaze as it swept across the marina. Without thinking, he leaned down and kissed her on the cheek. When she turned toward him, his lips caught hers full-on in a kiss that neither of them was expecting. She tasted of lemons and wine, and he knew that he would never again taste either of those things without thinking of this moment. Her lips were warm in spite of the cold, and soft, and he couldn't help but kiss her again.

"I've been wanting to do that for real since we were in seventh grade," he whispered. "Remember when you wanted me to practice kissing with you so that you'd know what to do when you went to that dance with Kevin?"

She laughed. "I do remember."

"After we practiced, I tried to think of some way to disable Kevin so that he couldn't take you. I was so jealous that he was going to get to kiss you for real while I only got to practice."

"Seriously? That bothered you?"

"Made me crazy."

"I guess I should have told you then . . ."

"Told me what?"

"That I never did kiss him." She took his hand and started toward the parking lot.

"Damn. And here I've held a grudge against him all these years." He realized he was smiling, realized, too, how silly after all this time that it still mattered somehow. "Why didn't you kiss him?"

"Didn't want to." Lucy shrugged. "And don't look so smug . . ."

He was still laughing when they reached the car. He unlocked her door and opened it, ignoring the fact that she'd reached for the door handle at the same time. When he slid behind the wheel, she'd already fastened her seat belt. He started the car and drove up

Kelly's Point Road to Charles Street, where he stopped for the light.

"So are you going to tell me what it was that I did that ended our friendship back in high school?" he asked.

"I never thought our friendship ever really ended, Clay," she said softly.

"You shut me out for all these years," he reminded her. "You've said more to me tonight than you did through the last three years of high school."

When she didn't respond, he added, "Okay, this may not be a very manly thing to say, but it really hurt that you just stopped talking to me. I know I must have done something that upset you or hurt you, but I've never known what it was, and it's bothered me all these years."

The light turned green, and he made the right turn.

"So I have to ask: What was it that I'd done back then that kept us from being friends all these years?"

"It wasn't something you did, Clay. It never occurred to me that you'd think that you'd done something." She spoke so softly that he could barely hear her words. "I'm so very sorry that you thought it was you."

"Then what was it?"

He turned into the inn's drive, and followed the lane to the back of the building. He stopped the Jeep near the back door and shifted into park. In the dark, he heard her breathing, ragged and uneven.

"Something happened that summer that changed me. It had nothing to do with you, and everything to do with me." She looked across the console, her eyes wide and haunted. "I am more sorry than I can say that I shut you out. You were the one person I could always depend on—you didn't deserve the way I treated you. It's embarrassed and shamed me all these years because you had been such a good friend to me, always, and I treated you unfairly and unkindly. Thank you for not holding it against me, for giving me a chance to tell you how much I've regretted my actions."

Before Clay could react, Lucy jumped out of the car and disappeared through the double doors into the lobby.

What, he asked himself, was that all about?

He sat outside the inn, watching to see if the lights went on in her old room, the corner room on the second floor, but the windows remained dark. He eased the car toward the NO PARKING sign, and sat in the silent car, wondering what the hell had just happened.

Diary ~

It's lovely to have a little time to reflect during the holidays. Of course, for just about everyone else, the holidays are over, but here at the inn, we're still celebrating. Lucy arrived on Wednesday afternoon, and that night we had Christmas all over again. I don't know who enjoyed the double holiday more, me or Daniel's children. Probably me—because Lucy was home and Ford called and we all had a few moments to speak with him. Still not clear on exactly where he is, but no matter. It was good to hear his voice. He sounded in good spirits and it was wonderful to see how everyone's face lit up when it was their time to chat with him. I do miss my youngest . . .

But I do have Lucy home until Sunday and that's a gift, so I will not complain. She had her meeting with Robert and Susanna about their wedding today. Trula called a little while ago—she tells me that both the prospective bride and groom are thrilled with Lucy and her take-charge attitude and her willingness to work with their ideas, not to mention the glorious plans they have for their wedding. I didn't share with Trula that arriving at a date might be a wee bit of a problem—not my place to get involved in all that. I'm sure Daniel will work it out, though—what a feather in the inn's cap to host such a high-profile affair. I know that

Lucy is accustomed to such grand shindigs, but other than the MacGregor wedding, we've been pretty low-key here. Looks like the times, they may be a-changing.

We're going to—reluctantly—undecorate the inn tomorrow. Daniel has done his best to keep the trees and decorations fresh for Lucy's Christmas, but alas, all has gotten pretty dry—though no one seems to mind so very much. Lucy is on a date with Clay Madison tonight—she keeps insisting that it's only dinner in that no-big-deal way of hers, but if you could see the look on that young man's face when he looks at her . . . it's pretty clear he doesn't think of her as just another old school chum. I think he's always been a little sweet on her. As for her, who knows what goes through that girl's head sometimes? If she can't see what everyone else sees in Clay . . . well, I shouldn't have to spell it out for her.

And speaking of spells . . . no, no, of course I wouldn't do one of those where my daughter is concerned, tempted though I may be at times. But I am thinking I'd appreciate a little help from the other side right about now. There's a strange vibration sometimes when Lucy is in the inn—I can't put my finger quite on it, but it comes from Lucy and it's unmistakable. I'm so frustrated because I can't interpret what she's feeling—not that I'd ever try to "eavesdrop" on my daughter—not intentionally—but there's something there that's just . . . off. Some sadness or sense of unrest . . . which doesn't really make much sense, since Lucy's always been happy and loved here. I was hoping perhaps my old friend Alice might have some input, but she's been scarce these past few weeks. Things are rough when a girl can't rely on her friends—in whatever dimension they might dwell— to lend a hand once in a while!

~ Grace ~

Chapter 9

T HE lobby was lit only by the lights on the twelve-foot-tall Christmas tree that stood in one corner and the lamp on the reservation desk, though Lucy was pretty sure there'd be no late or unexpected arrivals that night. Other than the good-natured chatter of the kitchen's cleanup crew—one of them loudly singing along to Lady Gaga's "Born This Way" on the radio—there didn't seem to be much activity in the inn. Lucy paused at the foot of the steps that led to the second floor and the family's quarters. She didn't fancy another night lying in bed staring at the ceiling, fighting sleep for fear of the nightmares returning. If she went upstairs now, she'd be expected to join everyone who was still awake while they watched the news in their shared family room and surely she'd be subjected to interrogation by her mother about her date with Clay.

She wasn't up to either—nightmares or interrogations—so she walked down the hall into the darkest part of the inn, to the library, where she'd always found peace. The white lights were still lit on the tree, though all of the candles were extinguished. Lucy took off her boots then curled up in the leather chair and tried to sort through the evening.

The good news was that she'd finally been able to voice a long-overdue apology to Clay for the way she'd treated him so many years ago, and that he hadn't pushed for any further explanation than what she'd offered, which, in retrospect, had been none at all. Why, she wondered, had it taken her so long to have gotten even that much out? Whatever else might have happened, Clay was still her friend, quite possibly the best friend she'd ever had. She hadn't realized how much she'd missed his friendship until she'd sat across the table from him that night and the years seemed to drift away. At his core, Clay hadn't changed much at all: his humor and good-natured earnestness had always been part of his personality, and as always, his enthusiasm—for his farming, his prospective brewery—had made her smile. Clay was a man who loved life, embraced it, and she was smart enough to realize that her life had been richer when he'd been a part of it.

And then there was that kiss—a lifetime in the making if you didn't count those practice kisses back in seventh grade. She smiled in the dark and wondered why *that* had taken so long, too. It had come as such a surprise that her normal defenses never had a chance. But that was okay. There'd been such an air of fate about the entire night—including the kiss—that she hadn't felt the alarm she usually felt when someone got too close.

Now if she could only work up the courage to tell him the rest of the story, to speak the words she'd never said aloud to anyone, maybe some part of her might be free.

"I was raped, Clay," she whispered to the empty room. "That summer? I was raped . . ."

Lucy carried a stepstool to the library to reach the star on the top of the tree and remove the top tier of ornaments. Her mother was there waiting for her, staring out the window, the boxes for the ornaments laid out on the table.

"You look as if you're having deep thoughts." Lucy set the stool next to the tree.

"I was just thinking about Vanessa," Grace told her.

"What about Vanessa?"

"Well, you know that she and Grady are getting married in a few weeks," Grace began.

"And . . ." Lucy leaned on the back of a nearby chair, certain that her mother was leading up to something.

"And, well . . . I was wondering if you could do a favor for me."

"Does this have something to do with Vanessa's wedding?"

Grace nodded. "Oh, I know you don't have time to plan her wedding for her, but she's at such loose ends, I was wondering if maybe you could stop at her shop while you're here and just give her a few pointers. She's really feeling overwhelmed, and she's such a dear girl—"

"Where's the wedding going to be?"

"At her house. I offered to let her use any of the public rooms that aren't booked on her date, but she really would like to get married at the house." Grace smiled. "I think she was afraid Alice would be offended and start acting up if she missed the wedding."

"Alice? You mean Alice Ridgeway? The woman who used to own Vanessa's house?"

When Grace nodded, Lucy said, "The same Alice Ridgeway who's been dead for, what, three years now?"

"Thereabouts." Grace smiled calmly. "Vanessa says she's still about from time to time."

Lucy rolled her eyes. "I'll stop by the shop and see what I can do to help." She turned her attention back to the tree, but not before adding, "I don't suppose Alice is in the wedding party."

"Don't be disrespectful, dear."

Lucy laughed and repositioned the stool.

"Are you sure you can reach the top?" her mother asked. "We could wait for Dan."

"I think I can get it." Lucy struggled to open the old stepstool. "How long has it been since this was used, Mom?"

"Probably too long." Clay entered the room, an old brown leather bomber jacket over a black crewneck sweater and jeans and a cardboard container of coffee in his hand. "How 'bout if I get that?"

He reached up and snagged the star from the top and handed it to Grace.

"You still want that stool opened up?" he asked as he set the coffee on the table.

Lucy nodded. "I want to take down those ornaments."

"You have the box for them?" He glanced around the room, then picked up a box from the table and handed it to Grace. "This looks like the one I took them out of. Why don't you hold it, Miz Grace, and I'll just pluck them off the tree."

"You don't have to do that," Lucy and Grace said at the same time.

"Really," Lucy told him. "You don't have to . . ."

"I found myself with some time this morning, so I thought I'd stop over to help out." He began to take the ornaments down. One by one, he passed them off to Lucy, who put them into the box in her mother's arms.

"That's very nice of you, dear," Grace told him, "but you've already done so much to help out . . ."

"We were always taught that the job wasn't finished till the cleanup was done." He grabbed a few more glass balls from the tree and handed them down to Lucy. "You know, like when you bake something, you clean up everything you used when you're finished, right? Bowls, spoons . . ."

"I don't bake," Lucy heard herself say.

"Never?" Clay looked over his shoulder.

She shook her head.

"Not even brownies?"

"Nope."

"Chocolate chip cookies?"

Lucy shook her head again. "None of the above."

"Miz Grace, are you listening to this?" He turned to her mother.

"I don't know where I went wrong," Grace deadpanned. "I tried to raise her right, Clay."

"Oh, stop it, you two." Lucy laughed. "I don't bake and I almost never cook because I'm never home when it's time to eat."

"Are you telling me you eat out three times a day?" he asked.

"I don't usually eat very much in the morning and I'm usually too busy at lunchtime to stop. I generally stay at the office until seven or eight—"

"Sorry to interrupt, but I need to keep track of the time. I promised my granddaughter I'd take her to Scoop after lunch." Grace glanced at her watch, then put the box down on the table. "Oh, my, it's much later than I thought. I guess the two of you can finish up this one little room without me."

"No problem, Miz Grace," Clay told her.

"I don't remember you and Diana talking about going to Scoop today." Lucy frowned, fully aware of what her mother was attempting to do.

Ignoring Lucy, Grace went up on her tiptoes to give Clay a smooch on the cheek. "Thank you very much for all of your help. You can tell your mother that she raised a fine boy."

"Will do." Clay smiled and turned to Lucy. "You might want to pick up that box your mother was holding."

"She's not fooling me one bit," Lucy grumbled, and wrapped the ornaments she'd been holding in tissue and put them into the box with the others. "Transparent as new window glass."

"What?" Clay asked.

"She's just trying to throw the two of us together, that's what."

"Works for me," he muttered. "Does it bother you that I'm here?"

"No, it doesn't." Lucy exhaled loudly. "It's just that she's so blatant about it."

"I think she thought she was being subtle."

"About as subtle as . . ." Lucy paused. "I'm glad you're here, and I appreciate all your help. You could be somewhere else, doing something more interesting."

"No place I'd rather be, LuLu." He turned and held out an ornament. "Nothing else I'd rather be doing."

Maybe it was the sincerity in his voice and in his eyes, or maybe it was just that he looked so damned good, but before she could talk herself out of it, Lucy put down the ornaments and took three steps toward the tree. Clay met her halfway and opened his arms to her, folded her inside. For just one moment, she felt safer than she had in years.

"Thank you, Clay."

"For . . . ?"

"For being you. For being here today. For being here . . ." She swallowed hard. "Just for being here."

"I've always been here for you, LuLu," he said softly.

"I know," she whispered. "I know that now."

"So anytime you need me . . ."

She nodded.

There was commotion in the hall outside the library, and Lucy turned as the door opened.

"Oops. Bad timing." Her brother stood in the doorway. "I'm interrupting—"

"No, no, Dan," Lucy broke from Clay's embrace. "I was just thanking an old friend for helping us out."

"Right." Dan was obviously not buying that, but she let it ride. "We're taking a bunch of trees over to the firehouse for recycling. I thought I'd take this one, but I see you're still working on it."

"We need about five more minutes," Clay told him. "Just a few more ornaments and the lights, and she'll be good to go."

"Dan, how are you doing with dates for the Magellan wedding?" Lucy asked.

"I'm working on it," he told her. "It's not as easy as it sounds, getting people to agree to give up the week they've had for years. In some cases, twenty years or more. We have people who came here as kids who come back every year with *their* families. They want the same week, even the same rooms. We've offered comps for a different week, but for some people, it's been a really hard sell."

"I understand, but at the same time I need to get back to Susanna with a couple of dates before she gets antsy and decides to go elsewhere."

"I definitely don't want that to happen. I'll just keep making phone calls." Dan turned to Clay. "I'll pull the pickup around to this door." He pointed toward the front of the building. "You can bring the tree out when you're ready."

"Want me to go with you over to the firehouse, help you unload the trees?" Clay asked.

"That would be great. Thanks," Dan replied.

"Okay, see you in five." Clay passed a handful of ornaments to Lucy as if they hadn't just been caught cuddling by her big brother.

She made a point of looking for the lid to the box they'd just filled. "I guess most of the houses that were on the tour have had their decorations taken down by now. One of these years, I'm going to make a point of being home the weekend of the tour so I can see the houses all dressed up. Mom said the old Enright mansion was on the tour this year."

"The highlight of the tour," Clay told her. "People are still talking about it."

"Damn, and I missed it. I would love to have seen that place all fancied up."

"That could be arranged."

"Really?" She stopped what she was doing. "How?"

"I happen to have an in with the Enrights."

"Do tell." She fit the lid onto the box and turned back to face him.

"My sister's hot and heavy with Jesse."

"So?"

"So Curtis is out of town visiting a granddaughter in Pennsylvania and Jesse has the key to the house. I have it on very good authority that the decorations are still up." Clay grinned. "All it would take is a phone call."

"Make it."

Still grinning, he took his phone from his pocket and hit speed dial. Brooke didn't answer but he left voice mail.

"How old is that phone?" Lucy asked when he'd closed it over.

"I don't know." He shrugged and started to slip it into his pocket. "A couple of years, maybe."

"Let me see that thing." She held her hand out and he dropped the phone into her palm. "Clay, this phone is, like, from the Dark Ages. No Internet . . . no email . . ." She looked up at him.

He took the phone back and put it into his pocket. "I don't want to read emails or use the Internet on my phone. I just want to make and receive phone calls. Maybe send a text once in a while, but that's it."

"Dark Ages," she whispered, and he laughed.

"I have thought about getting something newer, but I don't spend that much time on the phone. Besides, I like this one. It folds over."

"I think some of the newer ones fold over," she told him.

"Maybe I'll look around next time I'm near the phone store." The phone in his pocket began to ring. He glanced at the screen then answered it. "Hey, Brooke—we need a favor . . ."

After he explained what he wanted, he asked Lucy, "What are you doing this afternoon?"

She hesitated. "I need to stop in to see Vanessa Keaton. I don't know how long I'll be."

"Brooke, how 'bout tomorrow afternoon?" He glanced at Lucy and asked, "One o'clock?"

"Perfect. Thank you, Brooke!"

"Lucy says thank you. See you then." He put the phone away.

"Thanks, Clay. I'm really excited about seeing this place. I used to walk past it on my way to Miss Harriet's for piano lessons and I'd dream about what the inside looked like. I can't wait to see."

"Like I said. All it took was a phone call."

"Hey, Clay, you about finished in there?" Dan called from the lobby.

"We're good. I just need to get the tree out of the stand," Clay called back to him. "Give me one minute."

Clay turned the tree over and pulled off the stand.

"I'll take that," Lucy told him. "I'll clean it up and

put it back into the closet with the decorations. Thanks again for your help."

"Don't mention it." Clay hoisted the tree onto his shoulder. "I'll pick you up at twelve forty-five."

"I can't wait." She stood on her tiptoes and kissed the side of his face. "I'm so excited. Thanks so much for making that phone call."

"Whatever it takes, LuLu." He leaned down and kissed her on the mouth. "Whatever it takes . . ."

At three o'clock, Lucy opened Bling's door and stepped into Vanessa Keaton's shop, which, for all its upscale merchandise, still retained a cozy, inviting vibe. Vanessa was stacking sweaters, and when she saw Lucy, her face lit up with a smile.

"Lucy! I heard you were in St. Dennis this week." Vanessa put down the pile of sweaters. "So good to see you."

"I couldn't resist a chance to come in and see what new goodies you got in since my last visit." Lucy scanned the shop's walls, where shelves held bags and sweaters and shoes. She made a beeline for a tan leather tote. "Oh, this is perfect." She opened the bag and looked inside. "And yes! Interior pockets!"

She looked up at Vanessa. "It's so annoying when you have to go to a meeting and you have to carry a tote with your files and you have to carry a handbag, too. You can't put your handbag stuff into the tote because it all rolls around together on the bottom and you can't find a thing. But these pockets organize quite nicely. There's even a deep pocket for a wallet or e-reader."

Still smiling, Vanessa leaned on the counter. "You'd make a fabulous salesperson, you know that?"

"It's perfect." Lucy held it up. "Does it come in black?"

"Absolutely." Vanessa pointed to the wall behind Lucy. "Three short steps away . . ."

"I'll take it." Lucy plucked the bag from the wall shelf.

"Easiest sale I made all week," Vanessa said. "Thanks, Lucy."

"I love it. I'm so glad I stopped in today."

"How long are you staying this time around?" Vanessa took the bag from Lucy and began to wrap it in tissue.

"Just till Sunday." Lucy opened her wallet and handed over a credit card.

"I heard you're planning a big wedding." Vanessa ran the card through the machine and returned it along with the slip for Lucy to sign.

"Everyone in town has apparently heard about it." Lucy made a face. "We'll see. We're still in the talking stages. But I hear there's to be another wedding soon."

"Isn't it great?" Vanessa held up her left hand to show off her sparkly ring. "I can hardly believe it myself, but yes, Grady and I are getting married in a few weeks."

"How are your plans going?" Lucy asked as if she didn't know that Vanessa was stumbling where the wedding reception was concerned.

"More slowly than they should, I'm afraid." Vanessa leaned on the counter and sighed.

"Anything I can help with?"

"Oh, if only." Vanessa sighed. "I could never afford you, and I know your time is valuable and that you won't be here . . ."

Lucy waved a hand dismissively. "I always have time to help a friend. We can make time to talk over what you want to do, if you like. Maybe I could help you to streamline things. Consider it a wedding gift."

"I just can't seem to make up my mind about anything and the day keeps getting closer and closer . . ." Vanessa's eyes began to take on a desperate look.

The bell over the shop door rang and several middle-aged women came in.

"This is the place where I got those darling tops last summer," one was saying. "Oh, and there's Vanessa!"

"Oh, hi," Vanessa greeted the ladies. "Nice to see you back again."

"I've been telling my friends all about St. Dennis and about how fabulous you are and we just had to take the trip down today." The woman placed a hand on her chest and said. "I was here in September. Margo? Elizabeth, New Jersey?"

"Of course. Margo." Vanessa nodded, and only someone who knew her could tell that she had no recollection of ever having seen this woman before.

"I'll leave you to your customers." Lucy patted Vanessa's hand. "But how 'bout we try to get together before Sunday morning?"

"Are you free tonight?" Vanessa asked. "I mean, if you didn't have any plans, maybe we could sit down for a while . . ."

"Sure. Do you want to come to the inn . . . ?"

"How about at our house? That's where the wedding is going to be. One of the problems I'm having is how to decorate the rooms to look like a wedding is taking place. And since it's the weekend before Valentine's Day, I know everyone will be expecting red roses, which I so do not want to do."

"I understand," Lucy assured her. "Would seven be too early?"

"Seven is perfect."

"I'll see you then." Lucy gathered up her purchase.

"Oh, yay! I'll call the girls!" Vanessa all but beamed.

"The girls?"

"Steffie, Mia, Brooke. This will be so much fun!"

"Vanessa, are these sweaters on sale?" Margo from Elizabeth, New Jersey, called.

"Go take care of business," Lucy told Vanessa. "I'll see you tonight at seven."

"Thanks, Lucy. I so appreciate this . . ." Vanessa came around the corner of the glass case and did a little dance. "I'm going to have a wedding and now it will be perfect . . ."

Lucy laughed. "I can't promise perfect, but I can promise perfectly organized."

"At this point, I'll take it." Vanessa gave Lucy a quick hug. "I can't wait to see what you'll come up with. . . ."

Chapter 10

"So nice you're getting out for an evening with girlfriends," Grace said as Lucy buttoned her coat in the lobby.

Lucy looked up, puzzled. "I'm just going over to help Vanessa organize her wedding plans, maybe give her a few pointers."

"Well, it's nice that you're doing it, and I know Vanessa will appreciate any help you can give her. The girl just seems overwhelmed. The wedding, a baby on the way . . ."

"Who's having a baby?" Lucy opened her bag and checked the contents. A notebook, a pen—just in case she needed them—her reading glasses . . .

"Vanessa." Grace folded her arms across her chest. "Didn't you know?"

"No. I wouldn't have guessed. She didn't look pregnant . . ." Keys? Where did she put the car keys?

"Just a very few months, from what I understand." Grace smiled. "It will be lovely to have a new baby in the family."

"Vanessa's family? Is there something I don't know about our relationship with her?" She could hear the keys jingling in one of the pockets in her bag, but couldn't find the right one.

"Family in the greater sense, dear."

Lucy located the keys in the bottom of the center pocket—what was the purpose of that big center pocket, anyway?—and kissed her mother on the cheek. "I'll see you in a while," she said. "I doubt I'll be more than an hour or two."

"No hurry."

Lucy checked her phone for messages while the car warmed up—thank goodness for heated seats—and answered a text from Bonnie about the flowers for the following week's wedding. She'd spent all afternoon tending to business and had thought she was totally caught up. She sat in the warm car and waited for her partner's response. After it arrived, she sent one more reply, then put the car in gear and headed off to Vanessa's house on Cherry Street. By the time she got there, the car was toasty inside and she hated getting out.

"Shouldn't be such a wimp when it comes to winter," she grumbled as she turned off the engine and gathered her bag. "It's not like I didn't grow up here. Not like I don't know what cold is."

There were several other cars parked directly in front of Vanessa's bungalow, making it a longer walk from Lucy's car to the front door. She rang the doorbell with cold fingers. (*Note to self: Gloves are good. Buy a pair.*) Vanessa opened the door before Lucy could ring twice.

"Come in!" Vanessa greeted her with open arms. "Thanks so much for coming, Lucy. I'm excited already."

"Well, save the excitement for when we actually come up with an idea or two that you might like." Lucy dropped her bag on the floor and unbuttoned her coat. She rubbed her cold hands together even though the house was cozy warm.

"Come sit next to the fire," Vanessa said, "and let's see if we can chase that chill."

"It really isn't even that cold out tonight." Lucy followed her hostess into the living room, where she was shown to a wing chair next to the fireplace. "I'm just so used to the weather in Southern California. They don't call it 'sunny' for nothing."

"I've never been," Vanessa told her, "but I've heard it was—"

"Hi, Lucy." Steffie emerged through double doors with a tray on which sat four glasses and two bottles of wine. "I was just telling Ness how totally cool it was to work with you on our wedding. Everything went so smoothly with you there."

She placed the tray on the coffee table and asked, "White or red?"

"Red, thank you," Lucy replied.

"Great choice. The wines are from Hunter's Vineyard over in Ballard," Vanessa was saying. "Of course, I'm not drinking because of the baby—it's strictly club soda for me these days—but I've had their wines before and have really enjoyed them.

"I heard the vineyard and the winery are for sale." Vanessa ducked into the kitchen and returned with a tray piled with cheese, fruit, and crackers. She set it on the table next to the wine. "We're hoping some innovative someone will buy it. Though it will be a shame to see the Petersons' name off the label. They've been making wine there for years."

"Must be after my time," Lucy said. "I don't remember the name or there being a vineyard in St. Dennis."

"It's out on New River Road, down about three miles. Past the Madison farm, you know, where it wraps around the corner of Charles and New River?" Steffie told her. "Which reminds me: Brooke should be along soon. She's trying to finish up tomorrow's cupcake orders, but she didn't think she'd be too late. She said not to wait for her. She's been really crazy busy trying to get her bakery ready to open— she's calling it Cupcake because, you know, she's only making cupcakes. Plus she's getting ready to move . . ."

Steffie opened the wine bottles, poured first from the red, and passed a glass to Lucy. Vanessa sat on the edge of a chair nursing a tall glass of sparkling water with lemon and lime slices from the kitchen.

"I've been in such a tizzy these past few weeks, it's been hard for me to focus. First Stef's wedding, then Christmas and all of Grady's relatives were here. After that was the big sale I had at Bling. All of a sudden the wedding is just a few weeks away and I don't know what I'm doing." Vanessa frowned. "The only thing I know for certain is that the ceremony is going to be in here, by the fireplace. I thought maybe we'd have chairs set up going this way." One hand made an invisible line from one side of the room to the other. "What do you think, Lucy? What would you do in here to decorate?"

Lucy got up from her chair and gazed around the

room, then walked into the foyer, which was wide and bisected by a wide stairwell leading to a landing, then to the second floor. From the foyer, she walked back into the living room.

"If I could make a suggestion . . . ," she said.

"Absolutely. Suggest away." Vanessa followed Lucy's line of vision. "You like the bay window . . . ?"

Lucy nodded. "You have this lovely antique table here, and with candles and some flowers on this beautiful lace cloth, it could be quite the focal point. Having the ceremony at one end of the room instead of in the middle will give you more space for guests to gather."

Vanessa walked to the table where Lucy stood. "So I'd have one solid section of chairs instead of two with an aisle," she said thoughtfully.

"Unless you're planning on a long ceremony, you might want to forgo the chairs altogether," Lucy suggested. "People can stand for ten or so minutes. Except, of course, if you have elderly or infirm guests."

"None that I can think of offhand, but we could have a few chairs here in the front. That would save us from taking the sofa and the wing chairs out of the room."

"No need to do that," Lucy told her. "You could move the sofa to the other short wall so that your guests aren't tripping over it, and the chairs could stay there by the fireplace."

"That could be pretty cool," Steffie noted. "Not what you'd expect—I mean, you'd almost expect to see the ceremony in front of the fireplace. Which could get very warm for you and Grady if you stood there for too long in front of a roaring fire."

"I'll run that past Grady, but I definitely like the idea. Now, what would you suggest for flowers?" Vanessa asked. "All I see this time of year are red roses and I don't want this to look like a Valentine's Day party."

"White tulips," Lucy told her. "Masses of white tulips. Assuming, of course, that you like tulips."

"I love tulips." Vanessa's eyes lit up. "I have tons of them planted out front. All colors. They are glorious when they all bloom and the yard is so colorful, but that won't be for a few more months. But white tulips . . ." She glanced at the navy paisley wallpaper. "Yes, I can see white tulips in here."

"Would you be ordering from Olivia at Petals and Posies?" Lucy asked.

Vanessa nodded.

"Tell her you'd like frosty white vases, all in the same size and shape. I'll sketch one out for you, if you like."

"I'd love that, thank you."

"You want five, all identical, to march right across the mantel." Lucy pointed to the fireplace, where, in her mind's eye, she could see the vases, the flowers, come to life. "You want the same there on the table in the bay window, only much larger, fuller." Lucy held her arms to form a circle. "Enormous."

Vanessa nodded. "Got it. Gorgeous."

"Out here . . ." Lucy headed toward the foyer. "Another huge spray of white tulips on this marble-topped table, with maybe your guest book alongside it. Then over here, on either side of the steps, white urns filled with curly willow spray painted white with little white fairy lights wound through them."

She paused for a moment, looking back into the living room, then smiled. "Maybe something fun, something whimsical."

"Like what?"

"Like maybe silvery-white helium balloons in different sizes, all congregated up around the ceiling like champagne bubbles."

"I like that a lot." Vanessa nodded. "But we'd need tons of them to get the right effect. I'll talk to Grady about that, maybe put him in charge of the balloons. Cool idea, Lucy. Thanks."

Lucy went into the dining room that opened from the other side of the foyer.

"You have pocket doors here?" Lucy investigated. "Maybe you could close these over during the ceremony. Hang wreaths of white baby's breath on each door, not in the middle, though. Hang them close to the open edge, so that when the ceremony is over, you slide the doors open partway, and the wreaths are still visible on either side of the opening."

"I love that idea." Vanessa followed Lucy into the dining room.

"In here, again, white tulips. Big display on the table, then across the back of the sideboard—I am assuming you'll be serving food on that piece?"

Vanessa nodded.

"So instead of flowers at one end, try tall narrow vases that only hold one stem each, and line them right across the back of the sideboard. They'll look like twice as many with the mirror there behind them, but won't interfere with the space you need for serving dishes."

"I never would have thought of that," Vanessa told her, "but I love the idea."

"What are you wearing, by the way?" Lucy asked.

"Short white dress, a little on the froufrou side," Vanessa replied.

"Vanessa's our resident girlie-girl," Stef joined them in the dining room. "Not that there's anything wrong with that."

"I hesitated about wearing white," Vanessa admitted, "because I've been married before." She paused. "Well, twice, actually."

"The first when she was way too young, the second when she was way too foolish," Steffie told Lucy. "We told her those didn't count when deciding what color dress to wear, because this is the marriage that counts." Stef put an arm around Vanessa's shoulders. "This is the right guy and the right time, and this time is the only one that matters."

"Thanks, Stef." Vanessa looked as if she were about to tear up. "You're right about Grady being the right guy. He is the only one that matters."

"So a white wedding is totally appropriate," Lucy noted.

"I can't thank you enough." Vanessa gave Lucy a hug. "You're making this seem so easy."

"It is easy, once you decide what you want to do, and you keep things relatively simple," Lucy told her. "Are you having a caterer?"

"Yes. We were lucky to get Deanna Clark. She's the best on the Eastern Shore, and thanks to Dallas, we were able to get her to squeeze us in that weekend."

"Ask her to serve everything in or on white pieces. That will sort of tie it all in," Lucy said as they all began to drift from the dining room back across the foyer toward the living room.

"We're having cupcakes instead of a cake," Vanessa was saying.

"Not to mention white ice cream, compliments of *moi*."

"What flavor of white are you making for the occasion, Stef?" Lucy asked. Steffie's homemade ice cream was famous on the Chesapeake.

"I haven't decided yet," Stef confessed. "I keep going back and forth between coconut, which isn't so original, and white peach. Which could possibly be my favorite of all time. Unfortunately, this is not peach season."

"It must be peach season somewhere in the world," Vanessa said.

"It's a matter of finding a sufficient supply of good fruit, which I haven't been able to do yet. But I haven't given up." Steffie patted Vanessa on the back. "I'm doing the best I can."

"I know you are, and I know that whatever you make will be delightful. I've never tasted any of your ice cream that hasn't been fabulous. And trust me," Vanessa told Lucy, "I have tasted everything Stef makes and it's all been perfection."

"You make me blush." Steffie took a seat on the sofa. "But it's all so true."

"So if you can't find white peaches in sufficient quantity, what are the other choices?" Lucy asked.

"White chocolate mint, or white chocolate mousse." Stef leaned over and refilled her wineglass. She held up the bottle and asked, "Anyone?"

"I'll have a splash more," Lucy heard herself say.

She hadn't planned on staying for a second glass, but it was delicious and the fire was so nice and warm, why hurry back out into the cold?

Stef refilled Lucy's glass.

"Of course, there's the old standby, vanilla bean," Stef continued, "or vanilla with macadamia nuts. I found a terrific supplier in Hawaii when we were on our honeymoon."

"I think I'm just going to say 'surprise me.'" Vanessa sat on a hassock in front of a wall of books.

"I am humbled by your trust in me."

"Then again, maybe we should ask Alice," Vanessa said thoughtfully.

"Since when does Alice know from ice cream?" Steffie asked.

"Alice?" Lucy asked.

"Alice Ridgeway. She lived here in my house for about, oh, I don't know. Ninety years, maybe."

"I know about her. She was a friend of my mother's," Lucy told them. She recalled her mother's recent comment about Alice. "My mother somehow thinks that Alice might still be about."

Vanessa nodded and moved to the wing chair opposite the one Lucy was sitting in. "Your mother's been very helpful in interpreting Alice's journals and notebooks."

"Interpreting . . . ?"

"You know, Alice's spells." Vanessa's voice dropped an octave. "That woman had a spell for damn near everything you could think of."

"Why would my mother know about any of that?"

"Well, because . . ." Vanessa paused. "Because . . ."

"Because when your mother was younger," Steffie said carefully, "Alice sort of *guided* her."

"'*Guided*' her . . . ?" Lucy asked.

"Your mother is . . . sensitive," Vanessa blurted out.

"She's always been a very sensitive person," Lucy agreed, "but what does that have to do with Alice Ridgeway's journals? I'm sorry, but I'm confused."

"Don't you remember, growing up, everyone—all the kids, anyway—thought that Alice was a witch?" Stef whispered the last word.

"That was kid stuff." Lucy waved a hand dismissively.

Steffie and Vanessa both shook their heads from side to side.

"Not kid stuff," Stef told her.

"Alice was the real deal." Vanessa nodded.

"Are you two crazy?" Lucy started to laugh, then stopped. "You are crazy, aren't you."

"I know it sounds that way, but I live in her old house, and believe me, she's still here."

Before Lucy could comment, Vanessa added, "Did you know that she was agoraphobic?"

"And that she and my mother's cousin Horace Hinson were in love but didn't marry because she wouldn't leave the house?" Stef said. "Well, she still hasn't left."

"Stop. You're making my head spin," Lucy told them.

"Believe it or not, but I'm telling you, Alice is here sometimes," Vanessa insisted. "Not all the time, just sometimes."

"How do you know when she's here?" Lucy could

not believe she'd actually asked that. Still, she looked around the room. "Is she here now?"

"Uh-uh. I know when she's here 'cause I can feel her." Vanessa took a few sips of her club soda.

"You mean, like, breathing down your neck? Or does she pinch you . . . ?"

"No, no. Nothing like that. I just sense her. She's not mean at all, she's really rather sweet and protective. It's comforting, actually. Grady still has his wilderness guide business and he's often out west for a week or so at a time, which means I'm often here alone at night. Sometimes I just feel her here, and it's like, I don't know, like having your grandmother stop in to see if you're doing all right."

"I don't believe we're having this conversation," Lucy muttered.

"I can see you're skeptical." Vanessa smiled. "I used to be, too. So did Stef. But you live with something, you start to run out of explanations for things happening. You hear footsteps and tell yourself that it's the heater, but then you remember that it's July and the heater hasn't been on in months. Or the curtains move, and you tell yourself it's just a breeze, but the windows are all closed. You smell flowers when there aren't any in the house. After a while, you just come to accept."

"Does Grady believe she's here?" Lucy asked.

"Grady won't go so far as to say he believes, but he's not saying he *doesn't* believe," Vanessa said. "He's being pretty cagey."

"I can't say I believe either. I do think there are things that happen that can't be logically explained,"

Lucy admitted. "But I am confused about how my mother fits into all this."

"I think Alice taught Grace stuff, or told her stuff. I'm not really sure of the details, but she seemed pretty happy when I gave her Alice's Ouija board." Vanessa sliced a piece of cheese for herself.

"My mother has a Ouija board?" Lucy's eyes widened at the thought. Mom? Playing at Ouija?

"She has Alice's." Stef nodded. "Ness found it upstairs in the attic and gave it to Grace. But not before we used it right here one night—Grace and I— remember, Ness? Remember it kept spelling out 'Daz' and we couldn't figure out what that meant?"

"And then we found the heart written on the wall under the wallpaper in your house . . ." Vanessa reminisced. " 'Horace loves Daisy.' "

"And we found something in one of Alice's journals that made us realize she was Daisy . . ." Stef continued.

"Sorry but my head is spinning again." Lucy raised a hand to her temple and laughed.

"I think I told you when you stayed with me in December before the wedding that my house used to belong to my mom's cousin Horace and that he left it to me when he died." Stef turned to face Lucy. "When Wade and I were stripping the old wallpaper, we found a big heart drawn on the wall. Inside the heart it said, 'Horace loves Daisy.' How romantic is that?"

"It's terribly romantic," Lucy acknowledged. "But I'm still not clear on what all this has to do with my mother."

"Just that Grace was a friend of Alice's and I think they can communicate, that's all," Vanessa said.

"You think my mother can communicate with ghosts," Lucy said flatly.

"Maybe just with Alice. I don't know if she's in contact with anyone else. Stef, did Miz Grace ever mention anyone else?"

Steffie shook her head. "Nope. Just Alice."

"Curiouser and curiouser," Lucy murmured.

Stef leaned over and refilled Lucy's empty glass, and Lucy took a sip. Everything she's just heard about her mother was at odds with the mother she knew. Mom—her mom—in league with the town witch? That would be crazy talk even if there *was* a town witch. Which there wasn't. Alice Ridgeway had been a nice old lady. A bit eccentric, sure, but still, just a nice old lady. Lucy took a sip of wine and glanced from Vanessa to Steffie. Surely the two of them just fed off each other's fanciful natures. If she looked at this in that context, it was sort of amusing.

"It's starting to snow." Brooke Bowers blew in through the front door, a sprinkling of white in her hair and on her coat. She carried a flat white box that she deposited on the coffee table the second she entered the room. "Good thing I made extras. In case we get snowed in here, at least we'll have cupcakes." She turned to Lucy. "Hi, Lucy. I hear we have a date tomorrow."

Lucy nodded. "I can't wait. I always wondered what the inside of that old house looked like."

"It's fabulous," Brooke assured her as she stripped off her coat, then draped it over the newel post in the front hall. "I had a ball dressing it for the house tour. I'm so glad we'll get to show it off one more time before we have to start taking the decorations down."

"If you're talking about the Enright house, it is fabulous," Steffie agreed. "Wade and I went through when it was open. Brooke did an amazing job." Stef turned to Lucy. "If you ever want to move your business back to St. Dennis, you should hire Brooke to help you decorate."

"I'm sure she's terrific, but I'm not moving back to St. Dennis. I'm just doing this one more wedding at the inn because it's too big to turn down." Why, Lucy wondered, did she suddenly feel defensive?

"Just don't break my brother's heart, okay?" Brooke said nonchalantly. "He's bug-eyed over you, so just let him down easy."

"Clay and I have been friends for . . . forever," Lucy told her. "He's not bug-eyed, he's . . ."

"Bug-eyed. Over the moon. He can't help himself. He's always been sweet on you." Brooke sat on the floor, cross-legged, and poured herself a glass of wine. "I'm only having one glass because I have cupcakes cooling at home that will need to be frosted and I have some packing to do."

"Do you have a moving date yet?" Vanessa asked.

"Maybe the end of next week. Cam thinks the electricians will have finished by then. I can't wait." She snagged a cracker and topped it with a bit of cheese. "I love my family, but I need my own place. Mom is happily living in her new town house, and while I love and adore my brother, we both need to have our own space. Logan is excited about the move because I promised him he could have a dog once we were in the house." She looked at Steffie. "Your brother said he has a great group of rescue dogs from down south someplace that we can pick from."

Stef nodded. "He does. We're getting one, too. Wade thinks Austin needs a companion."

"I told Clay he should get one. There hasn't been a dog at the farm since Harry the hound died ten or twelve years ago. Clay always loved his dogs."

"I remember a dog you used to have. He was really huge and all black," Lucy suddenly recalled. "He used to chase the geese around the pond."

"Midnight." Brooke nodded. "He was a great dog. Clay and I both cried for months over that dog when he died."

Lucy remembered. She'd cried, too. They hadn't had a dog at the inn—too many people had allergies, her dad had told them—and she'd secretly thought of Midnight as hers. All of a sudden she found herself wanting a dog, too.

Must be the wine, she told herself. She put her glass on the table, out of her reach.

"Okay, now that we have the famous Hollywood event planner here, maybe we can get her to dish just a little." Brooke grinned mischievously. "What was it like to do that fortieth birthday party for Julia Lucas? I read she's an absolute diva . . ."

For the next half hour, Lucy related some of her more memorable moments as an event planner. By the time she'd finished, everyone's sides hurt from laughing, and somehow, Lucy's wineglass had been filled and emptied again.

"So, Lucy, can you think of anything else we could do to make our wedding special?" Vanessa asked.

"Your wedding is going to be special because it's yours. Everything else is just trappings. You have a good caterer, you'll have fabulous ice cream and cupcakes and gorgeous flowers. I'd say you're set." Lucy opened her bag, took out a card, and handed it to Vanessa. "Don't be shy about calling if you have any last minute questions about anything."

"I couldn't. You've been all too generous with your time as it is." Vanessa slipped the card into her pocket.

"I was happy to stop over. It was fun." Lucy stood.

"Are you all right to drive?" Brooke reached out a hand to steady Lucy, who wobbled just a tad when she stood.

"I'm okay." Lucy stared at the empty glass in her hand before she placed it on the table. Had she really had three glasses of wine tonight?

"How 'bout I drive you home?" Brooke raised herself from the floor. "I can just swing by the inn, drop you off, and tomorrow on your way back from Enright's, Clay can drop you off here for your car."

"I hate to admit it, but that might be for the best." Lucy turned to Vanessa. "I'm embarrassed to admit it, but I think the wine's crept up on me."

"It can happen to anyone." Vanessa put an arm around Lucy's shoulders. "Actually, it has happened to all of us, at one time or another. You get together with the girls, you open a few bottles of wine, and the next thing you know, a couple of hours have gone by."

Lucy glanced at her watch. "It has been a couple of hours. I can't believe I've been here all this time . . ."

"It flies when you're having fun." Steffie handed Lucy her coat.

"I did have fun." Lucy slipped into the coat.

"So did we. Come back next time you're in town and we'll do it again."

"Thanks. I will." Lucy followed Brooke to the door. "Good luck with the wedding. Take lots of pictures so I can see how gorgeous you look."

"I guess there's no chance you'll be around that weekend." Vanessa's hand was on the doorknob.

"Sorry, no. I have a sweet sixteen party that same Saturday."

"Well, then, next time . . ." Vanessa opened the door.

"Next time." Lucy nodded.

"I'll talk to you tomorrow," Brooke told Vanessa as she followed Lucy outside and closed the door behind her.

They hurried through the chilly air to Brooke's ride, a big pink van with a huge cupcake painted on its side.

"Wow, way to advertise," Lucy said.

"Clay had been using this old van to haul around produce. It had a lot of body rust and the paint was worn in places, but I needed a van to distribute my cupcakes. So I asked him if I could paint it, and he said sure." Brooke laughed.

"So he was okay with the pink paint job and the big cupcake?"

"Let's just say that now he uses his Jeep more and the van less to make deliveries." Brooke unlocked the passenger door.

Lucy climbed into her seat and slammed the door just as Brooke got in and slid behind the wheel. "Thank God Clay has such a good sense of humor."

"He does, that," Lucy agreed. She leaned back in the seat and stared out the window.

Brooke started the van and drove to the end of

Cherry Street, then made a left onto Charles. St. Dennis was quiet at this hour of the evening: there were no pedestrians and no other cars.

"I guess they really do roll up the sidewalks early around here," Lucy remarked.

"I guess it's early to you, being from L.A., but around here, eleven o'clock is practically the middle of the night." Brooke put on her turn signal and pulled onto the drive leading to the inn. The big sign out front was floodlit, the only light on the street at this end of town. The van followed the winding path to the back of the inn and Brooke stopped outside the double doors.

"Just so you know," Brooke said, "I wasn't kidding about my brother. He really does have a thing for you. I'd hate to see you hurt him."

"I have no intentions of hurting Clay," Lucy all but snapped.

"I doubt you intended to the last time, but you did." Brooke put the van into park. "Are you going to try to tell me you weren't aware of how much you hurt him back then?"

"I . . . I wasn't. I didn't know . . ."

"You were as close friends as anyone I've ever known, and you stopped speaking to him without warning. You dumped him as a friend, and you didn't think that would hurt him?"

"I didn't think," Lucy said softly. "I just didn't know."

"Didn't know or didn't care?" Brooke's words stung.

"Didn't know. I never didn't care." Lucy opened the door and jumped out. "I never thought . . ."

"Maybe you should have."

Lucy reached in and grabbed her bag from the floor where she'd dropped it.

"I should have," Lucy admitted. "Yes. I should have. I'm sorry I didn't."

"Have you told Clay that?"

Lucy nodded. "I told him."

"Look, I don't know what happened back then, but I know it affected my brother for a long, long time. I just don't want to see him go through that again. I realize it's none of my business, but if you really only think of him as someone you used to know, please don't encourage him." Brooke's voice softened. "Clay's a great guy. He deserves someone who appreciates what a truly great guy he is."

"I understand." Lucy backed away from the van. "Thanks for the ride. I'll see you tomorrow."

"See you." Brooke waved.

Lucy slammed the van door, and watched the taillights snake back toward Charles Street, her shoulders hunched against the cold. When she finally went inside, the warmth felt positively tropical.

To her surprise, the family's living quarters were dark except for a lamp in the hall. She went into her room and tossed her coat onto the bed, toed off her shoes, and sat in the chair next to the window. She pulled her legs up under her and leaned close to the glass. There was moonlight on the Bay, and the shadow of an owl swooping across the quiet lawn.

All in all, it had been an interesting evening, mostly because the past few hours made her aware of the lack of friendship in her life. Oh, she and Bonnie were friends as well as business partners, but they never got together just to chat or to have a fun social evening. If they met for dinner, it was always a working dinner to discuss an upcoming event. How had it happened that she had spent fifteen years in California and had developed no social friends? She and Bonnie had worked equally hard to build up their business and to make it a success, and she'd be lying if she said she hadn't enjoyed the work and the satisfaction it brought.

But she found herself envying Vanessa, Stef, and Brooke for the network they'd formed, the friendships they shared. She'd enjoyed the evening at Vanessa's, enjoyed the companionship and the laughter.

For just a little while, she'd felt at home there.

And then there were those comments Brooke made about Clay, the ones Lucy'd been trying all night to push to the back of her mind.

"Bug-eyed. Over the moon," Brooke had said. "He can't help himself. He's always been sweet on you."

As hard as she'd tried to pretend it wasn't so, Lucy had known in her heart that Clay thought of her as more than an old friend. If there'd been any doubt, there was that kiss . . .

She sighed and sank deeper into the chair. That Clay felt that way was one thing. That she was starting to feel the same way about him was something else entirely. After all these years, he was still the best guy she'd ever known, still could make her laugh in ways that no one else could. The difference now was that he was also the one who made her heart beat faster. When he'd kissed her, there was no sign of her usual defenses—that urge to pull away she always felt when someone got too close to her. While that feeling of being suffocated, of having her space violated, generally did pass within an instant, she couldn't remember the last time someone had been that close to her when her initial reaction hadn't been to flee. Actually, she wasn't really certain that *she* hadn't been the one to kiss *him*.

And the confusing part was that she couldn't decide whether she should be happy about it, or scared to death.

Chapter 11

So, are you ready?" Clay held Lucy's hand as they ascended the front steps of Curtis Enright's house, which took up the whole last block of Old St. Mary's Church Road.

"I'm so ready." Lucy's face was a study in joyous anticipation. "I've waited all my life to get a peek inside this place." She nudged him with an elbow. "Knock already, or I will."

Clay raised a hand to the large polished brass lion's head that served as the door knocker, but before he could do the deed, the door opened.

"Hey, Clay. Hi, Lucy." Jesse Enright stood in the doorway of his grandfather's home. "Come on in. Brooke tells me we're giving a private tour this morning."

"This is so nice of you," Lucy told Jesse. "I was just telling Clay that I've waited forever to get a glimpse inside this house."

"Glad we could accommodate you." Jesse stepped aside to admit them. "Brooke's around here somewhere."

"Oh, wow." Lucy stood in the center of the entry

hall that was dominated by one of the biggest Christmas trees she'd ever seen. "This place is even grander than I expected."

"It's something, all right." Jesse closed the door softly. "I have to admit, the first time I stepped through that front door, I was as dazzled as you are."

"It's a pretty amazing place," Clay agreed. "I got my first look at the house during last month's tour, along with all the other gawkers. I don't know too many people in town who'd been in the house before, so there were a lot of 'oohs' and 'aahs' that day."

"I can understand why. Look at that tree . . . and the garland on the stairwell. Oh, and that crèche there on the table." Lucy appeared to be at a loss as to where to look first.

"All Brooke's work," Jesse told her with no small amount of pride. "All I did was follow orders."

"I'll bet she had a ball." Lucy stepped closer to the tree. "Antique ornaments?"

Jesse nodded. "We found boxes of them in the attic. I thought Brooke was going to pass out, she got so excited."

"I don't blame her. They're exceptionally well preserved. The colors haven't faded a bit."

"They were wrapped up pretty well and hadn't seen the light of day since my grandmother died twenty-some years ago."

Lucy stepped closer to the wall on the right side, where numerous portraits were hung. "Relatives?" she asked.

"Earliest to the latest. From Elias Enright there on the end to my grandfather, farther on down the hall.

Not all of them lived here, though. The house has only been in the family since around 1864."

"The paintings are all exquisite," she said.

"Thank you." Jesse was smiling. "I really like that three of them—the most recent—were painted at almost the same spot outside. You can see how the property changed over the years." He pointed to one portrait. "In the background here, you can see the tenant houses that once stood along the stream at the back of the property. The place was built by a tobacco farmer who moved here from South Carolina around 1840. He based the floor plan on a plantation owned by a cousin. When the Civil War broke out, he joined the Confederate army, died at Gettysburg, and his widow sold the house to my great-great-grandfather the following year. In the next painting, though, those houses are all gone."

"There was a big flood around 1898," Clay said. "My grandmother wrote about it in her diary. They lost all their crops that year, almost lost the farm."

"My granddad said that the stream overflowed and washed out every one of those houses, and two children were lost. My great-grandfather had the cabins torn down rather than risk another tragedy. They planted a line of trees, but nothing ever was built again from the back of the carriage house to the edge of the stream."

"Hey, guys." Brooke came toward them from the back of the house, clutching an armful of amaryllis and ferns. "Sorry. I was out in the conservatory looking for something to replace the flower arrangements that have pooped out."

"There's a conservatory here?" Lucy's interest was clearly piqued.

"A real one, with plants that have survived since Jesse's grandmother's time. Curtis has kept them going." Brooke headed into the room on the left. "Come on in, look around the parlor."

"You don't need to ask me twice." Lucy followed Brooke, her eyes wide.

Seeing Lucy so carefree and happy tugged at Clay's heart, and he was grateful to have been able to bring that smile to her face. There'd been a time when she'd laughed easily and often, and smiled freely. It made him happy to know that that happy young girl who'd always found joy in her everyday life—his LuLu—still lurked inside the serious woman she'd become. Now that he'd had a glimpse of her, he was determined to not let her slip back into that place where she'd been hiding.

"Jesse, this is really nice of you to let Lucy and me stop over. As you can see, she's really enjoying this."

"I don't mind, and my granddad didn't mind. I know Lucy's only in town for another day and that she isn't here very often."

"Not so often at all."

"Is this wise?" Jesse lowered his voice.

"Is what wise?" Clay frowned.

"You know. Lucy."

Clay smiled. "She's the only girl who ever broke my heart."

"Maybe that's the attraction," Jesse said. "You know, the one who got away."

Clay shook his head. "It isn't that. I've been dumped plenty of times, once by a girl I thought I was in love with about five years ago. It hurt my pride, but it didn't break my heart."

"Brooke's worried that Lucy will do just that."

"What can I say? I've been a fool for lesser things, as the saying goes." Clay watched through the doorway as Lucy exclaimed over the arrangement of greens and berries and ornaments on the mantel. "I've been missing her in my life since the summer I turned fifteen. Every time I see her, I feel the same way inside as I did when we were kids."

"That's not necessarily a good thing," Jesse noted. "You're not kids anymore."

"I just mean that back then, I always knew I could be myself with her, that she'd never judge me, that she knew me for who I really was, and that I never needed to be anyone or anything other than who I am. I still feel that sort of comfort when I'm with her. I've never felt that with anyone else, not even my college sweetheart, who I almost married."

"Just be careful, okay? Brooke doesn't want to see you hurt. Hell, neither do I."

"I appreciate that, but if there is any way . . . well, I figure this could be my last chance."

"Last chance for what? What is it you want?"

Clay considered the question for a moment.

"I want to not have regrets. I want to know that I did whatever it took to see . . . well, just to see what's really there between us. I know there was a time when she and I meant a lot to each other. I guess I want to see if there's any of that left, and if there is, what are the chances that it could be more."

"I wish you luck, but you know that even if you're right, long-distance romances don't always end well."

Clay could tell Jesse was choosing his words carefully.

"Like I said, I don't want to regret what I didn't do when I could have. We'll see what happens. But either way, I appreciate your concern and Brooke's."

"Hey, you two," Brooke called from the parlor. "What are you doing out there?"

"Chewing the fat," Jesse called back.

"That expression always raises the most unpleasant visuals for me." Lucy appeared in the doorway and gestured for the two men to enter the room. "However, I will ignore them because the visuals in here are just heavenly."

She took Clay's hand and led him into Curtis Enright's parlor.

"Look at this tree," she urged. "Did you ever see anything so glorious?"

Clay stepped closer to get a better look. "It's very pretty . . ."

"It's ethereal." Brooke grinned.

"Yeah, it's really pretty," Clay repeated.

"Don't you notice anything about the decorations?" Lucy asked.

He took a closer look. "They're all really old?"

"They all have angels on them, you clod." Brooke tossed a bit of fern at her brother.

"Oh, yeah, I noticed that right away." Clay nodded, knowing full well his sister wasn't going to buy it.

Brooke and Lucy both rolled their eyes at the same time, and Clay laughed.

"Yes, I do see that they are all angels," he said.

"Aren't they just beautiful?" Lucy stepped closer to the tree, her eyes shining.

"Found them in the attic," Jesse told them, "under the eaves in a big dusty box. Brooke flipped out when she opened it."

"And I still flip out every time I look at them," Brooke noted. "They are so unique and so beautifully painted."

"Any idea where they came from, Jesse?" Lucy continued to walk around the tree.

"My grandmother had a great-aunt who never married. Pop said she painted some for my grandparents the first year they were married, but my grandmother loved them so much that her aunt painted several more every year until she died." Jesse stood in front of the tree, his hands in his pockets. "If you look closely, you'll see that every angel has something in common."

"Wings?" Clay couldn't resist.

"Something a little more personal to my grandmother," Jesse told him.

After studying the tree for a moment or two, Lucy observed, "All the angels are holding roses."

Jesse nodded. "My grandmother's name was Rose."

"So very cool." Lucy took one last walk around the tree. "I love that you brought them down and put them on a tree of their own. It's a nice way to honor your grandmother. I'm sure Mr. Enright appreciated that you did this. I'm sure it reminded him of his wife."

"He doesn't need any reminders," Jesse replied, "since he believes she's still here."

"Oh, not you, too." Lucy glanced from Jesse to Brooke and back again. "Seriously?"

"Seriously. Jesse's granddad says that every once in

a while he smells gardenia, which was the only fragrance she ever wore. And when that scent is there, so is she." Brooke removed a few spent roses from a vase and replaced them with a stem of amaryllis. She turned and added, "I've been aware of it myself."

"Lucy isn't a believer, are you, Luce?" Clay sat on the arm of a nearby chair.

"No, I'm not. And I do find it odd that so many homes in St. Dennis claim to have unseen residents," she said.

"Oh?" Brooke slipped the fresh ferns into the vase amid the flowers. "Who else?"

"Well, Vanessa, for one." Lucy turned to Brooke. "You came in last night after the discussion about—"

"Alice Ridgeway." Brooke smiled. "Everyone knows about her. I thought you meant there was someone else."

Lucy looked at Clay first, then at Jesse. "Do either of you buy into this stuff?"

"It's hard to know what to think, when you've experienced the phenomena," Jesse admitted. "I've been here, in the house with my grandfather, when a very strong, unmistakable scent of gardenia came out of nowhere. Where or what or how . . . I can't say."

"What does your grandfather say?" Lucy asked. "As I recall, from what I knew of him, he was pretty much a matter-of-fact kind of guy."

"He still is, about most things. But he believes that his wife is still here—I've heard him talking to her several times, as if he's carrying on a conversation." Jesse shrugged. "Who am I to say she isn't here, in some form, at least to him? Which of course, doesn't explain the fact that Brooke and I have both caught the scent. And last year, when my siblings were all here, one of my sisters smelled it as well, and my cousin Elizabeth says she's often smelled gardenias when she's been here. And before you ask, there are no gardenias in the conservatory."

"How about you?" Lucy addressed Clay. "Do you believe in such things?"

"I don't *not* believe," he told her. "I know too many people who I know to be intelligent and otherwise stable who have had some sort of experience that they can't explain."

"I suppose in a town as old as St. Dennis, with houses as old as we have here, it's inevitable that there's going to be some sort of rumors going around," Lucy conceded. "Sort of a mass hysteria thing, without, of course, anyone actually being hysterical."

"Don't you have any spirits hanging around the inn, Lucy?" Brooke asked.

"I certainly hope not." To Clay, Lucy's laugh appeared slightly uncomfortable.

"All spirits aren't evil or scary," Brooke told her. "Rose is a very sweet and gentle presence. Vanessa says that Alice's spirit feels protective." She shrugged. "Who's to say what can linger, that a person or even an event can leave behind certain emotions, feelings . . . ?"

"I just don't believe in anything like that. Sorry." Lucy brushed her off casually, but Clay thought a look of uncertainty had flickered across her face. "Gone, done . . . is gone and done, and it's best to leave it that way."

"Whatever." Brooke smiled. "You ought to talk to your mom, though. She's been known to—"

"I don't believe any of that either. I'm sure she's just been playing along with everyone," Lucy insisted.

"Maybe. Maybe not." Brooke rolled up the discarded stems and lifted the bundle. "Ready to move on? We still have the study, the dining room, the sitting room, the conservatory. Oh, if you like orchids, wait till you see the orchids! They were big favorites of Rose's, too . . ."

"Yes, please. I love orchids and I want to see every inch of this place." Lucy's smile returned, but Clay wasn't sure if a little bit of unrest remained behind that smile.

It seemed to Clay that they had, in fact, seen every inch of the Enright mansion before they left. From the first floor to the third, from the fancy parlor and Curtis Enright's library to the former maids' rooms in the attic, they'd gone up and down the two stairways and poked into the bedrooms, all of which had been turned out for the holiday.

"I've never seen such decorations," Lucy told Brooke after they'd made their way back down to the first floor. "I don't know anyone who has your touch. What you've done here with greens and berries alone is breathtaking. Then add in all those antique tree ornaments and the effect is just one big wow. If you ever think about moving to the West Coast, you could come to work for me that very day. I could use someone with your sense of style."

"Thanks, Lucy. I've seen your work, so coming from you, that's quite a compliment." Brooke beamed. "But I won't be leaving St. Dennis again. I know where I belong."

Brooke looped her arm through Jesse's and smiled up at him.

"But if you ever need a helping hand when you're here, give me a call," she added. "I'm pretty busy most of the time, but maybe I could fill in for a few hours."

"I will definitely keep that in mind. I might need extra hands for the Magellan wedding," Lucy told her.

"I'd love to work with you. The inn has the most amazing possibilities, and when you think of what you could create, well, the mind boggles."

"Magellan's wedding will be outside, tented, and all I can say right now is that it will involve truck-loads of flowers. I was hoping to meet with Olivia while I was here, but we haven't signed the contract yet and I don't want to get her hopes up. It will be a massive job. I just hope her wholesaler can get everything we'll need." Lucy placed her bag on a side table while she put on her coat. "And I'll have to find a really good landscape designer. We'll need to move the gazebo and have some roses planted around it."

"I can recommend my former brother-in-law, Jason Bowers. He sold his previous business and is thinking about starting up again here. You might want to give him a call when you're ready."

"He's in St. Dennis now?"

Brooke nodded. "He's renting one of Hal Garrity's cottages down near the river while he's deciding what to do. Of course, we're hoping he sticks around for a while, if for no other reason than for my son Logan's sake." Brooke explained, "Jason is my late husband's only living immediate family, and he and Logan have gotten pretty tight. I never knew Eric as a boy, so there's so much that Jason can tell my son about his dad that no one else can."

"If we lock up the Magellan wedding, maybe I'll give him a call, see what he can do with the property," Lucy said. "Maybe give him a reason to stick around for a while longer." She glanced at Jesse. "It looks as if you're okay with that."

"I don't have a problem with Jason. He's a good guy." Jesse shrugged. "Besides, if it's good for Logan, it's good."

"Thanks again for letting us invade your family home," Clay said. "We both really appreciate it."

"I live to serve my brother's whims," Brooke told them as they walked to the front door.

"Does that include chocolate ganache cupcakes today?" Clay asked.

"Ah, no." Brooke smiled and opened the front door. "But nice try."

"So much for my whims." Clay took Lucy's hand. "Guess I'll see you at home later."

"Only if you want to help me pack." Brooke waved good-bye to Lucy. "Don't forget to call me if you need any help with the wedding."

"I've already made a mental note," Lucy assured her.

"That was so fun," Lucy told him when they were both in the car and headed toward Charles Street. "That house is just amazing. I still feel starry-eyed. It's so hard to believe that one person lives there alone."

"My mom said a lot of people thought Curtis would have sold the place by now and moved to something smaller, but it's unlikely he'll ever do that now."

"Especially if he believes his wife is still there,"

Lucy noted. "I wonder what will happen to the place when he's gone."

"That's apparently been the topic of much speculation. Jesse said Curtis is considering leaving it to the town to serve as a museum, but I don't know if that's gone beyond the talking stage as yet."

"It would make the most glorious event site." Lucy sighed. "I can see weddings in the garden, or in tents outside on that beautiful expanse of lawn, or in that magnificent hall and parlor. And that dining room— gorgeous. A lot of towns have historic homes that they rent out for events. It's a great moneymaker, pays the taxes on the place, draws people to the area—"

"Um, isn't that what your brother is doing at the inn?" Clay grinned. "I doubt he'd appreciate you encouraging anyone to go into direct competition with him."

"It would be competition, but only in the sense that it would be another event location. I think couples who want the inn want the relaxed ambience, that classic Chesapeake Bay experience. Couples who want something much fancier and more lavish would be more attracted to the Enright place."

"Of course, if that were to happen, St. Dennis would need a world-class event planner right here in town full-time."

Lucy leaned back in her seat and smiled. "And if that day ever came, I'm sure I could help find someone."

He made a left onto Charles Street, then a right onto Kelly's Point Road.

"Where are we going?" she asked.

"There's no way you can leave St. Dennis without a visit to Scoop and some of Steffie's amazing ice cream," he said solemnly. "It would be wrong."

"It would be wrong," she readily agreed, "except that I did have some at Vanessa's the other night. But we can stop if you're in the mood for ice cream."

Clay drove past the municipal building and headed to the far end of the lot across the road. He parked in the section nearest the ice-cream shop and turned off the engine.

"I wonder if she has any of that peppermint divinity fudge ice cream that she brought to Vanessa's." Lucy got out of the car and slammed the door. "That was amazing."

Clay slammed the driver's-side door and offered his arm to Lucy. "You don't sound like someone who's only stopping in to keep me company."

"Well, as long as we're here, I wouldn't want Stef to think I didn't like her ice cream."

The sign out front—ONE SCOOP OR TWO—blew slightly in the wind that was kicking up from the Bay.

"It feels like snow again," Lucy observed, "but we've only had that one little bit since I've been home."

"Were you hoping for more?" he asked as he opened the shop's door.

"Not particularly. I don't really like the cold." Lucy waved a greeting to Steffie, who was behind the counter filling one of the containers in her freezer case.

"Hey, Lucy," Steffie called to her. "How was your tour?"

"It was fabulous. I've been in a lot of really spectacular places since going into business, but that place is unlike any other I've ever seen." Lucy took off her coat and placed it on the back of a chair. "There's something so special about it. It's gloriously elegant, and there's all that history, and at the same time, the atmosphere is so warm and inviting. I loved it."

"That's exactly what everyone said after the house tour. That the place is gorgeous, like right out of a magazine, but that you feel at home there." Stef came around the side of the counter.

"That's it exactly," Lucy agreed. "I was telling Clay that it would make the most wonderful event site."

"Oh, my God, could you imagine the weddings they could have there?"

"Exactly."

"So what flavors do we have today?" Clay wandered to the display case.

"We have the standards—vanilla, seven variations of chocolate, pineapple-coconut macadamia nut . . . what are you in the mood for, Clay?"

"I know what I want," Lucy told her. "If you have any of that—"

"Peppermint divinity fudge?" Steffie shook her head. "Alas, I ran out of white chocolate. But I do have a chocolate chili that I just made this morning."

"Chocolate chili?" Clay repeated, one eyebrow raised.

"Just enough of a chili pepper kick to be a manly flavor," Stef deadpanned. "At least, that's how my husband described it."

"Manly or not, I'd like to try it," Lucy said.

Steffie dipped a small plastic spoon into the container and handed it to Lucy.

"Wow. It leaves just a hint of heat in the back of

your throat." Lucy nodded. "I'll have one scoop in a dish."

"Clay?" Steffie held up an empty spoon. "Sample?"

"I'll take Lucy's word for it. Make mine two scoops, also in a bowl," he told her.

Clay took off his jacket and put it on the chair over Lucy's. He'd thought they'd just pick up cones and walk along the Bay, but Lucy apparently had other ideas. Which was perfectly fine with him. If they were outside walking, sooner or later, she'd get cold and they'd leave. Scoop was nice and warm, cozy and inviting, and he'd have that much more time to spend with her.

He walked back to the counter, paid Stef for the ice cream, then carried both bowls to the table Lucy had selected by the window.

"One scoop," he said as he passed her dish and spoon to her.

"Thanks." She smiled up at him when he sat next to her.

Her smile always took him back to a time when they were both younger and had shared all their secrets. Those days were obviously gone, he reminded himself. These days, there was almost as much mystery as there was familiarity about her.

"It's such a pretty view from here," Lucy was saying. "I'll bet it's lovely to sit here on a summer day and watch the sailboats out there."

Clay nodded. "It's a pretty view at any time of the year. Even today, when it's overcast and gray, you have the whitecaps and the geese flying overhead, the gulls swooping down around the docks. Doesn't matter the time of the year or the weather, St. Dennis is a good place to be."

"Tough to argue with that," she replied. "Though in California, we have such lovely weather all year round."

"Don't you miss the change in seasons?"

"We have seasons. The changes just aren't as dramatic." She paused. "But yes, I do miss the way the landscape changes around here. I don't think about it so much, unless I've been here for a few days. Then when I go back to L.A., I look out my windows and wonder where the Bay is."

"You always did love the water," he recalled.

"I still do." She ate a few spoons of ice cream. "Remember when we were little and your granddad took us fishing down at the cove and taught us how to put bait on the hooks?"

Clay laughed. "What made you think of that?"

"I don't know." She was grinning at the memory. "I remember sitting down on the dock and getting splinters in my butt and not wanting to say anything because I didn't want him to make me go home and have the splinters removed. I remember it was early in the morning and it was warm and quiet and there were swans on the other side of the cove watching us because they had a nest there." She dipped her spoon into the ice cream again, and paused with it halfway to her mouth. "Do the swans still come back to the cove, Clay?"

"They've never left, LuLu. Next time you're home, I'll show you."

"I'd really like that."

"When will that be?" He tried to sound casual. "The next time you're home?"

She shook her head. "I'm waiting for Dan to give me an open date for the Magellan wedding. Hopefully he'll have that worked out before I leave tomorrow because this wedding is going to take months to arrange. Once we have a date, I'll be able to schedule my trips back and keep my work out there running smoothly as well. I have the feeling Susanna is going to have me here every chance she has."

"I hope she gets her wish."

"She's the boss," Lucy told him. "At Shaefer and Sinclair, we aim to please. The client is always king. Or in her case, queen."

"Please give her my thanks." Clay put down his spoon. "What time's your flight tomorrow?"

"Early. I have meetings on Monday that I can't postpone."

"Can you have dinner with me tonight?"

"I would love to. I really would." She looked as if she meant it. "But I think I need to spend tonight at home with my mother. The only night I've been home since I got here was the day I arrived. I think she'd like to have some mother-daughter time."

He nodded. "I understand. We'll do it next time."

He did understand. He knew how much Grace missed her only daughter and he knew, too, that he'd spent more time with Lucy this visit than Grace had.

They finished their ice cream and chatted with Steffie while they got into their coats. Stef came around from the back of the counter to give Lucy a hug.

"Come back soon," Steffie told her. "We'll do another girls' night. My place, next time."

"You're on." Lucy hugged her back. "I'll look forward to it."

They took the long way back to the parking lot, walking hand in hand along the Bay until it became obvious that neither of them was dressed for the change in the weather. The tiny flakes that had started to fall while they were in Scoop were turning to ice. They headed back to the car and sat for a moment while the engine warmed up.

"Thanks again for a terrific last day in town," she said when he began to back out of the parking space. "I really enjoyed myself."

"I'm glad. I enjoyed the day, too." He made the light at Charles and drove back to the inn.

"I am sorry you're leaving tomorrow," he told her after he parked in front of the double doors.

"I'll be back soon."

He nodded, then leaned across the seat and took her face in his hands. "It can't be soon enough for me."

She turned her head and kissed him, taking him by surprise. He could taste the last little bit of heat from the chili peppers in the ice cream on her tongue, hot and spicy. He could have sworn it tasted even better now, and he went back for a second dip. When she finally sat back, she touched the side of his face with her fingertips.

"I'll let you know when my next meeting with Susanna is going to be," she told him.

He pushed a strand of hair back from her face and nodded. "I'll be here."

She kissed the side of his face and jumped out of the car before he could grab her and kiss her again. He looked out the window and saw her mother in the doorway. Grace waved and he waved back, then with a final wave to Lucy, he drove around the loop and headed back down the lane.

He took the long way home, driving somewhat aimlessly, and tried to sort out his feelings. He found himself at the cove they'd talked about earlier, and parked and got out of the car. The sky was the same shade of gray as the water, and the afternoon had already made its first turn toward dusk. The swans he knew still nested there were nowhere in sight, and slivers of ice pelted his face. He stood looking out over the water until his face stung.

He didn't want her to leave tomorrow. He didn't want her to ever leave again, but there was nothing he could do about it. He understood that she had a thriving business—one she'd worked hard to build and was justifiably proud of. She had a whole life somewhere else that he wasn't a part of, and while he didn't like it one bit, that was the reality. He wished he could do something that could change what was, but those were foolish thoughts and Clay wasn't generally a foolish man. But Lucy owned a big part of his past, and with luck, perhaps there'd be a place for him in her future.

Whatever it took, he'd told her, and he meant it. As far as he was concerned, he was in this for as long as it might take and wherever it would lead. Of course, he was hoping it would all lead her back to St. Dennis, and to him.

Time would tell. He was in no particular hurry. After all, he'd already waited twenty years.

Chapter 12

O N Monday afternoon, Lucy was just wrapping up a call with a potential client when Bonnie swept into her office. Lucy held up one hand in a give-me-a-minute gesture, and Bonnie paced until the conversation concluded.

"Sorry. That was a possible November wedding," Lucy said as she hung up. "What's doing? Where'd you go?"

"I was in Sacramento," Bonnie replied. "Just for yesterday and this morning, but I needed to spend some time with my honey."

"Your honey?" Lucy raised an eyebrow. "Who's your honey?"

"Bob, of course."

"How did he go from 'the ex' to 'my honey' so quickly?"

Bonnie shrugged. "When it works, it works."

"So it's going well."

"It's going . . . well, yes, surprisingly well. He's a different man since he stopped drinking."

"Just take it slowly, Bon. You know what they say about a leopard and his spots."

"No one is more cautious than I am," Bonnie told her. "Believe me, no one knows better than I. But he really has changed, in big ways and in more subtle ways as well. I'm willing to take it day by day. I'm still in love with him, what can I say?"

"And he . . ."

"Says he's still very much in love with me, and I believe him. The move up north was the best thing he could have done for himself. He's painting again—good stuff, too. Gorgeous landscapes." Bonnie slumped in the closest chair. "He should never come back to Southern California. Not even for a visit. It's like poison for him."

"Because of his family being here?"

Bonnie nodded. "But enough about me. How was your little vacation in charming little St. Dennis?"

"Too short." Lucy smiled. "But charming."

"Do we have a date for the Magellan wedding?"

"We do. My brother had to do all manner of finagling with other reservations, but they have nailed down the last Saturday in June."

"Which is what the bride and groom wanted, right?"

"That was their first choice, yes."

"Well, then, hallelujah. Get that contract signed." Bonnie took off her shoes and lifted her feet to rest on the chair next to the one she was sitting on.

"I'm working on it right now, but it's massive. I called Susanna, told her we could confirm the date, but I need to work our pricing. She said send the contract ASAP and she'd sign it, to put in a flat fee for me and add an 'as required' clause plus estimates for all the extras." Lucy sighed. "I'm not comfortable doing that—I like the numbers solidly nailed down—but this woman is tenacious. She said just put in a clause to the effect that all numbers are estimates and subject to revision. She wants to get moving on this since now we're down to a little more than five months till the wedding and there's a lot of work to be done."

"As long as you have her name and Magellan's name on the contract and he signs it, I don't know what else you can do at this point but send it."

"That's what she wants, that's what we'll do. I am trying to be as thorough as possible, but some of the things she wants I can't get a price on right now. Some things will have to wait until my next trip to St. Dennis."

"Which will be when?"

"End of the month."

"Do what you have to do to keep her happy. We're going to make a killing on this one. The publicity alone is going to be priceless. Just look at the mileage we got from the MacGregor wedding. We're still getting calls from brides who saw the pictures in *People*."

"As long as we don't have to turn away too many other affairs because I'm tied up with Susanna and there's no one here to handle them."

"Not to worry. We have Corrine Miles lined up to start in . . ." Bonnie pulled up her sleeve to look at her watch. "Four days. And Ava handled the Carlton wedding on Saturday like a pro. Which she is."

"All well and good, but I still think we need more support staff, more assistants. We can afford to hire more people."

"True enough. So let's work up an ad and have

Angie place it in all the appropriate places. How many assistants do you think?"

"The way things have gone so far this year—and remember, it's only January—I'm thinking another full-time assistant for each of us. That would be four, with the addition of Ava and Corrine as full-time event planners."

"Then we'll hire four new assistants." Bonnie eased herself off the chair. "By the way, how'd you make out with the Tollivers this morning?"

"Better than I expected," Lucy confessed. "The contractor really knows his stuff, for which I am infinitely grateful. Knows exactly what to do to build that skating rink and can do it in under six weeks, so we're good."

"What's he going to do? The least technical version, please. Keep it simple."

Lucy laughed. "Basically, he'll build a modular rink. Wooden sections that he'll piece together on their grounds. Then he'll put some kind of thick plastic liner down, install a refrigeration system, and then just flood the thing and let it freeze. It's going to use a ridiculous amount of electricity, because he's going to have to do at least one test run to make sure it freezes, then keep it cold until the party. But the party girl will have her skating rink and everyone will be happy." She paused. "I still have to find some cattails to plant around the sides." She made a note on a small pad, then looked up. "Beverly wants as much 'authentic atmosphere' as possible."

Bonnie rolled her eyes and lowered her legs from the chair. "No one can say that Shaefer and Sinclair doesn't deliver the goods." She stood and stretched.

"I have about fifty calls to make, so I'll be in my office if you need me."

"I'm glad you and Bob are making an effort to work things out," Lucy said when Bonnie had reached the door.

Bonnie shrugged. "I don't know that it will work out, but I do know that I could not live with myself if I didn't at least make the effort. Some things are just worth it, you know?"

"I suppose." Lucy tapped her fingers on her desktop and watched Bonnie cross the hall to her office.

For her partner's sake, Lucy did hope that Bonnie and her ex-husband could work out their problems, but if, as Bonnie seemed to feel, Bob was better off in Sacramento than in Los Angeles, what exactly did that mean for the "Shaefer" in Shaefer & Sinclair if they did get back together? It would make for one hell of a commute.

Not my decision, Lucy reminded herself. *Not my life.*

She opened the electronic file she'd started on the Magellan wedding. First up was to put everything in order of priority—those details that would take the longest to work out, the items that would take the most time to order, what could be accomplished from her office and what could only be done in St. Dennis. She'd need a schematic of the tent and of the gazebo, which, she recalled, would have to be moved. She had to get the contact information on the landscaper Brooke mentioned. She'd need to bring Dan into those discussions, since he was the majority owner of the inn.

She'd have to meet with Olivia from Petals and

Posies and go over all the florals they'd need. Would the peony season stretch into June this year so that Susanna could have all the flowers she wanted? Lucy doubted that they would, but she'd ask. She'd also ask Olivia to sketch out a design for the inside of the tent based on the comments Susanna had made, then they'd go over it with her and see if it met with her approval. If not, it would be back to the drawing board, literally. If it was approved, they'd have to figure out how many dozens of each flower they were going to need and get them on order to ensure they'd be in reserve.

She made a list of other vendors they'd need so that she could discuss the possibilities with the bride, and the groom, if he decided to participate. Based on his involvement the previous week, Lucy suspected he would not, but he could change his mind. There were a lot of decisions that would have to be made fairly quickly, so the sooner Lucy and Susanna addressed those issues, the better.

She wrote up all her ideas in an email and sent it off to Susanna, asking for her thoughts and confirming their earlier conversation. She'd also attached photos of some very cool and original invitations, and again asked about the guest list, to which Susanna replied that she was still working on it. They'd agreed to meet at the inn in three weeks—Susanna had wanted to meet in two, but Lucy had a wedding that she'd been working on for over a year and there was no way she could pass off the handling of the Big Day to someone else, not even Bonnie. Her bride had counted on her for every decision that had been made for the past thirteen months, and she'd be counting on Lucy to make sure that each carefully chosen detail was just so. Lucy had made a commitment and she would keep it.

She pulled up her online calendar for the year and, after studying it for a few moments, wished she hadn't looked when she felt a tickle of anxiety creeping up her spine. The next few months would be murder, there was no way around that. She'd be chained to her iPhone and her laptop straight through the summer. Well, she and Bonnie had set out to be the best, hadn't they? When they first opened their doors, they'd dreamed of a day when they'd be in such demand, they'd be turning away clients. They hadn't quite reached that point yet, but Lucy could see the day approaching, especially after the news of the Magellan wedding broke.

"It's the whole reality-TV thing," Bonnie had said once. "Everyone watches what the celebrities do, then they want to do the same thing, because basically, everyone wants to be a celebrity."

Lucy was starting to believe Bonnie had been right. They'd had more than a few calls from brides who wanted the same flowers/decor/favors/cake that Dallas MacGregor had had.

It was all good, though. Last night, at dinner with her family, Daniel had mentioned how the income from the Magellan wedding alone would make it possible for him to have the inn's roof replaced, and maybe even replace the rotted dock they'd had to remove two summers ago. It had given her the strangest sensation to realize that her West Coast party business could have such a positive effect on her family's East Coast inn. The inn was part of her heritage, part of her family's history, and knowing that she was contributing to its preservation had made her secretly proud.

"If we booked a few more events like that," Daniel had said, "I could redo the bathrooms, make them more like the spa types you see in the really high-end hotels. Wouldn't Dad be proud?"

"I think Dad would be very proud of the way you've run this business, whether or not you get those new bathrooms," she'd replied.

"I'm sure he's proud of both of you," Grace had assured them. "And I'm sure it's making him just as pleased as punch to see the two of you working together. I think it was always his dream that his children would run the inn as a team."

"Well, I'm afraid that's one dream that isn't likely to come true," Lucy'd told her, "not beyond this summer, anyway. And even at that, Ford's not here. Who knows where he'll end up, once he decides he's had enough?"

After dinner, Daniel's kids, D.J. and Diana, had pulled out the board games and insisted on several games of Clue. Grace had begged off the last game and gone to her room, and Lucy lost the hope she'd had of asking her mother about the Ouija board and the other insinuations that had been made about her relationship with Alice Ridgeway. Next trip back, Lucy had promised herself. Next time, she'd make time to get to the bottom of all that.

For now, she had a mountain of work in front of her and all of last week to make up for. She closed the Magellan file and opened the one for Saturday evening's Considine wedding. She pulled up her "week before to-do list" and went to the page she'd headed *STATE OF THE WEDDING PHONE CALLS.* She reached for her phone and dialed the first number on the list, that of the floral designer. After Lucy checked in with him, she'd call the band, the photographer, the videographer, minister, the string quartet for the church, the limo service, the caterer, and her "day of" staff. After all those calls had been made and she was assured all the ducks were in a row, she'd call the bride and give her a little reassurance that everything was on target.

It took all afternoon.

Bonnie called to her when she passed her office on the way out at seven thirty.

"See you in the morning." Bonnie's voice trailed down the hall.

"Right. See you." Lucy glanced at the clock. How had it gotten so late? "Wait! Bonnie!"

She got up from her desk and shot into the hall.

"Want to grab some dinner?"

"You mean, right now?"

Lucy nodded. "I skipped lunch and I'm just realizing how hungry I am."

"Is there a problem?" Bonnie paused.

"No. I just thought it would be nice if we had dinner together," Lucy told her.

"Maybe some other night. I'm really exhausted, and I still have a bunch of calls to make." Bonnie turned toward the door. "Don't work too late. I'm sure you're tired, too. See you in the morning."

Lucy stood next to the receptionist desk, which had been cleaned off for the night. Angie was nowhere to be seen. She had a vague recollection of someone—

could have been Angie—appearing in her office to say good night, but Lucy'd been on the phone and had barely paid attention.

On her way back to her own office, Lucy poked into Ava's and the conference room, but there was no sign of life. She went back to her desk and made her last three calls for the night and sent her last half-dozen emails. She slid her laptop into her bag, turned off the lights, and stepped into the quiet hall. At the front door, she got out her keys, set the alarm, and relocked the door. She stopped for takeout on the way home, and went back to her empty apartment, where she changed into light sweats and a T-shirt.

On the drive home, she'd tried to think of someone else she could have called for a spontaneous dinner, but came up dry. It wasn't that she didn't like people, or that she wasn't interested in having friends. It was just that the business had kept her so busy that even when she met people she liked, people she clicked with, she just didn't have time to follow up. When she'd first moved into her apartment, she'd met several women who, like herself, were busy professionals who seemed like they'd be fun to get to know. But she just never got around to going out after work for that drink they'd talked about, or that Saturday shopping and lunch that had been proposed. Lucy was learning the hard way that even rain checks expired if they weren't cashed.

She ate at the dining room table, then set up her laptop and logged on to the Internet. She went to weather.com and typed in the zip code for St. Dennis. According to the site, it was snowing lightly and twenty-nine degrees in her hometown. She could almost see whitecaps on the Bay and the evergreens across the back of the inn swaying against the wind that would be huffing across the water. On such nights, she and her brothers would gather in the living room after homework was completed and they'd sit around the warmth from the fireplace and sip hot chocolate. She guessed that maybe her brother's son and daughter were doing just that right now.

Soon enough she'd be back there with them. Maybe there'd be another such night while she was home.

She Google-mapped St. Dennis and used the arrows to locate the Madison farm. The farmhouse was partially hidden by the trees, but the pond and the barns were visible. She wondered if Clay was, at that moment, sitting in what used to be his dad's study, maybe looking over the renovation plans for the barn, or maybe making a list of the plants he was thinking about growing this year. She remembered how his father would always start to plow up the fields in March, to get the soil ready for the spring planting. She suspected Clay might follow his dad's lead.

She moved the arrows on the map to the center of town and moved in closer. There was Kelly's Point Road, at the end of which stood Scoop. At the opposite end of the boardwalk stood Captain Walt's, where she and Clay had dinner last week. She leaned an elbow on the table and rested her chin in her palm, remembering. She'd smelled snow in the air when they walked along the dock, and Clay had kissed her. They'd practiced kissing when they were kids, but those practice kisses had been nothing like the real thing. He'd kissed her again on Saturday, but it was the memory of that first real kiss that stayed in her head. It had been both completely unexpected and totally inevitable.

She returned to the mail page on her screen, but instead of checking her email, she wrote one.

> Free 4 dinner on 1/31?
> L

Moments later came the response.

> Will pick you up at seven. Lola's Café this time around?
> Wish you were here.

Lucy smiled and stared at the screen for a minute before replying.

> Me too.

Chapter 13

CLAY sat in the front seat of his Jeep, his cell phone up to his ear.

"No, I understand," he was saying. "It's okay. Do what you have to do."

"That's just it," Lucy replied. "There are too many things I have to do in too short a period of time. I'm so sorry to cancel, Clay. I just didn't realize how jammed the schedule was. I mean, I should have, I've been doing this long enough, but you just can't always predict when something is going to go wrong. And it seems that when one thing goes wrong, everything else falls like dominoes."

"How did Susanna Jones take it?"

"She's disappointed but she's trying to understand. The good news is that she and Robert did sign the contract, so they're locked in for their wedding at the end of June, which will take a crazy amount of work to pull off in just a few months. I did explain to her that if similar circumstances arose during the week before her wedding, she'd want me to drop everything and take care of her crisis, which she totally would." She made an exasperated *grrrr* sound deep in her throat, and he could tell she was getting worked up all over again. "Honestly, you spend years building up a list of vendors you feel you can trust, and then something like this happens."

"You have other caterers you can call on, though, right?" he asked, trying to sound reasonable and coolheaded.

"Yes, but none of them are available on such short notice."

"Maybe you'll need to try someone new," he suggested.

"I did think of that," she admitted. "I've even printed out the emails from caterers who have contacted us in the past trying to get onto our preferred list. I hate to use someone I don't know, because if they're terrible, there goes our reputation. Then again, perhaps bad food could be perceived as better than no food."

He laughed to lighten the mood. "I'm sure there's someone in that pile of emails who would be so happy to have the chance to make your A-list that they'll do a bang-up job."

"I'm hoping you're right. I'll check each of their websites before I start making calls, maybe see who's got the best résumé, and who's available to bring me some samples between now and Saturday." Lucy sighed. "And then I can turn my attention to convincing the bride that having colored calla lilies—which are the only kind the florist tells me she can get this week—will be so much better than the all-white ones she'd had her heart set on."

"What happened to the white ones?" he asked.

"Something about a crop failure, though why it affected only the white ones, who knows?"

"So what are you going to do about the Magellan wedding?"

"Susanna is going to fly out next week and we'll go over everything that we would have gone over if I'd come east. Right now we need to run through the basics, and we can do that from here. Frankly, we could do that by phone and email, but she needs her hand held a little at this point. But I think we can accomplish enough so that I won't have to come back there until the spring. Then it will be full steam ahead, because, like I said, there will be a lot to be accomplished."

"Spring?" He frowned. He'd have to wait until spring to see her again?

"Probably not until April."

"What happened to February and March?"

"Clay, we're so overbooked it isn't funny. We have three weddings, one sweet sixteen party, a fiftieth wedding anniversary, and two major fund-raisers between now and the first week in April. Under normal circumstances, it wouldn't be an issue, but if I take myself out of the picture here for three or four days at a time to fly out there every few weeks, there will be chaos. We have hired a new event planner and we've promoted someone who's been assisting us for the past two years, but they still have to go through a sort of apprenticeship before they can go off on their own to one of these big-ticket affairs. So I'm making all the contacts for the Magellan wedding that I can from here, then by April, I figure both Ava and Corrine should be ready to step in for me, and I can stay in St.

Dennis for at least a week to get everything lined up.
I'll be having each of them gradually take over for me
on events in the spring so that the brides aren't trau-
matized when 'their' wedding planner doesn't show
up on the big day."

He pondered the possibility of having Lucy in St.
Dennis for a week or better when he could see her
maybe every day, as opposed to one dinner this week,
and had to agree that her plan had merit.

"I thought you had a partner. Can't she handle
some of the events?"

"Bonnie has her own events to handle, and frankly,
these past few weeks, she's been a little distracted."
Clay heard her sigh. "She and her ex-husband are
sort of working toward getting back together again,
and she's taking time off that she didn't use to take to
fly up to Sacramento to be with him. Not that I be-
grudge her the chance to work things out with him,"
Lucy hastened to add, "but it just seems that everything is hitting the fan at the same time."

"That's when it usually happens," he noted. "That's
what my dad always used to say. But look, this is just
a temporary situation, right? I mean, you'll get everything under control out there and then you'll be able
to devote more time to what you need to do here."

"In an ideal world, yes."

"Think positively."

"I'm trying to. Then I look at my incoming email
and I want to crawl off into a quiet corner where
there is no Internet and suck my thumb."

"Is there such a place?"

"Doubtful."

Clay laughed softly. "Hey, this is just a little setback. Take care of your business, then come home for a week or two."

"That's what I'm focusing on right now." She hesitated before adding, "I'm disappointed. I was looking forward to coming back, and to seeing you."

"So was I. You can make it up to me when you get home."

They chatted for a few more minutes before ending the call. Clay remained in the car, behind the wheel, until the cold seeped through and his hands were beginning to chill inside his gloves. *Disappointed* barely said it. Ever since Lucy left, he'd been thinking about the things they might do together while she was home, where they'd go to spend some time alone—and now it would be months instead of weeks before he could see her again.

Then again, the delay could work in his favor. By April, the snow would be gone, and with luck, there'd be a day to spend out on the Bay, a day to revisit some of the places they used to go, places that could remind her of who she used to be, and what he'd once been to her. And maybe, just maybe, she'd let her guard down enough to talk to him and tell him just what it was that had caused her to turn away from him so many years ago. She'd already told him it hadn't been because of anything he'd done, which meant he could lay down that burden of guilt he'd carried for so long, thinking he'd inadvertently done or said something that had hurt her so much that she couldn't stand to be around him. He thought she'd been just about ready to share whatever it was with him, then something made her pull back. Clay's instincts told him that, whatever it was, it somehow stood between him and Lucy, and that alone made him determined to lay that beast to rest, one way or another.

He got out of the car and walked to the house through the snow that had fallen that afternoon, reminding himself with every step that he'd already waited more than half his life for her to come back. It wouldn't kill him to wait a little longer.

Brooke was dragging a box toward the back door when he stepped inside the kitchen.

"Need a hand with that?" Clay asked.

"Yeah, thanks." She stood up and slid the elastic out of her ponytail, then smoothed her hair before pulling it back into a tail. "I guess I bit off a little more than I could chew. Jesse offered to come over to help me, but I told him I could handle it. Silly me."

"You want this over to the tenant house?" He lifted it with ease.

"You did it again. Called it the tenant house." Brooke frowned. "I'm thinking about putting a sign out front that says BROOKE'S COTTAGE. Do you think that would help?"

"Not really." He started through the back door, then called back over his shoulder. "Is the door open?"

"Yes. Logan's over there putting his books on his bookshelf."

"You coming over?"

"In a minute."

"See you there." Clay went down the back steps and cut across the backyard to the path that led to the old house that hard work and a whole army of contractors had turned into a home for his sister and her son. It was late in the day and the sun had almost set, and when he tripped over a rock in the path, Clay was reminded that they should have some sort of illumination back here.

His eight-year-old nephew was standing in the doorway before he reached the house.

"Mom called to tell me you were coming," Logan called out to Clay. "She said to open the door."

"Thanks, buddy. I appreciate it."

The door opened directly into the large living area that was stacked high with boxes.

"Any idea where your mom wants this box?" Too late, Clay realized he should have asked Brooke where she wanted it.

"Nope." Logan shook his head.

Clay put the box down inside the front door. "I can move it when she gets here." He looked around the room where he himself had once hung his hat. The place had come together nicely since Brooke had decided to make it her own. "It's looking good in here," he told his nephew.

"Uh-huh." Logan nodded enthusiastically. "Wanna see my room? It's upstairs."

"Sure. Lead the way." Even though Clay already knew which room belonged to Logan, he gestured for the boy to go first.

Logan bounded up the steps and Clay followed.

"See? I got all these shelves built in for my stuff." Logan pointed to one of the short walls.

"I do see." Clay scanned the rows of books, games, and action figures. "You've got some pretty cool stuff here."

Logan nodded and pulled a pair of books from the top shelf where they stood between bookends. "My uncle Jason gave me these. See? The Hardy Boys. That's who the books are about, these two guys named Joe and Frank and their last name is Hardy. They have all these adventures."

He held up *The Missing Chums*. " 'Chums' is another word for friends," he explained. "Their friends are Biff and Chet. They got disappeared."

"I read that one when I was a boy." Clay held out a hand to look at the book. He opened it, and inside found the name "Eric Bowers" printed in green ink. Underneath, Logan had printed his own name in black. "This was your dad's book," Clay noted.

"Uh-huh." Logan leaned over Clay and pointed to the two names. "That's why his name is in it. I wrote my name in there, too, because it's my book now."

"That was very nice of your uncle Jason to give this book to you."

Logan nodded. "I like having my dad's stuff." He went to the bottom shelf and picked up a baseball glove. "This was my dad's, too. I don't use it so much."

"I remember." Clay had coached Logan's baseball team the year before, and had purchased a new glove when it became apparent that the boy was afraid to use his father's glove, lest something happen to it.

"And I have a new lamp." Logan picked up the desk lamp.

"But an old desk," Clay pointed out.

"*Your* old desk. From when you were a kid."

"I did a lot of homework on that old desk," Clay told him.

"Ugh. Homework." Logan grimaced. "I'd rather watch TV."

"Sure. Who wouldn't rather play than work?" Clay leaned against the doorjamb. "But you know the rule . . ."

" 'Work first. Play after.' " Logan made a face.

"Right."

"Hey, are you guys up there?" Brooke called from the first floor.

Clay turned in the direction of the steps. "Logan's showing me his new room."

"If you're done, could you come help me get a few of these boxes into the kitchen?"

"Are we done?" Clay asked Logan, who was getting himself comfortable on the floor with *The Missing Chums.*

Already lost in the story, Logan nodded.

Clay took the steps two at a time. When he reached the first floor, he hoisted the box he'd brought over minutes before.

"Does this go in the kitchen?" he asked Brooke.

"That one goes into my office, which is the room right through there." Brooke pointed to an arched opening. "Thanks, Clay."

He made the delivery, and then came back into the living room. "How about these boxes?"

"Kitchen," she said as she lifted one. "Honestly, it's going to take me weeks to get this place straightened out." Her voice trailed toward the kitchen.

Clay stacked two boxes, one atop the other, and followed her. Once in the kitchen, he placed them on the floor in what would be Brooke's breakfast nook, once she had a table. "Any others out front belong in here?"

"All the boxes along the fireplace wall."

"I'll get them."

After they'd brought in the last box, he asked, "When will your furniture arrive?"

"It's all supposed to be here next week." She leaned back against the counter. "I have some things in storage that Jesse is going to help me with tomorrow. The new stuff will be here on Tuesday."

He opened the refrigerator door, hoping to find a beer or, at the very least, a bottle of water. Nada.

"I'm afraid all I can offer this time around is water." Brooke opened a cabinet and took out a glass, which she handed to him. "The well is hooked up."

"Thanks." He poured a glass of water from the sink and took a long drink. "What else has to be done before you can move in?"

"Just the furniture delivery and emptying the boxes. I'm hoping it doesn't take me too long to get organized. I have a business to run."

"Moving into a new home and opening a new business at the same time—I'd say you have no sense of timing."

"Could have been better," she agreed. "But when Mom decided to close up her shop and offered me the space for my cupcake bakery, it was too good to pass up."

"What will the residents of St. Dennis do, now that there is no Bow Wows and Meows?" he asked, referring to the specialty pet supply shop their mother had owned on Charles Street.

"Not to mention all those tourists who liked to buy

those froufrou outfits for their little dogs." Brooke grinned. "Their loss will be their gain, once they taste my cupcakes."

"It's been my gain. About five pounds' worth since you started baking."

"Don't blame my cupcakes. Blame your lack of willpower."

"You bake a mean cupcake, sister."

"I do, indeed." Brooke beamed and pointed to her new stove with the double ovens. "And I'll be able to bake even more with my newly installed appliances."

"It's pretty fancy, all right," he agreed.

"I figured I'd bake a sampling and dazzle Lucy with my creativity when she's here next week."

"Oh." Clay frowned. "About that . . ."

"You didn't go all Neanderthal on her and scare her off, did you?"

"Of course not. She called a little while ago to let me know she had to postpone her trip."

"Why?"

"Work overload."

"So when's she coming?"

"Probably not until April." He took another long drink of water, then refilled his glass. He could feel his sister's glare on the back of his neck.

"April? April as in February-March-April?"

"That would be the one."

"Humph." Brooke crossed her arms over her chest.

"What?" he asked.

"Nothing." She turned her back and started to unpack a box.

"What, Brooke?"

"Why the delay?"

"She's just overwhelmed. Overbooked and under-staffed, apparently." He leaned back against the counter. "What's with the attitude? From the way you were acting at Enright's, I thought you and Lucy were going to be BFFs."

"I don't like that she's jerking you around, okay?"

"She's not jerking me around."

"She knows how you feel about her and she's putting as much distance, timewise, as she can between you and her."

"Lucy is running a business, Brooke. A very successful one. You of all people know how hard that is. Right now she's a little over her head. She lost time out there because of the MacGregor wedding, and she's going to lose more time with the Magellan wedding. She's just trying to get through the events she contracted for over the next couple of months so that she can spend a couple of weeks out here taking care of what she needs to do for Magellan."

"I think it's really nice of you to defend her, but I still think she's jerking your chain." When he opened his mouth to speak, she held up a hand to stop him and said, "Just remember you heard it here first."

"As if you're likely to let me forget," he muttered.

"I don't want to see you hurt, Clay. You deserve someone who's going to be here for you. That someone isn't going to be Lucy."

"Well, that's too bad for me, then, because Lucy is the only someone I want." The words were out of his mouth before he could stop them. "I had this discussion with your boyfriend not too long ago, and I'll tell you what I told him. I appreciate your concern. I thank you for caring. But Lucy is the only woman

I want, and this—this time she's going to be spending here—may be the only chance I'll ever have. I really wish you'd respect that. I really wish you'd just wish me luck, and then shut up about how she's going to break my heart."

Brooke was silent for a long moment. Finally, she said, "I don't remember saying I thought she was going to break your heart."

"That's what you meant."

"Actually, yeah, I did. And I'm sorry. I just think you're a terrific guy, and you could have your pick of any single woman in this town." She smiled. "Maybe a few not-so-single ones as well. But I get that Lucy is the one who floats your boat. I do respect that, and I do wish you well. And now I will shut up about it."

"Really?"

"Well, for now anyway." Brooke's smile widened.

"I guess I should be grateful for that." Hoping to move past the subject, he opened a carton and took out a smaller box that he sat on the counter and opened. "Spices. Where will you be keeping this stuff?"

"Just leave it. It always takes me a while to move things around before I'm satisfied."

"What makes you think she knows how I feel about her, anyway?" he asked.

It took a moment for Brooke to respond. "I guess I sort of told her."

"Did you, now?" Clay glared. "How nice of you."

"I'm sorry. It just sort of came out the night we were at Vanessa's."

"So what did she say?"

"She sort of denied that you had anything but

friendly feelings for her, but I could tell that it gave her something to think about."

"I would appreciate it if you would leave my relationship with Lucy to me."

"I said I was sorry, and I meant it." She paused, then said, "Okay, since we're still on the subject—which you reintroduced even after we agreed not to talk about it—you know what I don't understand? Why you're not upset about Lucy not coming home next week."

"Look, you've been in business for yourself for what, all of three months now? Lucy's spent nearly fifteen years building her reputation. That's a long time. She feels she owes it to the clients she has to give them her best—which is why she's so successful. Taking time off right now, when she's booked to the max, means taking shortcuts somewhere down the line, and she doesn't want to shortchange her clients, who pay top dollar for her work. I understand that because I feel the same way about the people I grow for. I promise the best produce on the market, and that's what I deliver. I don't take shortcuts and when I say my crops are one hundred percent organic, people know they can trust that. When you are in business for yourself, your reputation is basically all you have.

"And besides, I know that when she comes back here in April, she'll stay longer, which means I'll have more time to spend with her."

"I hope you're right, Clay," Brooke said. "I really want you to be right."

"Hey, so do I," he conceded. "No one wants me to be right more than I do . . ."

"But, Clay." Brooke's tone softened. "Even if she

comes out here and spends some time and say you guys get together and everything is just skippy between you." She paused. "Where does it go from there? You said it yourself. Lucy has a successful business that she's spent a lot of time building out there. You have one thriving enterprise going here and you're embarking on another. What do you think is going to happen once the Magellan wedding is over?"

"I haven't thought that far ahead," he replied.

"Maybe you should."

"Maybe I will. For now, we'll just have to wait until April to see how it all shakes out."

Clay went back into the living room and, over the course of several trips, brought the rest of the boxes into the kitchen, making it clear he was done with the conversation. Of course he'd asked himself what would happen after Lucy's wedding planning duties were finished, but he hadn't come up with any answer he'd liked, so he'd dropped it, just as he was doing now.

"If you don't need me for anything else," he told Brooke from the doorway, "I think I'll run back to the house and order a few pizzas."

"I'm good here," she told him. "But maybe you could take Logan and get him started on his homework. I need about another half hour here. That's all the time I can spare tonight because I have some cupcakes to frost for tomorrow."

"You got it," he replied. "Pizza and homework, not necessarily in that order."

He bounded up the stairs to get Logan, who insisted on bringing his book back to the house. They walked across the snowy expanse, Logan chattering about the dog they were going to get as soon as they moved into the house and got settled. Together they tackled a list of spelling words and second-grade math, and when they were through, set out for Robotti's to pick up their pizza. Brooke arrived at the house about the same time they did, and the three of them ate together in the kitchen. When they finished, Brooke herded Logan upstairs to get ready for bed, and Clay put the plates and glasses into the dishwasher before going into his office.

There were plans for the new brewery to be signed off on, and orders for equipment to be doubled-checked. His sketch for the hop barn had been sent to the same architect who was retrofitting the larger of the barns for the brewery, and they were awaiting the final plans. He thought it would look pretty cool, and he was eager to get started.

Clay smiled to himself. He'd been right about Cam O'Connor and the old barn boards. When Cam saw what they had, what he could have, he was more than happy to do the demo for nothing. Every piece of siding that Cam removed had been afforded the type of respect that should be shown to something that had survived for well over a hundred and fifty years. Cam had been so happy that he agreed to make a table for Brooke's new house as a special thank-you.

He put the brewery aside and looked over the plans he'd made for planting. As soon as he could work the soil, he'd put in the barley he and Wade wanted to test for their first batches of beer. Of course, he couldn't control the weather, but he was hoping for a dry enough spring that the barley, which needed very dry soil, would be happy. The hops rhizomes would take a couple of years to mature, so while they planted what they hoped would be a bumper crop in three years, this year they'd be buying from a wholesaler. Wade had an entire list of flavored beers he'd brewed in Texas that he wanted to re-create in their new venture, so they'd be growing the herbs, flowers, and fruits he'd had success with in the past. In addition, Clay had large plots of vegetables and herbs to plant for his regular customers, so he would be doing double duty this year.

Pushing aside Brooke and her doubts—and his own—even those he had about Lucy—Clay flipped through the catalog of heirloom vegetables he'd received in that day's mail, and turned his attention to the crops he'd plant that spring. Truth be told, he wouldn't have had a whole lot of free time for Lucy these next few months anyway. By April, his crops should be in the ground, and he'd have a little more spare time, but it would take a lot of work to get them there, and the farm had to be his priority right now. It wasn't in his nature to brood or to focus too hard on things he couldn't control. He, too, had a business to run.

Diary ~

Well, this has been a most interesting week! Trula invited me to visit, the occasion being her birthday. She did tell me that Robert had a surprise planned for her, but she had no idea what it might be. He did tell her to tell me to pack a travel bag and bring my passport, but not another bit of information. So hard to pack for a trip when you don't know where you're going or how long you'll be staying! In the end, I did all right on that score, but the trip was more than either of us could dare anticipate!

There we were, boarding Robert's private jet (what a fun experience to fly without going through the whole airport security thing!), still no idea for where we were bound (I must admit to enjoying the bit of mystery!). It wasn't long before we knew we were headed across the pond—that great expanse of deep blue sea was a dead giveaway!—but as for our destination, everyone's lips were sealed.

Did I mention we were accompanied by Robert and Susanna, Robert's cousin, Father Kevin, and several members of Robert's staff at the Mercy Street Foundation—Mallory, Emme, and her darling daughter Chloe? We landed first in London, where we were whisked away to the Savoy and shown to our sumptuous rooms. Then a delightful lunch followed by a stop at the British Museum, one of those places that topped Trula's "bucket list." After the museum, high tea at the hotel, then shopping at Harrods. Dinner at one of Gordon Ramsay's restaurants, then back to the hotel, where Trula and I shared a room. How fun that was! Just like when we were young girls . . . oh, how many years ago was that!

The next morning, back on the plane for a quick trip to Paris, where we walked the Champs-Élysées, lunched at a favorite place of Robert and Susanna's, touristed a bit, then dinner at a restaurant in the Eiffel Tower. A stay at the Ritz. Breakfast in the morning, a few hours of shopping (I am ready for family birthdays!), then it was back to the airport, onto the plane, and homeward bound! An amazing forty-eight hours—April in Paris, indeed! It was a trip I'll never forget, and of course, a very happy birthday for my oldest and dearest friend.

We're back at Robert's home now, and settling in for the night. I'd planned on leaving first thing in the morning for St. Dennis, but I'm severely jet-lagged and Trula thinks I should plan to stay one more day, if for no other reason than to sleep! I just may do that. Lucy will be arriving on Thursday, and of course I want to be there for her, but since Susanna's appointment at the inn is on Friday and she has offered to drive back with me, I just may take her up on the offer. It seems I'm really not as young as I used to be, but oh, my, I certainly did enjoy myself! It was a lovely trip and a lovely birthday for my dear friend, who declared this to be her best birthday ever. I was so happy to have been included in the family celebration and to have shared in this special time with them. Bless Robert for his thoughtfulness.

And now back to work, sorting through the ads for next week's edition of the <u>St. Dennis Gazette.</u> I feel like Cinderella, the day after the ball . . .

~ Grace ~

Chapter 14

L UCY loved the view from the pinnacle of the Bay
Bridge—officially the William Preston Lane Jr.
Memorial Bridge, but few ever referred to it as
such. Staring straight ahead, the Eastern Shore in her
sights, she always knew she was as good as home
once she hit this spot. A bit of chill still clung to the
April air, but she could smell spring and the promise
of warmer days, and the very thought of it made her
smile. St. Dennis warmth wasn't the same as L.A.
warmth. It had a smell and a feel and a sound track
all its own, and she'd missed it. She rolled down the
windows in the rental car as she came off the bridge
and inhaled.

Delicious.

She turned on the radio and found a station to
match her mood, sang along with Heart's "Alone" at
the top of her lungs, and felt the stress and anxiety
of the past few months melt away with every mile.
She had survived three months of working nonstop, three months of weddings, anniversaries, sweet
sixteen parties, fancy luncheons—even a tea for the
duchess of something or other who hailed from some

small European principality Lucy'd never heard of, one that had been gobbled up by some larger country years ago. The duchess had kept her titles, her jewels, and her contacts abroad and was known for her elaborate soirees. Last year, she'd entertained in Shanghai and D.C. This year it was L.A.'s turn, and it had been a coup for Shaefer & Sinclair to have landed the event.

But it was all behind her now. She'd left careful instructions for Ava and Corrine for those events they'd be handling in her absence—events for which they'd shadowed her since the beginning of February. She had her electronic files and carefully constructed lists and had left them both with timetables for reporting to her. She felt as comfortable as she was ever going to be in leaving work behind for others to do. Her focus was now—had to be—on the Magellan wedding and everything that needed to be done to pull off something spectacular in a short amount of time.

Of course, she had her endless lists of things to do here in St. Dennis, but she was taking one thing at a time. She'd be meeting with Susanna at the end of the week, and they'd walk the grounds at the inn along with Daniel, whom Lucy had already warned about Susanna's wish to move the gazebo. She'd called Brooke's former brother-in-law, Jason Bowers, to discuss some thoughts she had for the landscaping, and he agreed to meet with her and Daniel on Saturday to go over her ideas. She'd get together with Olivia about the flowers on Monday, and sit down with the inn's chef on Tuesday. She still had to contact the owner of the golf course, find a tennis pro, and someone to give sailing lessons to the kids. There was no doubt in Lucy's mind that she could accomplish everything in ten days.

Well, maybe twelve . . . but by the time she left St. Dennis, she'd have it all under control.

She changed the radio station, found a country station that her mother listened to all the time, and tried to remember the words to Carrie Underwood's "Before He Cheats." Before she knew it, she was making the right onto the road that would take her into St. Dennis. She could smell the river that ran behind the trees, and a soft scent of new earth. She glanced at the Madison farm as she flew by and thought she saw Clay's Jeep parked next to the house. Without thinking, she made a U-turn at the first opportunity and turned into the lane leading to the farm.

She'd promised herself that she'd make a point to carve out more time to spend with Clay this visit. She'd found herself looking forward to their daily emails and nightly chats, and realized she didn't want to wait until later to see him.

She parked behind the Jeep, got out of the car and looked around, and took a deep breath. She started toward the back porch, planning to knock on the door, when she saw Clay on a tractor out in the field. She sat on the back steps and watched, and waited.

This farm, these steps, held so many memories for her. When they were kids, on hot summer days, they'd swim in the pond, then dry off on the grass. They'd wrap their wet towels around them and sit on the steps and Clay's mother would bring Popsicles out for them. The memory was so strong that Lucy could almost taste the cold icy sweetness, feel the sugary liquid trickle down the wooden stick to her fingers, leaving a sticky path in its wake.

She heard the tractor's engine cut, saw Clay park the tractor next to the barn. He jumped down and took a long pull on a plastic water bottle, then looked around. She knew the second he spotted her. He waved a hand and started toward the farmhouse. She watched him for a moment, watched his familiar amble pick up the pace as he drew nearer. She got off the steps when he was ten feet away and was in his arms before she realized what she was doing.

"Hey," he said softly, after he'd given her a quick kiss on the mouth. "I'm a little sweaty . . ."

"You look fine sweaty." She slowed him down for another kiss. "Farmers are supposed to be sweaty."

"I thought you weren't coming till tomorrow."

"I finished what I had to do out there, so I thought I'd take an earlier flight."

"How long have you been here?"

Lucy looked at her watch. "About a half hour or so."

"What were you doing all that time?"

"Reminiscing." She sat back down on the step on which she'd been sitting.

"About anything in particular?" He sat down next to her.

"Popsicles, for one thing."

"Those double ice jobs my mom used to give us?"

"You always took the grape and I always wanted the lime."

" 'Cause I didn't care if my mouth turned purple, but you did. You always thought the green wasn't as noticeable. I never had the heart to tell you that lime-green lips weren't an especially good look."

"Thanks for sparing me."

"So what else besides Popsicles?" he asked.

"Chickens."

"Chickens," he repeated flatly.

"Remember there used to be that chicken house next to the barn?" She pointed out toward the field. "And you had that big rooster that used to chase me every time he got loose?"

"Big Red." Clay nodded. "He used to chase everyone, even my dad and the dogs."

"What happened to the chicken house?" she asked. "Where are the chickens?"

"A hurricane took down part of the house about ten years ago. We haven't had chickens since."

"You should build another chicken house." She poked him in the ribs. "What kind of farm has no animals, not even a couple of Rhode Island Reds or a dog?"

"The dog is on the list. Brooke promised Logan a dog once they moved and got settled, which they have, so it's any day now for the dog. I figured I'd get one, too. And I'll make a mental note to put chickens on the list of things to do. After I build a henhouse."

She noticed lines of fatigue around his eyes and mouth. "I guess you've been pretty busy."

"Farming's pretty much a full-time thing, especially this time of the year."

"I've been getting that impression from your emails. Planting . . . how many kinds of barley? Three?"

"Well, it's four now. Wade found seed for some heirloom variety he's been stalking for the past couple of years." He nodded in the direction of the field.

"That's what I'm doing this week—getting it into the ground."

"And then there were those hops roots . . ."

"Rhizomes," he corrected her.

"Right. I lost track of how many different kinds of those you said you planted." She looked up at him. "How many kinds of beer are you planning on making, anyway?"

"How 'bout if we talk about that over dinner?" he asked. "Or do you think Grace would be upset if you didn't have dinner at home your first night here?"

"Mom won't be back until tomorrow. She's off celebrating Trula's birthday. I called my brother from the airport, and he said she was staying an extra day because she was jet-lagged." Lucy smiled. "Apparently Robert Magellan flew Trula and her entourage in his plane on a whirlwind trip to London and Paris as a surprise. Daniel said Mom was bubbling over like New Year's champagne when she called to tell him."

"Nice to have your own plane. Nice birthday present."

"Well, you know, Trula and Robert's cousin, Kevin, are the only family Robert has."

"I thought Trula wasn't related to Robert."

"Not by blood, but she was his grandmother's best friend from girlhood, and when his grandmother passed away, she made Robert and Kevin—who are really like brothers—promise to take care of Trula since she had no family at all. So she's been like a great-aunt/grandmother to both Robert and Kevin—he's a priest—and Robert has always made a place in his home for Trula."

"Sounds like Magellan is a nice guy."

"He seems to be." She put her arm though his. "And speaking of nice guys, did I tell you how much I appreciated the pictures you emailed me from Vanessa and Grady's wedding?"

"You did. I'm only sorry you weren't here for it. Their house looked great, and Vanessa told everyone that you were the one who gave her all her ideas."

"Aw, that was nice of her. I'm sorry I couldn't have been here, too. I hope someone took a video that I could watch sometime."

"Wade took one, since Steffie was in the wedding. I'm sure they'd be happy to show it to you while you're here, if you have time."

"I'll try to make time for that." And some other things, she'd promised herself. This visit, she would work her tail off for the June wedding, but the last time she was home, she'd had a taste of reconnecting with her St. Dennis roots, and the taste had left her wanting more.

"So was that a yes for dinner?"

Lucy nodded. "I would love to have dinner with you, but I want to go to the inn first and get settled."

"Great. I'll run in and take a shower and I'll pick you up in an hour or so."

"Make it two," she said. "There are a few things I have to discuss with Daniel and we agreed to sit down when I got home today to work out some of the details for the wedding. I'm meeting with Jason Bowers on Saturday, and there are some issues I need to go over with Daniel."

He walked her to the car and leaned in through the

open window to kiss the side of her face. "I'm really happy to see you, LuLu. I'm really glad you're home."

"Me, too. See you in a while." She smiled and made a U-turn in the wide lane, and waved when she passed him on the way to the road.

She'd been tempted to blow a kiss but didn't because she knew it would be too corny, but the thought made her laugh out loud.

She drove through the center of town at a leisurely pace, waving to Gabriel Beck, the chief of police and Vanessa's half brother, and to Barbara Noonan, who was closing up her shop, Book 'Em, for the day. She drove past Bling, and made a mental note to stop in first thing in the morning to tell Vanessa how much she enjoyed the pictures of her wedding that Clay had sent. *Or maybe,* she mused, *I'll just get up early and come down to Cuppachino for my coffee like the rest of the locals do.*

She'd meant it when she vowed to make time for the St. Dennis native within her. She wanted to spend an afternoon with her nephew, D.J., and Diana, her niece. She wanted to take long walks around the town and reacquaint herself with its streets and its houses. There were people she wanted to get to know a little better, and people she wanted to meet. It was a lot to cram into two weeks, but if she stuck to her schedule, she just might be able to fit it all in.

The parking lot at the inn had two full rows of cars, so she had to leave her rental at the end of the second row.

"I didn't realize you did such a business this time of the year." She poked her head into the office, where her brother was reading an email.

"Thanks to the Chamber of Commerce for being so foresighted, St. Dennis has something going on every month that draws the tourists." He looked up and smiled. "Good to see you, Lucy."

"Likewise." She took a seat in one of the wing chairs. "So what's the attraction in April?"

"Here at the inn, we do an April showers special getaway weekend. Reduced rates. Spring garden tour. Later in the month there's the wine festival." He grinned. "There's always something going on."

"Great marketing of the community."

"Like I said, thank the Chamber of Commerce for being so proactive." He spun halfway around in his chair. "So we have you for a whole two weeks now, I understand."

"I should be able to accomplish the bulk of what I need to do." She opened her bag and took out her notebook. "There's going to be so much to do for the Magellan wedding. I told you Susanna wants the gazebo moved—"

"I have no problem with that." He held both hands palms up. "I said, whatever she wants, and I meant it. Whatever we have to do, I'm for it, if it makes her happy. For one thing, this wedding is great for business. For another, Mom wants Trula to be happy, which means Susanna and Robert have to be happy. The details are all in your hands."

"I'm going to need some help here in St. Dennis. I was wondering if Madeline could give me a hand with some of those details."

"Absolutely. As long as she can balance the affairs she's running here with whatever you need her to do, I'm fine with it."

"We might have to hire someone part-time just to work on this."

"Do what you have to do."

"I'll also need some office space."

"There's the little annex right next door here. Mom uses it occasionally, but for the most part, it's just sitting there."

"I'll take it. I'd like to keep the wedding details somewhat confidential, so I appreciate the privacy."

"It's all yours."

"Terrific." Dan dangled a pen from between his index and middle fingers. "So is that it, for now?"

"For right this moment." Lucy nodded. "We will need to go over the garden plans with the landscaper, but I spelled that all out to you in that last email I sent."

"Right. Plant tons of roses. Move the gazebo. Plant flower beds. Got it. I'm fine with all of that."

"And I'm meeting with the chef early next week . . ." She paused. "Dan, your chef is really good, isn't he?"

"I wouldn't have hired him if he wasn't. No worries there, sis."

"Good, because he's going to be very, very busy that week."

"What else?"

"There are some odds and ends to talk about, but right now I have to . . ." Lucy stood and took two steps toward the door.

"Now I get to tell you my news," Daniel told her. "Sit back down, okay?"

"Sure. Is something wrong? You look so serious. . . ."

"This *is* serious." He leaned forward on his desk.

"Since it got out that Robert Magellan chose this inn for not only his wedding but for a weeklong stay for all his guests, we've been having trouble keeping up with all the calls."

"How did it get out there, anyway?" Lucy frowned. Her office never broadcast who their clients were, and she hadn't seen an article about Robert and Susanna in which the wedding was discussed.

"Mom and Trula were talking about it on their Facebook pages, and I guess—"

"Mom and Trula are on Facebook?" Lucy choked. "Our mom who can barely send an email has a Facebook page?"

"Diana set up the pages for them the last time Trula was here and showed them how to use it. Anyway, it's been great for business. Almost too great." He took a deep breath. "We have a shot at two very important affairs. One is the September wedding of Senator Francis's daughter. The other is an anniversary weekend that sort of blows back to the Magellan thing."

"I don't understand what that means."

"The family is one of those that's been coming here for like fifty years. The old man remembers Dad, used to sail with him. They always book that last week in June and did not want to give it up. I had to bargain with them to get them to move their week."

"What sort of deal did you have to make with them?"

"They agreed to move to the middle of July, but only if the anniversary party is held here."

"So, you can accommodate that, right?"

"Yeah, but there's a string."

"What's the string?"

"You have to do the party."

She laughed. "Uh-uh. No way will I have time to——"

"Lucy, it's that, or they don't give up their rooms."

She stopped laughing. "They're serious?"

"Oh, yeah."

"How big a party?" she asked cautiously.

"Maybe twenty-five, thirty people."

"They don't need me for that. Madeline can handle that."

"Madeline is not the party maker to the stars, or whatever it is that that magazine called you after you did the MacGregor weddings. Lucy, it's a small event. How long can it take?"

"All right, Dan." She sighed. "Is that it?"

"There's more."

"Of course there is."

"Senator Francis's daughter wants——"

"Oh, Dan, no . . ."

"I'm afraid so." He nodded. "They want you to do the wedding. Otherwise, they take it to Annapolis."

"That's blackmail."

Daniel shrugged. "What can I say, he's a politician."

"It would mean a lot to the inn, wouldn't it?"

"Are you kidding? Do you know how many of those D.C. pols would be staying here? How many could conceivably come back if they like what they see?" He shook his head. "I can't even begin to tell you what we could do with the revenue, Luce."

"Let me see what I can work out with Bonnie. I'll do the best I can, Dan."

"I know you will. I'm sorry to put you in this

position—I really am. But I had to ask. Thanks, Lucy."

"Right now I have to run up and change." She stood, gathered her bags, and went to the door.

"You going somewhere?" he asked.

"Yes. I have a date," she told him as she walked out of the office. Over her shoulder, she added, "Don't wait up. . . ."

Chapter 15

Wow." Lucy studied the menu at Lola's Café. "When did fine dining come to St. Dennis? Other than at the inn, of course."

"Seriously?" Clay peered over his menu. "Was that supposed to be a serious question?"

"It was," she replied. "It is."

"You've been away from home for way too long if you have to ask that. In addition to Lola's—and of course the inn—there's now Bancroft's on Charles Street right before you go over the bridge to Cannonball Island, and McClaren's over on New River Road. Not to mention Let's Do Brunch, which is gourmet from its sandwiches to its frittatas."

"Sounds like I've been put in my place." She smiled in spite of the mild rebuke she detected in his tone. "Looks like I have a lot of catching up to do."

"Hey, the foodie movement is alive and well in St. Dennis." He put the menu down. "I'm pleased to say that I've played a modest part in its success."

"Because your patronage keeps all these restaurants in business?"

"I don't deny I like to dine out. After all, I'm a

lonely bachelor, living by myself . . ." He unconvincingly faked a sad-sack face.

"Baloney. I'll bet you know your way around the kitchen."

"I have my moments."

"But back to your contribution to the success of all these new dining establishments."

"They all buy from me. Every one of them. Whether they buy some of the produce I raise, or only certain things, or just herbs . . . every chef around buys from the Madison Farms."

She detected the note of pride in his voice, and it made her smile. She understood what it meant to do something really well, then stand back and take a look at it through someone else's eyes. "You really do love what you do, don't you?"

"I'm a farmer. I never wanted to be anything else. I've never spent one day wishing I were somewhere else, doing something other than farming."

"Do you think you'll be able to continue to supply the customers you have now once you get more into the business of brewing beer?"

"I admit time is occasionally going to get tight. I grow certain specialty items for restaurants outside of the Eastern Shore. D.C., Baltimore, Philly, New York. I wouldn't give up that business. It's not only lucrative, but it's fun." Clay grinned. "Besides, I'm determined to get MacGregor out there in the fields with me."

"I take it that Wade's not much of a farmer."

"Not on his best day. But he's willing to learn because he wants to be involved in the total process. He can't afford to have the business collapse if something happens to me, so he has to know his way around the crops. Just like I have to learn his end of it. He's the one who knows how to brew a great beer, the one who has the formulas for all those flavored beers he wants to make."

"I thought beer's flavor was just beer."

"In the hands of some, that may be so." He raised an amused eyebrow. "But Wade's sort of a mad scientist when it comes to brewing beer."

"I'm conjuring up an image of him wearing a white coat puttering around in a lab full of bubbling test tubes."

"He's maybe more like Dr. Frankenstein, taking a little of this and a little of that for his creations."

The waiter stopped by for their orders, refilled their wineglasses, and took their menus.

"So what exactly are you growing that Wade will turn into flavored beers?"

"Chili peppers, heather, basil, oregano, raspberries, cherries, nasturtiums—"

"Whoa." Lucy held up a hand for him to stop. "You lost me at chili peppers."

"Wade said his chili beer was a big seller for him in Texas."

"The Eastern Shore isn't Texas," she reminded him.

"I think there's a market for it. As far as the fruit beers are concerned, they've been around for a long time. It's going to be an adventure to see what we can come up with and what sells for us, but we both agreed we have nothing to lose. I think the experimentation we do over the next year or so will pay off. Wade had a really successful brewery and he's applying everything he learned to this effort. He believes

MadMac can be even more successful because we're able to cut costs by growing so many of the raw materials ourselves. Besides cutting out the supplier, we'll have total control over the quality of our ingredients. We can make the best because we'll grow the best, and it can all be organic."

"Sounds like a plan that can't fail."

"Right. Unless, of course, the weather is too cold or too hot or too wet." He grimaced. "Or if our hops get hit by a fungus or insect invasion. Other than that, yeah, it's foolproof."

"I think it's admirable that you're willing to get into a totally new venture, to use your resources in a whole new way."

"Small farmers face a challenge. The big agricultural concerns dominate the marketplace. It's become harder and harder for legacy farmers to hold on. So anything I can do to keep my farm relevant, to make it prosperous enough to keep it going, I will do. I feel like I owe it to my dad and my granddad and all those other farmers in my family to keep it going."

"I guess I feel the same way about the inn," Lucy said. "An ancestor of my dad's built that place, and while it didn't start out as an inn, it's had a long and happy life as one. I didn't realize until today how much responsibility I feel for it." She stopped to take a sip of wine as her thoughts gathered.

"What happened today?"

"My brother told me that there were two events that could greatly benefit the inn financially which would require my planning, one this summer, one in September."

"More weddings?"

"One is a party for a family who are longtime guests of the inn who have to be rebooked because of the Magellan wedding. Dan said they agreed to move their booking to July but only if I do this party for them. I believe there may have been a lawsuit implied." Lucy sighed. "The other one—the September event—is Senator Francis's daughter's wedding."

"Oh, no pressure there."

"No kidding." Lucy tapped her fingers on the side of her glass. "If I say sure, no problem—which is what my brother is hoping I'll say—I'll end up neglecting my own business. I mean, the logistics of the senator's wedding . . . the time involved. It would take me most of the summer to pull that one off."

"So you'd be in St. Dennis all summer?" he asked.

"Pretty much, yes." She watched his eyes, saw the wheels turning, and she laughed in spite of herself. "Yes, I would be home for much of the summer, and I can see that possibility doesn't bother you at all."

"Not a bit." He toasted the prospect with a tilt of his wineglass before taking a sip. "I understand your dilemma, though. You're thinking you have to choose between your business and the family's business, and you're torn because you don't want to see either of them suffer."

"Yes. You get it. That's it exactly." She put her glass down. "Of course, I feel some responsibility to my brother. He's had to carry the inn for years by himself. He took over when my dad passed away, and he's done a remarkable job in making it the success that it is. He's brought it up to date as much as he could afford to, he's reinvented it so that it's almost a resort with all the activities, the tennis courts, the playground for the kids, the kayaks and the boats . . . he's been a genius at that. He's the one who started having weddings and big gatherings there, even before destination weddings became as big as they are now. He really has made the Inn at Sinclair's Point what it is today."

"I'll bet you worked just as hard to make your business successful," Clay pointed out, and she nodded.

"Bonnie and I have worked very hard." She thought of all the hours she put in on a daily basis, the weeks and the months—and yes, the years, when time off was almost nonexistent. There was no way she'd let Shaefer & Sinclair go off the rails. "I can't let that go."

"You don't have to. Do both." He reached across the table and took her hand. "You're talking about one event in July and the other in September. So you set up a temporary office here for the summer to do what you have to do, and then you go back to California after the senator's daughter's wedding and get back into your groove."

"That's pretty much the conclusion I'd come to," she confessed, pleased that he'd seen her predicament for what it was and understood why she couldn't abandon either. "Dan's giving me a small office to handle the Magellan wedding, and I suppose I could use it for as long as I have to. It would mean handing off a lot of work to the staff in L.A., but I suppose if I have Ava and Corrine working the planning stages now, it would work . . ." She mentally ran through the events that were already on the books. There were one or two for which no substitution would be acceptable, but most of the others, she thought, would be fine with either of the other planners and, of course, Bonnie.

She became aware of someone at her shoulder. She looked up to find their server, holding their salads and apparently waiting for her to move out of the way.

"Oh." She flashed a smile. "Sorry . . ."

When the waiter was finished and had walked away, Lucy looked across the table at Clay and said, "That's exactly what I'm going to do. I'll have two offices this summer and divide my time according to where I'm needed when." She sighed happily and dug into her salad.

"Let me know if there's anything I can do to help," he said.

She speared a tomato and raised the fork to her mouth, then paused. "Maybe you can. I'll be meeting with the chef at the inn this coming week to go over the menus for the Magellans. If he has any special dishes in mind, maybe we'll ask you to grow whatever it is he needs."

"I already grow for the inn," he told her, "but sure, tell Gavin to let me know if I have to put in anything special, though we're running short of time if I have to start something from seed."

She took a bite of the tomato. "I'll keep that in mind when I meet with Susanna. I've been trying to pin her down on the menu for the past month. If I tell her the farmer needs to plant now, it might spur her on."

"Tell her if she plays her cards right, there might even be a specialty beer available."

"Oh, that would be fabulous." Lucy put her fork back down. "If we could offer a special beer—like, call it Magellan or something—exclusive to them for a limited time . . ." Susanna would love that, she knew. "Is that possible? Can you make a beer between now and the end of June?"

"Not from our crops, but I'll talk to Wade."

"That would be really something." Her mind began to take off. "Oh, and maybe when you get your brewery up and running, you could make a beer that would be exclusive to the inn."

"I can talk to Daniel about that," Clay told her. "We'll call it LuLu Beer."

She laughed, and suddenly everything that she'd been fretting about over the past few months—the overbookings, the botched scheduling, floral designers who got their orders mixed up and caterers who backed out at the last minute, DJs who didn't show, cranky brides and their near-impossible mothers—all seemed somehow less important than they had just a few days earlier. In the flicker of candlelight, she saw the boy she used to laugh with, the boy who'd kept her early secrets and who shared the carefree days of her childhood, and she saw the man he'd become. The boy had once been her best friend. Something told her that the man still could be that friend, that keeper of secrets—and a lot more.

A whole lot more, judging by the way he looked at her.

The waiter brought them the dessert menu after they'd finished their meals, but Clay handed them back with a thank you and a smile. To Lucy he said, "I have a better idea."

"But they serve your sister's cupcakes here," Lucy protested. "I saw it noted on the menu."

"I know where there's a private stash of Brooke's best chocolate raspberry cupcakes, baked this morning."

Lucy raised her eyebrows. "And where might they be?"

"On my kitchen counter."

"Oh, wait." A smile played at the corners of her mouth. "Is this the Madison equivalent of 'want to see my etchings?'"

"Much better. Etchings aren't edible. Besides"—he signaled for the check—"I never was much of an artist."

"Not much of a baker either, if you're relying on your sister to deliver the goods."

"Ouch."

"However, since I have tasted your sister's cupcakes, I'd be a fool to decline."

"A wise decision. Best baker on the Eastern Shore."

He paid the bill and helped her drape her jacket over her shoulders. They walked out into the spring evening and he took her hand.

"This is such a beautiful time of the year here," she said as they walked across the street to the parking lot. "I too often forget the little things that make it special."

"Like what?"

"Like the daffodils and the tulips that are blooming everywhere. The English wood hyacinths. The dogwood and the azalea and the weeping cherry trees. The colors are just so perfect, and the air is so delicately scented. It's why you always think of pastel colors when you think about spring. In my head, spring is always soft yellow and pink and lavender and pale green like new grass."

"What colors are summer?"

"The colors of heat. Red and bright yellow," she replied without thinking.

"What about blue and green? Where do they fit in?"

"They're summer as well. The colors of the Bay, and shade trees."

"And fall . . . ?"

"Browns and golds, rusty reds and deepest orange." She smiled, anticipating his next question. "And winter is white and silver."

"And back in California?" he asked. "What do your seasons look like there?"

"Where I live?" She thought about it for a moment. "For me, mostly yellow and green all year round. There are other colors, I suppose, but that's what I think of, when I think of the colors of L.A. And haze on the freeways, but I don't know how to describe the color of that."

He laughed. "We get haze here as well, don't forget."

"But only in July and August, if my memory serves. When it gets so hot and the heat rises off the sidewalks and the mist rises off the Bay. That's a different kind of haze."

As they approached the Jeep, Clay opened the car with the remote and walked Lucy to the passenger side.

"I can get it," she said when he reached for the door handle.

"I'm sure you can," he replied as he opened it.

"If my grandma were here, she'd say that the Madisons raised you right."

"They did their best. Some of it stuck." He closed the door behind her, walked around to the driver's side, and got in.

Lucy rested her head against the back of the seat and watched from the corner of her eye as Clay fastened his seat belt and started the car.

"It's a pretty night," she said as he turned onto Charles Street.

"We have a lot of pretty nights here. I'm glad you'll be around for some of them."

"Me too."

When she'd set out for St. Dennis early that morning, spending the summer here was the last thing on her mind. Funny, she thought, how sometimes things happen and you realize that the something was exactly what you'd wanted—what you needed—without even being aware that you wanted or needed it. She hadn't spent a summer in St. Dennis since she was in high school, and suddenly it was the only place she wanted to be.

"Penny for them," Clay said as they approached the farm.

"I was just thinking that it would be nice to spend the summer here, that's all."

He parked the car close to the house and turned off the engine.

"Think you can still hold your own when it comes to crabbing?" he asked.

"With a net or with a line?"

"Either way. I'm betting you've lost your touch."

"That's a bet you're going to lose." She turned in her seat to face him as she released her seat belt.

"You've been away a long time. I doubt you've maintained any of your old technique."

"I figure it's a lot like riding a bike."

She welcomed his embrace when he reached for her,

lifted her face for his kiss. She waited for that momentary hesitation that always accompanied the first seconds of intimacy of any kind, whether the hug of a friend or the first exploratory kiss of a new relationship. She waited, determined to push past it, because she'd wanted Clay to kiss her, wanted to kiss him back, wanted to push back against the years and the darkness that every once in a while arose in her. She waited, but the little *click* she usually heard inside her head—that instinct that told her to run, she was in danger—never came.

It was an anomaly she'd ponder later tonight when she was back in her room at the inn, but for now, she simply wanted to savor the sensation of this beautiful man kissing her, of kissing him back. She held his face in her hands and let the warmth of his touch spread through her as his tongue teased the corners of her mouth. She found herself wanting more.

When had she ever wanted *more*?

This is what it's like when you're not afraid, she thought. *This is what it's like when you're with someone you trust. . . .*

"LuLu," he whispered between kisses. In his voice she heard longing, desire. It was like fuel to the flame, and she moved closer, wanting to feel his body next to hers.

"Hey, Uncle Clay!" She heard the childish voice at the same time as she heard the rap on the passenger-side window. She lurched backward, startled.

"Great," Clay muttered as he disengaged himself. "He has his mother's sense of timing . . ."

Clay rolled down the window. "What's up, buddy?"

"What are you doing? Mom made cupcakes. She

let me help. Are you gonna come in and eat them with us?"

"Sure." Clay sighed. "Where is she?"

"In the kitchen."

"Yours or mine?" Clay asked.

"Yours, silly. That's where the cupcakes are."

"Get your head out of the window, Logan." Clay looked at Lucy apologetically as he closed the window. "Looks like we're going to have to share. Which was not, by the way, in the original plan."

"It's okay." Lucy grabbed her bag from the floor of the front seat where she'd dropped it.

"No, it isn't." Clay squeezed her hand. "But maybe we can pick up where we left off later. Assuming my sister leaves . . ."

Lucy laughed and opened her car door. "Hi," she said to Clay's nephew. "I'm Lucy."

"I know. My mother told me." Logan seemed to be studying her.

"All right, cupcake eaters." Clay came around the front of the car. "Let's head on in and see what your mom made for us."

"Chocolate raspberry, like you asked." Logan led the way to the porch, up the back steps, and into the house.

"Hello, Brooke." Clay focused a laser beam on his sister, who was getting coffee cups from the cabinet. Three coffee cups. "Nice of you to stop by."

"Hi, Lucy. Good to see you." Brooke flashed a smile. "I thought you might like coffee with dessert," she said brightly. "I hope decaf is okay?"

"It's fine for me," Lucy told her.

"How was your flight?" Brooke asked as she prepared the coffeemaker.

"Early." Clay pulled out a chair from the table for Lucy and she sat.

"You must be exhausted."

"I'm a little jet-lagged," Lucy admitted, suddenly feeling more tired than she had before Brooke inquired.

"So, Brooke," Clay said as he took the seat next to Lucy. "Shouldn't Logan be in bed by now?"

"Nope." Brooke grinned as she measured coffee grounds. "Teachers' in-service day tomorrow. No school."

"Brooke, can I do something?" Lucy offered.

"Oh, no, thanks. There's really nothing to be done." Brooke poured water into the coffeemaker and hit the on button.

"Does that mean you'll be leaving?" Clay asked pointedly.

Brooke ignored the question.

"So, Lucy." Brooke pulled up a chair at the table. "How's the Magellan wedding coming along?"

"I'll know better after I meet with Susanna tomorrow," Lucy told her.

"Clay says you're going to be home for at least a week," Brooke said.

"At least a week, yes."

"I'm sure your mom is happy about that."

Lucy nodded. "She is." Lucy glanced at Clay. "I'm happy about it, too."

"Looks like Lucy is going to be around even more over the summer," Clay said.

"Really?" Brooke turned to Lucy. "Why's that?"

"A few more events were scheduled at the inn that I'll be handling. One in July, one in September."

"I see." The coffee finished dripping and Brooke got up to pour. "So I guess we'll be seeing a lot more of you."

"Bet on it." Lucy met Brooke's eyes.

Brooke brought a plate of cupcakes and some small dessert plates to the table.

"Uncle Clay, I can't find the Power Rangers channel," Logan called from the living room. "Will you find it for me?"

"I'll be right back." Clay touched Lucy's shoulder as he stood, and she reached up to touch his hand. Their fingers entwined for just a second as she looked up into his eyes.

As he left the room, he told Brooke, "Behave yourself."

"Not to worry." Brooke poured coffee and placed the cups on the table. "Cream and sugar?" she asked Lucy.

"Please."

Brooke stood with her back against the counter. "I saw the way you looked at him," she said. "You care about him."

"Why do you sound surprised?"

"I was all ready to put you on the spot, play the big-sister card for real this time, and here you like him."

"Guilty as charged."

Brooke obviously had been caught off guard in her attempt to protect her brother, which in itself was okay, as far as Lucy was concerned. She might find herself called upon to defend one of her own brothers' heart one day. Neither Daniel nor Ford had ever been all that astute where women were concerned. Would she be similarly protective if she thought one of them cared too much for someone who didn't appear to care for him? Or would she shrug it off as none of her business and stand by and let him potentially make a fool out of himself?

Lucy liked to think that she, too, would stand up for her brothers, especially the younger one, who'd always been so idealistic.

Clay came back into the room and Lucy followed him with her eyes. He caught her gaze, and she couldn't help but smile.

"On second thought, I don't think I want coffee after all." Brooke stood and called into the next room. "Logan, come on. We're going back to our house now."

"Noooooo," he called back. "Power Rangers just came on!"

"You can watch it at home," she told him.

"You don't have to leave." Lucy beckoned Brooke back to the table.

"I'm interrupting your evening," Brooke protested.

"Wasn't that your plan?" Clay asked drily.

"Yes, it was," Brooke readily admitted. "Before it wasn't."

"Was that code for something?" Clay stared at his sister.

"I understood." Lucy laughed and patted the back of Brooke's chair. "Sit with us. I won't be staying that much longer." She looked at Clay. "I'm more tired than I thought I was. I've been up since three this morning."

"Then you are due for a crash." He passed her the

cupcakes. "Eat. Drink your coffee. And then I'll drive you back to the inn."

The atmosphere lightened, and by the time Lucy left the farmhouse, she and Brooke were planning a party to celebrate Jesse's being named senior partner in Enright and Enright, Attorneys-at-Law. With the retirement of both his grandfather and his uncle Mike, the only thing that stood between Jesse and the firm was Curtis, his grandfather, who had come to the conclusion that no one was more capable of carrying on the family name than Jesse.

"I want to invite his entire family," Brooke had confided. "I want it to be a night he'll never forget."

"Where are you going to hold it?" Lucy asked.

"I'm not sure. My first choice would be at the Enright house, but I'm afraid that might be a little pushy on my part. I'm going to have to give it a little more thought. But I have plenty of time. Neither Jesse's grandfather nor his uncle has officially announced their retirements yet."

"Let me know if there's anything I can do to help," Lucy told her as she slipped into her jacket.

"I'll do that."

Lucy and Clay stepped out into a clear night with a sky crowded with stars.

"If we drive out to the point, I'll bet there won't be as much competing light," Clay noted. "We'd be able to see them better."

"*You'd* be able to see them better." Lucy yawned. "I'm sorry, but I am fading very quickly."

"Then I'll take you home, and you can get some sleep, and we'll do the stars another night." He reached across the console for her hand and gave it a squeeze, and he drove back to the inn holding her hand.

"So I guess you're going to be pretty busy these next few days." Clay stopped at the double doors behind the inn.

"I have a list a mile long."

"Can we grab dinner one night, or lunch one day?" he asked.

"Yes, to both. And maybe coffee in the morning at Cuppachino if I get up early enough."

"I'm usually there by eight," he told her.

"Save me a seat." She leaned across the console and kissed him. "Thanks for a great night, Clay."

She could have added, *And thanks for reminding me how good it is to laugh, to trust, to care . . .*

The receptionist was still at the desk when Lucy entered the lobby, and there were still some guests milling about, some early arrivals for a long weekend, some looking as if they'd just come back from an evening stroll from town. Lucy passed them all and went right up the stairs to her room, and managed to change into a sleep shirt before practically passing out on the bed.

She'd passed a milestone that night, she knew: her defense mechanism, her inner siren, hadn't felt the need to shriek inside her head when he'd reached for her. There'd been no panic rising in her, no fight-or-flight response, no cold fear in the pit of her stomach. There'd just been Clay, and kisses that had been heartbreakingly sweet and crazily erotic at the same time. Her last thought as she drifted off to sleep was that it was going be a very interesting summer.

Chapter 16

CLAY had looked up from his usual table, where he was reading the newspaper, when he heard the door open—an automatic response he'd developed after months of regular morning visits, one he'd once compared to Pavlov's dogs. The door opens, you look up to see who is coming in. Someone you know? You smile, wave, call a greeting, invite them to sit, or not. A stranger or someone you're avoiding? You go back to your coffee and your conversation or whatever it was that you were reading.

This morning, he watched Lucy follow a party of three through Cuppachino's door and go straight to the counter, where she ordered her morning coffee.

Clay was waiting for Wade, who could always be counted on to be at least fifteen to twenty minutes late, depending on whether or not Steffie had gotten Austin ready for his day before she left for Scoop. His partner's chronic tardiness was annoying as hell, but this morning—seeing Lucy stroll in unexpectedly, her red hair pulled back in a ponytail, her legs bare in shorts, running shoes on her feet, and a sweatshirt tied around her waist over her gray T-shirt—Clay was grateful that Wade had ignored his pleas to be on time just once this week.

"So what news is in that paper that I should know about today?" she asked as she approached his table.

"Well, let's see." He scanned the section he'd been reading—sports—and read through the headlines. "The Orioles are celebrating back-to-back wins, the Ravens are gearing up for the draft, and the high school lacrosse team was defeated in the second round of a tournament over in Annapolis."

"Those are just the sort of things I need to know. Thanks for sharing."

"Can you sit?"

"I have a few minutes. Thanks." She pulled out the chair closest to his and sat.

"Nice to see you up and about early. Is this part of your normal routine when you're back in L.A.?"

"I wish. I don't have a normal routine back there, unless you count staying up way too late working so that the next morning I am crawling out of bed, rushing to get dressed and out of my apartment to make an early morning meeting." She took a sip of coffee. "Carlo brews a mean cup. I really look forward to coming here when I'm home."

"He does," Clay agreed. "So you're not really a runner, then, you're just—"

"I am so a runner. At least, I am when I'm here." She looked around the coffee shop and waved to a few familiar faces. "Mornings are so peaceful here. No thousand cars to dodge, no incessant honking of horns. No clouds of pollution to run through. No eight A.M. meetings. It's quiet and the air smells good. I like to see all the changes the town has undergone between visits. The houses, the landscapes—it's all new to me every time, even though it's still all familiar."

"As tired as you looked last night, I didn't think we'd see you until Saturday, at the very least."

Lucy laughed. "I did hit the wall of fatigue headfirst last night. Sorry for crashing on you."

"You get a pass for jet lag." He sliced off half of his muffin and offered it to her. "Whole wheat, raisins, pecans, and cranberries."

"Oh, yum." She slid the piece of muffin onto a napkin. "Thanks. I will have a healthy breakfast when I get back to the inn, but this should tide me over nicely."

"So what's your schedule for today?"

"Well, on my way back to the inn, I'm going to stop next door to see Olivia because I have a question about flowers for the wedding." She nibbled at the muffin. "This is delicious. Did Brooke bake this?"

He nodded and handed her the knife. She grinned. "Are you sure you don't mind?"

"Go right ahead. There's another one over there," he told her. "But I should probably claim it before someone else does."

Clay got up, walked to the counter, and returned with the muffin. When he got back to the table, he noticed she'd already eaten all of hers. He put the plate down in front of her, handed her the knife, and said, "Have at it."

"Thank you. I won't eat much more of it, I promise."

"Eat whatever you want. So you're going to meet with Olivia about flowers for Susanna." He sat back to watch her take little bites of the muffin. Just watching her eat—hell, watching her do anything—was a pleasure. Just having her there with him—drinking coffee, chatting—elevated what had started out to be a very ordinary morning to a very good one.

"Then," she was saying, "it's back to the inn to get cleaned up. My mom and Susanna should be back by eleven or so. I thought my mother had driven herself to Robert's house the other day, but Daniel told me this morning that Robert sent a car to pick her up. Wasn't that nice of him?"

"Mm-hmm." Clay nodded.

"So anyway." She took another slice of muffin. "Susanna is driving back with Mom. We have so much to accomplish today."

"I can see that all those excuses I was thinking up for being late this morning weren't necessary." Wade seemed to appear out of nowhere. Clay had been so focused on Lucy that he never saw his friend come into the shop until he was there, pulling out a chair.

"Good morning, Lucy. Good to see you." Wade sat opposite Lucy at the table.

"Hey, Wade. How are you?" she returned the greeting.

"I'm good." Wade looked from Lucy to Clay. "Am I interrupting something?"

"We were just chatting." Lucy spoke before Clay could. "I stopped in for coffee to take out, but I saw Clay here and decided to stay and help him eat his breakfast."

Wade looked over the remains of the muffin.

"Whole wheat, raisin, pecan, and cranberry?" he asked.

"Got the last two," Clay told him.

"Damn. Wonder if they have any in the back. . . ." Wade got up and went back to the counter.

"I should get going. It's getting late." Lucy pointed to the clock on the wall.

"You might want to make a stop at the table up by the window and say hello," Clay suggested.

Lucy turned around in her chair to take a look.

"The ladies Mom has coffee with every morning. Yes, I should do that." She looked over the group. "Oh, there's Vanessa." She finished her coffee in one gulp, then started to push back from the table. "I guess you and Wade have business to discuss anyway, right?"

"It is time for our daily morning meeting. Past time, actually."

"Then I won't feel as if I'm abandoning you." She rose from her chair. "Thanks for sharing your breakfast with me."

"Anytime."

"Oh, would you ask Wade if a beer for the Magellan wedding is even a remote possibility? I'd love to be able to tell Susanna."

"Sure. I'll let you know."

"I'll see you later, then."

"Call me if you find yourself with some free time," he said as she started to walk away.

"If I have any free time at all, you are the only person I'd call."

She walked to the front of the coffee shop, where she was greeted warmly by the ladies there. Clay watched her until Wade came back and sat in the chair he'd claimed earlier.

"You're right in my line of vision, you know," Clay told him.

Wade looked over his shoulder, saw Lucy six tables directly behind him, and turned back to Clay.

"Got it bad, don't you, sport?"

When Clay didn't respond, Wade said, "You want to know something I learned about women?"

"Not really."

"I'm going to tell you, anyway." Wade took a sip of coffee and added half a raw sugar to the cup. "Accept no substitutions."

"What is that supposed to mean?"

"It means that when you find the right one, you pull out all the stops." Wade peeled the paper from the cupcake he'd brought back with him. "No more good muffins. I had to settle for a chocolate orange cupcake."

He took a bite. "Of course, stalking is out. I mean, sometimes a guy might think she's the one, but if she doesn't agree, he has to back away. However, if she's interested—and it's pretty clear that Miss Lucy is—then you have to go for it."

"I have all intentions of going for it," Clay told him.

"Make the most of your time, then, since I hear she's only here for a couple of weeks."

"She'll be home for the summer," Clay said. "Well, for much of it, anyway."

"Hey, that's good, right?" Wade took another bite. "Your sister can really bake. I don't know why you don't weigh eight hundred pounds."

"I could say the same to you. Your wife makes the best ice cream in the state."

"She does her best work at Scoop. Sometimes she does bring home a new flavor for testing, though."

Clay watched Lucy head to the door, then turn to wave at him before she left. He waved back.

Wade looked amused.

"What?" Clay asked.

"Nothing."

"What was that look for?"

"You smile every time you look at her, you know that?"

"So?" Clay shrugged. She did make him smile. No big secret there. "She's beautiful."

"So I guess that makes my next bit of advice irrelevant."

"What bit of advice was that?"

"That maybe you should play it just a little cool. But it's obviously too late for that."

"That was going to be your advice? To play it cool?" Clay smirked. "How cool did you play it with Steffie?"

Wade shook his head. "I'd known her for too long. She wouldn't have bought it."

"Lucy and I have known each other since we were five years old, Wade."

"Oh, well, then." Wade took a sip of coffee. "How 'bout this, then? Just tell her how you feel."

"I can't believe I'm getting tips about my love life from Wade MacGregor." Clay looked to the ceiling. "What is wrong with this picture?"

"Hey, am I not married to one of the hottest women in town?" Now Wade looked amused and smug.

"I can't argue that," Clay conceded. "Though how you pulled that off is still a mystery to me."

"Yeah, well, it is to me sometimes, too." Wade dropped his "Dr. Love" persona. "The thing is this: Steffie is sheer magic. She's brought magic into my life. And that's the bottom line: when it's right, it's magic. So if the magic's there, go for it."

"Slow down, I'm taking notes." Clay tried to brush off Wade's comments, but in his heart, he knew his friend spoke the truth about the right person bringing magic into your life.

Lucy was magic, pure and simple. Clay had already figured out that he would do whatever it took to keep that magic in his life.

I met briefly with the floral designer this morning," Lucy told Susanna when they settled into the library and both had spread their notes out in front of them. "I showed her the photographs you'd sent me and she agreed that the garden-rose–hydrangea–gerber-daisy arrangement would be spectacular as centerpieces with some more organic touches like lamb's ear and English ivy, dusty miller and hosta leaves."

Susanna nodded enthusiastically. "That was actually the arrangement I liked the best. It just looked so . . . friendly. Beautiful and sophisticated in a country sort of way. But what kind of container? I'm not wild about baskets."

"Olivia agreed. She suggests that we use silver pots and bowls and pitchers—she happens to have a lovely collection that she showed me. Different sizes, different heights."

"I love that." Susanna frowned slightly. "Although I was hoping for peonies. . . ."

"I mentioned that. Late June is, well, late for that flower, but she said she'll exhaust every possible resource. If there are any available, she will find them."

"Fabulous." Susanna smiled. "Now, about my bouquet—I'm liking that look of just roses in cream and white and shades of pink."

"Love it. I'm sure that won't be a problem." Lucy paused. "So, would you like to nail down Petals and Posies as your florist?"

"Absolutely. Can you take care of that contract?"

"Of course. I'll have it drawn up and I'll email it to you for your approval of the numbers." Lucy nodded. "Now, for your attendants . . ."

"Just two friends from the Foundation. Mallory Russo and Emme Caldwell. They'll be wearing navy. And Emme's daughter, Chloe, will be the flower girl— she's wearing shell pink. Rob's son, Ian, will be the ring bearer. That's pretty much it." Susanna had counted off the names on the fingers of one hand. "Oh, and of course Rob, and his best man. Mallory's fiancé, Charlie, will be an usher."

"Small wedding party," Lucy murmured.

"Just the people who matter most. Except, of course, for Trula, who will take the place usually reserved for the grandmother of the groom. Rob's cousin, Father Kevin, will perform the ceremony. That's it. That's our inner circle. It isn't wide, but it's strong."

"That's all you need, then." Lucy placed the magazine photo of the arrangement Susanna had decided on in a file and made a note to tell Olivia that she'd been approved and that Lucy would be getting together with her to obtain a number for the contract.

"Next, music. Have you and Rob made a decision . . . ?"

Over the next two hours, Lucy and Susanna crossed off a number of open items on the to-do list. The band was selected, the options for photographer—Susanna wanted Karyn Park, the former model turned celebrity photographer—and Susanna had given Lucy a list of the meals for which she'd like to see menus, including the rehearsal, a brunch for the guests on the day of the wedding, the reception itself, and brunch the following day before the guests departed.

"Gavin said he'd be available for us whenever we're ready," Lucy told Susanna. "Why don't we go into the dining room, have lunch, and we can go over everything that you want with the chef at the same time?"

"Sounds perfect. Two birds, one stone." Susanna picked up her bag and stood. "Which way?"

"Follow me . . ."

Lunch and the meeting with the inn's chef took almost another two hours, but by the time they were finished, Gavin had a good idea of what he'd need to prepare and serve the couple's guests during the last week of June.

"I hope I haven't overwhelmed you," Susanna said when Gavin was gathering up all his notes along with the lists Susanna had made up for him.

"Not at all," he assured her. "I like that you know what you want, that you want to mix in some casual dining with some gourmet meals. And I like that you've thought ahead for the children. Our young guests should be as well fed as their parents. I especially like that you are concerned with local sourcing.

We pride ourselves here at the inn on using local produce, seafood, and meats when it's possible. It's going
to be a pleasure to serve you."

"I'm looking forward to the tasting."

"So am I."

Susanna was duly charmed, and Gavin was whis-
tling as he made his way back to the kitchen. Happy
customer, happy chef. Happy Lucy.

Having two big items—the flowers and the music—
crossed off the list gave Lucy a boost. She waved
good-bye to Susanna feeling as if she'd gained control
over this upcoming event. The food was a huge item,
of course, but Gavin was on the case now and she'd
meet with him during the coming week, start narrow-
ing down selections for the various meals, and get a
date for the bride and groom to come for a tasting.
She could tell that he understood that this wedding
could well secure his reputation as a chef, and she
knew that no detail would go unnoticed.

She went into her office and pulled up the wedding
file on her laptop, then proceeded to type in her notes
from today's meeting. She called Olivia, gave her the
green light, and arranged to meet with her first thing
on Monday morning.

Lucy reached for her phone to call Bonnie, then
checked first the time, then the company's schedule of
events for the day. A luncheon was being handled by
Ava, so Bonnie should be in her office. Lucy dialed her
partner's private line but had to leave voice mail for
Bonnie to call her back. The sooner they discussed her
dilemma—the proposed events for July and September—
the better.

It was late in the afternoon when Bonnie returned Lucy's call.

"I'm sorry." She sounded a little breathless. "I'm on my way to the airport. I hadn't planned on visiting Bob this weekend, but he had an accident this morning and just called from the emergency room."

"What happened?" Lucy asked. "Is he all right?"

"He was riding this morning, something spooked his horse, and he fell. He broke one of his legs in three places and has a concussion. I'm at my apartment packing some things for a few days. Thank God we staffed up a few months ago. With you there for a week and me up north for who knows how long—"

"I might be a little more than a week," Lucy told her. "And there's something else . . ."

Lucy told her about the two events for which Lucy had been requested as the planner.

"Wow. A senator's daughter. Good for you. Good for us."

"Between the anniversary party and the wedding, I'm going to be in St. Dennis for a good part of the summer. We need to go over our schedule of contracted events to see how we're going to handle this."

There was a long pause on the line before Bonnie said, "I agree we need to rethink a few things, but we can talk about that at another time. Right now I have to get to the airport. I promised I'd be there as soon as possible."

"Let's plan to get together as soon as I get back to the coast," Lucy suggested. "Tell Bob I'm sorry to hear about his accident and I hope he mends quickly."

"Will do."

The call ended and Lucy sat at her desk, the phone

still in her hand. With Bonnie distracted and leaving town for a few days, she was going to have to take it upon herself to work out a schedule for the next week that would keep all the bases covered and ensure that none of their clients were shortchanged. She pulled up the list of June events and began to scrutinize each one to see what remained to be done for each, and which tasks she could do by phone and email from St. Dennis. Next she called the office and spoke with Corrine about taking a more active role in several of the up-and-coming commitments. It was a lot to put on their newest employee, but what better way to determine if she was as good as she said she was?

By the time Lucy was finished sending that day's emails, she was stiff from sitting and had the makings of a headache. She stood and stretched and downed a few Advil from the bottle in her purse. She closed her eyes and proceeded to meditate for a moment, thinking that this might be a good time to start going to yoga again.

It might also be a good time to call Clay and see if he had dinner plans. In one of his emails, he mentioned that on Friday nights, there was live music at Captain Walt's. It was country music, but still. Things had been heading in a definite direction last night before Brooke and Logan popped in. Lucy had known exactly what Brooke had been up to, and had to admit she might feel the same way if she thought either of her brothers might be in a position to have his heart broken.

Breaking Clay's heart was the furthest thing from Lucy's mind.

It had seemed so natural to meet him for coffee and

a little early morning conversation after her run. She'd been pretty sure she'd find him at Cuppachino, and hadn't been able to resist spending a few minutes with him. The brief interlude had been just enough to set her day in the right direction. She was hoping to make a morning run part of her daily routine while she was in St. Dennis, and with any luck, coffee with Clay afterward would become a regular part of her morning, too.

"There you are." Grace poked her head into the office.

"Mom." Lucy got up and gave her mother a hug. "So how was your trip? Did you take lots of pictures? Did you have a great time? I want to hear all about it."

"And you will, dear. The trip was great fun and I took a ton of pictures on that digital camera you and Daniel gave me for Christmas. I can't wait to share them with my Facebook friends."

"I can't believe you have a Facebook page."

"Why not? It's a grand way to keep in touch with old friends." Grace leaned on the back of a chair and, to Lucy's eyes, suddenly looked very tired.

"You look as if you could use a nap, Mom."

"I surely could, but I'm afraid I'm not going to get one." Grace sighed. "Andrew just called in sick, so I'm going to have to play hostess in the dining room tonight." She turned her wrist to look at her watch. "Which gives me all of forty minutes to rest up."

"Don't be silly," Lucy told her. "You go upstairs and get some sleep. I'll cover the hostess duties."

"Are you sure, Lucy?" Grace looked torn between relief and mounting a protest.

"I'm positive. Go. You look exhausted."

"It's been a long time since you worked the dining room," Grace reminded her.

"Nothing to it," Lucy assured her.

"Thank you. I won't even try to talk you out of it." Grace smiled. "It's so nice to have you home, to have you part of the inn again. I can't begin to tell you how happy I am that you're here and that you're staying for more than a day or two."

"So am I, Mom."

"Daniel tells me that you're going to run an event in July and another in September."

"It does look that way." Lucy put her arm around her mother's shoulders. "But don't get too used to it. I will be going back to California, you know."

"Oh, I know, but it's such a relief for me not to have to worry about you for a while."

"Worry about me? Why?"

"I worry about something happening to you, surrounded by all those crazy people you read about out there in Hollywood," Grace stated matter-of-factly. "When you're here, with us, I know you're safe. I don't have to worry about something bad happening because, well, where on earth could you possibly be safer than under this roof, with your family?"

Lucy forced a smile and walked her mother to the door.

"Go upstairs and take a good long nap. Sleep right through until the morning if you can."

"Thank you, dear. I'll do my best."

Lucy watched her mother cross the lobby and slowly climb the stairs. She hated to think about her mother getting older, but she certainly did look her age tonight. Of course, it was fatigue after her trip, and surely with a few nights to catch up on her sleep, she'd be herself again.

Lucy logged off her laptop, the irony not lost on her that in all the years she'd lived in Los Angeles, there'd never been an incident that had made her fear for her life. Yet it was here, where she should have been safest, that she'd been assaulted and terrorized and robbed of so much. Thank God she'd never told her mother what had happened to her, Lucy thought as she locked her office. Let Grace go on believing that her family home offered safety and sanctuary. The truth would cause her mother too much pain. Knowing Grace, she would blame herself for not being there when it happened, and she'd carry that guilt for the rest of her life.

Lucy hadn't kept too many secrets from her mother over the years, but this was one she planned to take to her grave.

Chapter 17

FOR all Lucy's good intentions of running every morning, she overslept on Saturday by almost an hour, which meant she not only had to skip her run, but had to skip breakfast as well in order to get down to the lobby to meet Jason Bowers and Daniel to go over the proposed changes to the landscaping that Susanna had wanted.

"You're very accommodating," Jason said after they'd introduced themselves. "Offering to redo your landscaping to accommodate a wedding."

"It's a pretty important wedding," Daniel told him as they walked outside.

"So you said something about moving a gazebo." Jason addressed Lucy. "Let's take a look at where it is now, and where you'd like it to be."

"This way." Lucy led him around the side of the inn. "It's been here for years."

"I can see that," Jason replied as he stepped inside the gazebo and took a look around. "You've got a few splintered floorboards in here, did you know?"

Daniel and Lucy followed Jason inside and looked at the offending floorboards.

"Boy, that doesn't look good," Daniel said. "I guess we could replace them. I should talk to Cam about that."

"You could paint the floor," Jason suggested. "It would look fine."

He walked out of the gazebo and walked around it, taking note of the plantings.

"You've got a lot of old, established vines here that probably look pretty lush when they're all in bloom." Jason knelt down. "Looks like clematis, morning glory, honeysuckle. I'll bet this smells wonderful in the mornings."

"It does. Our guests have commented on that very thing," Daniel told him. "A lot of people like to come out here and sit with a book and just relax. We have wicker sofas and chairs out here in the warm weather."

"You're sure you want to move it?" Jason asked.

Daniel looked at Lucy for a response.

"Susanna really wanted the ceremony in the gazebo overlooking the Bay," Lucy reminded him.

"Let's take a walk over there and check it out."

"This way." Lucy stuck her hands in the pockets of the light jacket she'd tossed on before leaving the inn. She just wanted this to be an easy decision, but the look on her brother's face told her it was going to be anything but.

They walked around to the Bay side, and Lucy led Daniel and Jason to the spot where Susanna had envisioned her wedding as taking place.

"I see your point," Jason said. "This is the perfect spot for a wedding. You have the grove of trees on the one side to give some nice shade during the hottest part of the day, and the view of the Bay could not be prettier." He looked from Daniel to Lucy. "It's your decision, of course."

"Wouldn't it be easier and less expensive to just buy a new gazebo, have it delivered and painted right here on the spot?" Lucy asked.

Jason nodded. "Could be close."

"Then why don't we do that, Danny? Get Cameron to bring in a new one and place it right there. That way, your guests who like to sit and read can still do so in the old gazebo and they won't be inconvenienced if you're having a wedding out here."

"That's a much better idea. Yeah. I like it. Let's do it," Daniel said. "I'll run in and give Cam a call, see how quickly he can get us a new one. Then he can replace the floorboards in the other one." He turned to his sister. "Lucy, I'm leaving this in your hands. You know what you need to have done out here."

"Right." Lucy assured him. "We'll stop by your office when we come in."

Daniel headed inside and Lucy turned to Jason. "We're going to need some rosebushes planted around the base of the gazebo. Medium pink, fragrant, preferably one that will climb up the sides of the structure. Is it possible to buy roses now, in April, plant them, and have them mature enough to be climbing and blooming by the end of June?"

Jason whistled. "That's going to be tough, unless I can find a grower who has bushes to sell that are already very well established. I can make some calls. There is a grower in Pennsylvania that might have what you need, but they're going to want top dollar."

"Go ahead and contact them, see if they have them in sufficient quantity, and see what they'd want for them."

"Are you thinking of a structure about the same size as the one you already have?" Jason asked.

She thought that over. "Maybe slightly bigger."

"For a structure that size, you'll need maybe . . ." Jason appeared to be mentally calculating. "Maybe four good-size bushes on each side, one on either side of the doorway." He nodded as if to himself. "And you wanted a medium pink climbing rose . . . maybe Social Climber. Maybe a David Austin . . ." He turned to Lucy as if remembering that she was there. "I'll call around and see if I can find something that will suit. I'll get back to you as soon as I can. We want to move on this, though, if we find your rose. You're going to want the plants to get their roots into the soil and start putting out a good display of flowers."

"Here's hoping you can find what we need." Lucy crossed her fingers. "Now, we're also going to want some flower beds."

Jason looked around the expanse of lawn. "Where were you thinking of putting them in?"

"I think along this side"—she gestured—"and maybe over there. The greater part of the lawn will have a tent for this wedding coming up."

He studied the areas she'd indicated. "Annuals or perennials?"

"Both, if possible. I'd love to see a lot of bloom here, spring to fall."

"Any particular style?"

She thought about it for a moment. "Maybe something structured for the area closest to the inn, something more casual, sort of cottage-y for the side."

"How big? What color family do you have in mind?"

She walked off the beds with him. "Maybe mostly

soft. Pinks, lavenders, peaches, creams. We want to use this area for weddings, so we want colors that can blend with just about any color scheme."

"Got it." Jason nodded. "I think I know what you want."

"Great. You'll work up an estimate for us?"

"I'll start on it this afternoon, and I'll get you some sketches as soon as possible." Jason gazed up at the inn. "It's a beautiful building. The landscaping you have here—all the shrubs and those ancient trees—it's all perfect. But you're right that you need more color."

"I agree. Shall we go in and talk to Daniel?"

Jason nodded. "Lead the way."

They were almost to the inn's door when Jason said, "So you're Clay's Lucy. I've heard a lot about you. Mostly from Clay."

Her hand on the door, she paused. "Oh. Of course you'd know Clay. You're Brooke's . . ." What had Brooke said?

"Brooke's late husband, Eric, was my brother," Jason told her.

"Right. And you've moved to St. Dennis to be near Logan."

"My nephew. Last of our line."

"I met him the other night. He's seems like a terrific kid. I know Clay dotes on him."

"We all do. And thanks, he *is* a terrific kid. He's my brother all over again."

They crossed the lobby and knocked on Daniel's office door. Lucy outlined the landscaping plans that she and Jason had discussed, then sat back while Jason and her brother went over them. After a few minutes, her mind began to drift.

"Clay's Lucy," Jason had called her. She thought about it for a moment, then realized that yes, that's exactly who she was. She hadn't set out to be his, or anyone else's for that matter, but sometimes life throws you a curve.

Clay's Lucy. She actually liked the sound of it.

As soon as Jason left, she went back into her own office, her phone already in her hand, her fingers dialing Clay's number.

"Hi," he said when he picked up.

"Hi, yourself. Are you busy?" she asked.

"I'm at Logan's T-ball game and I . . . Justin, bend your arms just a little, don't hold them out so straight. That's better . . . Sorry, Lucy."

"No, no. I'm sorry. I interrupted your game. I'll let you get back to it."

"Not before you tell me why you called."

"I was just wondering if, well, if you were free tonight, that maybe . . ."

"Yes."

"I haven't even said what—"

"Doesn't matter. If it involves me doing something—anything—with you, the answer will always be yes."

"I was thinking dinner, maybe someplace with music."

"I'll pick you up." He paused. Maybe something a little different tonight. "I'll come for you around six-thirty. Dress casually."

"How casually?"

"Very."

"I'll see you then."

Lucy wrote up her notes on her meeting with Jason on her electronic file, checked in with Corrine to assure herself that all was well on the West Coast, then turned off the laptop and headed directly for the second floor, where she changed into running clothes. She'd missed her morning run, but she'd make up for it now.

She made it as far up Charles Street as Bling, where Vanessa had just stepped outside.

"Isn't this a gorgeous day?" Vanessa waved to Lucy.

"Glorious," Lucy agreed. "And don't you look fabulous. Pregnancy clearly agrees with you."

"Oh, thanks. I feel terrific now, but I have a way to go yet. We'll see how fabulous I look by July." Vanessa rolled her eyes and laughed. "Now, are you into serious exercise, or can you stop and chat for a minute? We've been really slow today . . ."

"I'm serious about my running, but not so serious that I'd pass up an opportunity to stop by and visit for just a few." Lucy followed Vanessa into the shop. "You're on my list of people to see. I was going to stop in one day this week."

"So it's true. You *are* staying for more than the weekend. Steffie said Wade told her you'd be here for the whole week."

Lucy nodded. "I'm trying to get everything lined up for this wedding at the end of June, and there's so much to do and so many people to see."

"Can't you get someone local to help you?" Vanessa asked.

"I'm going to talk to the event planner that Daniel hired for the inn, see if she can pitch in. She's off until Monday since there's no event this weekend."

"Wade said that you were going to be around a lot this summer," Vanessa continued.

"I have events at the inn, July and September, that will keep me around for a while."

"We'll have to get together while you're here."

"I'd love to." Lucy opened the bottle of water she'd carried with her on her run and took a drink. "By the way, congratulations on your wedding. You were a gorgeous bride, and your house looked beautiful. I wish I could have been there."

"I wish you could have been, too." Vanessa paused, and then frowned. "Where did you see . . ."

"The pictures? Clay emailed them to me."

"That was nice of him." Vanessa looked as if she wanted to say more, but did not.

"It was. I really enjoyed seeing them." She took another sip before screwing the cap back onto the bottle. "Before I forget, there's something I wanted to talk to you about."

"What's that?"

"Our June bride wants to give her wedding guests the royal treatment, including a week's stay at the inn and a very lavish welcoming gift bag. One of the things she wanted was to offer her women friends tokens that could be used for discounts at various shops here in town, and I was wondering—"

"Is this June bride the one who's marrying Robert Magellan?" Vanessa's eyes widened slightly.

Lucy nodded.

"And she wants to draw shoppers into Bling by offering them discounts?"

"Right. I don't know how you feel about that, so if you'd rather not—"

"Are you kidding? Of course I'd rather. I don't know who'd pass up an opportunity like that." Vanessa's eyes took in the shop's inventory in one quick swoop. "I'll make sure there's all fresh stock in that week. Lots of cute walking shorts and skirts. Tennis clothes. Oh, and I have some really sweet knit dresses on order that can be very casual or a little dressy, depending on how they're worn." She smiled at Lucy. "This could be really fun."

"Then I'll put you down as a yes."

"An absolute yes."

"Oh, and one other thing. For the gift bags for her guests, my bride wanted to do canvas totes with a map of St. Dennis on them. Any idea where I could get something like that? I could do a search and have them made myself, but if someone local is already doing them, I'd just as soon use the time for something else."

Vanessa tapped her fingers on the countertop for a moment.

"You can ask Jackie at the gift shop where she gets her things, you know, the coffee mugs and the T-shirts."

"I'm going to need to get a bunch of those to go into the bags."

"Talk to Jackie. I'm sure she can order whatever you want."

"Great. Thanks for the suggestion." Lucy noticed the time on the wall clock. "I should get going. I want to finish my run with enough time to get back to the inn and take a shower . . ."

"Hot date?" Vanessa asked as if she knew.

She probably did, Lucy thought. This *was* St. Dennis, and Vanessa's best friend, Steffie, was married to Clay's business partner.

"Just dinner." Lucy tried to make it sound as casual as possible but didn't think Vanessa was buying it.

"Have a good time."

"Thanks." Lucy started to the door.

"Hey, Lucy," Vanessa called to her just as Lucy was about to push the door open. "Everyone's happy that you're going to be around this summer."

"Thanks, Vanessa. So am I . . ."

And growing happier by the day, Lucy admitted as she finished her run through town and headed back to the inn. It seemed that every day there was one more reason why she was glad to be back.

She chatted with her mother for a few minutes in the family's second-floor TV room, then took a shower and dressed for her date. Clay had said very casual, so she pulled on a pair of jeans and a knit top in a soft shade of gray that had fabric flowers around the slightly dropped neckline. She slipped her feet into a pair of ballet flats and started out of her room just as her phone began to ring.

"Luce, would you mind driving over instead of me picking you up?" Clay asked when she picked up.

"Is something wrong?"

"No, no, I just got a late start."

"I don't mind at all," she told him. "I'll be there in five minutes." She hesitated. "Are you sure everything is all right?"

"Positive. I'll see you when you get here. Just park out back and come in through the kitchen."

Lucy said good night to her mother and her nephew, who were watching a movie.

"Where's Diana?" she asked.

"She's at a friend's for a sleepover," her mother replied, her eyes still on the TV screen.

"Gramma, wouldn't it be cool to have a magic wand like Harry Potter's?" Lucy heard D.J. ask.

"Very cool, dear. Though magic isn't something to be taken lightly." Grace turned to Lucy. "Have fun. Tell Clay we said hello."

Lucy made a mental note to add "Magic isn't something to be taken lightly" to the list of things to discuss with her mother one of these days.

"Will do." Lucy kissed the top of her mother's head, ruffled her nephew's hair, and left the room. She bustled down the steps, waved to the night clerk who had just come on duty, and went to her car wondering what was up with Clay. He'd sounded distracted on the phone.

She parked near the back of the farmhouse and walked to the porch, enjoying the soft evening air that was perfumed by a mass of tulips that ran along the side of the house. There were large clumps of peonies that were a few weeks away from opening, and a huge lilac that was just about to bloom. The sun was drawing down, its fading light casting a golden glow across the fields where the grain was already up and moving gently in an easy breeze. Lucy paused for a moment on the steps to take it all in.

"I thought I heard a car." Clay appeared in the doorway. "What are you doing?"

"Just looking." She turned and smiled. "It's so peaceful and quiet here."

"Well, right now it is. About an hour ago, there were fourteen eight-year-old boys running around out there playing . . ." He stopped for a moment. "I don't really know what they were playing, but they were loud."

"Where are they now?"

"Brooke and two of the other T-ball team mothers took them all out for pizza." He opened the screen door. "Come on in."

"Thanks." She climbed the steps and followed him into the kitchen, where he put down the wooden spoon he'd been holding to give her a welcoming hug and a kiss on the side of her mouth. "Whoa, look who's cooking!"

"I thought we'd eat in tonight."

"Something smells amazing." She sniffed appreciatively at the air.

"Roasted asparagus, baked halibut, and brown rice," he told her.

"Sounds delicious. I've never had roasted asparagus, but I'm game." She glanced around the room. "What can I do to help?"

"You can set the table in the dining room, if you want," he suggested.

"These plates, I'm guessing?" She lifted two plates from the counter.

"Right. Knives, forks, spoons are in the first drawer there on your left." Clay pulled on an oven mitt and opened the oven door.

"Got it."

Lucy went into the dining room and turned on the wall switch for the overhead light. The ancient chandelier came to life and enhanced the now-pale light that filtered through the back window. She'd always loved this room, and felt oddly pleased that so little had changed. The walnut dining room furniture was the same; the china cupboards held the same dishes she remembered the Madisons using for Sunday dinners, and the sideboard held the same glass candlesticks. The red Oriental rug that was worn from years of footsteps still covered the wide plank floor, and the lace tablecloth was the same one she remembered. She set the table, then stood in front of the china cupboard.

When she sensed Clay in the doorway, she said, "I like that nothing's changed."

He shrugged. "When my mom and dad moved to South Carolina, they were going into a small place in one of those over-fifty-five communities and couldn't agree on what to take and what to leave. So they basically took nothing with them and bought smaller furniture for their condo. Then, when my mom bought her town house here last year, she bought all new furniture for herself."

"I'm surprised that she didn't want the antique pieces," Lucy remarked.

"She said they'd all come down through my dad's family and she'd never had a chance to have her own things. I expect Brooke will probably take some stuff, now that she's starting to get settled over in the tenant house."

"It was nice to walk in here and see the room the way I remembered it. It makes me feel . . . I don't know, like I'm home, in a way."

"I didn't see any reason to change things," he said. "I admit that decor isn't much of a priority."

Lucy laughed. "If you saw my apartment, you'd say it wasn't mine either. I've never really had the time to do much more than buy some furniture. I spend more time in my office than I do the apartment."

"You probably need to take a little time off now and then."

"I know. But look who's talking. You have more going on right now than anyone I know. You have all those crops in the ground. Stuff for the restaurants and stuff for your brewery, and then there's the orchard. Do you really think you're going to have time to pick everything you planted?"

"I'm hiring day pickers to do that part, 'cause you're right. I won't have time to do everything myself," he confessed. "But still, I take time to do other things. I walk into town around seven every day for my morning meeting with Wade. I coach Logan's T-ball in the spring and soccer in the fall." He grinned. "And I cook the good stuff I grow, and I'm damned good at it."

"Oh, aren't we the cocky one?" She laughed.

"You can judge for yourself in about—" Clay turned to look at the timer on the stove. "Five minutes. I need to get busy."

Clay returned to the kitchen, and moments later, Lucy joined him.

"There's a bottle of wine opened on the counter there and two glasses," he said. "Would you mind pouring for us?"

"Not at all."

Lucy poured wine into the glasses and took one to Clay at the stove, pausing for just a second to watch him at work. What, she wondered, was so appealing about a man in jeans and a pullover standing over a hot stove, his sleeves pulled up to his elbows?

She handed him his glass and took a sip from her own. The wine was delicious and she looked at the label. She took another sip and let it roll around on her tongue, and wondered if it was offered at the inn. She'd have to check.

"You look lost in serious thought," Clay noted.

"I was thinking about this wonderful wine, and wondering if it was served at the inn."

Clay nodded. "I had it there over the winter. It's from Hunter's vineyard in Ballard."

"I had one of their wines at Vanessa's." She picked up the bottle and studied the label. "I might have to look into this for the wedding. Maybe I'll drive over this week and pick up a few bottles for the menu tasting."

Clay pulled a baking dish out of the oven and set it atop the stove. He dished brown rice from a pot on the stove into a bowl, which Lucy took into the dining room. When she returned, he had the asparagus piled in another bowl and the fish on an oval white plate and was heading into the dining room with it. Lucy grabbed his wineglass and brought it to him.

"This was such a great idea," she said as she took her seat. "Thank you for inviting me."

"You're welcome."

He handed her the fish platter and she helped herself before passing it back to him.

"You are so not the boy I used to know," she told him.

"What's that supposed to mean?" He made a face but she could tell he wasn't offended.

"The Clay Madison who was my best friend growing up couldn't even spread jelly on a piece of bread without glopping it onto the floor."

"I've come a long way, baby."

"I'll say you have."

Midway through the meal, he said, "I almost forgot. You wanted music." He got up and went into the kitchen. A moment later he returned with a CD player in one hand and a stack of discs in their cases in the other. He set the player up on the sideboard and handed the CDs to Lucy. "Your choice."

"No one can ever say that you don't have eclectic taste." She glanced through the plastic cases. "Bruce Springsteen, Nickelback, Tim McGraw, Maroon 5, Kenny Chesney, Bruno Mars, Rascal Flatts, Cream . . . Really?" She held up the psychedelic picture on the case. "Is this a test? Find the one that doesn't go with the others?"

"My dad was a big Clapton fan." Clay shrugged. "I'd replaced a lot of his old albums with CDs one year for his birthday. When my mom moved back, she gave them to me."

"Hannah's not a classic rock fan?"

"Hannah's deep into country now."

"And she let you keep the Rascal Flatts?"

Clay laughed. "I think she left that one here by accident."

Lucy handed him the Tim McGraw. "Let's live like we're dying."

"Good choice." He slipped the disc into the player and turned the volume on low.

"So have you gotten a lot of work done since you've been in St. Dennis?" he asked.

She brought him up-to-date on all she'd accomplished in the past several days.

"Sounds like you've got things under control," he noted.

"For the most part, yes. Things may be a little dicey back home, but I think we're okay. There was an event today that Bonnie was supposed to handle, but her ex-husband broke his leg horseback riding. She flew up to Sacramento to be with him, so she passed the event on to Corrine. I'm waiting for her to check in to let me know how things went today." She patted the pocket of her jeans to make sure she still had her phone.

"Nice of your partner to take care of her ex."

"I don't think he'll be her ex for much longer. I think they're getting back together." Lucy considered what that might mean for their partnership. Bonnie had said that Bob would never move back to L.A.

"How's your new office working out in the inn?"

"It's fine. I could never work there permanently, though. There isn't enough room."

They finished their meal and cleared the table, then rinsed and stacked the dishes in the dishwasher.

"This was a wonderful dinner," Lucy told him. "Thank you again. I'd like to say I'll reciprocate, but I don't have a kitchen and I'm not much of a cook. However, you could come to the inn one night and see what you think of the new chef."

"I'd love to do that, but I have to confess, I'm already a fan of Gavin's," he said. "I took my mom to the inn for her birthday dinner a few weeks ago."

"Ah, that's right. You did tell me that."

"Want to take a stroll outside? There's a skyful of stars tonight. I could see them from the dining room window."

"Sure." She picked up her wineglass on her way to the door.

Once outside, she shivered against the evening air. "I didn't realize how cool it had gotten."

"I'll get you something to put on. Be right back."

Clay disappeared into the house and returned a few minutes later with a fleece-lined jacket that he put over her shoulders. "Brooke left this in the front hall the other day when she stopped by for her mail. She still doesn't have a separate mailbox, so the mailman leaves everything in our box," he explained.

"Thanks. That's much better." She looked up at the sky. "It really is a beautiful night, and a beautiful sky. When you live in a place where there's so much light for the stars to compete with, you forget how many there are, and how dark the nights can be when you're in the country."

Clay put his arm around her and she leaned against him. "'Member when we used to sit out here in the dark and watch for shooting stars?" she asked.

"I do."

"That time seems so long ago, Clay. Sometimes it seems as if I was never really that young."

"Well, I can attest to the fact that you were. You were not only that young, but you were a happy, carefree kid with a great imagination for making up games and a great sense of fun."

"I was, wasn't I?" she murmured. Sometimes it was so hard to remember that time. Tonight wasn't one of them. Tonight she felt like that carefree happy girl again. She wondered how long the feeling would last.

He snapped his fingers. "Wait here."

Clay went inside, then came back out with the CD player under his arm. He plugged it into an outlet on the porch. When the music began to play, he took her in his arms.

"You wanted music," he reminded her. "I thought you might want to dance. . . ."

She smiled. "This is an oldie. Michael Bolton?" Lucy swayed against him. "This song was out when we were in high school."

"Ah, but it's a classic," he told her. " 'When a Man Loves a Woman.' Every guy in school knew all the words to this one. Great make-out song. They played it several times at our junior prom."

"I wouldn't know," she said. "I didn't go."

"I know." He rested his face against the side of hers. "I looked for you all night. The dance was almost over by the time I figured out that you really weren't there."

Lucy sighed. There was no explaining some things. Like why she barely spoke to any guys all through high school, or why, on prom night, she sat in her dark bedroom wondering what it would be like to feel like a normal girl.

Clay tipped her face up to his, and she leaned into a kiss that she'd been expecting. His lips were so soft, so undemanding at first, and he tasted of wine and memories. She held her breath for a moment before reminding herself where she was, and who she was with, and she gave herself over to the moment and the man.

This is the way it's supposed to feel, she thought as his kisses—and hers—grew hungrier and the warmth spread through her. When his lips trailed the side of her face to her throat and he whispered, "Stay, LuLu. Stay with me," she could only nod.

Forgotten, the music continued to play softly as they went into the house and he turned the key in the back door to lock it. Hand in hand they walked through the kitchen into the hall, where, at the bottom of the steps, Clay lifted her in his arms and started up the stairs.

"Hey." Lucy laughed softly. "Isn't this just a little . . . well, dramatic?"

"Just go with it, okay?" She could hear the amusement in his voice. "Every guy has this secret fantasy of sweeping his girl off her feet and carrying her to his bed. Don't women dream of being swept away?"

She didn't want to ruin the moment by telling him that no, she didn't have such fantasies, that the thought of anyone—anyone but him, anyway—grabbing her and carrying her off terrified her. But she suspected that maybe other women might feel differently. So instead of answering him, she nuzzled his neck and closed her eyes, and reminded herself that, with Clay, she was safe.

The rest of the night seemed to pass in a haze of want and need. His hands and his mouth seemed to have been everywhere at once, and she'd given in to every sensation without hesitation. There'd been a moment—a split second—when she'd felt a twinge of panic begin to curl inside her, but it passed quickly. It was true, what she'd read: it really was different when you were with someone you really cared for, someone you trusted with your whole heart—and there'd never been a man she trusted more than she trusted Clay.

Lucy pushed away the past and allowed herself to feel and touch and experience pleasure, to feel cherished by this wonderful man who only wanted to love her. She hoped that by the end of the night, she'd have found the piece of herself that had been stolen so long ago.

Most of all, she hoped that this feeling of peace, this joy, would last beyond the night.

Chapter 18

CLAY lay in a state of contented semiconsciousness, not quite asleep, not quite awake. He'd wanted Lucy so badly for so long that he could hardly believe she was here, in his bed, and that they'd just shared the most unbelievable night together. He reached out for her, and touched . . . nothing. He opened his eyes and sat up. In the pale light from the moon, he could see Lucy standing near the foot of the bed silhouetted against the window.

"Lucy, what are you doing?" he asked.

"Getting dressed," she said.

"Why?"

Her fingers paused on the button of her jeans and she seemed to freeze.

"You weren't going to leave me in the middle of the night, were you?" He pushed the pillows up behind his head. "Don't you know that when two people share what we shared, one doesn't leave without a good-bye and a good reason?"

"I just . . . I thought . . ." She sounded confused.

"Come here, please," he said softly. Something about her voice made him go cold inside.

She walked to the side of the bed and stood there. His hands drew her to him and she went without protest, but she felt stiff in his arms, not at all like the willing lover who'd shared the night with him. Whatever it was that was causing this . . . *disconnect* in her, he was going to get to the bottom of it.

"LuLu, tell me what's wrong. Is it something I did, or said? Did I hurt you somehow?" It occurred to him then that perhaps there was something else going on. "Lu, is there someone else, someone you're involved with back in California? Is that what's bothering you?"

She shook her head. "There's no one else, Clay. I'm just not used to . . ." She struggled with her words. "I'm not used to staying."

For a moment, he wasn't sure he'd heard her correctly. "You mean, after . . . ?"

She nodded. "I just always . . . I need to leave."

"Stay this time." He held her closely, certain he hadn't gotten the whole answer, but not sure she was ready to tell him more.

She nodded again, and he pulled up the blanket to cover her. There were so many things he wanted to say, so much was in his heart, but she seemed so fragile suddenly that he feared she would bolt. She lay with her back against him for a long time, her breathing at first slightly ragged. She was so still that he thought she'd fallen asleep.

"Clay, remember when you asked me why I acted like I did back in high school?" The room was so quiet that her whisper filled it.

"I remember."

"That summer . . . I was raped." She swallowed so hard that he could hear it. "At the inn."

His breath caught in his chest.

"He was there with his family. My parents were away, on that trip to Maine. My parents wanted all of us to be able to do all of the jobs at the inn. My job that summer was with housekeeping." She paused briefly to swallow again but continued. "He came into his room when I was starting to change the bed linens. He started saying how he was so glad that I'd been waiting there for him and how he knew I'd been wearing those short shorts just for him and how he knew I'd been wanting him to notice and how he knew what I wanted from him. And then he pushed me down on the bed and started kissing me, and the next thing I knew, he was tearing at my clothes."

She spoke in a near monotone, her emotions all beneath the surface. Clay held his breath. Had she really just said she'd been raped? How could something so terrible have happened to her, and he hadn't known?

"I was so scared I could barely speak, and when I started to call for my brother, he put one hand over my mouth and just continued raping me as if I wasn't trying to scream and kick him. When he was done, he told me not to tell anyone what happened because he'd deny it and no one would believe me. He said he'd kill my little brother. Then he went into the shower as if nothing had happened. I lay there for a long time, till I heard the shower turn off. Then I wrapped up the sheet and my clothes and ran back to my room."

"No one saw you?"

She shook her head. "There were sailboat races

out on the Bay, and everyone was out on the lawn watching."

"What happened next?"

"I went back to my room and I took a shower and tried to scrub him off me. He wore this aftershave and it seemed like the smell was in my skin and I couldn't wash it away. It seemed like I smelled that for weeks."

"But I mean, what happened when you told Dan? What happened when you called the police?" Clay knew that Hal Garrity was the chief of police back then. He would have skinned her assailant alive.

"I didn't tell Danny. I told him I was sick and I stayed in my room until the weekend, when I figured he'd be gone," she said. "I didn't call the police."

Clay sat up a little straighter but never let go of her. "You didn't tell anyone?" he asked in disbelief.

She shook her head.

"But when your parents came back . . ."

She shook her head again. "I never told anyone. Not anyone. Just you. Now."

It took him a moment to take it all in.

"You were raped when you were fourteen and you never told anyone?" Incredulous, he asked, "Why not?"

"Because I was afraid no one would believe me, like he said, and I was afraid he really would hurt Ford. And, Clay, I was very, very scared that Danny would have killed the guy and then my parents would have had to come back from their vacation early and—"

"Lu, this guy *raped* you. He hurt you and forced you to do something you didn't want to do. Do you really think your parents would have cared about their vacation?"

"Everyone had made such a big thing about it. They'd never taken a vacation, Clay. They'd spent every summer here at the inn working their tails off. They finally got the chance to get away. They trusted Danny and me and Ford to take care of things." She sat up and turned around, her hands covering her face. "Do you have any idea how guilty my mother would have felt that she'd left us?"

"It isn't as if she'd left you guys unsupervised. There were adults at the inn with you, weren't there? I seem to recall that there was a manager here who looked after you kids a lot."

"Mrs. Englewood."

"You couldn't have told her?"

"I couldn't tell anyone." She wiped the tears from her face with the sheet. "I never wanted anyone to know."

"You haven't talked to any of your girlfriends—"

"I don't really have any girlfriends," she told him.

"How 'bout the guys you've dated . . . ?"

She shook her head. "I never felt like I could share that."

"That's why you don't feel comfortable staying over?"

She nodded.

"LuLu, have you thought about talking to someone professionally about this?"

"I've thought about that. I thought it might help me to deal with . . . relationships better. I know I'm always so guarded. But then, there was never anyone I cared so much about that I thought it was worth going through the pain of talking about it."

"How are you feeling now?"

"Better. I'm glad I told you. I've wanted to forever. Even back then, I wanted to, but I went through this stage where I didn't want anyone close to me, didn't want to have to talk."

"So you pushed everyone away." He was starting to understand.

"It was easier than talking about it. It was always on my mind, and I was always afraid it would slip out." Her voice softened even more. "Even you. I knew what you would have done if I'd told you."

"Damn straight." Anger, then rage, began to replace the shock he'd initially felt listening to her recounting of the attack. Now it was all he could do to keep his hands from forming into fists, and for those fists to keep from punching something—like the nearest wall—but he figured physical violence was not the best way to comfort and reassure her that she was safe with him. "But you can still press charges. It's damn near impossible to hide these days, you can find anyone on the Internet. You were a minor, and I doubt there's a statute of limitations on assaults on minors. Besides, rape is a felony—no statute there. You could—"

"I don't even know who he was. I didn't even know his name."

"But you could have found out. You had the room number and you could have checked—"

"Don't you understand? I didn't want to know. I wanted to pretend it hadn't even happened. Since then, I have second-guessed myself a thousand times.

I keep thinking, what if he did this to other girls back then? What if he's still doing it? If I'd called the police when it happened, would it have saved someone else? But even if I knew who he was and wanted to press charges now, how could I prove it? How do I prove that it was rape and not consensual? What evidence do I have that it even happened?" She shook her head. "I kept quiet and he got away with it, and there's nothing I can do about it now."

"I wish I'd known, LuLu. He wouldn't have gotten away with it if I'd known."

"I know." She reached up and touched his face. "And I'm so sorry that you thought somehow it was you. I never thought you'd think it had something to do with you. It was all about me back then. I should have thought about the way other people were feeling."

"No, you shouldn't have. You were victimized. You suffered a trauma. But you should have talked to someone, LuLu."

"In retrospect, I wish I had."

"That's why you don't like to come home so much." The obvious finally occurred to him. "Why you put so much distance between yourself and St. Dennis."

"I have the worst nightmares when I stay at the inn. Though I have to admit, this time around, it hasn't been too bad."

"Maybe now that it's out in the open . . . well, not exactly in the open, but at least you've talked about it . . . maybe now coming back won't seem so terrible."

"I hate feeling that way about my home. I hate that feeling of panic when I wake up in the middle of the night and wonder if he's come back, if he's in the building. I hate what he did to me and I hate what it did to my life and my relationship with my family. I know it hurt my mother that I spent part of my time here in December sleeping at Steffie's. I told my mother Stef needed help making her wedding favors."

"Hey, you can always stay here."

"Thanks. You're a sport." Her smile was faint, but still, it was the start of a smile.

"I *am* a sport." He gathered her to him and rested her head against his chest. "No more slipping out in the middle of the night, okay? You need to stay with me." Clay paused, then rephrased his statement. "I need you to stay with me. I've waited a long time for you."

They sat in silence for a moment, Clay gently stroking her arm. Finally, he said, "I was in a serious relationship with a girl for three years when I was in college. We got engaged, and we almost got married."

"Why didn't you?"

"Because I realized that the biggest part of the attraction was that she reminded me of you. She was about your size and she had kind of reddish hair, like yours, but she wasn't you, and I couldn't go through with it." He brushed her hair back from her face. "You're my girl, LuLu. I think I've always known it."

"Clay, I'm not staying. My home and my life are back in L.A. You need to remember that." Lucy sat up. "It's just for the summer . . ."

"I understand." He did. He tried not to think about it, but he did understand. "I'll take whatever I can have of you. 'Just for the summer' is better than never."

Still, he knew that he wanted more, wouldn't be satisfied with less than all of her. How he'd make that happen, he didn't know. The only thing Clay knew for sure at that moment was that he wanted *always*.

Chapter 19

WHEN Lucy awoke to the sound of water running somewhere in the distance, her first thought was that rain was beating against the windows at the inn. She opened her eyes, and looked around, and remembered.

"Not in Kansas anymore," she whispered.

She looked over her shoulder and found the other side of the bed empty, and figured the sound she heard was the shower. She tossed off the blanket she'd been wrapped in and sat on the edge of the bed.

It had been one hell of a night.

Had she really poured out the whole story to Clay? She was pretty sure she had.

He'd been visibly upset by what she told him, but thankfully, there'd been no sign of the judgment she'd feared, no indication that he blamed her for what happened. Her rapist had told her repeatedly that she was to blame for what happened, that she'd been blatantly "asking for it." Lucy knew that hadn't been true, and Clay seemed to know it, too. He never once questioned her or doubted her recounting of the event. On the contrary, he'd been angry that she'd never reported the assault, that her rapist had never been made to face the consequences for what he'd done to her, though she was pretty sure he understood why it had taken her so long to talk about it.

In retrospect, maybe she could have—should have—handled things differently, but the child she'd been had lacked the wisdom and the foresight of the woman she'd become. And truthfully, while the memory had hindered her from forming close relationships in the past, it hadn't stopped her from forming one with Clay now, or from becoming a strong and independent woman who had been taking care of herself for years, and doing a damn fine job of it.

"You're my girl," Clay had said the night before. "Just for the summer is better than never . . ."

She wished she'd been able to offer him something more than "I'm not staying."

"Hey, she rises." Clay walked back into the room, dressed in only a pair of jeans, drying his hair with a towel.

He walked to the bed and kissed her on the mouth. "How 'bout breakfast?"

"As much as I'd rather stay, I think I should be getting back to the inn. My mom—Danny—everyone's going to think I've been kidnapped."

"They knew you were coming here, right?"

"I told Mom."

"Then they know where you are." He grinned. "And your mom is probably not too distressed about it."

"You're probably right. She's always reminding me what a wonderful young man you are."

"Of course you don't argue with her."

"Certainly not." Still dressed from having gotten up to leave in the middle of the night before Clay stopped her, Lucy began to look for her shoes. "Of course, if I marched into the inn wearing the same clothes I had on when I left, I imagine tongues would wag."

"This is St. Dennis. It's part of the culture. Some people actually believe that tongue wagging will be the next big Olympic sport. They train for it from birth."

She found her shoes and sat back on the bed while she slipped into them, and thought for a moment. She wasn't ready to say good-bye just yet.

"How about we have breakfast at the inn?" she suggested.

Clay raised one eyebrow. "That will give the tongues plenty to wag about."

"If we wait until later in the morning, I would agree. However, at this early hour on a Sunday morning, the dining room could be fairly empty."

"I'm game if you are."

Lucy found and used the bathroom at the end of the hall while Clay finished getting dressed. As they were leaving, each in their own car, Lucy rolled down her window, pointed to the BMW parked near the garage, and asked, "Did Brooke get a new car?"

"That's Jesse's. I guess Logan ended up staying over at Dallas's with Cody last night, and Brooke decided to take advantage of being child-free by having Jesse stay. He doesn't sleep over when Logan is there. Brooke's not comfortable with it and Jess wants to ease into their lives rather than move too quickly so that Logan can get used to him, develop a relationship of his own." Clay began to roll his window back up, then paused. "Before I forget, the party to celebrate Jesse's grandfather turning over the family law practice to him is next Saturday night. Want to be my date?"

"Sure. I'd love to go. It'll be my last night here before I have to go back."

Clay signaled for her to go first down the drive, so she turned the car around and headed off to the inn.

The sky threatened rain and the streets were almost empty of traffic, though Lucy suspected the churches' parking lots were filled or would be before too much longer. The inn's lot, too, was filled, and Lucy and Clay both had to park back by the cabins and walk up to the back door.

Lucy had been right: there were plenty of empty tables in the dining room, and they took one overlooking the Bay. Lucy had grabbed menus on their way into the room, and once they made their selections, she went into the kitchen to place their order. Moments later, a waitress delivered coffee to them.

"Shall I leave the pot?" the waitress asked after she'd poured for them.

"Please," both Clay and Lucy replied at the same time.

"Great view from here," Clay said as he sampled his coffee.

"It's too bad it's so cloudy this morning. The inn has great views from every side," Lucy told him. "The back and one side have views of the Bay, the front and the other side look out to Cannonball Island and the sound. My I-forget-how-many-greats grandfather who designed the inn sited it so that they would have water views whichever window they looked out of. His wife was from England, and she liked to think of her family being on the other side of the water. Which, of course, they weren't because the Bay isn't the Atlantic, but I suppose she may have been thinking about the Bay flowing into the ocean."

"How do you know that? That that's what she thought about?" he asked.

"Besides being a well-known and, may I say, a respected travel writer of her day, Cordelia Sinclair kept personal journals. One every year. They're all in the library here."

"You read them all?"

"Her travel books were wonderful, but her journals were fascinating. She was a terrific storyteller. She wrote about how she met the first Daniel Sinclair and how they fell in love. How she came to live here, the fun she had buying the furnishings—many of which are still here, by the way, though most of the best pieces are upstairs in our family quarters. How she'd had to adapt to living in America, how she missed her family. All about their children and their grandchildren. I still take down a volume every now and then."

"This is the woman in the portrait in the lobby?"

"Yes. She was quite something, in more ways than one." Lucy's phone began to vibrate in her pocket. She took it out and checked the caller ID. "Clay, would you mind if I took this? It's Corrine."

"Go right ahead."

Lucy went into the lobby and paced while Corrine gave her a rundown of the event she'd covered for Bonnie from the night before. Other than a few "uh-huhs," Lucy hadn't had to say much because apparently, everything had gone off without a hitch. Corrine obviously had proven to be a more than adequate substitute for Bonnie, and Lucy made sure she heaped on the praise before she hung up.

"Is everything okay?" Clay asked when Lucy returned to the table.

"Better than okay. It seems that our newest hire may be a superstar." She gave him an abbreviated summary. "Which is very reassuring, since I'm not sure when Bonnie will be back."

"You look a little anxious about that."

"I *am* anxious," she confessed. "I know she wants to be with Bob, especially now when he needs help, but the business isn't set up for anyone to be absent for too long a time."

"Even you?"

"Especially me." The more she thought about it, the more anxious she became. "When I agreed to do this June wedding, I assumed that Bonnie would be there to pick up the slack for me. The thought of going into the wedding season with her not there makes me extremely nervous."

"But you have good people working for you, right?"

Lucy nodded. "We do. But there's only so much one person can do. If we have two big events scheduled for the same day, we need two people to cover each one."

"So when's wedding season?"

"Starts in May, goes right into the fall. But May through the end of June is the peak. We're booked solid for eight weeks, both days. Some days, there's more than one wedding." She frowned. "Bonnie and

I are going to have to have a talk. I know she's doing a lot by phone and email, but there are times when she's going to have to be on-site."

"I think before you get too worried, you should have that talk."

"As soon as we can sit down face-to-face. There are some things you shouldn't do by phone or email."

Their breakfasts were served, and Lucy fell silent as she began to eat.

"Are you that hungry or that worried?" Clay finally asked.

She looked up and smiled. "A little of both. I'm thinking now about the Magellan wedding and everything that has to be done this week."

"I'm betting you've got a game plan."

Lucy laughed. "Oh, do I. My lists have lists. Every day broken down by who I need to speak with directly, who I need to email, and who I need to text."

"What's on the list for today?"

"About two dozen phone calls, including the one to the woman whose anniversary is being celebrated here at the inn in July. The one who blackmailed Danny into having me plan their event." She poked at her eggs Benedict with her fork. "She threatened to sue the inn for breach of contract if I didn't agree."

"She's the woman who was bumped from June for the Magellan wedding?"

She nodded. "It's not just her, it's her entire family. Dan said they've been loyal patrons of the inn forever. In all fairness, longtime guests do deserve special consideration, which is why Danny is comping a few days for the people whose reservations had to be changed. I just don't like that she threatened him. I'll be happy when that event is over. Usually I enjoy the parties I've put together, but I'm going into this one not loving the client."

"It's only one day, right?"

"Right. And it's a pretty small event, so I shouldn't have to have too much contact with her directly once the nuts and bolts are figured out. She's already emailed me a list of what she has in mind. I can make it happen without her being too involved from this point."

"Isn't that the idea of having someone else plan your event? So that someone else does all the work?"

"One would think," she said, "but you'd be surprised at how many people hire someone to plan the event but want to have their fingers in every stage of the planning."

"Like the future Mrs. Magellan?"

"Yes and no. Susanna knows what she wants and is capable of putting this thing together on her own. She's highly organized, and if she wasn't so involved in her husband's foundation, she could do this. But she doesn't have the time, and she doesn't have the contacts. Besides, she's so nice and she's so happy to be marrying her love, I don't mind her being all over this. She's waited a long time for Robert."

"I know how she feels."

She could have said, *I think maybe I've been waiting for you, too.* Instead, she merely reached across the table and touched her fingers to his hand.

After breakfast, they walked outside so that Lucy could point out the changes that were in the works for the big June wedding. The air was still cool and the clouds darker and lower in the sky.

"New gazebo here, garden beds there and there, and one big tent over there." She paused, thinking about the tent. "No, maybe two tents. We could have the cocktail hour in one while dinner is being set up in the other, then have the band and the dance floor in the tent where we served cocktails."

In her mind she could already see it. There'd be white furniture—sofas and love seats and some big ottomans—in one part of the cocktail/dancing tent. The bandstand would be used by the string quartet during the cocktail hour. It would be perfect, assuming that Susanna liked it. Timing, of course, would be everything, but . . .

"Lucy." Clay waved a hand in front of her face.

"What? Oh, sorry. I just had the best idea."

"I know. Two tents." Clay looked amused. "I'm guessing you just added one more name to that list of people to call this week."

"I'm sorry. The thought just sort of caught me by surprise."

He stood behind her and wrapped his arms around her.

"Look to your left. There's a bald eagle," he said.

"I see it. It's so dramatic, sweeping right over those whitecaps on those big wings, against that dark gray sky that you know is going to let loose any minute now. I always forget how big eagles are until I see one. I wonder where it's going."

"They've been nesting out on Goat Island for the last five or six years," Clay told her.

"Anyone ever figure out why it's called Goat Island?"

"Not as far as I know."

They stood close together, taking in the morning and watching the boats heading out into the Bay as the very first of the raindrops began to fall.

"One day while you're here, we're going to go crabbing," he told her.

She smiled, remembering all the times they'd crabbed together as kids. Those were happy times, and the thought of reliving them cheered her. "It's a date."

Clay's phone began to ring.

"Damn cell phone. I should toss it," he muttered, but took it out of his pocket and answered it in spite of himself. "Okay, buddy. Sure. No, I didn't forget. As long as it's all right with Cody's mom, it's okay with me. I'll pick you up in . . ." He peered around Lucy to look at his watch. "I guess that would be now. Ten minutes. But you have to be ready, okay?"

He returned the phone to his pocket.

"That was Logan wanting to know if I would pick him up at Cody's house now because I'd promised him lunch out and a movie today if he got an A on his science test this week, which he did."

"Isn't it a little early for lunch?"

"Yes, but he just spilled grape juice on his pants, so he has to go home first to change, and the show we're going to starts at twelve-thirty in Ballard, and he's afraid it will start without him."

"You're a good uncle, Clay."

"He's a good kid."

"I'll walk to the car with you."

The rain began to fall faster and they hastened their steps to the parking lot. Clay left Lucy at the back door rather than have her run with him through the rain to his car.

"We can say good-bye right here," he said as they ducked under the inn's overhang.

"I'll talk to you soon." She reached up and kissed him on the lips. "Have fun with Logan."

"I will." Clay took off across the lot. His quick step turned into a jog just as the downpour began.

Lucy stood near the door, her arms folded over her chest as if to ward off the chill, and watched the Jeep as it emerged from the back of the lot and swung past the porch. Clay raised his hand in a wave and soon disappeared behind the trees that grew along the drive. She missed him the minute he was gone, and the realization startled her.

The rain dripped through the overhang and ran down her back in cold streams. By the time she turned and went inside, her shirt was soaked. It took a hot shower, an old sweatshirt, and a cup of tea to warm her again.

She worked in her office until two, when she stopped to have lunch with her mother. Then, the rain having stopped, she drove to Scoop to talk to Steffie about offering tokens to the Magellan guests. That she could get a dish of world-class ice cream while she was there was purely incidental.

There wasn't much of a crowd when she arrived, so after she ordered, at Stef's urging, the flavor of the week—jelly-bean fudge—she had a few minutes to talk to Steffie about her proposal.

"Vanessa told me about your idea," Steffie said. "I was hoping you'd ask me to be part of it, too."

"I'm delighted that you're in," Lucy replied. "I was thinking maybe we could offer tokens for a free cone. Robert and Susanna would, of course, pay you for however many tokens they decide to go with."

"I'll go one better. I'll make an ice-cream flavor just for them. After all, Wade and Clay are talking about making a special beer."

"Something special, an ice cream never seen before . . . ?"

"Well, never seen before at Scoop. You know they say that there's nothing new under the sun, but yes. Something very special that I'll come up with just for them." Stef handed Lucy her dish. "Tell me something about the bride."

"Like what?" Lucy helped herself to napkins.

"Like, what colors does she like?"

"I know she wants lots of pink roses. Medium pink, not pale. She specified that." Lucy took herself to a table and sat. "Oh, and she's pretty sophisticated."

"I'll have to think about it."

Stef went into the back room, where she concocted her flavors, and Lucy picked at her ice cream with a plastic spoon. The door opened and a couple in their fifties entered the shop and went directly to the ice-cream cases. They chattered about the various flavors.

"I never heard of some of these," the woman said. "What do you suppose is in walnut surprise?"

"You mean besides walnuts?" her companion replied.

"Dried cherries and rum." Steffie emerged from the back room, a mischievous grin on her face. "We don't sell it to anyone under eighteen," she deadpanned.

"I'll have to see your driver's license if you want a taste."

Lucy took her iPhone out of her bag to check messages. There were three new texts. One was from Clay, so she opened that first.

Miss you already.

She sighed and wished for once in her life that things could be easy. She'd never shied away from work or asked anyone who worked for her to take on something she herself would shirk from. But this . . . this falling-in-love business . . .

Had she really just thought *falling in love*?

"Lucy, I've got it!" Stef called to her as she served the couple. "Balsamic strawberry!"

Lucy thought about it for a moment. "It's perfect. It's sophisticated and it's pink."

"And the strawberries, of course, will be local," Stef continued. "Though I'll either have to freeze them as soon as they're picked, or make the ice cream a few weeks early and freeze it, since berry season will have passed by the end of June. Damn. We'll miss the season by about two or three weeks."

"Stef, you really are good at this. Are you sure I can't talk you into coming back to L.A. with me and opening up a shop there and making special ice creams for all my events?"

"Not a chance. I know where I belong. I have everything I could ever want right here." Stef flashed her thousand-watt smile, obviously pleased at having come up with the perfect flavor in record time. "Now all I have to do is find a name for my creation."

"What's wrong with 'balsamic strawberry'?"

"Nothing, except it's not special enough. It should reflect the person for whom we're making it."

The couple at the counter paid for their cones and took a table a few away from Lucy.

"O Susanna!" Steffie shouted gleefully.

Lucy looked around to see if anyone responded.

"Lucy! That's it!" Stef all but danced across the small shop.

"That's what?"

" 'O Susanna.' That's what I'm going to call the ice cream."

"O Susanna," Lucy repeated, a smile spreading across her face. Of course. What could be more perfect? "Stef, you really are a genius."

"I have my moments," Steffie said modestly.

"It's inspired. I can't wait to tell Robert and Susanna. They're going to love it." Lucy ate the last bite of her ice cream, dabbed at the corners of her mouth with a napkin, and grabbed her bag. There were several other items she'd wanted to discuss with Susanna, but the ice-cream shop wasn't the place, and besides, her list was on her desk. She couldn't wait to get back to her office, pull out her notes, and make that call. "Thanks, Stef."

"Let me know what they think of it," Stef called as Lucy headed out the door.

"I will."

The song—"O Susanna"—was in her head all the way to the inn, but as earworms went, she decided, it wasn't so bad. It was a song she'd learned as a child but hadn't thought of in years. Leave it to Steffie to come up with something like that. Lucy hadn't been kidding when she'd said she wished she could take

Stef back to L.A. with her. What fun it would be to be able to offer brides their own ice-cream flavor to be served at their wedding reception.

Then again, no.

What would St. Dennis be without Scoop and places like Bling, Cuppachino, Book 'Em, Lola's Café, Sips, Cupcake? They were all part of what made their town unique. Like the Inn at Sinclair's Point, she reminded herself, each lent its own special something to the flavor of the community.

And today's flavor, apparently, was O Susanna.

Chapter 20

I F Madeline was surprised to find Lucy's note on her desk on Monday morning asking to meet after Lucy returned from her meeting with Olivia at Petals and Posies, she gave no sign.

"I hope you won't mind giving me a hand with some of the things on my to-do list for the Magellan wedding," Lucy started by saying. "Dan tells me you're wonderfully organized and great with details."

"Thank you." The young woman looked pleased at the compliment. "My mom always said the devil was in the details."

"Very true." Lucy handed Madeline a file. "I'm the same way. So I hope you'll understand why my lists have lists."

Madeline laughed, opened the file, and scanned the typed pages. "You weren't kidding."

"Sadly, no. This wedding is going to be a mega-production. There will be so much going on that week, my head threatens to explode every time I think about it."

"Wow, I heard this was going to be involved, but I had no idea it was going to be this involved."

"Which explains why I need your help. Are you in?"

"Are you kidding? Other than the fact that it is my job, and Dan's my boss, would I pass up the chance to work with you?" She rolled her eyes. "I am definitely in. Where do I start?"

"Let's go over the entire week's worth of events and see where you can best assist."

"Fine with me. I'll do whatever you need . . ."

Lucy breathed a sigh of relief. She'd been worried that Madeline might not be happy that someone else was coming onto her turf and taking over what some might think should be her job. The meeting lasted over two hours, with Lucy explaining each detail and Madeline taking notes. By noon, they had a game plan.

"I can't thank you enough for pitching in," Lucy told her. "I know you have a few events of your own scheduled."

"All under control," Madeline assured her as she swept her notes into the file and headed back to her own office.

"If you have any questions, or have any problems, let me know right away," Lucy called after her.

"Will do." Madeline's cheery voice trailed down the hall.

The work divided—certainly not equally; there were some things that Lucy had to tend to herself— Lucy began to make the calls she needed to make and read a few emails while she was on hold for this call or that. She stopped for a quick lunch before heading into town to approach other merchants about the discount tokens Susanna wanted to give out to her

guests. She figured if she could line all those up between today and tomorrow, she could arrange to
have the tokens made by a company she'd used for
something similar in L.A., and that would be one
time-consuming thing off the list. Madeline suggested
that instead of buying the mugs and T-shirts from the
gift shop in town, she order them from the supplier
herself and have them made with a picture of the inn
on one side and the town's slogan, "Discover St. Dennis," along with the bride and groom's names and the
date of the wedding on the other. She offered to draw
up the map of St. Dennis and arrange for the tote
bags to be made locally. She knew someone who had
a craft shop who could hand-make them.

All of the merchants Lucy met with loved the idea
of giving out tokens to the wedding guests that would
bring them into the town and entice them to shop.
Not surprisingly, no one turned Lucy down. Besides
assuring that Susanna would have what she wanted
for her guests' gift bags, stopping into each of the
shops gave Lucy the opportunity to reacquaint herself
with some people she hadn't seen in years as well as
to meet the newcomers. By late afternoon, she'd been
to every shop except Cupcake, which she'd saved for
last.

"Hey, Brooke," Lucy called when she went inside
the pretty pink shop with the striped awning and,
oddly, a FOR RENT sign on the side door.

"Be with you in a minute," Brooke called from the
back. A moment later, she emerged with a tray of
freshly frosted cupcakes.

"Hello, Lucy Sinclair." Brooke smiled when she
saw who her customer was.

"What's with the 'For Rent' sign out there?" Lucy asked. "You just opened a few months ago."

"Oh, that's for upstairs. The last tenant used it as a photography studio." Brooke placed the tray on the counter. "So what's up? I doubt you stopped in just to ask about that sign."

"I've been stopping by some of the shops this afternoon . . ." Lucy began.

"I heard. I was hoping you'd be stopping here as well." Brooke lifted the tray in Lucy's direction. "Cupcake?"

"I really shouldn't . . ." Lucy glanced at the beautiful confections.

"Oh, of course you should." Brooke set the tray on the counter. "Lemon supreme, mint chocolate, strawberry chiffon—"

"Couldn't you make this easy and just make something ordinary, like vanilla?"

"My friend, in the right hands, vanilla is never ordinary."

Lucy picked the mint chocolate and took a bite. "Heaven. You're too good at this. You should do a bang-up business come summer when all the tourists are in town."

"I hope so. I do pretty well with the restaurants and they all tell me that my fancy cupcakes sell really well as desserts, but they're really labor-intensive, so it's good to be able to make some that are simply frosted without all the flowers and such. I do keep a few of the fancy models for those times when someone rushes in and wants something special, but for the most part, the best sellers are just frosted with maybe a few sprinkles."

"I love the mint in the frosting," Lucy told her. "It's delicious."

"Thanks." Brooke leaned on the counter. "There's coffee over on the counter if you'd like a cup."

"I would love one. I didn't realize it until you said the word, but coffee is exactly what I need right now."

"Help yourself. I'll have one, too, and we can sit at that little table there by the window. I'm usually pretty slow at this time of the day."

"Great idea. I could use a break."

"Hey, Clay tells me that you're coming to Jesse's party on Saturday. You'll get to see the old Enright place again."

"The party is definitely there? He left that part out. Now I'm really excited."

"I was trying to work up the nerve to ask Curtis about having the party there, but he offered before I asked. Of course I jumped at it. The only other option is my house, and it's a little small for all the people I was inviting."

Brooke waited until Lucy had poured her coffee before pouring her own.

"This is lovely to sit and visit and have such a delicious treat." Lucy sat and shrugged out of the cardigan she'd tossed on before leaving the inn. "I could definitely get used to this."

"So could I." Brooke sighed. "So, aren't you going to ask me if I want to take part in the 'shop St. Dennis' movement you're planning?"

"It isn't exactly a movement, and I can't really take credit for the idea, though I think it's terrific. I love that so many new people will get to experience our pretty town."

Brooke stared at her. "*Our* pretty town?"

Lucy nodded and took another bite of cupcake.

"I thought you considered yourself a West Coast-er these days," Brooke said.

Lucy stared at her for a moment. "I have lived out there for a long time, but when I'm here . . . I still feel part of it. St. Dennis is my hometown, after all."

"I'm happy to hear you say that."

Lucy put her cup down. "This is about Clay again, isn't it."

"I saw your car there the other night," Brooke said gently. "I know it's going to just about kill him when you leave."

"I've never done anything to make him think I was staying here, Brooke. I'm not leading him on. . . ."

"I don't mean to imply that you are. I'm sorry if it came out that way." Brooke touched Lucy's arm. "I have a business, too, so I know how hard you have to work to become successful. And God knows, your business is a huge success. I always see your name mentioned in those upscale wedding magazines and sometimes in the celebrity weeklies. 'So-and-so's wedding planner was Shaefer and Sinclair.' I know you must have busted your butt to achieve that level of success, so I get that part and I congratulate you for having made it."

"But . . ."

"But my brother is in love with you . . . and as much as I applaud your success and appreciate that your life is somewhere else . . ."

"I get it. I do. And for the record, I care about Clay

a great deal—more than I ever thought I'd care about anyone—and I don't know what to do about it. I have a lot of commitments and a lot of people depending on me. Right now I just want to get through the Magellan wedding. It means so much to Robert and Susanna, and frankly, it means a lot to the inn. Dan's been working really hard to make the inn the premier destination wedding spot on the Chesapeake, and if we pull this off, coming on the heels of Dallas's wedding, it will put the inn permanently on the map."

Brooke nodded. "I understand. But I also understand that Clay is so psyched for this summer, for spending time with you. I know he's hoping for some miracle and that you won't leave. So what happens at the end of the summer, Lucy? What happens to Clay then?"

"I don't know, Brooke. I haven't had a lot of time to think about it. This thing with Clay is so new . . ."

"New?" Brooke raised an eyebrow. "Honey, Clay has never *not* loved you. 'This thing' has always been—"

The door opened and Barbara Noonan from the bookstore came in.

"Hi, Barb." Brooke got up from the table to wait on her.

"Hello, Brooke," she said. "Lucy, I haven't seen you in years, and here we are, twice in the same day." To Brooke, she said, "My nieces are coming for dinner and I just realized I have no dessert. What can you tempt me with today?"

"I strongly recommend the mint chocolate," Lucy said as she rose from her seat. "Brooke, thanks for the coffee break and the conversation. We'll get back to you on the tokens."

"Thanks, Luce. Take care."

Lucy pulled on her sweater and left the shop, a knot in her stomach. Brooke hadn't told her anything she hadn't already known. Of course she was aware that Clay cared for her. More and more, she was feeling the same way.

She just didn't know what to do about it.

After having fallen asleep at her desk, Lucy awoke at two A.M. and walked through the silent inn to her room. She tossed off her clothes and crawled into bed and fell back to sleep within seconds. It wasn't until around noon the following day that she realized that since telling Clay about her attack, she hadn't had any of the nightmares that had plagued her for so many years.

Her phone rang and she was happy to see Bonnie's name on the caller ID. Hopefully, Bonnie was on her way back to L.A.

"Hi," she answered the call. "How's Bob doing?"

"Not good," Bonnie replied, obviously upset. "Not good at all."

"What's going on?"

"They couldn't operate on his leg last week because they couldn't sedate him due to the head injury. They're planning the surgery for Wednesday, and, Lucy, I can't leave him while he's going through this." Bonnie began to cry into the phone. "I hate to ask you to do this because I know you're over your head as it is, but I don't have a choice." Lucy heard her take a deep breath. "Could you take over the Ruskin wedding for me on Saturday? I know that Ava and Corrine have both been doing a great job, but this is a big-deal wedding and these people are going to want to see me or you at the helm."

"You mean, this Saturday?" Lucy's jaw dropped. Was Bonnie kidding?

"Yes. I'm sorry, I know it's short notice and I know that you have a lot to do there, but I can send you the file. Everything's in order, all you have to do is acquaint yourself with what we're doing, call the vendors and let them know you'll be on board, and let the bride know."

"Bonnie, I've never met these people," Lucy protested. "I can't just show up on Saturday at their wedding not having met them and expect them to be okay with that."

"I thought about that. The bride's luncheon is on Thursday and the rehearsal dinner is Friday night, so you could—"

"I can't meet the bride for the first time at her luncheon. You know we don't work that way."

"I know, I know! I just don't know what else to do. I can't leave him like this. He's in so much pain and he doesn't have anyone else here . . ."

Lucy blew out a long breath. "All right. I'll fly back tomorrow and I'll meet with the bride tomorrow night. But, Bon . . ." Lucy's voice softened. "We have to talk."

"I know. And we will, as soon as Bob stabilizes and I can leave him. Maybe another week or so . . . I'll let you know."

Lucy ended the call and all but fell back into her

chair. She didn't want to go back to L.A. tomorrow, didn't want to leave St. Dennis yet.

"Damn."

Bonnie's electronic file arrived with a *ping* and Lucy opened it, read it through, then made the calls she knew she needed to make. Her mother stopped in to see if she wanted to join her for a late lunch, but Lucy explained why she had to pass.

"Oh, dear." Grace shook her head. "That arrangement can't go on . . ."

"You're right, Mom. I told Bonnie that we needed to talk, and she agreed, but she's not going to come back to the office until she feels she can leave Bob."

"What a shame," her mother said. "But of course, her place is with him."

Lucy looked up sharply. "She has obligations to fulfill."

"Of course she does, dear. But she has an obligation to herself and to her husband."

"*Ex*-husband."

"Perhaps not her *ex* for much longer," Grace pointed out. "Put yourself in her place, Lucy. What would you do? Would you leave someone you love when they needed you? Granted, this puts a burden on you to carry the business for a while, but you and Bonnie are partners. You need to be there for each other just as she has to be there for Bob. Owning a business doesn't mean that you're not entitled to a life, dear."

"You're right, Mom." Lucy sighed. "Of course you're right."

"Go on and do what you have to do. I'll have lunch

sent in for you." Her mother pushed herself from the chair.

"When will you be leaving?"

"Early in the morning."

"I'm sorry, sweetheart. These things do happen. Thank goodness you do have Madeline to help you here."

Lucy nodded and watched her mother walk from the room, then turned her attention back to work. She ate the sandwich and salad that was brought in to her, and worked for the rest of the day. By the time she finished at seven that night, the tents had been ordered as well as the furniture to go in the cocktail party tent, the bandstand, and the tall potted trees. Madeline was working on the big white paper lanterns and the chairs for the ceremony. Lucy and Clay had been sending texts back and forth all day, but she hadn't told him that she'd been forced to cut her week short. She wanted to do that in person. She turned off her laptop and the light switch on her way out of the office.

"I'm going out for the evening," she told her mother.

"Just don't miss your plane, dear," Grace said as if she knew where Lucy was going.

Maybe she does, Lucy thought as she drove from the parking lot. Her mother hadn't mentioned the fact that Lucy hadn't come home on Saturday night, but then again, Lucy was an adult and it wouldn't be like her mother to intrude into her affairs. Not that she wouldn't want to . . .

Clay's Jeep was parked next to the old John Deere tractor when she arrived at the farm. She got out of the car and walked toward the house. Through the open kitchen window, she could see him doing something at the sink.

She went up the back steps, knocked on the screen door, and called, "Clay?"

"Lucy?"

He came to the door in jeans and bare feet, his shirtsleeves rolled to his elbows.

"Come in." He dried his hands on the towel he was holding. "Why didn't you call to let me know you were coming over?"

"Because . . . because . . ." She followed him into the kitchen.

"What's wrong?" He tossed the towel onto the counter and reached for her.

His arms folded around her and she could feel the warmth and strength in his embrace. His lips brushed against the side of her face and his breath was soft against her skin. "Tell me . . ."

She did.

"Wow. Way to screw things up." Clay looked as dejected as she felt. "I was hoping you'd be here at least through Saturday."

"Me too. I was really looking forward to going to Jesse's party with you."

"Well, I don't like it much, but I don't know what else you can do. It sounds like the guy's really in bad shape."

"Bonnie was really upset." Lucy rested against him. "And I'm afraid I wasn't as sympathetic as I should have been. I'm not ready to go back tomorrow."

"Would you be ready to leave on Sunday?" he asked.

She nuzzled her face into his neck. "I don't think so."

He turned her face up and kissed her full on the mouth. Her lips parted slightly and she savored the sensation of his tongue flickering against her own. Her hands fisted in his shirt and she pulled him closer. Every inch of her cried out for his touch, and she gasped quietly as his hands began to caress the curves of her body.

"I want to stay," she whispered. "I want to stay with you."

"Let's try this again." He lifted her from her feet and this time she made no jokes about being swept away. She busied herself kissing his neck as he carried her up the stairs and into his room, and when he laid her across his bed, she pulled him down with her.

This time, there was no tickle of fear in her gut, no second-guessing, no doubts to distract her. This time, she welcomed his kisses and arched to meet his hands, and encouraged him to touch and taste and explore. This time, she unbuttoned her shirt and shivered as he slid her jeans over her hips. This time, his mouth and his hands on her breasts caused her to cry out in pleasure. This time, she ached to feel him inside her, moaned softly as his fingers found her core, then waited impatiently while he shed his clothes. And this time, when he came to her, she reached eagerly for him, and prayed it would last all night.

Chapter 21

Lucy reached for the ringing phone without looking and struggled to open her eyes.

"So how did the wedding go? Any problems?" Bonnie was asking as Lucy tried to sit up in her bed.

"It went really well. Thanks to your mad organizational skills, all I had to do was walk in and introduce myself." Lucy covered a yawn with her free hand. "Is it really nine?"

"Sorry, Lu. It never occurred to me that you'd still be sleeping. You're always such an early riser."

"I'm afraid I must have bottomed out. Between the travel and trying to handle big affairs on two sides of the country, I'm beat."

"I know I'm partially to blame, and I'm so sorry. I swear, once Bob is up and around and able to take care of himself, I will be your slave."

"How long do you think before that will happen?"

"The fracture was really bad, Lu. The bone in his lower leg was shattered, and they had to put a rod and pins and all manner of things in there, but they don't know if the bone will heal. The doctor said the surgery they performed was the only thing they could do, but an infection has set in and they're hoping they can resolve that."

"And if they can't?"

"If the infection in the bone continues to spread, or if the shattered bone cannot heal, the next step would be to take his leg off below the knee." Bonnie's voice shook as she relayed the news.

"Holy shit. God, I'm so sorry. That must be hell for both of you." Lucy remembered Bob as a tall strapping guy who loved pickup basketball games and competitive cycling.

"Mostly for him. I try to keep him upbeat, but it's a struggle sometimes. He's so scared. I'm so scared."

"I can only imagine." Lucy sat up in bed and pulled the light covering with her. "I'm really sorry you two have to go through this."

"Thanks, Lucy." Bonnie cleared her throat softly. "I suppose we need to talk about the business."

"When you get back, we'll talk."

"I'll fly down as soon as I can. We can talk then."

"Take what time you need, Bon."

"I appreciate that, but I know how crazy you must be right now. With all you have to do in St. Dennis to get ready for the big wedding, and now to be pulled back here . . . I know it isn't fair. I know I was the one who was supposed to be helping you by covering your events out here so that you could devote your time to the Magellan wedding."

"Don't give it another thought," Lucy told her. "It'll all work out. We have Ava and Corrine here and I have Madeline back in Maryland, and you'll do what you can do long-distance. We'll get through this."

"You're reminding me why I wanted you for a business partner." Bonnie sniffed back what Lucy knew to be tears. "I love you, Lu. You're a great friend and I'm so sorry to have put you in this position."

"Love you, too, Bon," Lucy told her. "We'll work things out. Bob is going to be fine. The business will be fine."

Lucy got up, showered, dressed in soft Sunday sweats, and made herself a pot of coffee. She sat on her living room sofa with a cup in one hand and her phone in the other. Last night was the first night since she came back to L.A. that she hadn't spoken with Clay before she went to bed. She was still at the wedding reception when he sent his last text of the night— around midnight eastern time—when he was turning in. She wanted to ask about the party, who was there and how much fun it was. But most of all, she wanted to hear the quiet reassurance in his voice. She speed-dialed his number.

"Hi." He answered on the first ring. "I was hoping this would be you."

"Hi. How are you?"

"Mildly hungover. Wade brewed some mean beer for Jesse last night and he made everyone taste it."

"I thought the brewery wasn't built yet." She frowned. "Did I miss something?"

"He bought some home-brewing setup and was experimenting. I'll bet everyone in town has a headache this morning. Including your mom."

"My mom doesn't drink beer," she told him.

"She did last night." He chuckled. "And from all appearances, she enjoyed it."

"I'm having a hard time picturing that, but I know

you couldn't be making it up." Lucy pulled her legs up under her and tried to picture him . . . where? "Where are you?" she asked.

"Sitting on the back steps drinking a bottle of water. I just came in from walking across the back field. I wanted to see how the barley was doing."

"How's it doing?" She was glad she asked. She could see him sitting there, taking long drinks of water until the bottle was empty, at which time he'd toss it end over end into the recycling bin he kept outside.

"Pretty good. I think we'll have a decent harvest." He paused to take another swallow. "So how did it go last night?"

"It went well. Bonnie did a great job setting it all up."

The silence that followed was painful. She knew what was coming next.

"When do you think you'll be able to come back?" he asked.

"I don't know. I don't know how long Bonnie is going to be up north. Bob's leg is badly fractured and they had to put a rod in it. She'd doing a terrific job considering that she's at the other end of the state, but on game day, it's tough on the rest of us. We have a full book from now into June."

"What about Robert Magellan and his fiancée? Weren't you supposed to meet with them and with Gavin soon?"

"Yes, but they're going to have to be content with Dan and Madeline in my place. I just can't see a free day on my calendar. Madeline can handle it. She's done a lot this past week. She has good skills. Not a whole lot of imagination, but she's well organized and that's critical." Lucy sighed. "I know that's not what you wanted to hear. Believe me, I wish I could say I'd be back in a few days, but it's going to be weeks." She hesitated, then said words she never expected to hear herself say. "I miss you. I want to be with you."

"I miss you, too, LuLu. Do what you have to do, then come home. I'll be waiting . . ."

On the Tuesday of the week before the Magellan guests were to arrive, a happy Lucy got off her plane at BWI and hurried to pick up her luggage. She had an appointment at the inn in the morning with the woman for whom she was planning the July anniversary party, but she planned to spend the rest of tomorrow with Clay. She caught the shuttle to the car rental facility, and had just taken a seat when her phone pinged to announce a text. She opened the message and found a picture of Clay standing out in front of the car rental lot that he'd obviously taken with his phone.

She laughed and texted back: *See you in . . .*

"How long?" she asked the driver.

"Maybe five minutes," he replied.

"Thanks," she told him, and completed her text.

When the van arrived at the lot and the driver opened the door, Clay was standing there, waiting for her.

"You didn't have to do this," she said after she'd kissed him soundly. "But I love that you did."

"I couldn't wait to see you." He grabbed her suitcase. "I'll bet you paid a hefty fee to fly this baby. Did you bring one of your assistants home in this?"

"Just clothes and stuff that I'll need," she told him.

They chatted all the way to the inn, Clay filling her in on what was going on in St. Dennis, she telling him about the NFL players who attended their teammate's wedding the weekend before.

Clay parked in his favorite "No Parking" spot near the inn's back door. When he started to take her bag from the back, she said, "Leave it. It's going home with you tonight, and so am I."

He slammed the hatch closed and smiled. "I was hoping you'd say that."

"For now, let's go in and have dinner. I need to see my mom and she's going to want to see me, but I'm not finished looking at you yet. I can't believe how tan you are already."

"If you spent as much time outside as I do, you'd be tan, too."

"I hope you're using sunscreen," she said as they went inside, where Grace was waiting for them in the lobby.

Lucy had called her mother when they reached the Bay Bridge, so Grace knew when to expect them.

"So nice of you to pick up our girl, Clay," Grace said after she'd hugged her daughter. "I hope you'll stay and let us feed you. There's a pretty full house, but I'm sure there's at least one table for two in the dining room."

"That would be great, Mom. I could eat a horse. But aren't you going to join us?" Lucy asked.

"Perhaps for dessert and coffee. Right now I'm due to interview one of our longtime guests." Grace held up a notepad. "One of the families who was displaced due to next week's festivities agreed to stay this week instead. The patriarch of that family has been coming here for seventy-five years, and his entire family is here to celebrate his ninetieth birthday on Friday. I think his kids and grandkids and great-grandkids are already starting to gather for dinner in the dining room, but he agreed to chat with me for a few minutes and let me take his picture for the *Gazette*."

"What fun. We'll be inside if you decide to join us later." Lucy took Clay's hand as they went into the dining room. After they were seated, she nodded toward the back of the room, where several tables had been pushed together to form a single long one. "That must be the family Mom was talking about."

Clay turned to take a look. "They've been coming here for seventy-five years? Do you recognize anyone?"

Lucy studied the faces right down the line, then shook her head. "No, but remember, I haven't spent a summer here in twenty years, and there are a lot of children there. Like Mom said, kids and grandkids and great-grandkids."

They ordered drinks and dinner at the same time and watched the room fill up with diners.

"I guess Gavin's reputation has been growing," Lucy said.

"There was a great write-up in the *Baltimore Sun* last weekend."

"Mom emailed it to me." She smiled up at the waitress who placed her salad in front of her. "They had nice things to say about the inn and its ambience too and they—"

Movement from her left caught her eye, distracting her as an elderly man in a wheelchair was brought into the room and positioned at the head of the table where the large family sat. Lucy found herself staring at the man who was pushing the chair and felt the blood drain from her face.

"What?" Clay turned to follow her gaze. "You look as if you've seen a ghost."

"No, it's all right." She shook her head. "It's nothing. For a moment, I thought maybe I recognized . . ."

"You thought what? You think that's him? The dark-haired guy in the navy blazer pushing the chair? Is he the guy . . . ?"

"No, no. Just for a second . . . but no. All I remember about that man was that he had dark hair and an athletic build, which pretty well describes at least fifty percent of the men who stay here." She nodded in the direction of the man they were discussing. "He just happens to fit the description, but he's too young."

She watched the man as he maneuvered the wheelchair to the table. A little girl of five or six jumped from her seat and skipped to him, and he lifted her up and planted a kiss on her cheek.

"No," she told Clay. "That's not him."

"You're sure."

"Positive. And to tell you the truth, I don't know if I'd recognize him after all these years. People change." She reached for Clay's hand. "I'm going to be here a lot this summer. Neither of us can start looking at every guest as a suspect. We're both going to have to accept the fact that he's out there somewhere, maybe, but he's not here. It's more than likely that he never came back because he was afraid I'd recognize him and would call the police."

"I hate the thought of him being out there."

"So do I. But I've come to the conclusion that I can either spend the rest of my life looking back—in which case I won't be looking ahead—or I can leave it in the past, where it belongs. And frankly, I've had enough of the past. I can't change what happened. All I can do now is live in the present and look forward to the future." She smiled and pulled him closer. "You're my present, Clay. Let's focus on now. Us. To-night. . . ."

"And the future . . . ?" he asked.

"Will take care of itself." She kissed him lightly on the lips. "We'll have the summer, Clay. Let's take it one day at a time, and see where it leads . . ."

Chapter 22

AT one in the afternoon on Sunday, a stretch limo made its way up the long drive from Charles Street to the inn and parked in the front of the building. If there'd been any hope of shielding Robert Magellan and his bride from the photographers that flanked the very edge of the property—having been warned by Gabriel Beck and his officers that trespassing would not be tolerated—it had been tossed aside as Robert, Susanna, Robert's young son Ian, Trula, and Father Kevin Burch took their time getting out of the car. The photographers knew there'd be a big payday when Robert walked with his bride-to-be and his cousin down to the water's edge and pointed out several sights across the Bay.

Lucy watched from the steps, and sighed. If Robert and Susanna weren't concerned that by tomorrow the pictures would be all over the Internet, she shouldn't be either.

Trula shepherded Ian directly to the inn, and they were followed by the limo driver, who carried her bags. She hugged Lucy and pointed the driver to the lobby.

"I'll get some help for you," Lucy told him. "Trula, Mom's been watching for you. She was at the front desk, last time I saw her."

"I'll find her. Oh, there she is." Trula beamed, obviously as happy as the wedding couple that this week had finally arrived. She guided the three-year-old into the inn, and Lucy heard her call, "Hello, Gracie! Ian needs the bathroom. This way, Ian . . . let's go with Gracie. . . ."

Lucy flagged down two of the bellhops and asked them to assist the limo driver. In a matter of minutes, the flurry of activity had begun. A second limo carrying the wedding party arrived, and several women and two men got out. Soon the lobby was filled with laughter and chatter at the desk as everyone signed in, got their keys, and admired the inn.

This is going to be a very long week. Lucy sighed. She walked down to the water's edge to greet the wedding couple, and to invite them to come inside for the welcome luncheon she'd had prepared for them.

"Lucy!" Susanna waved to her and opened her arms for a hug. "Isn't the weather glorious?"

"It is." Lucy returned the hug. "It's supposed to be beautiful straight through until next week."

Even the normally reserved Robert had a hug for Lucy before introducing her to Father Kevin.

"Lucy's the person who's making this all happen," Robert told his cousin. "She took Susanna's wish list—and it was a whopper—and made it all come true. Lucy, meet Father Kevin Burch."

"It's Kevin," the priest said as he offered his hand. "And I've heard wonderful things about you. I'm looking forward to the week. I understand you've arranged golf and sailing. Where do I sign up?"

Throughout the afternoon, the parking lot continued to fill as more and more guests arrived. Either Lucy or Daniel was there to greet everyone as they signed in, and both made it a point to try to remember the names of each of the guests. By four in the afternoon, all of the Sunday arrivals had checked in, and were eagerly exploring the inn and the printed agenda of the week's proposed activities that everyone received with their room keys and their welcome gift bags.

"I can't believe you managed to pull this all together, Lucy." Susanna held the list of daily things to do in her hand.

"I had excellent assistants," Lucy admitted. "No one person could have arranged all this in six months. Unless, of course, they did nothing else. Madeline here at the inn was a godsend. She kept track of everything here in St. Dennis, and my staff out in Los Angeles helped keep track of things."

"Well, whatever you did, it worked." Susanna was glowing, the perfect picture of the happy bride-to-be. Lucy prayed that nothing would happen during the week to dim that joy.

And for the most part, nothing did. All the instructors Lucy had hired—for golf, sailing, tennis, and boating—had satisfied students. The golf course and tennis courts were filled morning through dusk, and the boats the inn had chartered for fishing went out every day with enthusiastic would-be fisherman. The older children learned how to sail, and the little ones looked forward to their pony rides and story hours. The ladies enjoyed afternoon tea every day—the first had been so well received that Gavin had suggested they offer it every day, much to Susanna's delight. Gavin himself had been a huge hit, preparing every meal as if for royalty, and the guests had been impressed enough that some had already booked weeks toward the end of the summer to return.

The hit of the week, however, had been the shopping trips into town. Every one of Susanna's women guests had made it to Charles Street, where they cashed in their tokens for discounts on clothes and food and books and antiques.

"Honestly, I can't keep madras anything in the shop this week," Vanessa had confided to Lucy. "Every pair of shorts, every little sundress . . . gone. Not that I'm complaining, but I'd have stocked in twice as much merchandise if I'd known ahead of time what a preppy crowd this was going to be."

"I'm so happy to hear that you're doing well," Lucy'd replied.

"It's not just me," Vanessa told her. "Every merchant in town is saying the same thing. Brooke says by four in the afternoon, there's not a cupcake left in her shop. And Stef has had to double the amount of ice cream that she's been making. O Susanna has been a huge hit."

"Susanna and Robert loved that idea." Lucy grinned. "And it certainly didn't hurt that the ice cream is delicious. We're serving it at the wedding reception on Saturday."

"I know. Stef is about dead on her feet trying to keep up. She said there's been a steady stream of kids in the shop from lunchtime right through till dinner.

She's had to reorder from her suppliers three times this week."

"But that's all good, right?"

"Of course. Even Carlo at Cuppachino has had to bring in extra counter help this week. Not that that's a bad thing. It's been business bonanza here all week long."

"Maybe we'll do those discount tokens again," Lucy said, thinking out loud.

"Just make sure everyone knows you're doing it so we're all well stocked. Barbara at the bookstore said she was sold out of bestselling hardcovers by Tuesday and had to put in rush orders to get in enough books to last the week." Vanessa added, "But I can attest to the fact that everyone who's participated in this token thing has gone home every night with a smile on their face. We all think you're a genius for thinking of it."

"I'd love to take the credit, but it was Susanna's idea."

"Then please tell Susanna we all think she's brilliant," Vanessa told her.

Lucy did just that, at her first opportunity.

"I'm glad it's worked out so well." Susanna had been all smiles. "My friends come back from shopping every day and tell me what fun things they've found. Of course, it helps that you have some terrific places to shop and to eat here in St. Dennis. I'm thrilled to know that this week has been so much fun for our family and friends."

By Friday, Lucy's head was about to explode. The tents had all been set up and the chairs and tables delivered. The new gazebo had been perfectly sited and the roses Jason had planted in April and had tended so carefully had burst into bloom as if on cue, and the beds he'd designed and planted had filled in nicely with colorful, fragrant flowers. The rehearsal and dinner afterward was casual and fun, and everyone was in high spirits.

"Everything's going right on schedule," Madeline whispered to Lucy. "I'm almost afraid to say the words out loud."

"Then keep it to a whisper," Lucy replied. "I can't believe there hasn't been at least one thing that went wrong."

"Well, except for that pony taking off across the lawn with the four-year-old on its back yesterday," Madeline reminded her.

"Amazing that kid held on, and to think he'd never been riding before."

"No one's called in sick all week and all of the deliveries have come on time. It's almost as if the inn and everyone in it are under some sort of magic spell."

Madeline's comment reminded Lucy of something she'd been meaning to discuss with her mother. She had the chance later that night. Grace was in the family room with Trula, who was on her way to bed.

"Big day tomorrow," Trula all but sang. "We're all having such a good time, Lucy. Everyone is so enjoying being here this week. You've certainly gone above and beyond to make sure everyone has a good time."

"Thanks, Trula. It has been unlike any wedding I've ever done before." Lucy sat in a chair that faced her mother.

"Well, as I told your brother, you should certainly

give some consideration to expanding your wedding business," Trula said.

"Don't be surprised to see a lot of what we did this week make its way into the premium wedding package offered here before too long," Lucy told her.

"Madeline couldn't possibly handle it, dear. She's a darling girl and we all like her, but she doesn't have your skill or your imagination."

"She did a great job," Lucy protested.

"After you told her what to do," Grace reminded her.

"She's very well organized," Lucy insisted. "I wouldn't have been able to pull this off without her."

"She's a good first mate, dear, but she's not a captain." Grace got up to see Trula to the door. "I'll see you at breakfast, dear."

"Gracie, thank you for all your help. Seeing Rob so happy after all he went through . . . well, it does my heart good." Trula gave Grace a quick hug. "Good night, Lucy. See you in the morning."

Grace closed the door behind Trula.

"I think I'll turn in now, as well," Grace told Lucy. "As Trula said, tomorrow will be a very big day."

"Mom, what did Trula mean when she thanked you for all your help?"

"Oh, I guess she meant over all the years that we've been friends." Grace dismissed it.

"That isn't how it sounded. It sounded as if somehow she was thanking you that Rob was happy."

"Now, why would she do that, dear?"

"I don't know." Lucy turned in her chair. "Mom, where's your Ouija board?"

"In my closet." Grace stopped and turned to Lucy. "How did you know I had a Ouija board?"

"Someone might have mentioned it."

"Someone like Stef and Vanessa?"

Lucy nodded. "They seem to think you have some kind of power over that board."

Grace looked uncomfortable, as if she wished to flee. "Lucy, it's getting late, and I think this is a discussion for—"

"Gramma, you said we could read on your Kindle." Diana appeared in the doorway.

"Why, so I did, dear." Grace smiled. "Sorry, Lucy. Perhaps another time . . ."

Grace put her arm around her granddaughter's shoulders. "Now, which book tonight?"

"The Lion, the Witch and the Wardrobe," Diana replied happily.

"Didn't we read that one last week?"

The voices of Lucy's mother and her niece trailed down the hallway.

"Dodged a bullet there, Mom."

Lucy chuckled as she grabbed her bag and left the inn for Clay's. It was already late and she'd have to be back here at the very crack of dawn to oversee the rest of the setup for the wedding and to take care of every last-minute detail. She'd need her wits about her and she was already exhausted from a very full week, but she'd come to rely on the peace she felt when she was with him. She'd come to love the farm and the farmhouse, and, she realized, she was loving Clay. She wasn't sure where it would lead, and right then, she wasn't up to thinking about it. She had one very big, very high-profile wedding tomorrow, and she was determined that everything would be perfect. Right now the Magellan wedding was priority. Everything else would have to wait its turn.

Mention of the wedding of Robert Magellan and Susanna Jones would appear in all the major newspapers during the following week, and every tabloid and weekly celebrity magazine would run photos of the festivities that had been taken with high-powered lenses from various spots at the edge of the inn's grounds. Fortunately, the gazebo had been situated in such a way that the structure itself blocked the view of anyone on the north side or the Bay side of the property, so the only photos taken of the actual ceremony were taken by the photographer that the wedding couple had hired.

Lucy arrived at the inn just as the sun was rising. She went into the kitchen and begged for a cup of coffee from the breakfast crew, then took it outside to oversee the setup of the chairs in such a way as to form an aisle. There was a light mist off the Bay, but the sun would soon burn it off, and if the weather forecast was correct, the temperature would not exceed eighty and the humidity would remain relatively low.

The chairs were placed as directed and the rose petals that would be strewn along the path to the gazebo were in a cooler to be tossed about a half hour before the ceremony. Lucy went into the tent and spoke with the member of the inn's crew who was in charge of placing the furniture in one end of the tent to be used for cocktails.

"Sofas here and here." Lucy pointed. "Love seat there, chairs there, there, and there. Questions?"

"None," she was assured.

"Great. Now where's the guy who's supposed to be putting down the dance floor? He was supposed to have done that yesterday. . . ."

She checked to see that all the paper lanterns would be lit when the time came, then greeted Madeline, who arrived at seven thirty.

"Find the guy with the dance floor, please." Lucy handed off the sheet with the specifications to Madeline and went inside to make sure all was ready for the champagne breakfast they would soon be serving on the veranda that looked out on the Bay.

The kitchen was ready, but the centerpieces for the outside tables had somehow been taken into the dining room instead.

"Crap," she muttered, and began the task of moving the centerpieces.

"What can I do to help?" Clay came into the room as if she'd conjured him.

"Ordinarily, I'd say thanks, but I've got this under control." Lucy stood with her hands on her hips. "Today, however, I'll ask you to help me move the centerpieces." She stopped to kiss him on the lips. "And thanks for ignoring me when I said there wouldn't be anything you'd have to do today. How did you know . . . ?"

"I just figured you could always use another pair of hands." Clay carried the flower arrangements, two at a time, back to their boxes in the lobby. "I never saw vases like these. They look like they're made out of tree trunks." He held one up to take a closer look.

"They *are* made from tree trunks. We had holes cut into them large enough for the glass vases to fit, see?" Lucy pulled one of the glass cylinders from the wood.

"Very cool."

"They are, but they go on the veranda. The arrangements in the silver containers are for the reception, but those tables aren't set up yet, so they have to stay in here for now."

"I can handle this," he told her. "You go ahead and do whatever else you have to do."

"Thank you. You shall receive a suitable reward."

"I'm counting on it."

Lucy laughed and checked in with the kitchen, where preparations were in high gear. It seemed as if only minutes passed before guests started streaming in for breakfast. She checked the time and realized it was already nine.

The rest of the day went quickly. When she was satisfied that all was on schedule, Lucy ran upstairs and changed into the light silk sheath she'd brought home for the occasion. She pulled her hair back into a neat ponytail and put on a little makeup, then went to the room they'd set aside for Susanna and her attendants for hair and makeup and to dress for the wedding. Lucy knocked on the door, then went in. Susanna had just arrived and was checking on her dress, which had been delivered earlier.

"I can't believe the day is finally here." She was all but singing.

"Believe it." Mallory Russo, one of the investigators for the Mercy Street Foundation and, as Lucy figured out over the course of the week, Susanna's closest friend, entered the room and went straight to the closet to hang up her dress. "Where's the lady who's doing hair?"

"She should be here any minute." Lucy checked the time. The hairdresser was almost ten minutes late. She was just about to call the woman when she arrived with her assistants. Lucy breathed a sigh of relief and stepped back as the last of the attendants, Emme Caldwell, came into the suite with her daughter, Chloe, the flower girl.

"I'm wearing pink," Chloe announced to the hairdresser, then held up her feet. "And I have pink shoes. Trula bought them for me. . . ."

The photographer knocked on the door.

Lucy let her and her two assistants in, then told Susanna, "I'm going downstairs to check on things. You have my number and I have my phone. Please call me with any questions or if you have problems."

"We're fine. No problems. Scoot," Susanna told her.

Lucy scooted.

At noon, she had a tray of fruit and cheese and freshly made fruit breads taken up to the dressing room.

At one-thirty, the ceremony musicians arrived and set up near the gazebo. The string quartet began to tune up as Madeline finished draping the aisle chairs with airy white tulle and pink-and-white-striped paper cones filled with pink roses.

"I thought Olivia did those earlier," Lucy said.

"She wanted to hold off as long as possible so that the roses stayed fresh for the ceremony."

"Doesn't she have them in water?" Lucy frowned.

"She has each stem in its own little vial of water.

But she said the direct sun wouldn't be good for them, so to hold off." Madeline looked up. "In another half hour, the sun will be behind those trees, so the flowers will hold up for the afternoon."

"Why are you doing them? And where is Olivia?"

"She's in the tents finishing up the flower garlands for around the tent poles. They proved to be a little more complicated than originally thought, so I offered to do this."

"And the trees with the white lights?"

"Already set up and turned on."

"Great." Lucy made her way to the inn and checked in with Gavin.

"Are we good to go for the cocktail hour?" she asked.

"Good as gold," he told her. "Did you eat anything today?"

"I had coffee."

Gavin signaled for one of the line cooks to bring him a plate of some of the pasta he made that morning.

"Pear-and-goat-cheese *agnolotti*. Take this into the dining room, sit, and eat before you pass out." He carried the plate for her and ushered her to a quiet table. "Rocco, bring Miss Sinclair a glass of iced tea, please."

"Are you going to sit here and watch me eat?" Lucy asked.

"Of course not. I have work to do and you're far too smart to let yourself run down when you have a very long day ahead of you."

"Thanks, Gavin."

The pasta was perfection, the cream sauce delectable, and for almost ten minutes, Lucy permitted herself to relax. Then it was back to work, her iPhone with its checklist in hand.

"What else?" Daniel asked her when she walked into the reception tent.

Lucy shook her head. "Nothing. Thank God, I think we've got it together after all." She looked around. "Is Clay still here?"

"He said something about helping Wade deliver some beer," he replied.

"So they did it? They made beer just for today?" Her eyes lit up. "That stinker didn't even mention it."

"He wanted to surprise you."

"So did he say what's in it? What makes it special?"

"You'll have to ask him. He said it would be here in time for the reception."

"Before we can have the reception, we have to get them married." Lucy glanced around and saw that a few people had started to gather behind the chairs. "Oh, damn. I forgot the programs. Have you seen Madeline?"

"She was headed back to the inn, last I saw her."

Lucy pulled her phone from her pocket and dialed Madeline's phone. "The programs for the ceremony—"

"—are in my hands and I'm on my way outside."

Lucy looked toward the inn and saw Madeline walking across the lawn.

"You're good," Lucy told her in passing. "I'm going to go check on the bride. I think we're okay out here now."

"Everything is under control here. The groom and his guys should be here in"—Madeline checked her watch—"less than thirty minutes now."

"You know what to tell them when they get here," Lucy said. "I'm going to check up on the bride. I'll call you if it looks as if there will be a delay."

She passed Daniel on the way to the inn and said, "Don't forget, Susanna wanted flutes of champagne served while their guests are waiting for the ceremony to begin."

"Isn't she worried that some people might overindulge?"

"Apparently not, but I think someone should be vigilant if it appears anyone is asking for too many refills before the wedding."

More guests were beginning to flow from the inn to the lawn, and Lucy hurried up to the second floor. Everyone was dressed, hair and makeup applied, and the photographer, Karyn Park, had already been shooting for an hour.

"Susanna, you make a stunning bride," Lucy told her.

"Thank you. I tried on a dozen dresses, but the second I saw this one, I knew it was mine." Susanna turned slightly so that Lucy could get the full effect of the gown. It was a slim column of white silk, with a halter neckline and a wide belt of chiffon flowers.

"Gorgeous."

Susanna beamed and turned her head so that Lucy could see the orchids that were wound into hair.

"Like I said, gorgeous."

"Thanks, Lucy." Susanna turned to her two attendants, who wore strapless dresses in navy silk with obi sashes in navy, pink, and orange. "Ladies, are we ready?"

"We are so ready," Mallory replied.

"I'm ready." Chloe jumped up.

"Get your little basket of flowers," Emme told her daughter.

"Susanna, are you ready to walk down the aisle?" Lucy asked as they filed out of the room.

"I am." She took Lucy's arm as they approached the steps.

The musicians were ready, the guests were in place, the groom waited patiently and calmly for the appearance of his bride. One last check to make certain that all was as it was supposed to be, and Lucy gave the musicians the nod. Clarke's "Trumpet Voluntary" began to play as Mallory and Emme began their walk through the rose petals to the gazebo. Next came Chloe, who seemed confused to find that there were already rose petals on the ground, but she tossed hers anyway, and Ian, who carried the rings tied to the satin pillow, which was just as well since he bounced the pillow all the way up the aisle.

And then it was Susanna's turn. To the strains of Pachelbel's Canon in D, she walked unassisted to her groom, who met her halfway up the aisle to take her hand.

The ceremony was beautiful, filled with personal stories about the bride and the groom delivered by Father Kevin with great humor and warmth, the vows lovingly exchanged. Lucy looked around the crowd for her mother, and found her seated in the first row next to Trula, who looked elegant in a silk dress the color of a creamy latte. She tried to recall if she'd ever seen Trula dressed up before, and came to the conclusion that she probably hadn't.

The strings began to play the recessional—Vivaldi's "Spring"—the newly married couple made their way back down the aisle, and Lucy breathed a sigh of relief. The ceremony was over, the Magellans were married, and now, all she had to do was get everyone happily through the afternoon and evening.

Clay watched from the second-floor balcony as Lucy orchestrated the events of the afternoon and the evening. It was the second time he'd seen her at work—he'd been a guest at Dallas MacGregor's wedding—and had to give the woman credit for knowing her stuff. The entire affair flowed seamlessly from ceremony to cocktail party to dinner and dancing. Even to his eye—which admittedly wasn't experienced when it came to evaluating social events like this one—it looked like one hell of a party.

One-third of Lucy's reason for being here was over, though, and that was a problem. She'd as much as said she wouldn't be needed on-site very much for the July event, which meant she probably wouldn't be around much until August. From the way things looked now, she might be here for a week or so in July, but it wasn't what he wanted. He'd counted on her being home for the entire summer.

He almost laughed at himself. Who was he kidding? As if Lucy spending the summer in St. Dennis would be enough to make him happy. Oh, sure, that would make him happier than home for a few weeks here and there, but still. If she was only around for a day here and a day there, she'd be working and there wouldn't be time to do any of the things he'd planned on doing with her.

Clay leaned on the railing and looked down to the lawn, where Lucy was hustling from one tent to the other then back to the inn. She was working her butt off for this wedding but looked totally happy doing it. He could relate. Was it a whole lot different from spending a day up on the old John Deere plowing up a chunk of acres? Didn't that give him the same satisfied smile he saw on her face?

Wade came to the door and said, "Magellan beer is ready to make its debut, if you're ready."

Clay nodded. "I'm ready."

He turned from the scene below and followed his partner downstairs. The problem wasn't going to be solved today, and since she was leaving early on Monday to go back to the coast, it wasn't likely to be solved anytime soon. But they had today, and tonight, and tomorrow, and he planned on savoring every minute.

Chapter 23

A s Lucy had predicted, photos of the Magellans were everywhere the week following the wedding, many of them given freely by Karyn Park at Susanna's request, so that most of the unauthorized photos taken found no paid home. Lucy had to admit to a twinge of pride when she passed by the newsstand in the airport on her way back to Los Angeles on Monday and saw a big photo of the inn on the cover of one of the weekly magazines. Everyone at Shaefer & Sinclair congratulated her on another job well done, and most importantly, well publicized.

She spent a good portion of the flight back looking over the calendar for the next six weeks, and found one brief window of time—three days—that she could spend in St. Dennis. It just wasn't enough. She'd been counting on at least the week before the anniversary party in St. Dennis, but with Bonnie basically out of the picture for who knew how long, Lucy was needed at the office. The plans for the anniversary party were, for the most part, finalized, and though Lucy's presence at the actual event had been part of the deal, Madeline could do much of the legwork between now and the end of July. Unless, of course, Bob made a miraculous recovery and Bonnie came back to Los Angeles and stayed.

"Not counting on that," Lucy muttered.

"Excuse me?" the woman seated next to her asked.

"Oh, sorry. I was thinking out loud." Lucy smiled apologetically, then closed her eyes and pretended to sleep.

She was tired to the bone and wished she could sleep, but there was too much buzzing around in her head. She was still worn out from the wedding on Saturday and all the end-of-the-week festivities, the brunch, and the last of the afternoon teas yesterday afternoon for the few guests who remained and apparently thought that afternoon tea was an everyday occurrence. Though it probably should be, Lucy thought. It had been a lovely way to spend an hour.

She couldn't blame her fatigue completely on the wedding, after having spent both Saturday and Sunday nights with Clay. When she left St. Dennis that morning, it was with the growing realization that somehow, while she hadn't been paying attention, she'd fallen in love with him. It hadn't been planned, but there it was, and truth be told, she hadn't fought very hard against it. Loving him had seemed the most natural thing in the world. It had hurt her heart to leave his bed and get on the plane. She went because she knew she had to, but it had taken all of her will-power, because she hadn't wanted to go.

Of course, now she'd have work to divert her attention from the pain of missing him, but she knew it wouldn't be enough. Something would have to be done, and that something was going to have to start with Bonnie. If she couldn't come to L.A. to talk about the situation, Lucy would go to Sacramento. One way or another, they both would have to face the fact that while their business was booming, both of their personal lives were suffering.

Madeline is worth her weight in gold, Lucy was thinking as she hung up the phone. Besides having straightened out a small glitch in the menu for the anniversary party, Madeline had quietly taken care of a very important personal matter for her.

Tomorrow Lucy would make the requisite appearance at the party and would stay until the last guest departed. Today—and tonight—she had other plans.

She'd picked up the rental car and driven straight to the inn from the airport. She'd called Clay to let him know what time she'd be arriving, and suggested that he meet her at the inn.

"We'll have dinner," she told him. "And then, well, who knows what the evening will bring."

He'd sounded a little down, but she hoped that was due to the work schedule he'd set for himself. It seemed he was always busy, always too much on his plate. Always crossing something off the list and moving on to the next.

Much like myself, she thought drily.

She visited with her mother and Dan for a few minutes, then begged off. Once in her office, she made a phone call, then sat at her desk feeling not a little smug. She spent the next half hour reading a contract that had just come in from her and Bonnie's lawyer on the coast and making notes about two points she wanted to discuss.

When she looked up and saw Clay standing in the doorway, she smiled and asked, "How long have you been there?"

"Just a few minutes."

"Are you going to come in?" She got up from her chair and walked around the desk. She wrapped her arms around his waist and kissed him. For a moment, she thought he'd hesitated, and it caused a whisper of concern.

"Is everything all right?" she asked.

Clay leaned back against the desk and seemed to be studying her face. Finally he shook his head. "No. Everything's not all right."

She started to ask, but before she could get words out, he said, "I thought I could do this. I thought it would be easier than it is. I thought if I worked myself into a stupor during the day, I wouldn't miss you so much at night. I was hoping that once you went back to California, you'd find out that you couldn't live without me any more than I can live without you. But that apparently hasn't happened. I don't think I can spend the rest of my life like this, LuLu, and I don't know what to do about it."

Lucy thought about all the things she could say to reassure him, but decided that at this moment, showing might be better than telling.

"Come with me," she said. When he started to protest, she repeated, "Just . . . come with me."

She took him by the hand and they left the inn. When they got outside she told him, "I'll drive." They got into the rental car without discussion, and she drove into the shopping district. When she parked in front of his sister's shop, he raised an eyebrow.

"Cupcakes, Lucy? I've poured my heart out to you, and you want a cupcake?"

"Trust me." She got out of the car, and he followed her into the shop.

"I guess you know what I came for," Lucy said when Brooke came out of the back room.

Brooke reached into her pocket and pulled out a key, which she handed to Lucy.

"Thanks, Brooke."

"My pleasure." Brooke smiled.

"What's going on, you two?" Clay regarded them both with suspicion. "What are you up to?"

"Follow me." Lucy reached for his hand. "And all will be revealed. . . ."

She led him out of the shop and stopped in front of the door at the side of the building. She unlocked it with the key Brooke had given her, and together they went up the steps.

At the top of the stairs they entered one large room.

"I figured I could get Cam to divide this space for me. You know, a small reception area, an office for me, and one for an assistant. Then upstairs we'll have a conference room and storage and a place for me to keep my props." She paused and added, "I have a lot of props. We spent a fortune on those trees with the white lights that I used at Dallas's reception and I can use them again."

Clay looked confused.

"I'm not sure I'm following this," he said.

"Bonnie and I had a come-to-Jesus while I was in California, and we both agreed that in consideration of the fact that she wanted to stay in Sacramento, and I wanted to stay in St. Dennis, and neither of us was happy being tied to L.A., some decisions had to be made." She leaned against the wall and watched his face. She knew the second the light dawned and he got what she was telling him. "So in view of the success we've had, we decided to open two other offices and leave the L.A. office in Ava and Corrine's capable hands. It was time. Actually, it's past time that we expanded the business, but we were both too busy to give it as much thought as we should have. We both met with Ava and Corrine last week and agreed that in five years, they would become equal partners as long as the L.A. office continues to make money."

"Now, when you say you're opening two other offices . . ." he said tentatively, "you mean . . ." His hand gestured around the room they were standing in.

"Right. Here and Sacramento." She grinned. "So, what do you think?"

"Is that a trick question?" He scooped her up in his arms and swung her around. "When did you decide to do this?"

"After the Magellan wedding. I went back that Monday and I was miserable. Everything made me cranky. The traffic, the people, the weather, the view from my balcony, and the guy who delivered the Chinese takeout. Nothing made me happy. And then I realized that the traffic was the same as it always was. The people hadn't changed. The weather hardly ever changes. God knows, the view is always the same, and the poor delivery guy, he never did have much to say. The only thing that had changed was me. I didn't want to be there anymore. I wanted to be here, with you. I wanted to wake up early in your bed at the farm and meet you for coffee after my morning run. I wanted to have lunch with my mom and see my friends in the afternoon for ice cream or a cupcake if the mood struck. But most of all, I wanted you."

"You're serious? You're moving your business here. . . ."

"Right where you're standing."

"Because you want to be with me?"

"Every day of my life."

"I never would have asked you to do that. I wanted to, but I wouldn't have."

"I know that. I know it had to be my decision. But once I realized how much I love you, there really wasn't any decision at all. Except about the business, of course, and since everyone else agreed, everything fell into place."

"Say that part again, about how much you—"

"Love you? I do."

"I love you, too. I always have." Holding her, he swayed gently from side to side.

"I wish I'd understood that, back when . . . when I was going through so much alone."

"You didn't have to."

"I know that now. Somehow things always work out the way they're supposed to. I like to think that we were always meant to be together, and that fate made it happen."

"Whatever made it happen, I am eternally grateful. But you're sure you won't regret this? You worked really hard all those years to build up your business."

"No regrets," she assured him. "Besides, the wedding business here in St. Dennis is pretty good and about to get better. I have at least two more weddings to work on."

"Whose weddings?"

"Brooke and Jesse's," she said, "and ours. Assuming that you accept my proposal."

"You're proposing to me?"

"I am." She nodded. "Will you marry me?"

"That's supposed to be my line. And I'm supposed to talk to Dan and your mother about it first, then I'm supposed to ask you."

"You can talk to them, but when you do, you make sure you tell them that I asked you first."

He kissed her full on the lips, then said, "Now it's your turn to come with me. I have something to show you, too."

"What?"

"I was allowed no questions, therefore you're not allowed any either."

She laughed and locked up her new office space and went back to her car.

"How did you arrange all that, by the way?" he asked as she pulled away from the curb.

"Brooke had mentioned that the two floors above her shop were for rent, so I asked Madeline to go look at the space for me but not to tell anyone, not even Dan or Mom. I didn't want to get anyone's hopes up, you know?" she explained. "She measured the rooms and took pictures and sent them to me, and it looked pretty good. So I contacted the owner and had him draw up a one-year lease and that was pretty much that."

"I can't believe you never said a word." He shook his head.

"It would have ruined the surprise," she said as she turned into the drive at the farm.

"Park back near the barn," he told her.

When she parked and they'd gotten out of the car, she said, "So what's the surprise?"

"Close your eyes." He walked behind her, steering her straight ahead, then turned her toward the left.

"Clay, where are you—"

"Open your eyes."

"Oh, my God, Clay!" She laughed. "The chicken house! You built a new chicken house!"

The small house was a replica of the original, with a Dutch door and windows on all four sides, and was surrounded by a tall fence.

Clay opened the gate and held it for her. "Go look inside the house."

She peered over the top of the half door. "Baby chicks! Oh, look at them!"

"There are several different kinds, see? I always liked the variety when my folks had them. There are a couple of Rhode Island Reds, a few Araucanas—they're the ones that lay those pretty light blue-green eggs—and a couple of Barred Rocks."

"They are so cute." She watched them peck and scratch at the feed in a pan on the floor, then looked back at Clay. "You did this for me. You built a hen-house so that there'd be chickens here again because you thought it would make me happy."

"Nah." He shook his head and shrugged. "I did it because my carpentry skills were getting rusty."

Lucy laughed. "I am happy. Thank you."

"We'll see how happy you are the first cold snowy

winter morning when you have to get up and gather your eggs for breakfast."

"Those would be oatmeal days." She nestled against his shoulder and stayed there, imagining herself living there on the farm where she'd always felt at home.

"It's funny how things work out," she told him. "I came back here to run a couple of events at the inn, but I never dreamed of staying. But something happened while I was working on the Magellan wedding. I started to feel more and more a part of the community, like I had a place here. I hated that I missed Vanessa's wedding. I wanted to be there for her and Grady. But the last straw was looking at those pictures you emailed me during the party Brooke had for Jesse. Looking at those made me feel apart from it all again, and I hated that because I knew I should have been there with all of you, celebrating. And I decided right then and there that I belonged here, with you and with my family, and I wasn't going to ever feel like I don't belong here again."

"You do belong here. You do belong with me." Clay bent down and picked a white clover from a clump that grew outside the chicken pen. He took her hand and wrapped the thin stem around her finger, then tied it off. "It's not much as rings go, but it will have to do until we can get something more permanent."

"It's beautiful, and it's exactly right for this moment." She held up her hand. "Let's go back to the inn and show Mom and Dan. I can't wait to tell them I'll be home for the summer, after all . . ."

Diary ~

Oh, my, what a happy heart I have these days! To say that my fondest wish has come true would be an understatement! My Lucy has come home for good! Yes, that's what I said: *LUCY IS HOME FOR GOOD!*

She and her partner have decided that three offices were better than one, and Lucy's one would be right here in St. Dennis. Strictly speaking, from a business standpoint, it was a stroke of genius, because thanks in no small part to her, the Inn at Sinclair's Point has become THE destination wedding spot on the Eastern Shore. And why not? I could modestly submit that we have everything one could want, but that's a diary entry for another day. BUT—the big news is that she and Clay are engaged! Yes! There are those of us who have always known that the two of them belonged together—Clay certainly had no doubt. It just seemed to take forever for Lucy to figure it out. But figure it out she has. She's rented office space and she's moved her things from her L.A. apartment directly to the farmhouse, where she says she intends to stay. I'd always dreamed she'd be a springtime bride, but it's looking like October might be the month. She says she has some fabulous ideas for the reception. All in autumn colors, she tells me—gold sunflowers and russet dahlias, orange and red zinnias, and other such things she saw growing in a field somewhere.

It's all happened so fast—funny thing, that. Why, Trula and I were just discussing the situation after Robert and Susanna's wedding. She'd asked if I still had Alice's journals—which, of course, I do—and asked me to show her. Well, of course, I didn't mind sharing them with her. I know how discreet Trula is, how she'd never tinker with any of Alice's spells because she knows how tempermental such things can be. Anyway, she was saying how I could probably help Lucy's "situation" along if I had a mind to, but I assured her that I'd never interfere with any of my children's lives like that—tempted though I have been on many, many occasions. I would dearly love to see Dan happily married again after these years as a widower, and few things would please me more than to have Ford settled— preferably here in St. Dennis, but what are the chances of that happening?

But no—I held fast and refused to give in to the temptation. Besides, as I told Trula, I was just too tired after all the activity to even begin to think of such things. A misread word, the wrong amount of herbs, and poof! Disaster! I excused myself to go to bed, and left her in my little sitting room, in a big cozy chair, with Alice's journal on her lap. I'm sure she appreciated the opportunity to relax and have some peace and quiet. I'll have to remember to ask her sometime if she found anything of interest in Alice's journal . . .

Anyway, I am a happy woman—and a very blessed one. Who knows what good fortune will follow next?

~ Grace ~

Turn the page for a preview of the next entry in

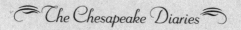

The Chesapeake Diaries

By Mariah Stewart

Available from Ballantine Books

Chapter 1

So this is St. Dennis.

Ellis Chapman drove slowly along Charles Street—slowly enough to earn her a few short polite beeps from the cars following her. At the top of the street, where she'd turned off the highway, there'd been an old farmhouse and an orchard on the left side of the road, and woods on the right. Where the farmland ended, a residential area began with a long block of lovely old homes set on nice lawns surrounded by old shade, mostly maples and oaks. The fallen leaves had blanketed many of those nice lawns with yellow and red and brown, all just waiting to be raked into irresistible piles into which the neighborhood children would surely jump.

The commercial district crept up gradually: It took a moment for Ellis to realize that the clapboard houses she'd passed were actually a restaurant, an antique dealer, a bookstore, a gift shop, a children's clothing store, and a candy store. The heart of the district had a handful of storefronts. There was a cupcake bakery, a women's clothing store, another restaurant with an upscale look about it, a coffee shop, a flower shop, and a small newsstand that apparently sold beverages, judging by its name, *Sips*.

Nice, she thought as she drove along. *All the basics, but with a slightly trendy touch.*

She continued on through the town, past a sign announcing a marina, yet another restaurant, and an ice-cream parlor.

Looks like the people around here like to eat.

"Works for me," she murmured.

The drive from Connecticut had taken longer than she'd anticipated, though she was still almost thirty minutes early for her appointment. She made a left turn and drove around the block. Once back onto Charles Street, she made a second pass through town, trying to decide how best to assuage her hunger. There was no time for a meal, but coffee and maybe a quick snack would be welcome. She parked across the street from the coffee shop—the sign read *Cuppachino* in a stylized script—and with her head down against the wind, she dodged the mid-afternoon traffic to cross to the other side.

She pushed open the coffee shop's red door and rubbed her hands together to warm them while she glanced around for an empty table. She was just about to head for one when a little wave from the teenage boy at the counter caught her eye.

"I can take your order here," he told her. He went on to explain, "We're counter service only."

"Oh. Well . . ." She squinted to read the hand-written menu on the chalkboard behind him.

"Take your time. No hurry."

"I'd like a large regular coffee with whole milk." She paused to survey the edibles. *I really shouldn't indulge,* she told herself, right before she heard herself say, "And one of the vanilla cupcakes with the pink frosting."

"Excellent choice." The boy nodded his approval and poured her coffee into an oversized blue mug. "Cream and sweeteners are over on the cart there behind you."

"Oh," she said for the second time, and turned to locate the station.

She paid for the coffee and the cupcake and took both to a table that sat off by itself next to the wall, then carried the mug to the cart where she added milk and a packet of raw sugar. She sat, sipped, and took a bite from the cupcake.

Bliss.

It was excellent, with tiny bits of strawberries in both the frosting and the cake. The coffee was equally good, and she sighed. If St. Dennis had nothing else to recommend it, at least there were great coffee and baked goods to be had.

The door opened and three chattering women entered the shop and went directly to the counter, where they were served coffee in mugs from what appeared to be a special shelf along the wall. Ellis watched surreptitiously while the ladies fixed their coffee at the station.

". . . so really, Grace, what else could I have done?" one women was saying as she added two pink packets of sweetener to her coffee.

"I don't know that I would have done anything differently, dear." The oldest of the three—Grace, apparently—shook her head slightly. "Sometimes you just have to go with your gut."

"My gut would have told me to smack her over the head with something," the third woman said dryly. "She's lucky that you have more patience than I, because, really, Barbara . . ."

The voices trailed away as the women passed by on their way to the table next to the front window. The woman called Grace, who had white hair tucked into a bun and a gentle face, turned to smile at Ellis.

"Hello, dear," she said softly without breaking her stride.

Ellis returned the smile and felt an unexplainable lump form in her throat. She turned her attention back to the cupcake and her coffee. So far, it seemed that St. Dennis was much like her mother had remembered it: a small welcoming town populated by nice people. For about the one thousandth time, Ellis wished she'd accompanied her mother on at least one of her trips back, but for Ellis, there'd always been somewhere else to go.

"Why waste your summer in some little nowhere place," her jet-setting father would say, "when you could be in London. . . ."

If not London, than Rome, or on the small island they owned off the coast of Greece. There'd been summer classes in Cairo when she'd been majoring in archaeology, and another in Paris the year she'd majored in art history. He'd take her anywhere she wanted to go, as long as it wasn't St. Dennis, a place that *no one* who mattered had ever heard of. In retrospect, it seemed that her father had been manipulating both her and her mother for more years than anyone realized.

Well, those days are gone—not just the travel, but

the manipulation . . . along with her mother, and any chance Ellis might have had to see St. Dennis through her mother's eyes.

She downed the last of the coffee and bused her table as she'd seen another customer do, returning the plate and mug to the counter.

"Thanks," the young man told her. "Come back again."

"I'll do that." Ellis tossed her crumpled napkin into a nearby receptacle and started toward the door, stood back while other patrons entered, then stepped out into the sunshine. She was standing on the curb, waiting for the light to change, when she had the inexplicable feeling that someone was watching her. She turned back to the shop, and saw the white-haired woman seated next to the window. The woman raised her hand in a wave. Ellis waved back, then realizing that the light had changed, crossed and went directly to her car.

She slid behind the wheel and glanced back to the window. The woman had turned from the glass and appeared to be once again engaged in conversation with her companions, but there'd been something about the way she'd looked at Ellis, almost as if she knew her. Impossible, of course, Ellis reminded herself, since she'd never set foot in St. Dennis before today.

She pulled away from the curb and drove east, watching for the street where she'd make her turn. The sign for Old St. Mary's Church Road was larger than the others because it also sported a plaque that marked the historic district. She made a right and drove the designated three blocks, made another right, and parked along the street, as per the instructions she'd been given. She got out of the car, locked it, and stood on the sidewalk reading the sign over the door on the brick Federal-style building.

ENRIGHT AND ENRIGHT, ATTORNEYS AT LAW.

This would be the place.

Ellis took a deep breath and walked along the brick path to the front door, which she pushed open. She stepped into a quiet, nicely furnished reception area where an elderly woman sat behind a handsome dark cherry desk. The woman looked up when she heard the door, glanced at Ellis, then did a double take.

"I'm El . . . Ellie Ryder. I have an appointment with Mr. Enright." *Ellie Ryder,* she reminded herself. From now on, that was who she'd be for as long as she stayed in St. Dennis, and possibly longer, depending on how long it would take before the shit storm subsided.

"I believe he's expecting you." The woman at the desk smiled uncertainly and got up from her chair. "I'll let him know you're here."

The receptionist disappeared into a room across the hall and stood behind the half-closed door. A moment later, a man who appeared to be in his mid-thirties emerged and came directly into the reception area, his hand outstretched to her.

"Ellie, I'm Jesse Enright. How was your trip? Can we get you some coffee? Have you had lunch?" His hand folded around hers with warmth and strength, and Ellis—*Ellie*—felt herself relax for the first time in days.

Reminding herself that he already knew the story, she smiled as she stood.

"The trip was fine. I arrived here in town with time enough to spare for a stop at the coffee shop in the center of town," she told him. "I had a great cup of coffee and a delicious cupcake."

"Vanilla with strawberry frosting?" he asked.

Ellis nodded. "You had one, too?"

"One last night and another at lunch. My fiancée, Brooke, is the baker." He patted his waist. "It's good news and bad news."

Jesse turned to the receptionist. "Violet, hold my calls, if you would . . ."

He led Ellis to his office and closed the door behind them.

"So how do you really feel?" He held out a chair for her, and she sat.

"Strange. It's strange to introduce myself as Ellie instead of Ellis. My father hated nicknames so I've never had one. Ryder is my middle name, but I never use it, so that's strange, too."

"You don't have to do this, you know." Jesse sat behind his desk in a dark green leather chair. "I think you'll find people here to be much less judgmental than you might assume."

"Over the past year, I've had more judgment passed on me than you could possibly imagine. Friends I thought for sure I could count on stopped returning my calls as soon as the news broke." Her best effort not to sound bitter was failing her. "My father has a fairly large family, but every one of them has turned their back on me. Even when my home was confiscated, my car, my jewelry, my bank accounts—no one would let me sleep on their sofa for even one night. If not for one friend who stuck by me, I wouldn't even have had a car to drive down here."

"The Mercedes you parked out front belongs to a friend?" Jesse asked.

When she nodded, he smiled. "Nice friend."

"The best," she agreed. "I don't know where I'd have been this past year without her."

"I understand that you've been treated unfairly, but I'm asking you to keep an open mind as far as the people in St. Dennis are concerned. You'll find them welcoming and friendly, if you let them."

"I'm not here to make friends, and frankly, I hope I'm not here any longer than it will take to sell the house my mother left me." She looked at him across the desk and added, "You don't know what it's like to have people judge you because of something your father did."

"Oh, but I do." Jesse leaned back in his chair. "My father was the black sheep of the Enright clan. Still is, actually. Suffice it to say, I had to earn my grandfather's trust to join this firm, prove that I was good enough to call myself an Enright here in this town where Enrights have practiced law for close to two hundred years. So yes, I do know what it's like to be judged because of something your father did. I overcame it, and so will you."

"But you were still able to work as a lawyer somewhere, right?"

"In Ohio before I came here, yes."

"I can't get anyone to even give me an interview or return my calls. I ran public relations for a major corporation for eight years, and I can't get anyone to hire me. Granted, the company was owned by my father—

hence the confiscation of my worldly goods, all being perceived as 'fruit of the poison tree,' as the FBI told me repeatedly—but still, I was very good at what I did. One of the investigators even said that one of the reasons the entire scheme came as such a shock to everyone was the fact that I'd done such a good job creating the company's image. So even though I had no hand in the scheme, I did have a hand in the public's perception of CC Investments." She blew out a breath. "When I think about all of the lives he ruined, I get sick to my stomach. All the retired people who'd trusted him with their pensions, their mortgages, their futures . . ."

"What your father did was unconscionable, but you're not responsible for the decisions he made. I think the fact that the FBI and the SEC have both totally exonerated you from any involvement in your father's scheme makes that clear."

"Intellectually, I do know that I'm not responsible. I do. But then I think about all the suffering he's caused, and I just feel sick all over again."

"I understand," Jesse said. "But you're here to pick up the pieces and put your life back together again. I want you to know that you can call on this firm for anything, any time."

"I appreciate that, Jesse. You've already done so much. My mother was wise to have entrusted the Enrights with her property."

"Actually, it was your mother's cousin, Lilly, who first came to us, as clear as I can figure out from reading the file and from talking to Violet."

"Violet?" Ellis tried not to panic. Someone other than Jesse knew?

"My receptionist. You may have noticed she's a bit . . . advanced in her years."

"She *knows*?"

"She knows that you are Lynley's daughter, and that you've inherited the house." Jesse held up a hand. "There's no way she wouldn't have known, Ellis. *Ellie*," he corrected himself. "Violet's been here forever—she worked for my grandfather for years. She knew Lilly—went to school with her, I think— and she knew your mother and your grandmother. She typed up the original wills. But she also knows there's a confidentiality issue here, and she will not discuss it with anyone, I can assure you of that. That woman has kept more secrets than either of us will hear in a lifetime. Your identity is safe with her."

"I trust you, so I will have to trust her, I suppose. Though the way she looked at me when I came in . . ." She paused, remembering the woman in the coffee shop. "There was another woman, one in the coffee shop, who greeted me as if she knew me."

"Don't let your imagination run away with you. I told you, it's a friendly little town."

"Be that as it may, I'd like to stick to the explanation we discussed on the phone."

"That you purchased the house from Lynley Sebastian's estate and you're fixing it up to sell it?"

"Yes."

"You're the client." Jesse pulled a thick folder to the center of the desk. "Now, I suppose you want to get on with the business at hand."

He pulled a sheaf of documents from the folder, explained each, and showed her where to sign. Twenty-two minutes later, he handed her a small envelope with the address, 1 Lighthouse Lane, written on the front in blue ink. She could feel the shape of keys inside, and her heart took an unexpected leap.

"The keys to your home," he said. "I went over this morning and turned up the thermostat, so it should be nice and cozy for you. There's wood stacked outside if you feel like building a fire. The chimneys were all cleaned out four years ago and to the best of my knowledge, none of the fireplaces have been used since. The bank account your mother set up years ago has paid the taxes and utilities and periodic repairs—we had to have the roof replaced a few years back—and from time to time we checked in to make sure that all was well, that the faucets weren't leaking, that sort of thing."

"I can't thank you enough for looking out for the place. I'm sure my mother appreciated it."

"She was the one who made it possible. She set up the account a long time ago, with money she made from her modeling career. Once it was verified that she'd earned that money and set it aside before your father even set up his investment fund, the Feds weren't able to touch the accounts. Because your father's fingerprints weren't on any of it, you still have that money to work with. I never personally met your mother—I guess she passed away before I came to St. Dennis—but Violet spoke very highly of her."

"Violet knew my mother?"

"Sure. I imagine there are more than a few of the old timers who knew her when she was younger. She did grow up here, you know."

"But she left so long ago, I didn't think about people having known her."

"I didn't grow up here, but I assure you, I remember Lynley Sebastian. After all, she was one of the first supermodels. Back in the day, every boy on the planet had one of her posters in his room." He smiled. "I know I did."

"Let me guess. The one where she's leaning on a fence and she's wearing a very thin pale pink dress."

"And the wind is whipping that long blond hair around her." Jesse grinned. "The very one."

"If I had a dime for every time someone brought that up to me . . ." She rolled her eyes.

"Speaking of money . . ." Jesse pulled another stack of papers front and center on the desk. "Here are the bank accounts I told you about. There's not a whole lot of money left at this point, but if you're careful, I think you can manage until the house is sold." He looked up at her. "You are still planning on selling the house?"

"Yes. The sooner the better. That's why I'm here."

"I can put you in touch with a Realtor when you're ready. Now, there might be some minor repairs that need to be done or perhaps some upgrades you might want to think about before you put it on the market. There's been no updating in thirty years, so I'm sure it all looks very dated. I can send Cameron O'Connor over to talk to you about all that. He's actually the one who's been taking care of the place."

"He's the handyman?"

"You could call him that." Jesse appeared to be suppressing a smile. "Now, here are the papers you need to take to the bank in order to have the accounts moved into your name."

"But if I put my real name on the account, then the people at the bank will know." She frowned. So much for her desire for anonymity.

Jesse tapped a pen on the desktop and appeared to be considering other options.

"We can do this: We can maintain the accounts as they are now, in the name of your mother's estate. As executor, I've been signing the checks on behalf of the firm. I can continue to do so until the house is sold. You can submit any bills you have for repairs or whatever to me, and I'll pay them. If you need cash, we can arrange that as well. We can work under the pretext that the estate has agreed to pay for any repairs to the property as part of the agreement of sale."

"Perfect." She sighed with relief.

Jesse gathered all of the papers and slid them into a brown legal envelope and tied the strings to secure it.

"Here you go, Ms. Ryder." He handed it over to her. "I wish you all the best." He paused, then added, "I hope you do give the folks around here a chance. Everyone isn't out to hurt you."

"I'll try to keep that in mind." She rose, the large envelope under her arm. "Hopefully, I won't be here long enough to find out."

Jesse opened the door for her and led her into the foyer.

"If you need anything, anything at all, let us know and we'll do whatever we can to help," he told her.

"Thank you, Jesse. I can't even put into words how much I appreciate everything you've done."

"You're welcome. Maybe we'll run into you at Cuppachino for coffee one of these days. It's the place where all the locals gather every day."

"I don't know that I could handle one of those cupcakes every day."

"They are lethal, but I'll be sure to tell Brooke that you enjoyed it."

"Please do." Ellis craned her neck to see if Violet was at her desk so she could say good-bye, but the room was empty.

Jesse held the front door open and stepped outside with her. "Glad to see the sun came out. It's been a little on the gloomy side the past couple of days."

"It's still chilly," Ellis noted.

"November moving head-first into winter," he said. "Hope you brought some warm clothes."

"I did, thanks."

Jesse accompanied her to the end of the cobbled walk, his hands in his pockets. "Check in from time to time and let me know how things are going."

"Will do. Thanks again for everything, Jesse."

He nodded and waited at the sidewalk while she walked to her car, then waved before turning and going back into the building.

Nice guy, she told herself, and said a prayer of thanks that her mother's family had selected such a firm to represent them. She was well aware that another attorney might have been willing to sell her out. She could see the headlines now:

Daughter of Clifford Chapman Found Living Under Assumed Name in Small Maryland Town!

King of Fraud's Daughter Dumps His Name, Hides Out on Eastern Shore!

Sad but true.

She slid behind the wheel and started the car. Following the directions Jesse had printed out for her, she drove around the square and made a left to head back to Charles Street. Once on Charles, she made another left and drove back through the center of town. Two blocks past the light, she took a right onto Lighthouse Lane and drove all the way to its unpaved end. The number 1 was painted in dark green on a white mailbox that looked surprisingly new. She stopped in the middle of the street and stared at her inheritance.

The house seemed to have nothing in common with the others she'd passed on her travels through town, those colonial and federal and Queen Anne styles that appeared on every block. This house, set back from the road, looked like an overgrown cottage, with a misplaced gable here and there. The white clapboard could have used a new coat of paint and the shutters were faded. Three brick chimneys—one listing slightly to the side—protruded from the roof. At the end of the driveway, which was covered in what appeared to be crushed shells, stood an outbuilding, a garage or a carriage house, its windows painted black. The shades in every window of the house had been pulled down, making it look as if it had something to hide. The entire property was encircled by some of the tallest trees she'd ever seen. All in all, the impression was far from inviting.

Like it or not, this was home.

She eased the sedan into the driveway and sat for several long moments before bursting into tears.